THE COLOUR OF DEATH

Michael Cordy

WINDSOR
PARAGON

First published 2011
by Transworld Publishers
This Large Print edition published 2012
by AudioGO Ltd
by arrangement with
Transworld Publishers

Hardcover   ISBN: 978 1 445 87507 1
Softcover   ISBN: 978 1 445 87508 8

British Library Cataloguing in Publication Data available

Printed and bound in Great Britain by
MPG Books Group Limited

For my father and my mother

Synaesthesia: (Origin—Greek *syn* = together + *aisthesis* = perception)

In its simplest form it is best described as a 'union of the senses' whereby two or more of the five senses that are normally experienced separately are involuntarily and automatically joined together. Some synaesthetes experience colour when they hear sounds or read words. Others experience tastes, smells, shapes or touches in almost any combination. These sensations are automatic and cannot be turned on or off. Synaesthesia isn't a disease or illness and is not at all harmful. In fact, the vast majority of synaesthetes couldn't imagine life without it.

The Synaesthesia Society

Synergy: (Origin—Greek *sunergos* = working together)

Cooperation of two or more things to produce a combined effect that is greater than the sum of their separate effects.

Oxford English Dictionary

PROLOGUE

Portland, Oregon

Sitting with his sister in the back of their parents' hired station wagon, the boy doesn't realize how close he is to death. His mind is preoccupied with thoughts of his eleventh birthday party in two days' time and how much he loves family holidays with his American aunt and uncle in Oregon. Everything about America's North Pacific coast seems more glamorous than England: the summers hotter, the beaches whiter, the cars bigger, the skies bluer. The giant sequoias his parents took him to see today dwarf the mightiest oak trees back home in Cornwall. Only his teenage sister interrupts his reverie, when she starts pinching her right forearm.

'Stop it, Ali,' he pleads. She gives a bored smile, pushes her forearm closer to his face and pinches harder. Sometimes he hates his big sister and wishes he could make her disappear.

His mother turns from the front passenger seat. 'What's going on?'

'She's pinching her arm.'

'It's my arm. He doesn't have to look.'

'Stop it, Alice. You know how it affects your brother.' His mother smiles at him. 'Don't look at her, Nathan.'

'We need some petrol,' his father says.

'We're coming into Portland, Richard. Surely we've got enough gas to get back to Samantha and Howard's?' Nathan loves the way his mother says gas instead of petrol. He sometimes wishes his

1

father were American too, then they would live here all the time.

'I don't want to risk it, Jenny. It's getting late.' His father points to a Chevron garage. 'We'll fill up there, use the phone and tell them when to expect us back.' He pulls into the forecourt then looks over his shoulder. 'You two stay in the car.'

'I want to get out. It's so *boring* in here,' groans Alice, as if boredom is the worst thing in the world.

'Let's all get out,' says his mother. 'Stretch our legs, use the restroom.'

The little bell on the kiosk door rings as they go inside. Nathan's father stays by the car while his mother uses the phone in the corner and Alice uses the toilet out back. Nathan flicks happily through the rack of comic books until he finds a Superman issue he hasn't yet read. The bell on the door rings again as his father comes in to pay for the petrol. Nathan keeps on reading and is so lost in the book that he doesn't notice his sister return, or the doorbell ring for a third time. Only when his mother grips his arm and pulls him towards her does he look up and register the fear in her eyes and the stony expression on his father's face. Alice is pale as their father gestures for them to move closer together. Something is wrong.

Then he sees the two men and a cold queasy lump forms in his belly. Both wear sinister black coats with hoods that obscure their faces. He watches as one pulls a pistol from under his coat, the other a sawn-off shotgun. They ignore Nathan and his family and focus on the Asian clerk behind the counter. Pistol points at the cash register, revealing a tattoo on his right forearm: a cobra coiled round the shaft of a strange-shaped crucifix,

2

topped with an oval loop instead of a vertical bar. 'Hey, Jackie Chan, empty the register.' The clerk nods nervously and reaches down below the counter.

There is a moment of eerie calm.

Then Shotgun shouts, 'The fuckin' gook's hitting the alarm,' steps forward and fires both barrels. Nathan squeezes his eyes shut just in time. When he opens them again the clerk has disappeared behind the counter. Blood drips like crimson treacle off a stack of cartons behind where he had stood.

'What do we do now?' Pistol says, agitated, pumped.

Shotgun leans across and empties the cash register. 'Get out of here, I guess.' As Shotgun moves for the door Nathan notices he has the same tattoo on his arm: a cobra coiled round a strange crucifix.

'What about them?' Pistol says, turning suddenly to Nathan and his family, who are standing in a line: Mum first, then Dad, Alice and him—a firing squad in reverse.

Shotgun shrugs as he opens the door. 'Killed one pig, may as well kill 'em all. I'll get the car running.' As Pistol raises the gun and flexes the muscles in his forearm Nathan watches the coiled cobra tattoo writhe into life.

'You don't need to do this,' Nathan's father pleads with an urgent calm. 'I'm a doctor. I might be able to save the clerk—'

Pistol's hand shakes, making the cobra dance. 'Shut the fuck up,' he snarls. 'You can't save anyone. You're not worth a fart in hell. You're not chosen. You're not one of us. You're all pigs.'

3

At that moment Pistol looks directly at the boy. Despite his hood, the angle of the light catches the dilated pupils of the man's bloodshot eyes and Nathan knows he is going to kill them. As Nathan's numb fingers drop the comic book to the floor his last instinct is to turn to his mother—

The first shot rings out.

The boy feels the bullet hit him.

Followed by searing, intolerable pain.

Then nothing.

Until Nathan becomes conscious of a young cop kneeling over him. The brass badge on his navy uniform says Portland Police. 'C'mon, son. Let her go now. We'll take care of this. Come with me.'

As if in a hideous dream Nathan looks down and realizes he is cradling Alice in his lap. Her eyes stare up at him but they are as lifeless as a doll's. There is a bullet hole in her chest, a well of blood so deep and dark it looks black. He remembers their argument in the car and feels sick. 'She's my sister,' he says numbly.

He turns to his parents but the cop pulls him to his feet. 'Don't look, son. No good can come of that.' As the boy stands, the policeman examines him. He is covered in blood but none of it is his. 'You weren't hit. Why weren't you hit?' He detects an almost accusing tone in the cop's disbelief. Nathan feels no relief at being unharmed, only confusion.

How can he still be alive?

'Come with me,' the policeman says. 'There's nothing you can do for your folks, but you're safe now.' The cop opens the door and the boy flinches when the doorbell rings one more time. There's a small crowd outside and police cars with bright

4

flashing lights. He squints, dazzled and dazed. He hears his name being called and turns in the direction of the familiar voice. In his confusion, watching her run towards him, he thinks for one blissful second that his mother has survived. Then he realizes it's her sister, Aunt Samantha, and the sweet illusion disappears for ever. She sweeps him up in her arms and squeezes him to her.

'You're OK now,' she says. 'We'll look after you.' Over her shoulder Nathan sees his uncle Howard. His face is white with shock and he looks angry.

The cop leans in close. 'What exactly happened in there, son?'

The boy buries his face in his aunt's coat. Her perfume reminds him of his mother. 'I don't know,' he says. 'Two men came in with guns. They killed the clerk but I don't know what happened after that. I can't remember.' He starts crying, big painful sobs. 'I can't remember anything.'

'It's OK, Nathan,' his aunt soothes. 'It doesn't matter. All that matters now is you're safe.'

But she's wrong. It *does* matter. Knowing how his parents and sister died, and understanding why he didn't die with them, matters more to him than anything else in the entire world.

PART 1
A Memory of Dying

PART I
A Memory of Dying

CHAPTER ONE

Portland, Oregon. Nineteen years later

It was June, summer in the city, and the night breeze felt cool on her skin as the young woman hurried through the quiet streets. An ambulance siren rang out and she could see its wailing sound unfurl before her eyes: a ribbon of reds and blues that flared across the dark sky. The alien city teemed with unfamiliar sounds, smells and sights that threatened to overwhelm her senses. Clouds obscured the moon and stars but the sodium street lamps held back the velvet darkness, revealing ghosts flickering in her peripheral vision. To keep them at bay, she looked straight ahead and walked down the middle of the sidewalk. Clutching the heart-shaped locket at her neck with one nervous hand, she stroked her cropped hair with the other, unconsciously feeling for the missing blonde curls she'd cut off to alter her appearance. Despite everything that had happened she yearned to forget the last few days and return to a state of blissful ignorance, homesick for the once-idyllic world she had fled.

Heading for the bus station, she passed houses with trees and yards, and began to relax. It was less enclosed here and quieter, as if everyone save her was asleep. Even the ghosts. She looked up at the sky and realized it would be dawn in a few hours. She smiled with relief and her face—sun-freckled, with razor-sharp cheekbones and pale haunted eyes—lit up. Perhaps she could survive out here among the children of men. She'd take a bus down the coast to California, to the place she'd been born, and start again. Her mother had said it was beautiful, that you could reinvent yourself down there and become whoever you wanted to be.

A police car approached, the sound of its engine a symphony of greens. Panicked, she gripped the locket tighter and backed into the side alley of the nearest house, hiding in the shadows. As the car disappeared into the night she sighed and leaned against the wall. Suddenly, she arched her back and jumped away, as if scalded by the red brick. The dark, silent house looked no different to the others—two storeys, shuttered windows and a red-tiled roof—but she had learned how deceptive appearances could be. Tentatively, she rested her palm flat against the wall, like a doctor placing a stethoscope on a patient's chest. Her face was sickly pale now, as white as the moon that made a sudden appearance through the dark scudding clouds. Every instinct screamed at her to get far away from here, as fast as she could. But a small internal voice counselled her to conquer her fear and make *it* flee. Using her hand like a divining rod she let it lead her along the wall. All the time her terror grew—along with the certainty that she couldn't turn back. The night was still but she could hear things, terrible things, and she could see . . .

She squeezed her eyelids shut but was unable to close her mind's eye. Looking down at the clear stone path, she stepped over something visible only to her, and then came to a solid wooden door. It was locked. Sick and frantic, she knew this was the moment of no return. Fight or flight. Run away or break down that door. Looking around in panic,

10

she noticed a truck in the large carport. Beside it was a pile of logs. And an axe.

As if in a trance she picked it up and tested the keenness of the blade. Her father would have scolded her for letting it get so blunt but it would suffice. The thought of him converted her fear to rage and hardened her resolve. Wielding the axe, she braced herself, took a deep breath and swung it as hard as she could. She slammed the blade into the door with practised, powerful blows that belied her slender frame. With each impact she willed the sound of rending wood to drown out the screaming in her head. Stepping through the splintered door she found herself at the top of mildewed stone steps, which led down into the dark underbelly of the house. She shivered, despite her exertions and the warm night.

More cries, some angry, some fearful, echoed in the dark but it was hard to know if they were real or coming from inside her own head. At the bottom of the stairs a dank passageway greeted her, illuminated by an infernal red glow. Like a lost soul entering hell, she walked towards its source, the sounds growing louder with each step. She passed a generator flanked by two cans of kerosene and a red wall light, then the corridor widened into a room walled with vertical wooden slats. It took a second to realize she was surrounded by cages, occupied by hollow-eyed young women. As they turned to her, half in terror, half in hope, she saw they were even younger than she was, little more than girls. She raised her axe and smashed the slatted, padlocked doors to tinder. 'Run,' she shouted, as she dragged them out of the cages and pushed them to the exit. 'Get out of here.'

Shepherding the last dazed girls down the corridor, she heard guttural male voices cut angrily through the screams. She turned to see two men running towards her. The nearest was bald, stocky and breathing hard, his face contorted with rage. In the far gloom two more men were descending a stairway from the house above. All carried guns and spoke a language she didn't understand. Their unfamiliar sounds tasted strange on her tongue. She dropped the heavy axe and ran for the exit. The sound of the first gunshot flashed crimson before her eyes, like a blood vessel bursting. The second shot hit her, grazing her temple and spinning her against the concrete wall of the narrow passage. Dazed and gritting her teeth against the pain, she got to her feet and stumbled past the generator. The impact of the third shot sounded—and looked—different: metallic.

The kerosene cans.

Time paused for a second, followed by an explosion that sent a kaleidoscope of colours flashing before her eyes. A ball of intense heat knocked her to the ground. Then the colours disappeared. Replaced by black.

CHAPTER TWO

A few miles across town, Dr Nathan Fox woke with a start and found himself in a dimly lit room, slumped in a chair, back aching. For a moment he didn't know where he was. It sure as hell wasn't his apartment. Then he saw the bed and remembered he was in one of the private rooms at Oregon

University Research Hospital. This had to be the first time he had spent the whole night in a hospital since his years as a medical student.

Tonight wasn't work, though. This was personal.

He stood and studied the patient lying in the bed. In repose, with his eyes closed, the man's gaunt face looked relaxed and at peace. In the low light Fox could almost imagine he was well, except for the sound of his ragged breathing, which told Fox that the pneumonia was now in its final stages. Since the antibiotics had been stopped the disease had advanced rapidly. Pneumonia hadn't been the real killer though: just the merciful coup de grâce. Fox stroked the patient's clammy forehead and the man's eyes flickered open, stared blankly for a moment then closed again. At least the morphine was minimizing his discomfort.

A sigh made Fox turn to the woman lying on the couch beside the bed. Like Fox, she too had been keeping vigil all night and as he straightened her blanket he was glad she was now sleeping. The glow through the shutters told him it was almost dawn. Yawning, he flexed his legs and checked his watch. His first outpatient would be here in a few hours and he welcomed the distraction of work. First, though, he needed to go for a run in the hospital grounds and wake himself up. He met the senior nurse in the corridor.

'You OK, Dr Fox?' She instinctively reached out a comforting hand but, equally instinctively, he shifted his body, subtly evading her touch. 'Can I get you anything?'

He smiled. 'Thanks, Kate. Just look after Samantha when she wakes. I'll be back to check on both of them but page me if anything changes.'

A little over two hours later—after a run round the grounds, a shower and a hot milky coffee with two sugars in the hospital canteen—Fox was sitting behind his desk in his small office in the psychiatric and neurology department with his first patient of the morning. Fox enjoyed the variety of his work. Although he treated outpatients here at the main hospital he spent much of his week at Tranquil Waters, the hospital's specialist residential psychiatric clinic, and still managed to squeeze in time for police forensic work. This morning's patient had been on Fox's latest experimental programme and the man's first words buoyed Fox's spirits:

'I can't tell you how much the treatment's helped me, Doc. You've given me my life back.'

'I'm pleased, John. Really pleased.' Fox contrasted the beaming young man sitting across the desk from him with the desperate, haunted patient he had met six months ago. Then, John Fontana had been tyrannized by obsessive–compulsive disorder triggered by spending several years in a religious cult. Fox prided himself on his professional objectivity but detested cults and the damage they caused. John's form of OCD didn't involve manifest behavioural compulsions but obsessive repugnant thoughts (he was convinced he was possessed by the devil), which made it notoriously difficult to treat with behavioural therapy. The condition had stopped John working, sleeping or having a social life—or any kind of life—for almost five years. Finally, after every other treatment had failed, he had joined Fox's experimental programme. Fox scanned John's notes and went through a checklist of questions.

14

'How would you rate your anxiety levels now?'

'Overall, I'd say they'd halved, down from a ten to a five. I even have moments when I actually forget about my OCD. I got my old job back, too.'

'You're working again. That's great. How's your sleep? Still need Valium or chlorpromazine?'

'Nope. My sleep's fine. Just taking the Prozac and risperidone you prescribed.'

'Any side effects?'

'Just the dry mouth I told you about last time and I've put on a bit of weight. But I can live with fat and happy.'

Fox smiled as he noted the improvement from earlier consultations. 'You're still attending the ACT sessions?'

'I haven't missed one. They're really helping me get some distance from my thoughts.'

'Excellent.' Fox checked the file one last time, then closed it. Of the thirty subjects on his study, twenty-eight had enjoyed significant improvements. 'In that case, John, I'd like to see you in a year's time to check on progress but for now just keep taking the medication and attending the sessions.' He stood. 'All the very best, John.'

'You've saved my life, Dr Fox.' John moved to embrace him but Fox reached out and shook his hand. 'I can't thank you enough.'

'Trust me, seeing you doing so well is more than enough.' Fox smiled. 'Thank *you* for taking part in this programme. Your courage in volunteering will allow us to help others.' Seeing John leave, Fox's thoughts returned to the man he had watched over last night, and his smile faded. He wished he could have done as much to help him. As the door closed behind John, there was a gentle knock and it opened again. The expression on the nurse's face, and the fact that she hadn't sent one of her staff, told him all he needed to know. 'It's time?'

'I'm afraid so, Dr Fox.'

Ever since the murder of his parents and sister, Nathan Fox had learned to distance himself from pain and loss but as he returned to the room of last night's vigil he knew it wasn't always possible. Fox was often asked how someone with his natural empathy could inhabit the minds of the mentally disturbed without becoming somehow infected or affected, and he always gave the same answer: detachment. If you became involved, or got too close, you became vulnerable and lost perspective. Applying this philosophy to his personal life didn't please girlfriends who mistook him for the marrying kind, but usually it served him well and kept him safe. Usually.

After taking the elevator to the third floor, he barely suppressed the urge to run the length of the corridor to the private room. As he approached the bed and the woman tending to the patient, Fox could feel his defences falling away. His uncle Howard and aunt Samantha, who despite planning on never having children had brought him up as their own, were the only people in the entire world to whom Fox's strategy of detachment and distance didn't apply. Howard had never tried to replace his father but in so many ways he had. He had stepped into the blackest part of his life, when Fox was drowning in almost intolerable grief, and like a beacon in the dark had provided unswerving guidance with unconditional love. When Samantha saw Fox, she reached for him. 'They say it's close now, Nathan,' she said.

Fox put his arm round her shoulder and kissed her cheek. 'His suffering will be over soon.' He checked his uncle's pulse, listened to his ragged breathing and accelerated the morphine drip. Fox's parents and sister had been ripped from him in an instant, when he was too young to understand fully what had happened. Alzheimer's had stolen his uncle away over a period of years, day by day, brain cell by brain cell, when the medically trained Fox had understood *exactly* what was happening.

Suddenly, Howard let out a rattling wheeze and opened his eyes. He reached out his hand and gripped Fox's arm. Samantha leapt forward. 'Howard, Howard. It's me, Samantha.' She stroked his face. 'Nathan and I are both here.' Howard looked at her and then at Fox and his fevered eyes cleared. In that instant, for the first time in a long while, Fox felt sure his uncle recognized them. Then Howard's grip slackened and his hand fell back on the bed. Samantha looked at Fox with red-rimmed eyes and smiled.

Fox nodded. 'He knows we're here. He knows he's not alone.'

Moments later Howard took a shallow breath, released a final, rattling sigh and was still. Samantha, who had always been so strong for Fox, suddenly collapsed in his arms and began to cry. 'He saw us,' she said, shock and wonder tempering her grief. 'I think he was trying to say goodbye.'

Fox said nothing, just enveloped her small frame in his arms, supporting her, making sure she didn't fall.

CHAPTER THREE

The flames reached high into the dawn sky, lending the silhouetted neighbourhood of nondescript brick houses an unfamiliar air of drama and menace. Red trucks from the Portland Fire Department were already on the scene while uniformed cops were holding back the small crowd that had gathered despite the early hour. More cops and paramedics were helping a group of blanket-wrapped girls into a bus.

Getting out of his car, Chief of Detectives Karl Jordache took a sip of black Arabica from the flask his wife had prepared for him. He was medium height and broad—too broad according to his doctor, who had him on a low cholesterol, low fat, zero-taste diet—but his charcoal-grey suit fitted well, and he was light on his feet.

'What have we got, Danny?' he called to the nearest policeman.

The cop checked his notes and indicated the girls getting on the bus. 'There were at least eleven in there, Chief. They claim they were abducted and caged in the basement. According to the fire chief, the wooden cages are why the brick house went up like a torch. Helped by the kerosene, of course. The basement reeks of it.'

'Who are the girls?'

'A couple of American runaways but mostly illegals from the old Soviet republics who paid a syndicate—part of the Russian mob—to ship them into the US and hook them up with jobs. See those Douglas firs at the back end of the yard? A couple

18

of girls who tried to escape were killed and buried under there.'

'Who says the slave trade's been abolished?' Jordache muttered wearily. 'The sleazeballs promise the girls money and a better life, then lock 'em up, take their passports, get them addicted to drugs and force them into the sex industry.' He sighed. 'Christ, the girls are little older than my two daughters. They all got out OK?'

'Yep.'

'The Russians?'

'They're being taken down to the station for processing. Two are badly burned but they'll live.'

'That's too bad.' Jordache watched an unconscious, blackened figure being moved to the ambulance on a gurney. 'Is that her? Is that their mystery saviour?'

A nod. 'The girls are calling her their guardian angel.'

'Avenging angel more like. I heard she appeared out of nowhere with an axe and busted them out.'

'That's what they say. The Russians confirm their story and claim she was alone. They assumed she was police.'

'Police? She's not one of ours.'

'She doesn't belong to anybody so far as we can gather. No agency knows anything about her: who she is, where she comes from, what she was doing here, or how she even knew the girls were down there. She's got no ID on her, just a silver locket round her neck.'

'A real mystery, huh?' Jordache watched the medics load her on to the ambulance and slam the doors shut. As it pulled out and the siren wailed into life he climbed back in his car. 'Finish up here,

Danny, I'm going to learn a bit more about our friend.'

Twenty minutes later Jordache found himself in the emergency room of Portland General Hospital, standing in front of a fiercely protective intern who was refusing to let him get beyond the green curtain screening the mystery woman.

'I need to ask her some questions, Doc.'

'She's not speaking to anyone,' the woman replied. 'Not till we've checked her out.'

'Help.' The cry from behind the curtain was so raw it didn't sound human. The doctor swivelled and pulled back the screen. The woman on the bed was sitting up, a blackened arm propped against the wall, the other pointing at an empty gurney to her right. 'Help him,' she rasped from her smoke-ravaged throat. The whites of her terrified eyes looked huge and unnaturally bright against her blackened face.

'What's wrong?' the doctor said, rushing to her side. 'Help who?'

The young woman collapsed back on the bed, arms falling by her side. 'The man with the knife in his chest. Can't you see the blood? Do something. He's dying.'

Jordache looked at the empty gurney. 'There's no one there,' said the doctor.

The young woman shook her head, dazed. Despite the soot and grime, she had an ethereal, otherworldly beauty. 'What's happening to me?' she whispered to no one in particular.

The doctor shone a light into her eyes and examined her head. 'You're hallucinating. You experienced a trauma above the left temple. The bullet only grazed your skull but you were

20

unconscious and are still in shock. The detective tells me you've been to hell and back.'

Jordache moved closer and noticed how luminous her eyes were. Her clothes were plain and simple, possibly homemade: cotton top, loose jacket and dark denim trousers. The only distinctive thing she wore was the silver locket round her neck. He could see a catch on the side and wondered what it contained. Who was this girl? How had she known about the girls in the basement? And where had she found the courage to go down there alone, armed only with an axe? When she saw him looking at her locket she clutched it to her chest like her life depended on it. He smiled. 'My name's Detective Karl Jordache. I'm here to help you. Can I ask you some questions?'

'Not now—' the doctor started to say.

The young woman rested a blackened hand on the doctor's white sleeve. 'Please,' she pleaded in a dry rasp, 'may *I* ask something?' Her speech was old-school polite, out of town.

'Sure,' said Jordache, leaning in before the doctor could object. 'Shoot.'

The young woman frowned, marshalling her thoughts, then posed the exact same question Jordache was going to ask her: 'What's my name, Detective? Who am I?' At that moment, he saw in her eyes a fear as raw as any he'd witnessed in all his years of policing: a realization that she had become lost from herself, unable to find the way back to the person she had once been. 'Help me,' she pleaded. 'Someone, help me.'

CHAPTER FOUR

Ten days later

Almost a week had passed since his uncle Howard's funeral and Fox had already phoned his aunt twice that morning. Once from his apartment in north-west Portland and once in the car driving over. Samantha was always out of bed by six and it was almost eight thirty. As he parked his battered second-hand Porsche outside the house he spotted her small Ford. She must be in, he thought, as he rang the bell on the door of the imposing Victorian house and banged the brass doorknocker. The funeral and the wake that followed had been surprisingly joyous, with his aunt taking centre stage and appearing to revel in the celebration of her beloved husband's life. Nevertheless, Fox had called or visited every day since, concerned that anticlimax and depression would descend once the well-wishers had left her to get on with the rest of her life. He usually called when he guessed she might be at her lowest ebb without Howard: just after she got up and before she went to bed. Though she was invariably in good spirits and dismissive of his concerns, he was determined to be there for her, as she and Howard had always been there for him.

He used his set of spare keys to enter the house that had been his childhood home since he was eleven. He heard voices. 'Samantha?'

The television was on in the lounge, tuned to one of the rolling twenty-four-hour news channels. *Who is the mysterious avenging angel?*

read a banner across the bottom of the screen. The mystery woman staring out at him looked lost and otherworldly. Her pale skin, cropped fair hair and beautiful eyes momentarily diverted his attention. A reporter's voice explained: 'The authorities are still no closer to identifying the mystery Jane Doe who broke eleven girls out of a sex traffickers' dungeon in Portland. Although recovering well from her burns and physical injuries, she's being moved to a specialist psychiatric clinic for further treatment. To date, all attempts to match her fingerprints, dental records or DNA in major databases here and abroad have failed, and no one has yet come forward to identify her. If *you* recognize her, then please call this number.'

He turned off the television and called again, louder. 'Samantha. Samantha.' Nothing.

He searched the rooms, passing photographs of his parents and sister and bookcases crammed with books. The house had always been filled with books. The kettle in the kitchen was warm and the glazed doors leading out to the garden were still locked but there was no sign of Samantha.

He ascended the stairs. At the top he turned and glanced down the landing to the two bedrooms at the end. The one on the right was his aunt's. The one on the left had once been his. As he walked towards them he passed two more rooms: twin studies. He looked in the first and his relief made him smile. His aunt was sitting at her desk, small and birdlike, ears covered by huge headphones connected to a black iPod, peering through thick reading glasses at a loosely bound typescript. As she sipped coffee from an oversized cup, her pale brown bob, streaked with silver, nodded gently to

23

the beat of whatever she was listening to, which, knowing Samantha Quail, could be anything from Tchaikovsky to U2. After all these years she still closely resembled the memory he had of his petite mother. Fox had inherited his height from his father, along with two other legacies he had stubbornly retained from his childhood: his surname and English accent. With her penchant for kaftans and bright colours, Professor Samantha Quail betrayed her roots as a fully paid-up member of the hippy, flower-power generation. Not for her the cashmere cardigans and tweed skirts of conventional academia.

Deciding not to disturb her, Fox moved on to the next study. Although it had been unused in the years since Alzheimer's had claimed her husband, Samantha had left it unchanged. Fox could still smell his uncle's Virginia pipe tobacco and feel his presence in the room. You could guess Howard Quail had been a professor of ancient history and archaeology from the artefacts in the display cases and the textbooks and periodicals on the groaning shelves, many written by him. Howard's controversial and outspoken theories had not only affected his career but also that of his brilliant wife. If Howard had been less of a maverick, Samantha would almost certainly be teaching quantum physics at some Ivy League school rather than at Portland State. Fox suspected, however, that even if Harvard or MIT had come calling she would have stayed where she was—a big fish in a small pond. As Fox studied Howard's books about the ancient past, the irony wasn't lost on him that in the months preceding their author's death Howard had been unable to recall anything of the present, least of all his own name.

Fox picked up a flat stone paperweight from the desk. The size of a hardback book, it was polished smooth and dyed a deep ruddy brown. His uncle had once told him that it was part of a Mayan sacrificial stone, upon which victims were held down and their hearts cut out to appease some ancient god. He replaced the stone and picked up a silver-framed photograph displayed prominently beside it. A small boy in a white uniform held a trophy almost as big as he was, flanked by a younger Howard and Samantha Quail who were smiling like proud parents. The boy was staring directly at the camera, blue eyes fierce. As Fox stared back at the boy his focus shifted and he saw his adult face reflected in the glass. The fire in his eyes was more controlled now, but its glowing embers remained. He remembered the time—about six months after the orphaned Fox had moved to America to live with Howard and Samantha—when his uncle had promised the principal of his new school that he would handle his nephew's constant fighting.

Resigned to punishment or at least a long lecture, a sullen Fox was surprised when his uncle drove him to a nearby department store, told him to stay in the car, returned with a wrapped package and then drove on to a strange-looking building on the outskirts of town. Inside, Howard had sat Fox in the lobby and returned with a small, stern-faced Japanese man. 'You're angry, Nathan, and I don't blame you,' his uncle had said. 'After what happened to your parents and sister, I can only imagine what you're going through, but you've got to harness and control your anger.' He had pointed to the Japanese. 'Sensei Daichi has agreed to help you.'

Daichi had bowed his head. 'Welcome to my dojo, Nathan-*kun*.' Then had gently touched Fox's black eye. 'If you're going to fight, Nathan-*kun*, I suggest you learn to do it properly. Karate is self-defence, not self-destruction; it's about protecting and developing the mind and body, not destroying them. I've been your uncle's sensei for five years and, if you wish, I will be yours.' Fox's uncle had then opened the package, pulled out a white karate uniform and told him to put it on.

Fox replaced the photo on the desk. If he closed his eyes he could hear his sensei's constant refrain: 'Never let them get too close and never lose control.' Reaching into one of the display cases, Fox picked up an ancient Minoan vase his uncle had excavated at Knossos. Holding the three-thousand-year-old vase in his hands he could feel the weight of history, as if it were a tangible thing. When he put it back he spied a dog-eared document on the top shelf above the desk. Intrigued by the title page, he blew off the dust and began to flick through the pages. Then his phone rang in his pocket. He pulled out the iPhone he had bought for personal calls but, inevitably, it was his work BlackBerry that was ringing. He checked the caller identity: Chief Detective Karl Jordache.

'Hello, Karl.'

'Nathan, you got a moment?'

'Sure. How can I help?'

'You know the Jane Doe who saved those girls from Russian traffickers? Well, we've got all the evidence we need to convict the Russians renting the house but we're now looking at the owner. We've found the bodies of two girls who tried to escape buried in the garden but a few other girls are unaccounted for. The Russians say they gave girls to the owner to keep him quiet, but he denies this. He claims the house is just one of many properties he owns in Portland and he knew nothing about what was going on in there. His paperwork's all in order but something smells funny.'

'What do you want me to do?'

'Do your thing: interview the guy, find out what makes him tick and give us your take on his story. We've got him at his hunting lodge, about two hours out of town. If I text you the satnav coordinates can you come over?'

Fox checked his watch. He had a commitment this afternoon but could shift his morning appointments. 'I'll be there as soon as I can.' He waited for the coordinates then replaced the phone in his pocket.

'Nathan, what are you doing here?' His aunt was standing in the doorway, headphones dangling from her neck.

He shrugged, suddenly self-conscious. 'I was worried so I came to check on you. I rang twice but you didn't answer.'

She tapped the headphones. 'I was working.' She sighed. 'You really must stop worrying about me, Nathan. I didn't lose Howard last week. I lost him years ago. My period of mourning isn't just starting. Hopefully, it's coming to an end.'

'I know, but . . .'

'Please don't give me any psychiatric gobbledygook. I'm fine. Really.'

He smiled. 'I was just trying to help.'

She kissed his cheek. 'I know. And I love you for it.'

He showed her the document he had taken from the shelf above his uncle's desk. 'What's this?'

She looked at it and sighed. 'It's the last paper Howard wrote before he got sick. He made me promise to try and get it published in *Archaeology* magazine but . . .' She grimaced.

'But what?'

'It's even more controversial than his other stuff and I was worried it would be dismissed as a product of his Alzheimer's.'

He read the title page again. 'What's it about?'

'You know how when you enter certain rooms or buildings you can sense something, an atmosphere?'

He glanced around his uncle's study. 'Yes.'

'Howard always claimed that the ancient sites he visited over the years had a distinct atmosphere, an echo of their unique history. For example, the Colosseum in Rome and, more recently, Auschwitz resonate with suffering and misery whereas some sacred sites or places of learning have a calmer, more peaceful ambience. Archaeosonics promises to explore and explain this phenomenon scientifically.'

'Really?' Fox had grown accustomed to his uncle's own brand of gobbledygook. 'Archaeosonics?'

'According to the old saying: walls have ears. Archaeosonics proposes that they also have memory, with the voices of the past invisibly but indelibly imprinted into their subatomic fabric— like a tape recording.' She took the dog-eared document from Fox and replaced it on the shelf, then beckoned him to follow her back to her study. 'As Alzheimer's took Howard from me I found

28

his paper comforting. It felt like my last link to his healthy mind. The more times I read it the more I wanted to use my knowledge of science to back up its bizarre premise. I wanted to prove that his paper contained the last flash of his brilliance and not the first signs of his madness.'

In her office she handed Fox a freshly typed document with the same title. 'So I rewrote his paper, trying to underpin his theories with hard science. The concept of archaeosonics has been around for decades but with our growing knowledge of quantum physics and state-of-the-art acoustic technology we could soon explain and unlock these trapped echoes.' Reading the scepticism in his face, she smiled. 'I know it sounds nonsense, Nathan, but read it first, *then* tell me it's rubbish. Be as ruthless as you like.'

Fox didn't need to be a psychiatrist to realize his aunt's reworking of Howard's paper owed more to love than hard science. 'It's not exactly my area.'

'I don't care, Nathan. You have an excellent mind and I'd value your opinion.' She kissed him again then waved him away. 'Now go to work. I know you're busy.'

CHAPTER FIVE

Two hours later Nathan Fox found himself in the Oregon wilderness, eyeball to eyeball with a suspected killer. 'What is it with you shrinks?' George Linnet spat. 'You think you can know me just by asking me a few questions and seeing where I live. You don't know me. You don't know me at

29

all.'

'I've no interest in *knowing* any patient, George.'

'I'm not one of your sicko, psycho patients, you Limey asshole.'

'No, you're the prime suspect in multiple homicides,' Fox said evenly. 'You're a puzzle to me. Nothing more. I don't need to know you, George, just *solve* you. So I can discover what you did with the girls.'

'I told you already. I knew nothing about the girls those perverts were stashing in that property. They paid their rent on time and that was all I cared about.'

'The Russians say they gave you girls to keep you quiet.'

Linnet glared at him. 'You calling me a liar?'

Fox allowed himself a smile. 'I think I'm calling you a lot worse than that.' Dressed in check shirt and corduroy trousers, Linnet looked more like one of Fox's colleagues at Oregon University Research Hospital than a killer but after meeting him and looking around his hunting lodge the psychiatrist was beginning to get the measure of the man. He had interviewed enough psychopaths in his time to know there was more to Linnet than met the eye. After finding nothing in Linnet's impersonal apartment, offices and rental properties in Portland the police had driven Linnet to the one place they hadn't looked: his remote hunting lodge. Standing in the kitchen, Fox registered the immaculate granite worktops, porcelain floor tiles and Smeg cooking range. Though obsessively neat and over-specified for a basic lodge, everything fitted the profile he was building of the owner. He might profess not to know Linnet but Fox already knew

30

him better than he knew his own neighbours in north-west Portland, which probably said as much about him as it did about Linnet. As Fox glanced around the lodge the idea of hunting and killing for pleasure mystified him. A city boy at heart, Fox cherished the illusion of order and civilization that man's footprint brought to the world.

He turned his attention to the crime scene investigators, *CSI* emblazoned in big yellow capitals on the backs of their blue boiler suits. He watched as they closed the kitchen blinds and prepared their spray guns of Luminol. Within seconds of spraying the chemical around the darkened room, hitherto invisible traces, *copious* traces, of scrubbed-away blood magically reappeared on the walls, worktops and floor as a ghostly blue glow. By highlighting these indelible bloodstains the Luminol acted like the building's conscience, revealing how on more than one occasion this apparently spotless kitchen had been used as a slaughterhouse. He followed one trail of glowing blood spatter and, in his mind's eye, saw Linnet dragging one of his victims into the back yard. More glowing stains led to stairs in the corner of the room.

'Did you kill them all, George?'

Linnet made a sudden move towards him and one of the police escort yanked at his cuffs, snapping his arms behind his back. Linnet winced in pain and Fox winced with him, feeling the cuffs cut into *his* wrists, the tendons stretch in *his* shoulders. Fox quickly averted his eyes—a protective gesture he had perfected over the years.

He was seven when he first realized he was the only kid in school who experienced the physical sensations of touch or pain whenever he witnessed

31

another being touched or hurt. Years later his hyper-empathetic condition would be given a name but at the time the other kids had just assumed he was plain weird and laughed at his discomfort when watching anything violent, even cartoons on TV. As a boy in England he had wanted only one thing: to fit in and belong. But after the death of his parents and sister, and leaving everything he knew in England to settle in the States, he'd stopped trying to fit in and accepted he would always be on the outside looking in.

He moved to the stairs in the corner of the kitchen and descended into the basement. There were no CSI down here yet; they were all in the kitchen or out in the back yard digging up the newly laid wooden deck. As soon as Fox saw the refurbished basement he knew instinctively that this was Linnet's private den. Rows of books lined one of the wood-panelled walls: cheap bodice-ripping romances with lurid covers, telling stories in which red-blooded men tamed wild women called Storm or Tempest. Not what most people would expect on a serial killer's reading list but it fitted the profile of a weak, inadequate man who could only court—and conquer—women in fantasy.

Or with a weapon.

His eyes moved to the locked case next to the books. It contained at least five assorted rifles and handguns, and three serrated hunting knives arrayed in ascending order of size. At the far end of the basement was a leather couch facing a plasma television screen. Beside the screen was a stack of pornographic DVDs and a display case of stuffed animals: chipmunks, raccoons and squirrels. No doubt caught, killed and stuffed by Linnet himself. Studying the stuffed animals and weapons, and mentally revisiting similar cases, Fox could guess what Linnet had done with the girls: he had brought them here, released them into the wild and hunted them down. But where were his trophies? Looking around the room Fox noticed something odd. Although the basement was directly beneath the kitchen . . .

'We've got something. There's something here.' The tired voice calling from outside sounded angry but triumphant. Fox hurried back upstairs. Through an open window he could see more police in boiler suits and white antibacterial masks standing on the wooden deck in the back yard. The middle planks had been prised open like the ribcage of a whale, revealing a trench beneath. He frowned, strode past Linnet and went outside. The air was warm and he could already smell the decomposing fruits of their digging.

Detective Karl Jordache was standing with his team, looking into the trench. He patted a colleague on the right shoulder and Fox felt it on his left shoulder as strongly as if Jordache had patted him. The detective beckoned to Fox and removed his mask. He had a strong Roman nose, thick dark hair streaked with grey, and quick brown eyes that missed nothing. 'Hey, Nathan, look what we got here.' He pointed down at the three corpses lying in the dirt and Fox experienced a sudden pang. Not because of the smell or decomposition but because they appeared so forlorn and abandoned. He found it perversely comforting that the bodies had each other for company and remembered some lines of poetry his mother used to recite:

*The grave's a fine and private place,
But none I fear do there embrace.*

Jordache glanced at Linnet. 'Gotcha, you bastard. At least we can now identify the victims and inform the families.'

Glancing back to the lodge Fox thought he caught the ghost of a smile on Linnet's lips. 'You only found three, Karl?'

'*Only?*' The detective frowned. 'You think there's more, Nathan?' Keeping his eyes locked on Linnet's, Fox considered the man's hunting lodge: the immaculate kitchen, the books, DVDs, guns and stuffed animals. The insight, when it came to him, made Fox groan. 'What is it?' said Jordache.

Fox stayed focused on Linnet. 'You need to control your immediate environment, don't you, George? Everything must be "just so". You like to keep everything you value close to you. There's only one reason you'd bury your hunting trophies out here.' Linnet paled but said nothing.

'What reason's that?' Jordache demanded.

'The house is full,' said Fox.

'What do you mean?'

'Check the basement, Karl. It's smaller internally than the kitchen above. I bet it's got false walls.' He took some satisfaction from Linnet's fading smile. 'You should find the rest of the bodies in the walls.'

As his team ran off to investigate, Jordache studied Fox for a moment. 'Christ, Nathan, your mind's an interesting place to visit but I'd sure as hell hate to live there.' Both men had known each other for years, ever since Jordache, as a young rookie cop, had escorted a ten-year-old orphaned boy out of a blood-spattered Chevron garage. Over the years the cop had kept in constant touch. When Fox had qualified top of his class from Stanford University's Department of Psychiatry and Behavioral Sciences, a newly promoted Detective Jordache had taken him out for a congratulatory beer and sought the younger man's psychiatric advice on interviewing a particularly difficult suspect. Since then, Jordache had become chief of detectives and Fox the youngest member of the psychiatry and neurology faculty at Oregon University Research Hospital. In many ways the older man was Fox's opposite. Fox was a commitment-phobe who jumped ship before relationships became too serious and lived for his work. Jordache was a committed family man who put his wife and two daughters before everything— including his work. 'How many bodies are they going to find, Nathan?' the detective asked, turning back to the lodge.

'My guess, given the space, would be about half a dozen.'

The sound of drilling, sawing and splitting wood filled the still air. Followed by silence and a muffled exclamation: 'JEEZUS.' A shout: 'Hey, Chief, the doc's right on the money. You better come see this. We got five more bodies in here. Maybe six.'

'I'm coming,' said Jordache.

Fox checked his watch. 'Look, Karl, you don't need any more help from me with Linnet's little house of horrors. You mind if I get going?'

Jordache stopped outside the doorway and shook his hand. 'No problem, Nathan. We've got it from here. Thanks for your help, as always. I owe you a brew next time we're at O'Malley's.' He

35

glanced into the lodge. 'Before you go, though, there's something I've been meaning to ask you.'

'What?'

Jordache stepped through the doorway and reached for a pile of magazines and newspapers on a small table by the window. He picked up the *Oregonian* and pointed at the unsettlingly beautiful face staring out from the front page. 'It's about the Jane Doe who saved the other girls. You want to know something strange? We don't need her testimony to put the Russians away—we got more than enough from the girls she rescued—but my people went the extra mile to help her recover her identity and discover how she knew those girls were in there. And you know what my finest detectives came up with? Nothing. Nada. Zip.'

As Fox looked at the picture an idea came to him. He took the paper off Jordache and walked over to Linnet, who was being pushed into a police car. 'Hey, George, do you recognize the girl who burned down one of your houses and ruined your party? Was she one of the girls you hunted? Was she one that got away?'

Linnet looked at the picture with cold eyes, then smiled. 'I've no idea who she is. All I know is that none of the bitches I hunted got away.'

'Like I said, Nathan,' Jordache said, as the car door closed on Linnet, 'no one knows who Jane Doe is or why she went into the Russians' basement, unless she had a sixth sense about the girls or something. I'm telling you, Nathan, she's the real deal: your classic riddle, wrapped in a mystery, inside an enigma. The thing is, although she's all over the news at the moment, no one's coming forward to claim her. The last I heard she was destined for the Oregon State psychiatric unit in Salem and no one deserves to rot in that snake pit. Certainly not her, not after what she did. I was wondering if . . .'

Fox smiled. Jordache didn't do detachment. He couldn't help getting involved with everyone and everything he dealt with. 'Don't worry, Karl. Jane Doe's coming to Tranquil Waters. The handover meeting's today. She's one of the reasons I've got to get back.'

Jordache nodded, satisfied. 'That's all I wanted to know.' He smiled slyly. 'Watch yourself, though, Nathan. She's got something about her.' The detective patted him on the shoulder and disappeared into the lodge. 'She's got a way of getting under your skin—even yours, my Teflon friend.'

* * *

Two hours later, entering the outskirts of Portland, Fox turned right when he should have turned left. The almost subconscious detour meant he approached the city from a different direction— on a particular road. After a few miles a familiar collection of run-down buildings came into view and he slowed the car. Usually, he sought out the Chevron petrol station then drove on. But today a new yellow sign forced him to change his obsessive ritual, brake hard and pull into the dusty car lot, gripping the steering wheel white-knuckle tight, forehead beaded with sweat.

He had lost count of the times he had altered his route to drive past the place where his life had changed, but he hadn't ventured inside once.

37

Apparently the interior had been transformed over the last twenty years—the merchandising of the products, the décor and even the location of the cash register had altered—but that didn't make the prospect of going inside any more bearable.

Although he had been only ten at the time, he still felt guilty about surviving the shooting and believed he should have done more to save his family. When he had told Jordache about the cobra tattoos, the police had identified the killers as members of Sons of the Serpent, a small anarchic cult whose followers took hallucinogenic drugs to reinforce their belief that they were immortals chosen by Satan to sow discord in the world. He had later learned that the strange looped crucifix tattooed on their arms was called an ankh, an ancient symbol for eternal life. Fox used to fantasize about hunting the killers down until Jordache had informed him that both men, model citizens before they had joined the cult, had been shot dead in a later robbery: ballistics had matched their guns to those used to murder his parents and sister. The Sons of the Serpent had disbanded shortly afterwards but Fox still possessed an almost phobic hatred of cults. Numerous therapists, attempting to recover his memory of the event, had encouraged him to revisit the scene of the crime and confront his fears but he had always refused, rationalizing that sometimes it was better to let sleeping dogs lie. The simple memory of arguing with his sister before she was murdered still had the power to upset him. Recalling the moment of her death and that of his parents would surely be intolerable.

Deep down, however, he knew he'd never be

at peace until he recovered those lost minutes. That was why the yellow sign had shocked him. It announced that the Chevron petrol station and many of the surrounding buildings would soon be pulled down to make way for a new shopping mall. For reasons he couldn't explain, he feared that once the petrol station disappeared all hope of ever remembering what had happened on that night would disappear with it.

CHAPTER SIX

Across town, a stranger entered the Shanghai, a seamy bar hidden among the run-down hotels, strip joints, whorehouses and derelict warehouses that lined the Willamette River. Vince Vega and other hardcore regulars looked up from their lunchtime beers to glare at the intruder who dared trespass in their domain. Vega, sitting alone in the corner, shook his head in disgust. Even the police knew to stay out of the Shanghai. This rube had to be from out of town, too stupid to know better.

Portland's Old Town, home of the original skid row, had a notorious and sordid past. Not so long ago, men who drank in its numerous bars could have found themselves drugged and dragged through the infamous Shanghai tunnels which ran under much of the neighbourhood, waking to find themselves on a ship in the middle of the ocean, forced to work for food and drink. Young women faced an even bleaker fate as white slaves sold into prostitution in some far-flung land.

Today, it was still one of the more dangerous

parts of the city, edgier than its fashionable neighbour the Pearl District, and this suited Vince Vega just fine. Over the years he had clawed his way to a position of power and now regarded Old Town, in all its seedy glory, as his fiefdom. Most of the whores who walked its streets or operated out of the low-rent flophouses came under his control. Many of the crack dealers who plied their trade in the district paid him a cut.

As Vega sipped his beer, his weasel eyes watched the stranger approach the bar and study the extensive array of Oregon beers chalked on the large blackboard. The man wore a collarless white shirt but everything else was plain black: trousers, long jacket, boots, the broad-rimmed hat that concealed his face, even the large bag he carried in his right hand. His pale skin and lips added to the monochrome look. The stranger was large, with a labourer's build, but size had never intimidated Vega, who was a wiry ferret of a man. In his experience bigger men were invariably slow and overconfident. And this guy looked like one of those Amish pussies who wouldn't step on a bug. Some discarded marker pens lay scattered on the bar and the man picked them up, obsessively arranging the colours in a particular order, before replacing them in their carton.

What an asshole.

He listened to the rumbling growl of the man's voice as he ordered a beer, and watched the way he inclined his head like a dog, to stare at the screen above the bar. The guy seemed mesmerized by the TV, like he'd never seen one before in his life.

'Fucking retard,' Vega muttered into his beer. Suddenly the man straightened and stepped away from the bar, literally taken aback by what he was seeing on screen: a news feature on the mystery Jane Doe. Did the retard know her? The man watched the screen intently, apparently in awe of how Jane Doe had gone into a dark basement armed only with an axe and single-handedly rescued eleven girls from the Russian Mafia. Vega scowled at the television. If that bitch had moved in on his merchandise he would have given her more than fucking amnesia, that's for sure. Nothing and no one got in the way of his business.

He shifted his attention back to the stranger and noticed he was sipping his beer and looking in his direction. That stupid hat still obscured much of his face but Vega could sense the man was checking him out. The stranger glanced at him and then back at the screen a couple of times, as if making some connection. Then he tilted his head and Vega saw the man's pale eyes for the first time. The bastard *was* staring directly at him. He looked surprised, like he recognized Vega. Which wasn't possible. Vega never forgot a face and he sure as hell had never seen this fresh-off-the-farm rube before.

He reached for the gun in his waistband, intending to stand up and confront the stranger, show this asshole the natural order of things. But something about his cold, unblinking gaze stopped him. Vega could usually read a man's eyes, detect his weakness and go for the jugular. He detected nothing from the stranger, though, not a flicker of humanity. It was like looking into the eyes of an animal—or a dead man. Vince Vega didn't even try to stare him down because for the first time in a long while he felt the chill of fear. The beer suddenly tasted sour in his mouth so he put it down slowly on the table, picked up his newspaper and walked out of the bar. As he passed the stranger he detected a faint, almost imperceptible sickly-sweet odour. He had smelt it before, on a number of occasions. It was the smell of death.

Outside, he immediately felt better and cursed himself for not confronting the stranger. He was Vince Vega, for Christ's sake, and Vince Vega didn't back down from anybody or anything. Yeah, he reassured himself, if the guy was still there when he went back to the bar then he'd teach him a lesson he'd never forget. Heading for the low-rent apartment he used as an office, he cut through one of the deserted alleys off Burnside Street. It was only when he reached the end that he sensed someone behind him. He turned, just as his nostrils picked up a waft of the cloying smell he had detected in the bar earlier, but he was too late. The man was upon him. Before he could cry out a large hand clamped over his mouth, something sharp pricked his arm and his legs collapsed beneath him.

Some time later his mind cleared. He had no idea how much later. All he knew was that his head throbbed and his mouth felt dry. His hands were bound and he was lying face down on cold concrete steps inside a dark stairwell that smelt of piss. He was no longer wearing his own clothes, but a bra and women's panties.

'Feel familiar?' rumbled the same low voice he had heard in the bar. The smell wafted by him again and the big stranger came into view. He had a cell phone taped to his forehead and it took Vega a beat to realize its video lens was recording everything the sick rube was seeing.

'What are you doing? What the hell do you want

42

from me?'

'Remember this place?' growled the man. Vega heard the stranger's excited heavy breathing and looked around frantically. Where was this place? Why should it be familiar? The fucking retard must have him confused with someone else. The man opened the black bag at his feet and Vega saw the carton of marker pens from the bar, a transparent box of large syringes and a copy of the *Oregonian* newspaper. Reaching beneath the syringe box the man retrieved a staple gun and a large knife.

'No, no,' Vega cried. 'You've made a big mistake. You've got the wrong guy, I tell you.'

'I'm going to cut your throat and throw you down the stairs. Does that help remind you?' Suddenly, despite his terror and panic, Vega realized what the guy must be talking about. But how did he know? How the hell *could* he know? Vega had told no one. The cloying smell intensified, became overpowering, as the stranger's massive frame bent over him. 'Who are you?' Vega screamed. '*What* are you?'

The stranger's pale unblinking eyes stared into his. 'A demon,' the man replied in his low growl. 'A fallen angel freed to walk among the children of men and spread my dark wings.' The man moved behind him and Vega's last scream was cut short as the cold steel of his tormentor's blade sliced through his throat. The final image Vega registered before he died was the face of the Jane Doe in the newspaper.

CHAPTER SEVEN

As the nurses bundled Jane Doe into the ambulance she felt for the locket round her neck, opened it and studied the picture inside of a smiling baby. Holding this one link to her past comforted her, although she had no idea who the baby in the photograph was.

Jane Doe had once been somebody but now felt as if she had been dropped into hell, a lost soul bereft of any bearings. The nurses reassured her how lucky she was to be heading to a special private clinic, but it was hard to feel lucky about anything when you couldn't even remember your own name. They told her that the vast asylum she was escaping being transferred to was the actual place where they'd shot the Jack Nicholson film *One Flew over the Cuckoo's Nest*, which might have meant something if she could remember the movie or who Jack Nicholson was—or anything before the night of the fire, ten days ago.

As she sat alone in the ambulance and watched the state hospital recede into the distance it didn't seem like she was escaping anywhere. How could you escape from your own mind? Physically she was much improved; her burns and the bullet wound to her head had been superficial. Mentally, however, it was a different matter. She caught her reflection in the window. Looking at the eyes of the stranger staring back at her made her feel as if she was peering into the windows of a forgotten home, for which she had lost the keys. The amnesia had left her adrift in the world, untethered from all things familiar, a stranger to everyone including herself. Her hallucinations frightened her more, though. And sleep brought little respite. The nightmares that visited her sleeping hours were as disturbing as any waking visions. The doctors clearly didn't know what to do with her, apart from trying to fill her with pills, most of which she had refused. How could she hope to find herself again if she was drugged up to the eyeballs?

After some time she felt the ambulance slow. Out of the window a freshly painted sign revealed that she had arrived at the Tranquil Waters Clinic and Residential Retreat. The ambulance drove down a long gravel drive, through magnificent grounds, past a peaceful lake sparkling in the sun, and stopped outside a large Victorian building, connected by a glass walkway to a new modern wing. 'You're lucky to be out of the state hospital,' said the ambulance driver. 'This place is the best in the area.'

She said nothing. The doctors, visibly relieved she was now someone else's problem, had already briefed her on Tranquil Waters. The original Victorian building had apparently housed the infamous Pine Hills Psychiatric Hospital, which once treated hardcore psychotic cases and the full-blown criminally insane. Since its closure, however, Oregon University Research Hospital had bought the site, totally renovated the old building, added the new wing and renamed it Tranquil Waters. The private facility now had an enviable reputation for research, treatment and the long-term care of patients with dementia, memory loss, and a range of neuroses and anxiety disorders.

As the driver helped her off the ambulance and

45

led her towards the forbidding Gothic façade of the original Victorian block, she didn't expect this place to be any better than the last, however fresh the paint and beautiful the grounds. Her problem, after all, lay in the shadows of her mind, not out here in the sunlit world. Her worst fears were confirmed when she saw the two white-suited orderlies and the smiling doctor waiting to greet her. They looked no different to all the others she had seen. How could they hope to understand her when not one of them was even the right colour?

*   *   *

A few yards away, in one of the main offices near the Tranquil Waters reception, Nathan Fox sat in a handover meeting with Dr Tozer, Jane Doe's doctor from Oregon State. The other three people in the room were Tranquil Waters' two other senior psychiatrists, Frank Miller and Walter Kolb, both considerably older than Fox, and their boss, the redoubtable Professor Elizabeth Fullelove (which she insisted was pronounced *fully love*).

The head of Tranquil Waters was in her late fifties, hair more grey than black, but her bright eyes and unlined black skin made her look younger. She was a formidable presence; Fox had known her for some years but still called her Professor. As did all the other staff. He didn't know anyone who called her Elizabeth, let alone Liz. He suspected that even her husband addressed her formally.

Tozer passed Fullelove a thin manila folder labelled 'Jane Doe', the name the authorities gave to all female patients—and corpses—whose identity was unknown. Fullelove flicked through it and

46

then passed it to Miller, who passed it to Kolb who handed it to Fox. Fox knew that both Miller and Kolb had already read the contents and wanted to treat the patient. Jane Doe was high profile and her unusual circumstances added up to a potentially reputation-making case study. 'Is this all you've got on her, Dr Tozer?' said Fullelove.

'That's all we've discovered so far, Professor. Not just medically, everything. Remember, she had no records of any kind before last week.' Tozer looked tired and harried.

Fox scanned the meagre notes. There were no entries prior to the date Jane Doe was admitted to Oregon State. 'She was wearing a locket?'

'Yes, a heart-shaped silver locket. Not particularly valuable or distinctive, I'm afraid. It contains a faded picture of a baby.'

'Does Jane Doe have any idea who the baby is?'

'No. All I can tell you is she's never taken the locket off—not even to let me study it.'

Fox nodded. 'I don't blame her. It's all she's got from her past life.' He recalled Jordache telling him about the night the police had found her, and how she had been unable to remember even her own name. 'She's really got full-blown retrograde amnesia?'

'Total,' said Tozer. 'It's unclear if it's retrograde amnesia caused by the physiological head trauma of her bullet wound or a psychological fugue state caused by what she experienced in the basement, but the result's the same: she's lost her memories, identity, everything. She can remember *how* to do certain things but nothing else from before the night she saved those girls. And there are other symptoms we kept out of the press.' Fox flicked

47

through the tightly typed assessment. When he came to the third page his expression must have changed because Tozer smiled. 'You found them, I see.'

'Hallucinations?'

'Not just any old hallucinations. Hers are high-definition visions in glorious Technicolor, with Dolby Surround sound. We moved her five times before we found a room in which she didn't hallucinate. Strangely enough it was in the new palliative ward—where terminally ill patients are sent to die.'

'Any brain damage?' asked Miller.

'Her head injuries were minor. MRI scans have shown nothing abnormal.'

Fox read the sketchy descriptions of her hallucinations. There was a recurrent theme. 'I suppose they could be repressed memories.'

'Pretty horrific repressed memories,' said Tozer.

Fox thought of his own inability to recall the murder of his family. 'Do you know of a patient who's repressed good ones?'

'*Touché*,' said Tozer.

'Drugs?' asked Kolb, adjusting his thick glasses.

'All the tox screens were negative,' said Tozer. 'No traces of drugs or alcohol. And she isn't taking any hallucinogenic medication.'

Fox studied the file. 'What medication is she taking?'

'None, apart from sedatives and analgesics in the first few days. She's clearly psychotic but when I prescribed risperidone she refused. She refuses to take any anti-psychotics. She won't even take diazepam for her panic attacks.'

'What about talk therapies?' asked Miller. 'Have

48

your people tried cognitive behaviour therapy or acceptance and commitment therapy?'

Tozer laughed humourlessly. 'My people? You mean me.' He crossed his arms defensively. 'We haven't enough staff to give her CBT, ACT, DBT or any talk therapy. I've recommended it but the earliest she'd get any with us would be three months.'

Fox nodded sympathetically. He worked long hours but they were varied and as a staff member of a well-endowed research hospital, he had access to first-class resources.

'Any parting advice for us, Dr Tozer?' said Fullelove. 'Anything you want to tell us off the record?'

Tozer gathered his papers together, keen to leave. 'Honestly?'

'Of course.'

'I'm glad the wealthy father of one of the American girls she rescued put up the money for Jane Doe to come here. She deserves the best care. But I'm also relieved to hand her over. Even here I think you'll have your hands full trying to treat her. It's not just the media spotlight, which adds obvious pressures. It's the patient herself. Aside from her psychiatric problems, Jane Doe is difficult, impatient, aggressive and uncooperative. She has zero respect for our profession. So far she's claimed that every doctor who's treated her, medical and psychiatric, has been the wrong colour.'

Professor Fullelove raised an eyebrow and her black skin creased into a frown. 'The wrong *colour*?' Before Tozer could elaborate, Fox heard a distant, terrified scream.

'Calm down,' soothed a far-off voice. 'There's

49

nothing to be frightened of.'

'Let me out,' the first voice cried. 'I won't stay here. Why don't you understand? I *can't* stay in this room.'

Tozer smiled wryly. 'That's her, the famous avenging angel. I'd recognize those dulcet tones anywhere.' He stood up, fastened his briefcase and hurried to the door. 'She's *your* avenging angel, now. Good luck.'

*   *   *

The commotion was coming from a room in the original Victorian building, at the end of the corridor leading to the new wing. The door was ajar and as they approached Fox glanced inside. A doctor and two orderlies in white coats were trying to reason with a tall, agitated young woman who was shaking her head from side to side and holding her locket like an infant clutching a security blanket. 'I keep telling you,' she shouted. 'I *can't* stay in here.'

Fullelove went into the room, flanked by Kolb and Miller, while Fox waited behind in the corridor. 'What's the problem, Dr Feinberg?'

'Jane Doe doesn't like her room, Professor Fullelove,' said the junior doctor. The room was typical of all the rooms at Tranquil Waters: freshly painted walls; comfortable bed; large window overlooking the beautiful grounds; TV; chair and desk; private bathroom.

'What's wrong with it, Jane? It's a nice room,' Fullelove reasoned gently. The terrified young woman kept blinking as if trying to see something more clearly—or trying *not* to see it. Fox couldn't take his eyes off her. He had thought her striking

50

on the television news but her sculptured features and haunted eyes were beautiful in the flesh. 'What's wrong with the room, Jane?' Fullelove asked again.

'You won't understand.' Jane Doe slammed her right hand hard against the door and Fox felt his left smart with the pain. 'You're the wrong colour.'

Fox could see Professor Fullelove stiffen. 'What colour's that, Jane?'

'Red.'

'*Red?*'

'You're *all* the wrong colour,' she shouted. 'Just leave me alone and let me out of here. I *can't* stay in this room.' She shoved one of the orderlies against the wall with surprising force, pushed her way past Fullelove, Kolb and Miller, and ran into the corridor.

Straight into Fox's arms.

For a moment she stared at him, transfixed, then her face relaxed. The orderlies ran to her but Fox signalled them to stay back. 'Are you a doctor?' she asked.

'A psychiatrist, yes.' He held out his hand. 'My name's Nathan Fox.'

She gripped it tightly in hers, as if frightened he might escape. 'I don't know *my* name, Dr Fox, but perhaps you can help me remember it.' She turned to Fullelove, eyes shining with relief. '*He* can help me find myself again.'

'Why him?' Fullelove said. 'Is Dr Fox the right colour?'

'Yes,' she said.

'What colour's that?' said Fox, intrigued.

'The faint glow around you is a deep purple-blue—indigo. The others have all been

51

shades of red, yellow, green and orange.'

'Why's *my* particular colour so important?'

'I can't remember.' She shook her head in frustration. 'I just know it means you'll be able to understand me better than the others.' Jane Doe looked imploringly at Fox, her haunted eyes so filled with naked need that every defensive instinct he had nurtured over the years screamed at him to keep his distance, remain detached and not get involved. The reticence must have shown in his face because she released his hand, slumped her shoulders and stared down at the dark carpet. She looked exhausted, hopeless, helpless and totally alone, a stranger to everyone, including herself.

Against his instincts, he took her hand again. 'Tell me about what scared you in that room,' he asked. She stiffened, alert like a hunted deer. He smiled. 'Hallucinations can be as vivid and terrifying as dreams and nightmares, but they're also just as harmless. Unlike dreams, they occur in a conscious, awake state. Clinically, hallucinations are perceptions of things in the absence of external stimuli. Things that *seem* to be there but *aren't*.'

'They feel real, though.'

'But they're *not*. And that's the crucial point because what isn't there can't harm you, however frightening it might seem.'

'You wouldn't say that if *you* saw them.'

'Then show me them.' He retrieved a pen-sized digital voice recorder from his jacket. 'Walk back into the room with me and describe exactly what you see. Try to ignore whether the experiences are real or not, what they make you feel, or how you think they reflect on you. Just report them objectively, like a journalist. Be my eyes and ears.

Can you do that?' He squeezed her hand. 'You said you think I can help you. So let me.' He led her to the open doorway. As he stepped inside she hesitated. 'Come,' he said. 'Follow me. Tell me what's so frightening. Tell me what you see.'

He watched her take a deep breath, on the cusp of panic, riding the waves of her anxiety. Then she turned to him, eyes cold and challenging. 'You sure you want to do this?'

'Absolutely.' He hoped his unflinching gaze gave her courage. 'I'm right beside you. Tell me everything.'

CHAPTER EIGHT

Encouraging Jane Doe to confront her hallucinations and describe them objectively was a classic defusion technique. Fox hoped to challenge her belief that she was responsible for the hallucinations and help her gain some emotional distance from them. It required an enormous amount of courage from the subject but, according to Jordache, Jane Doe had that in spades. You don't break into a dark basement armed with only an axe and take on the Russian mob single-handed unless you know how to face a few demons.

As he led her into the room he became acutely aware of her breathing and the tension radiating from every muscle in her body. Her wide eyes and flared nostrils brought to mind a wild horse about to bolt. It was obvious Fullelove and the others watching in the corridor weren't immune to the tension. As Jane Doe crossed the threshold he switched on his digital recorder.

'See anything yet?'

She shook her head. 'Only flashes. Disjointed images.' She looked exhausted.

'Just report what you see,' he said. 'Nothing more. Nothing less. Don't try to analyse or interpret anything.' She rested against the wall then, suddenly, her face changed. It had been pale before but was now ashen. Her nose twitched and again the image of a panicked wild animal flashed through his mind. 'What do you see now?'

'Nothing,' she said, barely above a whisper. She sounded very far away. 'I can *smell* something, though.'

'Smell?' Fox said, conscious of his own mounting unease. 'What?'

'Shit. And blood.' She spoke in a robotic monotone as if in a trance. 'Now I can hear buzzing and see the flies.' She took a sharp intake of breath and Fox felt her fingernails dig deep into the palm of his hand. She visibly shuddered. 'Now I see *him*.'

'Who?'

She focused on a space in the middle of the room, her face contorted with disgust and fear. 'The man.'

'What man? Tell me exactly what you see.'

'I keep seeing the same scene again and again, like it's in a loop. He's hanging in front of me, naked. His pyjamas have been knotted together, looped over the ceiling beam and tied round his neck.'

Fox looked up. There was no ceiling beam. 'Go on.'

'The pyjamas have blue and white stripes,' she continued. 'Shit is running down his legs and

54

dripping on the upended iron bed beneath his twitching feet. I can hear each drip on the metal frame like water from a faulty tap. There's an overturned chair by the bed.'

The level of multi-sensory detail was remarkable. 'You mentioned blood. Where's it coming from?'

'The other man.'

'The *other* man?'

She pointed. 'He's in the corner of the room. The hanging man is faint, translucent, like a ghost. But this man is more substantial. He looks as real as you. Every detail's in natural colours except for a slight tint, which comes and goes, as though I'm looking through a flickering filter.'

'What colour is it?'

She pointed to an African violet on the windowsill. 'Like that flower but much much paler.'

'Do all your hallucinations have this flickering colour wash?'

'Yes.'

'What's the man in the corner doing?'

'He's sitting on the floor, staring at the door. He's wearing an orange T-shirt embossed with a yellow cartoon figure and the word Cowabunga.' She swallowed hard. Perspiration beaded her forehead. 'His neck and both wrists have been sliced open, exposing white tendons and nerves in the wounds. It's like I'm in hell. I can feel what *he* is feeling. I feel his slashes on *my* wrists and *my* throat. I feel the despair I see in his eyes. I taste the blood in *my* mouth. I *am* him.' Her steady monotone had turned to a pained, keening whine. 'Blood's pouring on to the floor. There's a pool at my toes.' Suddenly she stumbled backwards, pulling Fox with her, and stared down at her feet. 'I *can't* let it touch me because then I'll *know* it's real—as real as your hand in mine. The blood isn't the worst part, though.'

'What is?'

She let go of Fox and put her hands over her ears. 'The screaming. The man's staring at the door and screaming the same words again and again: "Marty, Marty. I'm sorry, Marty, but you can't help me. No one can help me, Marty."' She turned and left the room.

Fox stayed for a moment, staring into the corner of the room, trying to see what she had seen, then followed her into the corridor.

*   *   *

Although Jane Doe couldn't stop shaking, sharing her experience with Dr Nathan Fox had normalized it somehow, made it less horrific. It had still been terrifying but for the first time since she could remember she'd felt a slight detachment from the terrible scenes, less like they were *hers*, less like she was mad or evil for being the only person able to see them. She felt a sudden rush of gratitude. She had been right about Nathan Fox's colour. Not one of the doctors at the other hospital had listened to her fears or even begun to understand her hallucinations. Although nothing had actually changed, Fox had given her something which she thought had been lost with her identity: hope.

'How are you feeling?' Fox asked, as Fullelove and the others looked on.

She nodded slowly, clutching the locket. 'I'm OK.' She glanced back at the room. 'I'm not going back in there, though.'

'There are rooms available in the new wing,' said Fullelove. 'Let Dr Feinberg show you them and you can choose whichever feels most comfortable. How does that sound?'

Jane nodded then looked back at Fox. 'Can he be my doctor?'

Fullelove smiled. 'We'll see. I need to talk with my colleagues.'

*   *   *

As Fox watched Jane Doe walk down the corridor with Dr Feinberg, he couldn't shake off a feeling of unease. He remembered Jordache's warning: *Be careful, my friend. She'll get under your skin—even yours.*

Fullelove turned to him. 'You heard her, Nathan. What do you think?'

'Are you sure I'm right for her? Her irrational dependence on my perceived colour might be a good reason for me not to be her primary therapist.' He turned to Miller and Kolb, who suddenly didn't seem so keen to treat her. 'Perhaps Frank or Walter might be better?'

'I disagree. If Jane Doe thinks you're the right colour—whatever that means—then it gives you an immediate rapport. You've effectively had one session with her already, which went pretty well. Any other objections?'

He could think of quite a few, but none that were defensible. 'I suppose not, Professor.'

Fullelove patted him on the shoulder. 'Good, you can have your next session with her tomorrow. I'd better go and see her settled in.'

Alone, Fox was walking back to the main

57

reception area when he heard a cough from inside the room. He looked in and saw one of the orderlies lingering by the doorway. He was a big man but looked small, broken. His pale skin was glazed with sweat, his thinning hair slick on his forehead.

'You OK?'

The man moved close and whispered urgently, 'There's something you should know, Dr Fox.' He glanced nervously out of the doorway, down the corridor towards Jane Doe's departing back, as if checking she was out of earshot. 'About the room. About what she said she saw.'

'What's that?' said Fox.

'I don't know about the hanging man, but the other man—the one in the orange Bart Simpson T-shirt who cut his wrists and shouted for Marty—that actually happened. His name was Frank Bartlett and he was a patient in the old Pine Hills Psychiatric Hospital seven or eight years ago. He cut his wrists and throat and died in that room exactly as she described.'

'That's impossible. It was a hallucination.'

The orderly shook his head. 'I used to work at Pine Hills before the new place opened,' he said. 'I found Frank. My name's Martin Zabriskie. I'm the guy he was screaming at when he died. I'm Marty.' Something cold uncoiled in Fox's belly. 'The point is,' the orderly hissed, looking down the corridor after Jane Doe, 'how could *she*, a woman who can't even remember her own name, have known what happened in that room all those years ago?'

CHAPTER NINE

Later that evening they found the first victim.

Detective Karl Jordache was sitting down to dinner with his wife and two daughters when he got the call. His wife was an excellent cook but tonight's chicken dinner didn't excite his palate: no sauce on the grilled chicken breast, no dressing on the salad and no butter or salt on the boiled potatoes. He knew it was for his health but, cholesterol or no cholesterol, he wanted some flavour back in his life. Nevertheless, he was hungry and groaned when his cell phone rang. He checked the caller, excused himself and took the call in his study. 'This better be important, Phil.'

'We've got a one-eight-seven you should see, Chief,' said Phil Kostakis, one of the older detectives on his force.

'Handle it and give me your report in the morning.'

'Trust me, Chief, you'll want to see this.' A pause. 'Could be kinda sensitive if the press got hold of it. You'll see what I mean when you get here.'

Jordache cursed under his breath. 'Where are you?'

'Old Town. One of the abandoned apartment blocks near the river.' He gave the address and Jordache wrote it down.

'OK, Phil, I'll be right there. Secure the scene, and don't let reporters anywhere near it.' They had only just tied up the loose ends of Linnet's involvement in the Russian sex-trafficking case and now this.

Putting on his coat, he bent to kiss his daughters goodbye, but his wife shook her head. 'You're not going anywhere until you've had your supper, Karl. You need to eat and if you go hungry you'll only be tempted by a taco or a burger. So sit down and finish your plate. The dead can wait.' He considered arguing but knew it would only delay his departure further so he sat down dutifully and finished his meal.

The drive to the address in Portland's Old Town took a little over half an hour. The crime scene was a block from the Willamette River, near Burnside Street. Signs on the padlocked gates and chain-link fence around the derelict apartment building warned trespassers and squatters to stay out, but the fence had been breached in so many places that the gates were redundant. As he got out of the car he was grateful for a fresh breeze blowing in from the Pacific. Discarded condoms littered the cracked concrete of the car park and the soles of Jordache's sturdy brogues crunched on used syringes as he ducked under crime scene tape and greeted the cluster of police by the main door.

Phil Kostakis led him into the apartment lobby. The detective was a short man with dark hair over most of his body, except on his head, which gleamed under the bare bulb hanging from the temporary electrical rig. Kostakis led him past a disused elevator that reeked of urine, to an open door.

'This is the emergency stairwell that serves the block.' Lamps had been set up in the dark stairwell and men in white forensic suits were checking the handrails for prints. The first thing Jordache

60

noticed was blood on the walls. Then he saw a Caucasian male in his fifties lying broken on the bottom step, naked except for a pair of women's panties and a bra. He was on his back but his neck had been twisted almost one hundred and eighty degrees so Jordache couldn't see the face.

'Any ID?'

'Name's Vince Vega, a local pimp and drug dealer.' Jordache knew Vega. The sleazeball had been a fixture of the neighbourhood for years. He wasn't a loved man and Jordache wasn't surprised he'd come to a bad end but, as warped as the scene was, he still wasn't sure why Kostakis had dragged him out here. 'There are significant traces of ketamine in his blood.'

'What else?'

Kostakis went to a large CSI kit bag and pulled out two pairs of white plastic shoe protectors. He passed a pair to Jordache, who slipped them over his brogues. They weren't intended to shield the shiny black leather from the blood and filth but to protect the crime scene from contamination. Following Kostakis, Jordache stepped carefully over the body and ascended the stairs, which had the discomforting distinction of being both sticky and slippery. As they reached the limit of the light supplied by the lamps, Kostakis pointed to a pile of men's clothes on the top step. 'Seems the killer drugged him, carried him into the stairwell and up this flight of stairs. After changing him into women's underwear, the killer left Vega's own clothes here, cut his throat and pushed him down the steps. The pathologist figures the blood loss would have killed him before he reached the bottom step.' Kostakis led him back down the stairs

61

and crouched over the corpse. 'The body's been staged. It didn't fall like this. The killer came down the stairs and rearranged Vega's arms and legs to fit some preordained pattern.'

Jordache frowned impatiently. 'Why did you call me, Phil?'

Kostakis reached down with gloved hands and turned Vega's head so the face became visible. 'Because of this.' Jordache's eyes were drawn initially to the deep vicious gash on Vega's throat. The killer was so powerful his knife had virtually severed the head with what appeared to be a single slice. Then Jordache registered the bloodstained sheet of paper stapled to Vega's forehead, obscuring his face. A two-line message had been written on the paper in coloured marker pen, each capital letter a different colour:

SERVE THE DEMON
SAVE THE ANGEL

Why had the killer invested precious time doing that? Jordache wondered.

'We don't know what the message means yet,' Kostakis said. 'But look at what it's written on.' Jordache peered closer at the soiled paper and finally understood why Kostakis had called him. 'See what I mean about sensitive?'

Jordache mentally raced through the implications. 'Yes, Phil, I see what you mean.' He instantly thought of Nathan Fox and wondered what the psychiatrist would make of it.

'What do you want to do, Chief?'

'I want to find the bastard who did this, that's what I want to do.'

62

'But do we tell—'

'Nope. We tell no one. Not yet. Think about it, Phil. What good would it do?' He thought of the message, wondering what it might mean. 'We got to be real careful about this. With all the media attention the only connection could be in the killer's sick mind. I figure we keep this quiet for now and focus on what we do best: examine the crime scene evidence for clues and motive— anything that explains what's going on in the killer's mind—and look for witnesses. Someone must have seen something.'

Kostakis nodded. 'But what do you think, Chief? Off the record?'

Despite his recent meal and current surroundings, Jordache had a sudden, irrational craving for the comfort of a cholesterol-rich cheeseburger. 'Off the record, Phil, I don't know. But I got a bad feeling we're going to find out soon enough.'

CHAPTER TEN

Oblivious to events unfolding across town, Jane Doe slumbered in her bed at Tranquil Waters. She had declined the 10mg of diazepam and 50mg of chlorpromazine prescribed to help her sleep. Her encounter with Fox had calmed her and she felt more comfortable in her new room, especially after moving the bed into the centre.

When sleep came, however, the fragmented recurring nightmares that had plagued her since losing her memory returned: crazed horses, nostrils flared in panic, galloping in ever-decreasing circles; a giant eye staring down at her from a high tower; a faceless figure—a man and yet somehow inhuman—chasing her frantically through the rooms of a silent hotel occupied only by the dead.

Hours from dawn, just as her malevolent pursuer reached out to grip her shoulder and drag her back from whence he came, she awoke screaming. All hope of sleep banished, she lay awake until the light came, waiting for Nathan Fox to help reassemble the pieces of her shattered identity and make sense of the madness that threatened to engulf her.

*   *   *

The *mawashi geri* hit the man cleanly and he fell to the mat with a satisfying grunt. After delivering the roundhouse kick, Nathan Fox instantly opened his eyes, regained his balance and stood over the fallen man.

'*Yame*,' shouted the sensei from the side of the mat, ordering the fight to stop. Fox was panting hard with exertion, his pounding heart pumping blood through his veins. His karate *giri* was saturated with sweat but he felt exhilarated. After leaving Tranquil Waters he had gone straight to the karate dojo for his weekly bout of *jiyu kumite*, advanced free sparring. Karate enabled him not only to vent his aggression and express his passion but also to relieve the stresses of the job. This evening, however, no amount of karate could take his mind off what the orderly had told him about Jane Doe's hallucinations. Fox bowed and helped his opponent to his feet.

'You OK, Leo?'

The man smiled. 'Only a little hurt pride. I swear, Nathan, I'm going to get you one of these days.'

As they left the mat, the aged but still formidable Sensei Daichi tapped Fox on the shoulder. 'Nathan *san*, you want to enter competition next month?'

'You know I haven't competed for years, Sensei. Anyway, I haven't practised enough.'

Daichi shook his head. 'I don't agree. I think you better now you don't train so hard. More relaxed. More natural.' He shrugged. 'Perhaps next time.'

Fox smiled at his mentor. 'Perhaps.'

'Hey, Nathan, some of the guys are grabbing a beer at Scooters,' Leo said. 'You coming?'

'Not tonight, Leo. Next week.'

Leo laughed. 'Hope she's worth it, my friend.'

After a hot shower Fox returned to his apartment in north-west Portland. The neighbourhood boasted many period houses and apartments but his open-plan home on the top floor of a brand new circular tower block was not one of them. He had always preferred the space and light of modern buildings to the draughts, rattling windows, cracked walls and overrated 'character' of older homes. He opened a cold bottle of local Deschutes Cascade ale from the kitchen and cooked himself a steak— medium rare with just a blush of red in the middle.

As he sipped his beer and prepared a Caesar salad he checked his voicemail. There was a message from his uncle Frank in England inviting him to come over to Cornwall to spend Christmas with his relations on his father's side. Christmas was half a year away. Fox smiled affectionately at the thought of his uncle Frank, who was not an organized man, planning so far ahead. He checked his watch. The time difference meant he'd have to wait to call his uncle back. Next was a bland message from Kate in New York and he felt a stab of guilty relief that he'd been out when she'd called. They had been casually dating for three months and Kate had been hinting at moving into his apartment when, thankfully, her company had offered her a promotion to New York. At first she had called him every day, now she only called him a couple of times a week, usually when he was out. The thought that she might also be avoiding him didn't upset Fox.

Sitting down to eat at the dining table, he ignored the plasma television on the wall above the fireplace and the panoramic views of Portland through the curved windows of the circular tower. Instead he found himself reaching for the typescript document his aunt had given him that morning. As he tried to concentrate on the words his mind kept wandering back to his encounter with Jane Doe and the orderly's revelations about her hallucinations. The same questions kept looping in his mind: how had a woman with total memory loss known what had happened in that room all those years ago? Could she have overheard someone talking about it and registered it subconsciously? She had only been at Tranquil Waters a few hours but perhaps she had heard something while in Oregon State or known about it in her earlier life, before her amnesia. But how? *How?*

When he went to bed and eventually fell asleep his unconscious continued trying to process what his logical mind could not. He woke the next morning exhausted, dragged himself out of bed, ate a quick breakfast, checked on his aunt, then hurried to the clinic. Professor Fullelove was in meetings all morning but he could guess her brisk response: 'There'll be a perfectly logical explanation, Nathan, so don't worry about understanding it now. Let it become clear as you treat her.'

Treat what? Her amnesia? Her hallucinations? Usually he would focus on the amnesia first, trying to discover the identity she had lost. Most amnesiacs retained good operational memory so he would try to gain a picture of her past life by testing her for unforgotten skills, such as languages, sports and social activities. Then he would take her back to the night of the fire, to the time when all knowledge of her old life had died and Jane Doe's new identity had been born. But the orderly's revelation had made him question this approach. Before seeing Jane Doe again, he decided to search the patient records of the original Pine Hills Psychiatric Hospital.

As he sat alone in the small windowless basement room that housed the clinic's computer archive, his unease increased when he found Frank Bartlett's file. The report on his death by suicide confirmed everything the orderly had told him. More searches revealed that twenty years before Bartlett's death, another man had committed suicide in the same room—using his pyjamas to hang himself from the ceiling beam, which had since been removed.

Fox played back the voice recording he'd made of Jane Doe recounting her hallucination, comparing it to the notes on Frank Bartlett's file and the report on the hanging man. They were virtually identical—chillingly so. He went back to Jane Doe's slim file. The police report from the night she had been found raised more questions than it answered. Dr Tozer's psychiatric assessments at Oregon State provided few useful insights, and he was beginning to doubt Tozer's assumption that she was psychotic.

Psychotic patients lost contact with reality. They believed and accepted their hallucinations, voices and urges unquestioningly—sometimes enjoying them. They had little insight into their own condition, felt no anxiety or guilt for their actions, no empathy for their victims and were convinced they were completely sane. People suffering with neuroses, however, were very different. They were aware that their experiences— whether hallucinations, anxieties, thoughts or compulsions—were irrational and found them terrifying and repugnant. Essentially psychotics embraced their irrational experiences while neurotics fought them. Jane Doe was fighting hers with every fibre of her being.

Only when he reread the brief accounts of Jane Doe's hallucinations at Oregon State and checked that hospital's online files did he discover something interesting enough to make him return to the Pine Hills patient records and conduct more searches. The pattern that emerged sowed a disturbing thought in his mind. Irrational and resistant to logic, the notion quickly took root and began to grow. When he printed off his findings and placed them in his briefcase, he discovered another document that fed the insane but insistent idea blossoming in his mind. As he studied it, he began scribbling more notes. Most were questions, impossible questions. He was reaching across to make a phone call when he noticed the clock on the wall. It was time to see Jane Doe.

CHAPTER ELEVEN

Jane Doe seemed comfortable in her new room so Fox had arranged to meet her there. As he walked through the new wing, he decided not to tell her about the suicides until it was necessary and helpful to do so. When he arrived at her room Jane Doe opened the door before he could knock. Her beautiful face looked tired but expectant.

'Hello, Dr Fox,' she said, ushering him into the room and gesturing to the chair by the window. 'Welcome to my humble abode.'

Then two things happened.

The first wasn't significant in itself, merely embarrassing, but Jane Doe's reaction *was* significant: when Fox placed his briefcase on the table and moved to the chair he tripped on a shoe she had left on the floor. As he broke his fall, he turned his right wrist. Anyone else would have missed the small hand movement she made as she apologized and tried to help him up, but it was the exact same gesture Fox would have made if he'd been sitting in her place and seen what she'd just seen: she rubbed her left wrist.

He sat on the chair and watched her sit cross-legged on the bed. 'Did you feel that?' he asked. 'Did your wrist hurt when I fell?'

'Only a little.'

He thought this interesting but not necessarily relevant as he looked around the room. 'Why's the bed in the centre of the room?'

'It feels more comfortable away from the walls.'

He considered this and her fear of being trapped in rooms and wondered again if she could have been one of the Russian traffickers' captives. 'Do you have any memory of the place you rescued those girls from? Or the men holding them captive?'

She shook her head. 'None at all. I can't even remember breaking the girls out. Did anyone there recognize me?'

It was Fox's turn to shake his head. 'No. No one claims to have seen you before that night.' He gestured to her neck. 'May I see that?'

Her hand shot up and gripped the locket protectively. 'Why?'

'I just wanted to see the photograph inside.'

'It's of a baby.' She made no move to show it to him.

'Do you know who the baby is?'

'No. But I must have done once.'

He smiled. 'The locket's important to you, isn't it?'

'It's my only link to who I was.'

He nodded and retrieved her medical file from his briefcase. 'I understand.'

Then the second thing happened.

As he laid her file on his lap she pointed to the name written on the cover and said, 'I kind of like my new name. I like the way it tastes on the tip of my tongue.'

'The way it *tastes*?'

'Yes.'

'What does "Jane Doe" taste of?'

'Salmon and chives.'

'What does my name taste of?'

'You don't know the taste of your own name?'

'What does it taste like to you?'

She closed her eyes and said his name slowly,

70

syllable by syllable, savouring it. 'Doc-tor Na-than Fox.' She smiled. 'Cider and cream. Quite yummy.'

This bizarre exchange, and the way she had stroked her wrist, made what was already an intriguing case even more so. Then he remembered how she attributed coloured auras to people and cursed himself for not making the connection earlier. He took a pen and notepad from his jacket and scribbled down a list. It wasn't exclusive but it covered every variety he could think of off the top of his head. He immediately ticked off the first two entries. Then on a blank page he wrote a large letter A in black ink and showed it to her. 'What colour is this letter?'

She smiled slyly like it was a trick question. 'You've written it in black but everyone knows the letter A is red.'

'Always?'

'Of course.'

'The letter E?'

'Olive green.'

'What about the number 1?'

'Turquoise.'

'Do you *know* it's turquoise or can you *see* it?'

'I see it.'

'Where?'

She pointed to a space in thin air, about a foot in front of her face. 'Here.'

Amazing. This was getting more and more bizarre. He ticked the third entry off his list: 'grapheme-colour'. He probed further. 'What's the letter O like as a personality?'

'Os are female,' she said without hesitation. 'And they're generally generous, open and kind. Although they can be a bit fussy.'

71

'What about the number seven?'

'Seven is tall and dark. And male.' She giggled, enjoying the game. 'He's elegant but dangerous.'

He ticked the next entry off his list: 'ordinal linguistic personification'. This was incredible. He took out his cell phone and played two of its ringtones. 'What do you *see*?'

'Blues and greens, but the last note is yellow.'

He took out his bunch of keys and shook them, making a discordant jangling noise. 'Do you see anything now?'

'A blur of yellows, reds and oranges.' He ticked two more entries off his list: 'sound-colour (narrowband)' and 'sound-colour (broadband)'. Then he selected the calculator mode on his cell phone. 'What are you like at mental arithmetic, Jane?'

'Try me.'

'OK.' He began entering numbers into the phone. 'Multiply eighty-seven by twenty-two, add sixty-one, divide by eleven . . .' As he pressed the buttons he noticed her finger stabbing the space in front of her, as though manipulating a virtual abacus. '. . . multiply by fourteen, subtract twenty-three, add six and divide by five point five.'

As the phone revealed the solution he heard her say it, exactly as it appeared on his display: 'Four hundred and fifty-three point nine three three eight eight seven.'

'Impressive. When you do your calculations, can you see the numbers in front of you?'

'Of course. They're laid out in colour-coded rows and columns, which I move around to do my calculations.' *Like a spreadsheet*, he thought, ticking the final entry off his list: 'number-form'. His head buzzed with possibilities. She frowned. 'Can't everyone do this?'

'No, they can't.' He looked back over his list. 'Ever heard of something called synaesthesia?'

She shook her head. Like most synaesthetes she didn't appear to think her crossed senses were unusual but, incredibly, no one else had picked up on her condition. No mention of it appeared in her file. 'What's synaesthesia?' she asked, anxiously.

'Don't worry, it's not an illness. It's not classified as a neurological medical condition and rarely causes problems or disability. Some even regard it as a gift. If you want to get technical, synaesthesia is defined as a neurologically based phenomenon in which stimulation of one sensory or cognitive pathway leads to automatic, involuntary experiences in a second sensory or cognitive pathway. Put more simply, it involves two or more senses becoming cross-wired. For example: sight and touch, sound and taste, sound and colour, symbols and colour.'

'Is it unusual?'

'Pretty unusual. About one person in every twenty-one has some form of the condition. One of the rarer forms is mirror-touch synaesthesia, in which a subject sees someone else experience touch or pain and then feels it himself. I happen to know a bit about this because I've got it.' He smiled at her. 'I'm pretty sure you've got it, too. I noticed the way you rubbed your wrist when I fell.' She nodded. 'But you don't just have my type, you also seem to have lexical-gustatory synaesthesia, in which individual words and sounds of spoken language evoke the sensations of taste in the mouth. This tasting of words is also very rare. What makes it rarer still is that synaesthetes—as we're known—usually have only one form of the phenomenon, one pairing of cross-wired senses, but you appear—'

'To have two,' she said. She was sitting forward now, forehead creased in concentration, hungry for answers.

'Not just two,' he said. 'Even your ability to see coloured auras around people is typical of emotion-colour synaesthesia.' He showed her his list. 'What's truly remarkable is you appear to have not only the rarest forms of the phenomenon but every form I know of.' He read through the rest of the list. 'Grapheme-colour synaesthesia; you see letters and numbers as colours. Ordinal linguistic personification; you associate ordered sequences such as numbers, letters and days of the week with personalities. Sound-colour synaesthesia, both narrowband and broadband; you see musical notes and other environmental sounds as colours. And, finally, number-form synaesthesia; you see numbers in a three-dimensional, colour-coded virtual matrix that allows you to perform mental calculations at amazing speeds.' Fox paused to process what he was saying. Jane Doe appeared to be some kind of super-synaesthete, each and every sense feeding off and into the others. At one level she experienced the world as everyone else did but at another sensory level she interpreted it completely differently. Suddenly his own mirror-touch variety seemed very pedestrian. 'Basically, you have every form of synaesthesia I can think of, without going back to my reference books, and probably many others I can't. There are at least sixty recognized variants, involving differing permutations of the five major senses. You might even have forms that haven't been diagnosed yet. I've never come across this before. This is unprecedented. You may be unique.'

'What does it mean, though? What's it got to do with my memory loss and the hallucinations?'

He opened her file again and focused on her head injuries. 'Synaesthesia is usually something you're born with and often runs in families. You can get it from head trauma and exposure to drugs but your injuries from the night of the fire weren't that acute and drugs don't seem to be a factor. I'm guessing you probably had synaesthesia *before* you lost your memory and that it's linked to your hallucinations.'

'You don't think my hallucinations and memory loss are connected?'

'Not directly, no. But now I know about your synaesthesia I'd like to focus on the hallucinations. You appear to have *total* synaesthesia.' He paused, uncomfortably aware he was entering uncharted waters of speculation. 'Perhaps it also breathes full sensory life into your thoughts and fears, which would explain why you smell, see, hear and feel your hallucinations in such acute detail. Your unique sensory perception could act like an in-built special effects department: your hallucinations aren't so much computer-generated images as synaesthesia-generated. Don't forget, a hallucination is basically a perception in a conscious or awake state in the absence of external stimuli. You might not need external stimuli, though, to project your thoughts and emotions into the sensory realm and experience them as the real thing.'

'But where do these images come from? My

imagination? My fears? Memories?'

'That's the million-dollar question.' For a moment he considered telling her about the suicides and asking her whether she had overheard anything about them on or before her arrival at Tranquil Waters. If she had heard something, even at an unconscious level, her synaesthesia might somehow have allowed her to recreate the event. But he wanted to check one thing first. 'I did think they might be repressed memories, at first,' he said, pointing to her file. 'But then I read the reports on your hallucinations at Oregon State. They were so varied and prolific I don't see how they could possibly all be memories. Certainly not *your* memories. What's strange though . . .' He stopped himself. The irrational notion that had been growing in his mind was too bizarre to say aloud. He reached for his briefcase and rechecked his notes. There was definitely a pattern and her synaesthesia made the insight—if that was what it was—only more credible. The implications defied every rational instinct but the notion was too compelling to dismiss. And it could easily be verified or, as he expected, debunked. 'I need to make a couple of calls and arrange a few things. Then I want to try something.'

'What?'

'I want to run a little experiment.' He got up and moved to the door. 'I'll be back in a few minutes. I'll explain everything then.'

CHAPTER TWELVE

As Jane Doe waited anxiously for Fox's return, a second victim was waking up to his fate in Old Town. Some time last night, in the back alleys near Burnside, Josh Kovacs had collapsed on the pile of discarded cardboard and newspapers that served as a bed, unconscious from cheap bourbon and every downer he could get his hands on. When he had fallen asleep Kovacs had been wearing worn trainers, a scuffed leather jacket and stained sweats. When he awoke, head pounding and throat sandpaper-dry, he discovered that his lips had been sealed with duct tape and everything had changed.

Opening his eyes, he realized he was no longer in the alley but inside a disused warehouse. The windows had been blacked out and there was a naked bulb hanging overhead so he had no idea what time of day or night it was. As he slowly grasped his predicament, panic seeped through his addled mind. He tried to stand but his wrists and ankles had been bound. Then he noticed his clothes piled neatly on the dusty floor beside him. Looking down he saw he had been dressed in a woman's blue gown.

What the hell . . .?

He heard footsteps then a figure loomed over him, silhouetted against the light bulb. The figure bent down and Kovacs detected a faint cloying smell. When he saw his captor's pale, unblinking eyes, Kovacs found no pity or humanity there. They looked down on him as coldly as if Kovacs were prey to be devoured, or a bug to be crushed. The

77

man had a cell phone strapped to his forehead with duct tape, its video lens staring at him like another eye. Suddenly sober and rigid with fear, Kovacs needed to urinate but some last vestige of pride stopped him emptying his bladder. Two strong arms reached down and moved his body and limbs into a pre-arranged design, then the man pulled out a large knife, knelt over Kovacs and began prodding his chest, feeling for his ribs: a butcher determining the best place to make the first cut. He looked into Kovacs' eyes. 'How old are you now?' he demanded in a low growl. 'Fifty-five? Sixty? You look so old and wasted I almost didn't recognize you.' He scraped the knife against Kovacs' bedraggled grey beard and pulled at his thinning silver hair. 'But your age can't hide you. I know who you are. I know what you did. Can *you* still remember?'

Remember what? Kovacs strained against the duct tape, blinking back sweat, trying to speak. *What the hell are you talking about?*

'Look around you and cast your mind back a few years. Perhaps the blue gown will help remind you.' Suddenly, Kovacs realized what the madman was talking about. But that had been ages ago, decades ago. Why now? The recognition must have shown in his eyes because his tormentor smiled. 'You remember.' He raised the knife and Kovacs could see the muscles twitching in the man's arm as he prepared to plunge the blade into his chest.

A sudden shrill ringing made his attacker freeze, the knife inches above Kovacs' heart. It took Kovacs' terrified mind a beat to realize it was coming from the cell phone attached to the killer's forehead. For what seemed an eternity the knife hovered above him, then the man groaned,

78

stood up and walked out of view. The relief was too much for Kovacs. He relaxed his bladder and the flow of warm urine down his thigh was momentarily comforting. He twisted his head to see his tormentor walk to a black tote bag, which had spilled open, revealing a carton of marker pens and a newspaper picture of the Jane Doe he had seen all over the news. The man used the knife to cut the ringing phone from his forehead, then stared at it as if unsure what to do. *Answer it*, Kovacs prayed, hoping to buy more time. *Answer the fucking phone.* Eventually the man pressed a button and held the phone to his ear. 'Yes?'

Kovacs could hear a harsh, guttural voice, thick with anger, shouting orders down the phone like some foul-mouthed Mafia don. As the man listened his body language changed. His shoulders stooped, his head bowed and his breathing became more ragged like an asthmatic child. 'No, not yet,' he said, glancing at the woman in the newspaper. 'As soon as I discover anything I'll call you. Yes, yes, I understand.' He began shaking his head. 'No. I won't fail you again. I'm close. I'll finish it soon.' Kovacs began thrashing around on the floor, trying to make the caller hear him. Perhaps he would make the man stop. His tormentor walked back and kicked him hard in the stomach. 'What noise?' he said into the phone. 'Just a dog. Yes, of course I'm exercising discipline and being discreet. No, I've done nothing to attract the attentions of the children of men. I'm totally focused on finishing the job. I'll call you as soon as I know more.' He hung up and re-taped the phone to his forehead.

Seconds later, he was kneeling over Kovacs again. 'Stop moving,' he said, as he tied the bonds

79

tighter and repositioned Kovacs' head. 'I need to get this just right.' He raised the knife again, this time pausing for only a second before bringing it down so hard that the blade went clean through Kovacs' ribcage, missing bone and driving out the breath from his lungs. As he arched his spine in agony he felt the tip of the long blade exit his back and jar against the concrete floor beneath his body. His killer pulled out the knife and raised it for another strike. In that instant, struggling for breath, Kovacs focused on the glistening blade, mesmerized by its ruby-red sheen, slick with his own blood. Then the knife descended again.

Kovacs was dead before the fourth stab shredded his pumping heart.

CHAPTER THIRTEEN

Back at Tranquil Waters, Jane Doe paced her room, brought to life by Nathan Fox's diagnosis. In one session he had discovered more about her than her previous psychiatrist had in over a week, but she was unsure of the implications of Fox's discovery and anxious about what to expect next. When Fox eventually returned he had been away only half an hour but it felt more like two. He carried his briefcase in his right hand and a clutch of sealed envelopes in the other. She glimpsed something scrawled on the top envelope. He stopped in the doorway, reached into the briefcase and pulled out some sandwiches and a small bottle of Evian. 'I got you some lunch. Come, let's take a walk.'

She took the sandwiches but felt too excited to

eat. 'Where are we going?' She stiffened. 'We're not going back to the other room?'

He smiled. 'No. But we are going to visit some of the other rooms in the original building.' He took her hand. 'Come. Trust me. It's going to be OK.' Reluctantly, she let him lead her down the corridor and along the enclosed glass walkway that linked the new wing to the original Victorian building. 'OK, this is how the experiment goes. I'm going to take you to four empty rooms and I want you to tell me what you experience in each of them.'

'Why?'

He led her to the lift and pressed for the second floor. 'To test a theory.'

'What theory?'

'I can't tell you yet because it might affect the experiment.'

'What's in the envelopes?'

'Predictions.'

'Of what?'

The lift opened on the second floor. He led her down another long corridor and stopped outside a room. 'In each of these four envelopes I've written messages that apply to the four rooms we're going to visit. The messages are effectively predictions, descriptions of what you're going to hallucinate in each room.'

She didn't feel comfortable about this. 'Is this some kind of test? Do you think I've been making this up?'

'On the contrary. This is simply a controlled experiment to check out a theory of why you hallucinate, and this building is an ideal place to conduct it. Also, for what it's worth, the only way you're going to conquer your fear of these hallucinations and gain some distance is to expose yourself to them, again and again.' He peeled off one of the sealed envelopes and held it up. The number 207 was scrawled on it. 'The number on each envelope tallies with the number assigned to each room. This contains my prediction of what, if anything, you're going to hallucinate in room 207.' He took a key from his case and unlocked the door. 'The normal occupant is at lunch. Step inside and tell me what you experience, if anything.'

'But what if—?'

'Don't worry. Just humour me and step inside for a moment.' His blue eyes locked on hers. 'If you do feel anything, remember what I told you yesterday. Try to be as objective as possible and distance yourself from whatever it is you're experiencing. Imagine you're standing on a bridge, looking down on your stream of consciousness. Let whatever you think, feel or experience drift past you, under the bridge. Observe everything but don't accept responsibility for it. After all, you can't control it. You're an innocent bystander. And remember, nothing in the stream can hurt you. If it gets too much, just step out of the room.' He smiled and his intense features softened, became almost boyish. 'Please trust me, Jane. I'm not doing this to make you feel uncomfortable. I'm trying to diagnose what's happening.'

He opened the door, stood back and gestured for her to go in. Aside from a few personal touches—a photograph by the bed and some books on the desk—the room was like her own. She hovered in the doorway then took three tentative steps inside. Fragmented images, smells and sounds intruded on her senses, but nothing other than the normal white

82

noise she was accustomed to.

'Anything?'

'No. Not really.'

'Walk around a bit. Get a feel for the place.' She did as he asked. 'Anything now?'

She shook her head. 'Nothing specific.' She wasn't sure whether to feel relieved or disappointed. 'What did you predict for this room?'

Fox kept his face impassive, folded the envelope in half and placed it in his jacket pocket. 'Come, let's go to the second room.'

The second room was down the corridor. He unlocked and opened the door then peeled off another envelope, which had the number 222 written on it. He stood back. 'In you go.'

She took a deep breath and took three steps inside. Nothing. She shook her head.

He frowned. 'You always move to the centre of a room—you even moved your bed away from the walls because you said it made you feel more comfortable. Walk to the side of the room. Touch one of the walls.' She walked slowly towards the window and found that her hand was shaking as she tentatively touched the wall, as if it might burn her or deliver an electric shock. It felt normal. 'Keep it there,' he instructed. The 'white noise' became slightly more intrusive, but still nothing concrete or cohesive. 'Anything?' he asked.

'Nope. Some low-level stuff but nothing much. In fact it's quite calming. If I had to choose, I'd say this was actually more peaceful than the first room.' He remained expressionless but, for a fleeting moment, she thought she saw relief on his face. He had predicted she would see something in here, she was sure of it. So why was he relieved? What was so frightening about his theory that he wanted to disprove it? 'What was I supposed to have seen in here?'

He folded the envelope, still sealed, and placed it back in his jacket pocket with the first one. 'I told you, I'll show you everything after the experiment. Let's try the third room.' By now she was impatient for the experiment to be over so she could hear his theory. When he unlocked and opened the door to room 302 on the third floor she didn't wait to be coaxed. She stepped straight into the room and casually reached out her arm to touch one of the walls, convinced it would be three strikeouts.

But this time it was different—very different. Immediately, she sensed something: heat. It didn't just come from the wall she was touching. It was in the air around her. She could smell smoke, sense its acrid taste on her tongue and feel the burning in her throat and lungs. 'Fire,' she said aloud. Then she saw a woman huddled in the corner, holding her nightgown around her as if the flimsy cotton would shield her. The apparition had a pale violet tint, which flickered on and off, but the woman looked real: Jane Doe could see and feel the terror in her eyes. She turned to escape and saw flames blocking her path. Fire was billowing into the room from the corridor outside, its searing fingers crawling across the ceiling and walls, reaching to claim the woman who was now coughing and screaming. As Jane Doe realized that she too was coughing and screaming, she felt strong hands grip her and pull her backwards, through the door and out of the room. Suddenly, the fire receded, the pale flickering violet was gone, and she could see Fox looking into her eyes. His now-familiar face

84

comforted her. 'What did you see and feel?'

As she told him about the woman in the fire his eyes widened. Her account seemed to affect him almost as much as the experience had affected her. 'Did you predict that? Is that in your envelope?'

He folded it and put it in his jacket pocket. 'One more room, then I'll tell you everything.' He paused. 'You OK for the last one?'

She was still trembling but she could tell from Fox's face that he was on to something and needed to know what. 'I'm fine.'

The last room, 410, was on the top floor. As Fox unlocked and opened the door she could feel her courage ebbing away so she hurried in before her nerve failed. The window was closed and the day was warm but even before she touched the walls she began shivering and felt the hairs rise on her forearms, as if a chill air was blowing. Steeling herself, she reached out and placed her palm against the wall.

'How are you doing?' she heard Fox ask. 'You look very pale.' She didn't answer because another sound immediately intruded on her consciousness: the smashing of glass. Then a sudden rush of cold air hit her face, making her take a step back. 'What's happening, Jane? Tell me what you see.' Suddenly, the flickering pale violet returned and the window in front of her changed—the frame was no longer freshly decorated but cracked with flaking white paint. Then a man appeared to her right, tall and thin with a beard. He was holding a chair aloft and using it to hit the window as hard as he could. The glass was strong and it took him four blows to break the pane. He looked over his shoulder and she felt the terror in his eyes. Then

85

she realized another man was coming into the room—with a knife. The bearded man grabbed one of the shards and held it like a blade. As he did so she felt the glass, cold and hard, in the palm of her own hand. With icy awareness she realized she was witnessing the scene in the third person but experiencing it in the first, from the bearded man's point of view. In that instant she knew the bearded man was about to die. He raised the glass shard, defensively, but backed away towards the open window. Then the other man rushed him and stabbed him repeatedly. She doubled over with each stab as if they were entering her own body.

'What's happening, Jane? Speak to me. Speak to me.' Fox's anxious voice reached her from some faraway place but she was too immersed in the nightmare to respond. She could only watch helplessly as the mortally wounded bearded man climbed on to the windowsill, desperate to evade his attacker, and jumped from the window. She felt herself falling, then all went black.

She awoke to discover herself shaking with cold and shock, being carried from the room in Fox's arms. In the corridor the cold left her but when she tried to stand she was still shaking. 'You OK now?' he asked, his blue eyes creased with concern. He was also shaking, as if he could feel her cold.

She leaned on him and nodded.

'What happened in there?' he asked.

As he listened to her he shook his head in disbelief. Pale, he looked as tired and drained as she felt. When she finished he pulled the sealed envelopes from his pocket and stared at them. 'Did the experiment work?' she asked.

He frowned and glanced behind him, as if

86

worried he might be overheard. 'Let's go back to your room. I'll explain everything there.'

CHAPTER FOURTEEN

Back in Jane Doe's room Nathan Fox laid the four envelopes in a line on the desk. Was it her imagination or were his hands still shaking?

'So what's in them?'

'Look for yourself.' He pointed to the envelope with the number 207 scribbled on the cover. 'Open them in order.'

She picked it up. 'This relates to the first room, right? The one in which nothing happened.'

'Right.'

She tore it open. Inside was a single line handwritten in black ink. She read it aloud. 'In room 207 Jane Doe will *not* hallucinate.' She smiled. 'You got that right.' She reached for the second envelope, room 222. Again she read the message aloud. 'In room 222 Jane Doe will hallucinate. The hallucination will feature a man lying in bed by the window. He will look peaceful and appear asleep.' She looked up at him. 'You got that wrong. I didn't see anything.'

He remained silent, just looked at her, unblinking. She opened the next envelope, pulled out the enclosed slip of paper and read the prediction. 'In room 302 Jane Doe will hallucinate. The hallucination will feature a woman being consumed by fire.' Her mouth felt dry. 'How did you know that?'

He didn't answer, just kept looking at her. 'Open

the last one.'

She reached for the final envelope and tore it open. As she read the last prediction, she could hear her voice shaking. 'In room 410 Jane Doe will hallucinate. It will feature a bearded man smashing the window with a chair before being stabbed repeatedly by another man and jumping out of the broken window. She may well feel intense cold.' The paper slipped from her hand and she watched it fall to the ground. 'How did you know that? How did you predict two of my hallucinations? That's impossible.'

'What *I* did was relatively easy. What *you* did was impossible. I simply recognized a pattern. What do all your hallucinations have in common?'

'They all have the same flickering pale violet tint?'

'What else?'

She frowned. 'They're frightening?'

He shook his head. '*Why* are they frightening, apart from the fact you're seeing and sensing things no one else can? What's the common theme in all your hallucinations, including the ones you had at Oregon State before coming here?'

She thought for a moment. Then it came to her, clear and cold. 'Death.'

He nodded. 'In all your hallucinations you see or sense a person on the point of death.'

He reached into his briefcase and pulled out a file. 'These are the patient files for the Pine Hills Psychiatric Hospital which used to be on this site. Those weren't predictions I wrote in the envelopes. Quite the opposite. They were records of historical events—deaths. Nineteen years ago there was a fire in this hospital. Most patients got out but Mary

88

Lopez, the woman in room 302, perished. Two years later, in midwinter, Bob Kesey, the bearded man in room 410, was attacked and killed by a psychotic patient with a knife. He tried to escape by jumping out of the window but was dead before he hit the ground.'

'But that's impossible.'

'That's what I thought.' He pointed to another entry. 'This is the record of Frank Bartlett's death. He was the man in the Bart Simpson T-shirt you saw committing suicide yesterday. The description matches your hallucination almost exactly. One of yesterday's orderlies was there when Bartlett died and he said you included accurate details that weren't even in the report. What's more, records show that decades earlier another man committed suicide in the same room. He hanged himself exactly as you described.'

She put her hands over her mouth. 'You're saying what I saw in those rooms actually happened?'

'That's exactly what I'm saying.' He pulled out another folder. 'Your medical file records most of the hallucinations you had at Oregon State. This is where I first noticed the pattern. They *all*, without exception, involved death.'

Numbness seeped through her as she tried to process what Fox was saying. 'Those happened too?'

'Yep. I found death records that matched the location and description of almost every recorded hallucination.'

'What about the second room today? Who was the man in bed you predicted?'

'His name was Jack Lee and he died peacefully

in his sleep from an aneurysm.'

'Why didn't I see him?'

A shrug. 'I don't know.' He frowned, reached into his briefcase and pulled out a typed loose-leaf document. 'Jane, this is getting a little out of my area. Unless you're perpetuating the most elaborate and pointless hoax, something unprecedented is happening. I can just about explain how your total synaesthesia unconsciously synchronizes all your five senses to create these vivid episodes of dying, but you're not just creating them—you're *recreating* them. These people *actually* died exactly as you described and your synaesthesia can't explain that. Even if your memory was intact you couldn't have known about all those deaths, especially in such detail.

'What's so bizarre is you have no memory of your own life but appear to have perfect recall of other people's deaths. More than that, you *relive* their deaths.' He leaned forward and, for the first time since she became Jane Doe, she looked into his intense eyes and didn't feel alone. 'What we need to do is discover where these memories are coming from and how you're accessing them.' He opened the document. It was peppered with yellow Post-it notes covered in scribbles. 'There's a theory . . .' He stopped suddenly, weighing his words. 'May I be totally frank?'

'Please do.'

'As I see it, we have two options here. The conventional approach: I treat this as purely a psychiatric problem and brief Professor Fullelove. She'll then brief other psychiatrists who'll try and diagnose your psychosis and draw up a treatment plan. The problem is, apart from your amnesia, I'm not sure the issue is purely psychiatric. And I don't want to turn you into a medical freak show.'

She shuddered at the thought. 'I feel enough of a freak already. What's the other option?'

'We assume this is more than a psychiatric issue and speak discreetly to someone with more relevant experience.' He waved the document. 'The author of this has a theory which kind of fits what's happening here. Although, to be honest, it defies normal logic.'

'So do my hallucinations.'

'The point is,' Fox continued, 'they might *not* be hallucinations. Strictly speaking, hallucinations are perceptions in the *absence* of external stimuli. But if the theory in here is valid, then there could be some external stimuli present.'

She craned her head to read the title page, expecting it to be on psychiatry or neurology, but the first words she saw told her otherwise. *'The Echo of History?'*

'Like I said, this is getting out of my area of expertise. I'd like to sleep on it and discuss this with the author tomorrow. Do I have your permission to talk about your case?'

'Can I come with you?'

He considered for a second. 'If you like. We've got to do it quietly, though. Your face is all over the news at the moment and the last thing we want is for the media to get any more curious about you.'

She indicated the document. 'Can we trust the author to be discreet?'

'Oh, yes.' He smiled at the question. 'I trust the author with my life.'

CHAPTER FIFTEEN

As the setting sun turned the Willamette River to molten bronze, Karl Jordache stood in a disused warehouse in Old Town, studying the corpse at his feet. He wasn't as shocked by the sight of the second homicide as he was by its speed. According to the pathologist, time of death was only a few hours ago, a day after Vega's murder a few blocks from here.

The grey-haired corpse lay on the floor, legs splayed apart, arms tied behind its back. The dead man was wearing a woman's blue silk dress and had four stab wounds in his chest. 'The vic's name is Josh Kovacs,' said Kostakis, scratching his bald, spherical head. 'Back in the day, he used to be a bit player in prostitution and drugs, before he took too much of his own product. For the past few years he's been nothing more than a wino and a junkie, hanging around the alleys off Burnside. The MO's different from the first killing but the signature's the same. Both victims were stripped of their regular clothes then dressed in women's clothing, and their bodies were bound and staged. Vince Vega was found in women's underwear and had his throat slit with a heavy-duty hunting knife. Kovacs was found in a woman's gown and stabbed four times. The knife was probably the same as that used to cut Vega's throat. Unlike Vega, there was no ketamine in Kovacs' blood but enough downers and booze to mean the killer probably didn't need to sedate him.' Kostakis pointed down at the sheet of paper stapled to Kovacs' forehead. 'And that, of course.'

Jordache read the message, each capital letter written in a different colour. The wording and lack of punctuation was identical to that stapled to the first victim:

SERVE THE DEMON
SAVE THE ANGEL

'What's the connection between the victims?'

'Both were scumbags with a history of narcotics and vice and may have moved in the same circles back in the day. Otherwise there's no obvious link.'

'What about the gown, and the underwear found on Vega? Do we know where the killer got them?'

'The women's clothes weren't from a regular store. They were factory rejects, with the brand labels cut off.' Kostakis checked his notes. 'It's hard to trace clothes like this but we do have one lead. Two days ago one of the storekeepers in a thrift market on the border of Old Town and the Pearl sold items that matched the fancy lingerie and gown. She remembers the customer because most of her clientele are women. He wanted the biggest size and was pretty specific about colour and type of clothing. Like he was buying it for a particular reason. She didn't get a great look at his face because he wore a broad-rimmed hat, but she says he was large, had creepy pale eyes and smelt funny.'

'Get one of our artists down there and get a likeness of this guy. What did she say he smelt like?'

'Weird, dead, like decaying meat.' Kostakis indicated the victim's obscured face. 'And that? What do we do about that?'

Jordache frowned. 'I don't know yet. First, I want

93

to find out all we can about the guy with the odour problem and the hat.'

94

PART 2
The Last Echo

CHAPTER SIXTEEN

Hundreds of miles from the man-made sprawl of Portland a storm was building. It was born in the Canadian Rockies and raced along the mighty Columbia River, through Washington State, towards a remote tract of privately owned land in the vast Oregon wilderness. The storm whipped through its high canyons and dense forests before reaching a remote cluster of timber and stone buildings nestled in lush, rolling meadows, between a dense forest of giant sequoias and a rushing river.

This isolated Eden was man's only footprint for miles around. The corral was so large that the horses within it appeared to be running free and wild. But these were not wild horses. They were neither the mixed breeds nor the dun-coloured Kiger Mustangs that roamed the region but the purest breed of all: thoroughbreds. The highly strung animals flicked their manes, snorted at the moon and galloped in circles, unsettled by the gathering storm and the three exhausted horsemen arriving in their midst. Perhaps they sensed the fury of the lead rider, the storm in his head a match for any raging in the night sky. His thick silver hair flailed in the wind as wildly as the horse's mane, and his intense green eyes seemed luminous in the night. He was not young but his tall physique was as lean and muscular as that of a man half his age. His followers called him the Seer but tonight he felt blind. He and two of his most trusted Watchers had spent days scouring the thousands of acres that made up his land but still hadn't found what he was looking for. Only a trace of where the object of his quest might have gone. He dismounted the exhausted mare, patted her wet flank, unhitched the saddlebag and draped it over his shoulder. Without looking back, he left the other riders to tend to his spent horse. His muscles ached but as he walked among the panicked horses he breathed in their wild energy. A stallion reared before him. He gripped its mane in his strong hands, stroked its neck and breathed into its flared nostrils. The horse calmed instantly and the Seer smiled through his rage. He released the horse and opened the gate leading from the corral.

As he strode through his dominion, past the slaughterhouse and the shed that housed the settlement's main generator, expectant faces stared out from lit windows. Some came out of their cabins to greet him, touching the centre of their forehead and bowing low, but all remained silent when they saw he had returned alone, without his prize. He strode on past the Great Hall, ignoring the figures painted on its large twin doors. As he approached his private quarters, he glanced up at the round stone tower that dominated the settlement. A flash of lightning illuminated its large blue eye, a glittering mosaic of embedded dumortierite crystals, which stared down from the top of the tower's white walls. The all-seeing eye seemed to taunt him. For all its power it could not find what he was seeking.

He pushed open the door to his quarters, and entered a timber-beamed chamber, one wall of which was lined with bookshelves crammed with reference volumes, academic texts and books on world religions. On the far wall a six-foot-tall tapestry depicted two men, one a shadowy twin of the other. Both had their legs and arms outstretched like Leonardo da Vinci's Vitruvian man, and had seven wheel-like vortices running up their spines, from the pelvis to the crown of the head, each vortex a different colour of the rainbow.

The Seer's three beautiful Wives lay on a rug by the fire: Maria, flame-haired and heavily pregnant; Deva, a brunette cradling a newborn in her arms; and Zara, a much younger Nordic blonde. Dressed in indigo robes, each had an indigo dot painted on the centre of their foreheads, like the Hindu tilak. When the Seer entered, each bowed her head, touched her tilak in greeting and jumped to her feet. The blonde took his saddlebag and the redhead poured him a cup of fiery poteen from the earthenware jug on the table.

He waved them away. 'Leave me alone. I need to think.' The Wives nodded obediently, but as they hurried to their private rooms he had a change of heart. He initially considered Deva—her newborn was still a neonate, less than a month out of the womb—or the heavily pregnant Maria. Both were suitable for his needs. Tonight, however, he wanted uncomplicated release. He rested a hand on the young blonde's arm. 'Not you, Zara. Stay awhile.' Barely out of her teens, Zara was fresh-faced with full breasts and large brown eyes. She smiled at him, blushing with pride and excitement, then proceeded to help pull the wet oilskins from his back. He drank deep of the fiery poteen, but the 90 per cent proof liquor brought him little comfort as he stared at the calendar by the fire and noticed that the next Esbat was only a few days away. 'Where can she be? Where has she gone?'

99

Zara stroked his forehead. 'You are the Seer. You see everything. In time you will find her and all will be well.'

He still couldn't accept what had happened. He felt a sudden stab of anxiety but quickly dismissed it: that she had left him was incredible, that she would betray him was unthinkable. He rubbed his temples. His mind felt muddled and blocked. He had always thought of her as the weak one. But now he realized that the very thing that made her weak also made her indispensable to his life's most important endeavour. How could he have been so blind to her value? How could he not have appreciated what had been staring him in the face? If—he corrected himself—*when* she returned he would not neglect her again. Not now he realized how crucial she was to the Great Work.

He took Zara's hand. 'Go to the bedroom and prepare yourself.' He waited until she had left, then picked up his saddlebag, walked past the bedrooms, down a long corridor and unlocked a door at the end, which led to the base of the tower. Inside he unlocked another door. The lock was unnecessary—only a fool would pry into his affairs—but he rarely left anything to chance. The small room was filled with incongruously modern electronic equipment. Closed-circuit television monitors lined one wall, showing video images from various concealed cameras around the settlement, which were recorded on a hard drive beneath the desk for him to check periodically. He ignored the screens, however, and unlocked the safe in the corner. Its shelves were piled high with banknotes, documents, keys, cell phones and other paraphernalia forbidden to others in the settlement. He considered what he might need, then reached for his saddlebag, retrieved the satellite phone inside and plugged it into the charger beside the safe. A good night's sleep would rest his body but first he needed to unblock his mind and clear his vision.

He locked the tower and went to his bedroom where Zara was standing naked, her robes folded neatly on the bed. She looked nervous but excited and her youthful beauty pleased him. He noticed that her breasts were slightly fuller than normal and he suspected that she too was pregnant. Without saying a word he stripped and stepped into the shower in the adjoining bathroom. As the water rained down, Zara began massaging his body, moving her soapy hands from the top of his head, down his spine to his buttocks and round to his groin. Her large eyes looked up at him as she took him in her hands, but his flaccid penis remained immune to her caresses. She knelt and took him in her mouth but he stopped her and turned off the shower. Increasingly, he found it required more stimulation to arouse him—much more. He put on a robe then led her down the long corridor, to the locked door that gave access to the tower. He saw her pupils dilate with excitement when she realized where he was taking her.

Immediately he began to ascend the stairs of the tower, he could feel his own senses awakening, intensifying—and his power returning. Already he could hear the whispering echoes, smell the scents and glimpse the ghosts. The sensory onslaught, far from confusing or disturbing him, energized and aroused him. He led Zara up the central spiral staircase to one of the higher chambers and made

101

her kneel before him. As his senses surrendered to the avalanche of stimuli flowing through him, the mundane concerns of the world dissolved, the fog in his mind cleared and he began to discern the path ahead.

CHAPTER SEVENTEEN

The next morning

Acutely aware he was heading into uncharted territory, Fox had avoided involving Professor Fullelove or anyone official in Jane Doe's case until he understood better what he was dealing with. The last thing Jane Doe needed now was to be examined and investigated as some kind of freak. The next morning, after lending Jane Doe a large baseball cap and dark glasses, he drove her to meet the one person Fox not only trusted but also thought might be able to explain what was happening.

Samantha greeted them at the front door with a smile. 'You must be very special, Jane. Nathan has never brought a patient here before.' After last night's storm the day was clear and warm and Samantha led them to the summerhouse in the back yard. Fox had always loved the simple wooden shack with its mildewed glass roof, teak table and chairs and old couch that folded out to make a bed. It had been his refuge from the world when he'd first moved in with his aunt and uncle. Back then he would often spend warm nights sleeping on the lumpy couch. Looking up at the moon and stars had always made him feel closer to his parents and sister. When schoolfriends came over he would take them to the summerhouse and Aunt Samantha would bring over homemade lemonade and sandwiches. Not ordinary sandwiches but freshly baked homemade bread packed with the most delicious and exotic fillings.

Today, as his aunt offered Jane Doe a glass of homemade lemonade and a platter of her legendary sandwiches, he was reminded of those childhood days. As they ate and drank, Fox briefed his aunt on Jane's amnesia, synaesthesia and hallucinations. Far from being shocked or sceptical, the scientist listened intently and made notes, especially when Fox told her about the envelope experiment. When Fox concluded that Jane, despite having no memory of her own life, exhibited full sensory recall of the deaths of total strangers—even those who had died before she was born—his aunt jumped to her feet and rushed off to the house. When she returned with a pile of papers and proceeded to expand on her subject Fox felt relieved that he had involved her.

'First, let me explain why nothing is scientifically impossible,' Samantha began, 'only scientifically improbable. Almost three centuries ago, science was convinced it had mastered the rules of the physical universe. Newton's discovery of gravity and his laws of motion had created order out of chaos and laid down the natural laws of physics. And they were *laws*: everything in the universe obeyed them.

'Then, in the last century, Einstein and others demonstrated that, although Newton's laws hold sway in the observed universe, they don't apply to the microscopic quantum world of protons and electrons. In this outlaw world, invisible to the human eye, nothing is certain. Subatomic particles obey only the supernatural *probabilities* of quantum physics.

'Experiments have shown, for example, that light can be both a wave *and* a solid particle, and that individual subatomic particles exhibit "impossible" attributes, such as consciousness, clairvoyance, the ability to be in two places at one time—and crucially, given what Nathan's told me about you, memory. To this day, science struggles to reconcile Newton's universe of certainties with the quantum world of probabilities.'

'You think this can explain my hallucinations?' Jane Doe asked.

'The quantum world explains many things that are apparently unexplainable,' Samantha said, studying her pad. 'Can I just confirm my notes? Your hallucinations vary in intensity. Some are clearer and more vivid than others. They all deal with relatively violent and sudden death. You experience them inside a building or structure and they become more intense and focused when you physically touch the fabric of the building. Correct so far?'

'Yes.'

'Is each hallucination specific to a particular location?'

'Yes.'

'Does it change at all, even subtly, or is it identical every time, like a video loop?'

'Identical.'

Samantha turned to Fox. 'And these hallucinations *all* tally with actual recorded deaths—violent deaths?'

'Yes,' said Fox. 'That's why I think her

104

hallucinations may have nothing to do with her amnesia but may in fact be some sort of gift linked to her synaesthesia.'

'Or curse,' said Jane Doe with a wry smile.

Samantha poured her more lemonade. 'Cheer up, my dear, this at least means you're not insane. It would appear you're sensing, remembering or channelling genuine *external* stimuli. Stimuli only you can detect.'

Fox sipped his lemonade. 'But what stimuli, and where are they coming from?' He retrieved from his briefcase the reason why he had consulted his aunt about this: the paper she had given him two days ago. He studied the title: *The Echo of History: the importance of archaeosonics and molecular memory in rediscovering the past.* 'Is the answer in this paper of Howard's?'

A smile. 'A little more thought-provoking than you expected, Nathan?'

'Especially with your science input. Can you summarize it for Jane?'

Samantha cleared her throat. 'That paper specifically relates to archaeosonics, which tries to explain the absorption and retrieval of residual *sound* in structures built from natural materials, but its arguments are relevant to vision and other stimuli. We already know the world contains a whole symphony of sounds inaudible to humans. Famously, dogs can hear higher frequencies than we can. We also know there are sounds audible to some humans but not to others. You may have heard of the electronic anti-loitering device called the Mosquito, which emits an irritating high-pitched whine only teenagers can hear.

'State-of-the-art acoustic equipment can now

105

pick up sounds even further along the inaudible spectrum. Using electromagnetic energy to stimulate submolecular particles in old buildings we've detected acoustic patterns that aren't white noise but are consistent with recorded natural sounds. Scientists in Okinawa in Japan claim to have played back human voices recorded in the fabric of an ancient Shinto temple.

'What no one agrees on yet is *how* sound is imprinted into the particle memory of a structure. Some scientists believe that all sounds are recorded automatically, others that only those with a particular pitch or resonance are picked up. What all agree on, however, is that, analogous to burning data to a DVD or other digital media, significant energy is required to burn sound memories into the quantum particles of a structure. Where this energy comes from, though, is another mystery.' Samantha smiled. 'But your experiences may help shed some light on that, Jane.'

'How?' she asked.

'Yeah, how do her experiences explain the energy source?' said Fox. His aunt sounded so logical and matter-of-fact that she almost made this nonsense sound reasonable. His remaining concern was how it might help restore his patient's memory and enable her to rediscover her lost identity. He suspected that until that happened Jane Doe's bizarre extra sense would remain a mystery.

'One of the big unknowns is what happens to the life force at the moment of death,' Samantha explained. 'This is a basic question of physics. I'm not talking about metaphysics, ghosts or the soul here, just the passage of energy. Energy can't just disappear. It must go somewhere. One theory that's gaining credibility following studies on the acoustically remarkable Neolithic stone tombs in Maeshowe on the Orkney islands is that our life force leaves a kind of scorch mark at the moment of death, an invisible but indelible echo seared into the surrounding matter. With a gentle, peaceful death this energy is dissipated and trickles away gently, leaving a negligible echo. The struggle of a more emotionally violent and painful death, however, such as a murder or suicide creates a more explosive transference of energy, a greater splash if you will, which leads to a more intense echo—or memory—in the surrounding subatomic particles. This explosion of energy could explain how sounds and other related stimuli are burned into the memory of a building. It would also explain why all Jane's hallucinations feature violent, difficult deaths.'

Fox considered the envelope experiment. 'It might also explain why Jane didn't sense the death in room 222. Jack Lee died peacefully in his sleep. There was no violent struggle, no emotional or physical suffering, just a gentle passing away that would have left a smaller, perhaps negligible echo.' He thought of the indelible but invisible blood spatter at Linnet's hunting lodge and the Luminol used to reveal it. Did all murders and violent deaths leave an indelible but invisible *psychic* spatter as well?

'It would also explain why I experienced fewer hallucinations in the palliative ward at Oregon State Hospital,' Jane Doe said slowly. 'Although I was surrounded by the dying, I was in a new wing with fewer memories and the deaths were managed, calm, expected.'

'Palliative wards are designed to help people fade away and slip gently into death,' Samantha agreed.

'Archaeosonics only explains sounds, though,' Jane Doe said, rubbing her temples. 'What about the stuff I see, smell, touch and taste?'

'We're currently only gathering data on sound imprints but the principles apply to all the senses,' Samantha said. 'Take sight, for example. The human eye can detect the colours of the rainbow, but these make up only a fraction of the entire electromagnetic spectrum. As humans, we exist within the forty-ninth Octave of Vibration of the electromagnetic light spectrum. Below this range are barely visible radiant heat, then invisible infrared, television and radio waves, sound and brain waves. Above this range is barely visible ultraviolet, then the invisible frequencies of chemicals and perfumes, followed by X-rays, gamma rays, radium rays and unknown cosmic rays. This means that a vast array of stimuli—from radio waves at the bottom end of the spectrum to unknown cosmic rays at the top—are invisible to us. Under the right conditions, however, more of this hidden world—*our* world—might be revealed to us.

'When entering certain buildings many people sense a generic atmosphere—good or bad—which they often dismiss. Some, however, see specific *visual* imprints. Sensational claims by so-called psychics have undermined the credibility of these sightings but there's prolific anecdotal evidence. Famously, there are the Roman legionaries in York in England. Under certain atmospheric conditions countless independent witnesses have testified to seeing them. All reported seeing exactly the same ghostly apparition, and all claimed that only the top halves of their bodies were visible above the ground. Interestingly the original and intact Roman road is about three feet below the modern road—which would explain why their legs weren't visible. Psychics like to call this a "residual haunting" but the soldiers aren't sentient ghosts. They don't interact with the viewer. They're simply a memory—a delayed visual echo—captured in the fabric of the road, a residual image that under certain atmospheric conditions—such as the hour before an electrical thunderstorm—becomes visible to those receptive or sensitive enough to detect it.' She looked hard at Jane. 'You, however, don't appear to need atmospheric conditions to detect and replay these dying echoes in all their sensory glory.'

'But why? How come I'm so different?'

'That's a question for Nathan.'

Fox shrugged. 'All I can think is your unique form of synaesthesia is somehow responsible. Whatever stimulus exists—a sound or a vision or a smell—your *total* synaesthesia interprets it through the prism of *all* your merged senses. This synergy may create a distinct extra sense.'

She frowned. 'Like a sixth sense?'

'I'd prefer to see it as a specific type of synaesthesia. Like I told you, synaesthesia isn't regarded as an ailment. In fact, many regard it as a gift.' He thought for a second. 'Using the traditional naming convention it might be called something like death-echo synaesthesia.'

'Death-echo synaesthesia?' Jane Doe considered the phrase for a moment. 'Giving it a proper name makes it sound more official and less like there's

109

something wrong with me. Does it explain the flickering pale violet tint I see when I have my hallucinations?'

'Possibly. To a synaesthete, sounds and smells can have colour. Perhaps death has a colour, too.'

'But why do I have this strange form of synaesthesia?'

'I have no idea. We'll probably have to uncover your identity before we can even begin to guess at that.' Fox remembered something Jordache had told him about the night Jane Doe rescued the girls from the traffickers and an idea came to him of how he might test Jane Doe's death-echo synaesthesia and use it to jog her memory. The shadows were lengthening in the garden but there was still time. 'We'd better get going, Jane. There's something I want to try before I take you back.' He rose and hugged his aunt. 'Thanks so much, Samantha. You've given us loads to think about. I'll keep you posted but please keep this to yourself, for now.'

'My lips are sealed.'

'Thanks for the delicious lemonade and sandwiches, Samantha,' said Jane Doe. 'And thanks for all your help.'

Samantha embraced her. 'It's been a pleasure, my dear. If I can be of any more help Nathan knows where to find me.'

Walking through the house to the front door, Jane Doe stopped in the hall and peered inside a glass cabinet. 'What are those?'

Fox felt suddenly self-conscious. 'My childhood karate trophies. My aunt and uncle were ridiculously proud of them.'

'Karate?'

'A Japanese form of unarmed combat.'

'There are a lot of trophies. You must be good.'

'I only competed when I was young and angry at the world. Now I just do it to keep fit.'

'What about your mirror-touch synaesthesia? When you hit people, don't you feel it yourself?'

He smiled. 'Not if I look away or close my eyes at the crucial moment.'

She strolled over to the large hall mirror and studied the photographs on the table beneath it. One was of Fox's karate class. His classmates stood together but he was a few steps removed, apart and alone. 'You look much smaller and younger than the others.'

'I was so . . .' he searched for the right word, '. . . enthusiastic that they put me in an older class.'

'You do look pretty fierce.' She smiled, bent closer and read the signed message on the mount. *'Never let them get too close. Never lose control. Sensei Daichi.'* She nodded slowly but passed no comment, then turned to another picture. 'Is that you with your parents?'

'And my sister. Yes.'

'Where are they now?'

'They're dead.'

She paused a beat. 'I'm sorry.' Then reached forward and traced a finger around his mother's head. 'She was the same colour as you. Your father and sister were normal colours but your mother was indigo like you.'

Fox found this link to his mother comforting. He had always felt closest to her, especially as she had also had synaesthesia. Perhaps that explained their colour, he realized suddenly. Could Jane Doe sense fellow synaesthetes? Was that why she'd made such a big deal about his colour when they'd first met?

111

'You said my father and sister were *normal* colours. Does that mean the indigo end of the colour spectrum is different, special?'

She shrugged. 'I can't remember. All I know is it's *my* end of the spectrum.'

'Your end?' He recalled the mnemonic for remembering the colours of the rainbow he'd learned as a child in England: Richard Of York Gave Battle In Vain. 'What colour are you, Jane? Are you indigo like me?'

She looked at herself in the mirror and smiled wistfully. 'I don't know. I can't see my own colour. I don't even know that about myself.'

CHAPTER EIGHTEEN

The basic apartment hotel was ideal. It was just outside the Pearl, on the edge of Old Town, blank, cheap, anonymous. It had a fully equipped kitchenette so he could eat when he liked without drawing attention to himself, and the staff obeyed the *Do not disturb* signs. As far as he could tell, no one had entered the sparsely decorated apartment in the four days he had been in the city. Best of all, it had a private entrance which meant he could come and go unnoticed.

Half an hour ago he had dispatched his third victim. Of the three kills, it had been the most violent and the least satisfying. As he laid his knife by the kitchen sink and stripped bloodstained clothes from his huge frame he promised himself it would be the last—especially as the odds of finding another worthy victim were slim.

Stripping naked, he put the soiled clothes in the small washing machine and showered, scrubbing himself with antibacterial soap to wash away his smell. After drying himself he picked up his cell phone and paced the apartment. His naked body was slabbed with muscle. Not the sculpted contours developed in a gym but the brutish power acquired from hard physical labour. The upper part of his broad back was textured with a criss-cross of raised welts and silver scar tissue: the legacy of childhood beatings. As he paced, he flicked obsessively through video images on his cell phone, trying to recapture the fleeting sense of peace he had experienced killing the three men. Regardless of how many times he watched the videos, however, the graphic images of his victims' last moments were too pale an imitation of the real thing to satisfy him. Ideally, he'd return to the scenes of his crimes but the risks were too high.

When he had first arrived in the alien city its unfamiliar smells, tastes, sights and sounds had left him breathless with excitement. He had roamed Old Town in a daze, feeling his way round its seamier edges, exploring the run-down warehouses, cheap hotels, whorehouses and back alleys. He had told himself this obsession with the city's dark underbelly was crucial to his quest, the reason he had come. But that wasn't true. He had roamed the darker places precisely because their perverse history had inflamed his senses. He had never felt more alert and alive. He was a child again, every experience as raw and fresh as a newborn's. Even the sweet, cloudy wheat beer he had sipped in the Shanghai bar on the third day had tasted like nectar compared to the fiery liquor he was used to.

When he had seen the object of his quest staring out from the television screen the shock of seeing her face had stirred up a confusing cocktail of emotions within him: excitement; frustration; anxiety. Only after he had learned of her amnesia did he realize he still had time, precious time.

Then he had spotted the man in the bar.

He had never met the man before and his face looked older than the images in his head but it was definitely *him*. He had glanced back to the face on the television and a giddying surge of power had coursed through him as a connection had fused in his troubled mind. He had realized that out here among the children of men, unfettered by the usual constraints, he could be himself: a powerful demon free to act out his darkest instincts.

Not only did he have time. He had time to kill.

He itched to kill again now, if only to escape the war raging in his head. His temples ached with the constant pressure of trying to resolve the conflict between the sense of duty and destiny instilled in him from birth, and the burning desire—the primal *need*—to break free and follow his own path. Only killing the men as he had, especially the first victim, had momentarily eased the conflict between the steel grip of duty and the irresistible pull of desire.

The time to kill had passed, though. His duty could no longer be ignored. He walked into the bedroom and threw the cell phone on the crumpled, unmade bed. The floor was strewn with clippings of the woman the children of men had rechristened Jane Doe. After collecting all available information he had discovered what clinic she was in and even which room. But he hadn't acted on the knowledge until now. He glanced back at the cell

114

phone on the bed, expecting it to ring at any time, remembering the two main demands from the last call:

'*Have you found her yet?*'

'*Are you exercising discipline among the children of men?*'

He had lied when answering both questions, the chill frisson of fear warmed by the glow of rebellion. When the phone rang next, however, he wouldn't be able to stall. He had to decide what to do and do it quickly. There was no more time.

He pulled his one change of clothing from the black bag on the bed and dressed. Then he prepared a syringe, found the keys to the anonymous Japanese four-wheel drive parked beneath the apartment and retrieved the large hunting knife from the kitchen, still encrusted with the blood and viscera from his last victim. He cleaned its blade under the tap. Now he was filled with a fresh sense of purpose, the turmoil eased in his burning mind. He put the knife and syringe in his bag and checked his notes on the whereabouts of Jane Doe.

Finally, when all was ready, he sat on the bed, returned to the flickering video images on his phone, and waited for night to fall.

CHAPTER NINETEEN

Leaving Samantha's house, Jane Doe couldn't remember feeling so positive. With his aunt's help, Nathan Fox had encouraged her to view the terrifying hallucinations as a kind of unwanted gift, rather than an illness. The psychiatrist hadn't assumed, patronized or judged. Instead he had listened, observed and, despite his own obvious misgivings, reached beyond what he found comfortable to understand her problem. For that alone she owed him a debt. Still, despite all the talk of synaesthesia, archaeosonics and quantum physics, she felt no closer to answering the question that preoccupied her most. *Who am I?*

She found Fox an interesting and complex man. Although she was only his patient she suspected Fox was a hard man to get to know well even if you were a friend. She thought of the message on the photograph at his aunt's house: '*Never let them get too close. Never lose control.*' Seeing those photographs of Fox as a young boy had increased her respect—and affection—for him and made her think she understood him a little better. It couldn't have been easy losing his family so young, and the picture of him as the brave little boy in his karate uniform, standing apart from the others, chimed with her own sense of separation and loss.

For all his detachment, though, she didn't find him aloof or cold. He was too compassionate. She caught herself stealing glances at the psychiatrist, noticing the deep blue of his eyes, the generosity of his lips and the way his dark hair curled over his ears.

'I bet your other patients aren't as peculiar as me.'

The blue eyes flashed. 'You'd be surprised. But I'll admit you're more interesting than most.' He smiled. 'A friend said I needed a challenge.'

'Well, you certainly got that.' She laughed and the unfamiliar sound took her by surprise. They

116

drove on in silence and she noticed Fox was taking a different route to the one he had taken to his aunt's that morning. As they passed a group of nondescript buildings he slowed the car almost to a stop. Although the petrol gauge showed a full tank, he seemed about to pull into the Chevron garage. At the last minute, however, he accelerated and drove on. She wanted to ask him why but the tight expression on his face stopped her.

'Is this the way back to Tranquil Waters?'

'We're not going back just yet.' He pointed ahead to a street of residential houses. 'We're going to the place you were born.'

'What?'

He smiled. 'The place Jane Doe was born. We're going back to the last place you were seen before you lost your memory.'

Her earlier calm deserted her as a gutted house came into view, surrounded by crime scene tape and signs forbidding entry. The brick walls and the line of the roof were intact but the charred beams were exposed and half the tiles had gone. Most of the bricks and the surrounding ground were blackened with ash and she could still smell kerosene and acrid smoke in the air. 'Is this where I saved those girls?'

He parked the car. 'Yes. Remember anything?'

She looked at the deserted site. 'Not yet.'

He pointed to a blackened doorway in the side of the building. The door was gone, save for a few splinters of wood. 'That's the door to the cellar you destroyed with the axe. All I want you to do is to go up to the wall by the door, run your hand along the bricks and tell me what you feel.'

'Why?'

'You have no memory of anything before the night you went into that house and rescued those girls from the Russian traffickers. No one else remembers you either. The authorities have no record of you. The Russians you fought, the owner of the house and the girls you saved had no idea who you were. To all intents and purposes you appeared out of nowhere.' He gestured to the burnt-out building. 'Apart from your identity, one of the major mysteries is how you knew what was happening in that house. What prompted you to pick up the axe, break down the door and go inside? Detective Jordache joked that you must have had some kind of premonition, a sixth sense of what was going on in there. According to my aunt, perhaps you did.'

'You think I sensed something from the building?'

'According to the police report, two of the captive girls were murdered in or near the house and buried in the back yard. My guess is they didn't die peacefully so if Samantha's right then one or both would have left a big, fresh echo somewhere in the fabric of the building.'

'Which I sensed and acted upon?'

'That's the theory, and the building's still there so the echo should be too. By touching that wall again you should relive the identical experience you had as the person you were before you became Jane Doe, one of your last visceral experiences before losing your memory. That could spark a connection with your past self and build an emotional bridge back to who you were. Put simply, I want both to test your death-echo synaesthesia and use it to jog your memory. Understand?'

118

'Yes.' She felt suddenly nervous about what she would discover when she touched that wall. She knew Fox was right, though, and got out of the car.

'Don't worry, you're not going inside,' he said, as if sensing her nervousness. 'Remember, stay detached from whatever you experience. They're just memories and memories can't hurt you. Stand on your imaginary bridge, observe whatever flows beneath you and emotionally disengage. I'll be with you all the time. You ready?'

'I'm ready,' she said, feeling anything but. She walked to the broken door with Fox at her side. 'You sure I don't need to go inside?'

'No. If you sensed something that night then it must have happened before you went inside. Just touch the wall.'

She did as she was told. Instantly, the smell of fear-induced sweat cut through the acrid stench of ash and charcoal. Pale violet flickered across her vision, then a girl with beautiful long blonde hair emerged screaming from the doorway and ran directly along the wall towards her. Behind the girl, male voices were shouting in a foreign tongue. The girl was almost upon her when Jane heard a silenced gunshot and saw the girl drop at her feet, eyes blank, blood pouring from her head. Jane pulled her hand from the wall and collapsed into Fox's arms, clutching her own head.

'You OK?' she heard Fox ask. She pushed him away, trying to stay focused on what had happened. The experience of watching the girl's futile escape attempt was terrifying but it was the secondary emotions it stirred within her that disturbed her more: images from her dark recurring nightmares, especially the malevolent presence chasing her. The experience inspired in her a black rage even more intense than her fear—directed not only at the men hunting down the girl, but also at her own shadowy pursuer.

She told Fox everything. 'What does it all mean?' she said, exhausted.

'First of all, it validates your death-echo synaesthesia. One of the murdered girls was blonde, exactly as you described, and had a bullet hole in her skull. As for the stuff from your dreams, that's less clear. The dark unknown character chasing you could be a symbolic expression of a repressed fear. Perhaps you were running from something before your amnesia?'

'Or someone?'

'Possibly.' He shrugged. 'We're only speculating here but when you sensed the girl fleeing, you may have identified with her terror and decided that enough was enough. You had to fight back—even if it was against *her* demons and not your own—so you found the axe and went inside. The stress of fleeing from whatever was terrifying you, combined with what followed in that basement, may have contributed to your fugue state. Rare retrograde amnesia like yours can be triggered by intolerable stress.' He paused and studied her face. 'But, aside from this connection to the dreams you've been having, do you remember anything else? Any glimpses of your past life?'

'No.' He had obviously hoped for some kind of breakthrough and this wasn't it. She searched his face for disappointment but he gave nothing away.

He smiled. 'Well, it's a start. We've validated your death-echo synaesthesia and you appear to have made some kind of connection with your past self.' He checked his watch. 'Which we'll explore another time.'

She felt she had failed him and wanted to do more. 'I could try again now—for longer. I might have a breakthrough.'

'Or a breakdown. You look exhausted. It's getting late and I've already pushed you harder than I should. I've got a time slot tomorrow. We'll come back then.'

'But I'm here now . . .'

His phone rang and he checked the screen. 'Sorry, I better get this.' Fox put the phone to his ear. 'Hi, Karl.' Something the caller said made Fox glance at her. 'Sure. Yes. Why?' His face flushed. 'What kind of development?' Then he walked away towards the car, out of earshot. When he returned, moments later, he looked pale and troubled.

'What's wrong?'

'I'm not sure yet. But you'd better get back in the car. I'm taking you back to Tranquil Waters.'

CHAPTER TWENTY

As they left the site of Jane Doe's rebirth, Nathan Fox was disappointed her death-echo synaesthesia hadn't helped her make a more profound connection with her past self. He was, however, convinced of her gift now. It made him think of the Chevron garage and the yellow demolition sign they had passed on the way back from his aunt's. What would Jane Doe have sensed if he had stopped the car and led her into the garage kiosk? Could she have filled in the missing minutes that had haunted

121

him these long years? More importantly, did he have the courage to find out?

Not yet, he decided, pushing the thought from his mind. Jordache's call had raised more pressing concerns: *How the hell could Jane Doe be connected to three homicides?* After returning her to Tranquil Waters, he drove on to meet the detective, who had directed him to the Grand Hotel Excelsior, a run-down flophouse a couple of blocks from the Willamette River that rented out rooms by the hour. As Fox parked he was grateful for the battered state of his ancient silver Porsche. This wasn't a neighbourhood in which to leave expensive cars. Noticing that the G in Grand and the E in Excelsior had blown on the illuminated sign, Fox pondered why the sleaziest hotels so often boasted the most luxurious names. A crowd of reporters had gathered so he walked round the side, where Detective Phil Kostakis escorted him through the cordon.

Jordache greeted him in the lobby, led him down a dark corridor that smelled of damp, and filled him in on the homicides. 'This is the latest. We've had three in as many days, all with the same signature.'

'What's the link to Jane Doe?'

'I'll show you. Walk the scene with me, both as her shrink and as a forensic psychologist. I need to know *why* the guy's doing this. There's no obvious financial motive, no evidence of sexual activity and no real link between the victims, except they all were male, over fifty and scumbags.' Jordache pointed to an open door ringed with yellow crime scene tape. There was an emergency fire door beside it, which led directly outside. Men in white forensic suits were already in the room. 'The guy at

122

the check-in desk vaguely remembers a large man paying cash for the room.'

'Any other description?'

'This ain't exactly the Four Seasons, Nathan. The staff here make a point of *not* remembering clients and the man was wearing a large hat that obscured much of his face.' Jordache checked his notes. 'All the guy at the desk remembers is he had fair skin, intense eyes and a low rumbling voice. The description fits one we have for a suspect on the other killings.' He read out the statement from the witness at the thrift store.

'What about the bad smell?'

'The guy at the desk here had a cold and didn't pick anything up. The smell might be a dead end. The killer could have stepped in something or have been carrying some food that was off.' He indicated the fire door. 'We figure the killer cased the joint out earlier, paid for the room keys then carried his victim into the hotel through that fire door.'

'Carried him in?'

'Yeah, the pathologist took a blood sample and found traces of ketamine again. The killer waited for the guy to wake up in the room, then killed him.' He pulled back the crime scene tape and led Fox into the room.

The first thing Fox noticed was the blood spatter. No Luminol was required here. Sticky blood matted the threadbare carpet, and marked the furniture. Part of the pine wardrobe in the corner had been stained as dark as mahogany. 'Where's the body?'

Jordache pointed to the small adjoining bathroom. The door was open and a police photographer was inside taking pictures. 'In there.'

Fox walked in and saw a man's naked body

crammed into a bath, brimming with a rosy soup. The smell of blood hung in the air, its yeasty stench catching in the back of Fox's throat. The bled-out corpse was pale, its hands were bound with blue twine and it had no head. There were cut marks on the neck but otherwise the break was butcher-clean.

'All three victims were changed out of their own clothes,' Jordache said. 'The first two were found in female clothing, this one was naked. Forensics say the killer used a knife, large and razor-sharp but pretty standard. Not surgical. The kind of thing you'd find in most hunting and gaming stores. It was almost certainly the same weapon used at the other two scenes.'

Fox grimaced. 'The killer's got to be a pretty powerful guy to carry a man as big as him in here, tie him up, undress him and cut off his head with a knife—however sharp it is.' He stared at the body, which no longer looked human, more like a gruesome mannequin or a sick prop from a movie. But this had once been a person with a life, perhaps a wife and children. 'Who found him?'

'The cleaner.'

'This dump has a cleaner?'

'Comes in once a day, would you believe.'

'You got a name for the victim?'

'An old guy called Luis Paz. Was a small-time enforcer for the local mob. Retired some years back. We got an ID from his head.'

Fox looked around the bathroom. 'Where is it, by the way?'

The detective led him back into the bedroom, donned white latex gloves and pointed to the wardrobe. 'In there.'

'Where's the link to Jane Doe?'

'I'll show you.' Jordache stepped forward and, with a flourish, opened the wardrobe. Fox was not easily shocked but what he saw made him step back a pace. The interior of the wardrobe was divided into hanging space on the left and shelves on the right. On the middle shelf, sitting in a pool of dark congealed blood, was a severed human head. The skin visible around the pale lips and on the jowly chin was already turning grey like that of a diseased fish but the eyes and upper half of the face were obscured by a sheet of newspaper, which had been stapled to the victim's forehead. Despite the blood, Fox could see a message written in coloured marker pens.

He read the message aloud: ' "*Serve the demon, save the angel.*" This the same as at the other killings?'

'Yep.'

'Written the same way? In capital letters of different colours, on two lines with no punctuation?'

'Exactly the same. Look at what the message is written on.' Fox stepped closer to the wardrobe, ignoring the butcher's-shop smell of cold, bloody meat, until his nose was inches from the severed head. Suddenly, he understood the connection. The message had been written over the photograph of Jane Doe's face featured in all the news stories. 'All three male homicide victims had the same newspaper photo from the *Oregonian* stapled to their foreheads,' Jordache said.

'You think the killer knows Jane Doe?'

'It's possible. More to the point, she might know the killer. I want to talk to her, Nathan.'

Fox considered this for a moment. 'But Jane

125

Doe doesn't even know her own name, Karl. How do you expect her to know the killer's? You'd only scare her for no good reason and this may have nothing to do with her.' He thought of the messages. 'The killer might *think* he knows Jane Doe but he's just as likely to be obsessed with the guardian angel persona presented by the media. The only connection could be in his head.'

'But she's the only connection we've got, Nathan. The killer *might* know her and she *might* know him.' Jordache frowned at him. 'Why are you being so protective, Nathan?'

'I'm her doctor. It's my job to protect her. The point is, even if she does know the killer, she won't *remember* knowing him. She has no recall of anything before the night of the fire. Before we involve her, we need to go over the three crime scenes and work out what's going on in the killer's head. What are the messages all about? Who's the angel and who's the demon?'

'Jane Doe could help us do that,' Jordache persisted. 'Perhaps she'll remember something when confronted with all this?'

'You've got to be kidding. People lapse into a fugue state because they've undergone or remembered something so traumatic they retreat from their own identity.' He spread his arms wide, taking in the bloody room and the photo of Jane Doe stapled to the severed head. 'Speaking of traumatic, how the hell will confronting her with a fresh crime scene help her remember anything?' Even as the question left his mouth Fox knew the answer.

'I don't mean expose her to the goddamn bodies, Nathan. We'll remove those. I mean *tell* her about

126

the murders. Show her mugshots of the victims. Who knows? Perhaps she'll recognize one of them. Explain how her photo was stapled to their faces, and show her the messages. See if anything registers.'

Nathan thought for a moment. 'I'll make you a proposal.' Jordache frowned but said nothing. 'I'll talk to her about this, but you've got to let me do it my way. Jane Doe's fragile and her condition's complicated. OK?' He extended his hand.

Jordache frowned but shook it. 'Whatever you say.'

'Good. Now show me the other two crime scenes.'

CHAPTER TWENTY-ONE

It was late by the time Fox left the final crime scene. As he drove home he received a call from his aunt, who was in good spirits and had enjoyed meeting Jane Doe.

'What a lovely and beautiful girl,' she said at least three times. 'It was obvious you liked her too, Nathan.' He could see her teasing smile in the tone of her voice.

'She's a patient of mine, Samantha. That's all.'

'If you say so, Dr Fox.' He decided against telling Samantha about the murders and their connection to his patient but after he hung up he could think of nothing else. Images of the three victims kept surfacing in his mind, and each time he kept seeing Jane Doe in their place. He imagined pulling back the photo stapled to the severed head and revealing her real face beneath it, skin grey with death, eyes milky with decomposition. The thought made him nauseous.

Fox believed the killer had become fixated with Jane Doe's media persona and didn't know her personally, but that didn't neutralize the threat. Statistically, most victims know their killer, but strangers often target media personalities because they *think* they have a relationship with them, even though they have never met. Fox opened the car window, breathed in the fresh night air and reassured himself that Jordache had assigned a discreet police protection detail to Jane Doe, starting tomorrow, once Fox had briefed her on the murders.

What about tonight?

Fox considered calling Tranquil Waters, but the thought of disturbing one of the night nurses and having to explain why he wanted her to check on a sleeping Jane Doe stopped him. In the rear-view mirror his tired eyes stared back at him. *Get a grip, Nathan. You're losing perspective. She's a patient, asleep in a clinic. She's absolutely safe. You're the one who's exhausted. Go home and get some rest.*

He breathed deep and tried in vain to heed the advice he had given Jane Doe earlier, and distance himself from the fears invading his head. He tried all the mind games in his arsenal but, despite his best efforts, nothing helped him shrug off the irrational but obsessive certainty that Jane Doe was in danger, or soothed his sudden and overwhelming compulsion to check she was safe.

*　　　*　　　*

128

Lying in her bed at Tranquil Waters, Jane Doe took some time to fall asleep but tonight it was excitement that kept her awake, not anxiety. After Fox had returned her to Tranquil Waters she had gone for a run on the marked trail in the grounds. She had pushed herself hard and it had felt good getting to know her body again. After a shower she had eaten surprisingly good pasta in the canteen and met some of the other residents—as Tranquil Waters liked to call its patients. Some of them had made her realize she didn't have it so bad. She had watched a cheesy movie in the TV lounge with a few of them before going to bed.

Now, as she tried to sleep, her mind kept replaying the earlier events of the day: listening to Fox's aunt explaining archaeosonics; discussing her synaesthesic 'gift' with Fox; and returning to the burnt house where she had lost her memory and identity. She was beginning to accept what Fox called her death-echo synaesthesia but still couldn't understand *why* she had it and—given the remarkable nature of this 'gift'—why no one from her old life had come forward to claim her.

Who had she once been? Where had she come from? These questions, which had once unnerved her, now excited her. She was confident that with Fox's help she would eventually discover the answers. Before she eventually fell asleep, her last conscious thought was of seeing the psychiatrist the next morning. It made her smile.

As she descended into REM, the deep sleep when dreams come, the smile faded from her face and the anxiety returned, along with the nightmares that had plagued her unconscious since she could remember. This time, however, the recurring nightmares felt more real and immediate: she was running from her shadowy pursuer, through the empty rooms of a deserted hotel, occupied only by the ghosts of the dead. Outside, horses galloped in crazed circles while a large all-seeing eye looked down on her every move. As her pursuer got ever closer, she could hear his breathing and smell his scent in her nostrils. Still asleep she shook her head, as if to purge the smell, but it only grew stronger, reaching deep into the primitive, reptilian part of her brain, invoking a terror so primal it woke her.

It took seconds for her to focus and grow accustomed to the gloom. The first thing she became aware of was the open window and the breeze blowing the curtains into the room. Then she noticed a large figure standing over the bed, silhouetted in the moonlight, watching her. As her panic surged she mentally recited Fox's mantra: *observe your visions but remain emotionally detached; what isn't there can't hurt you; let your experiences flow past you.* Gradually her breathing steadied.

Then the apparition leaned towards her. He was wearing a broad-rimmed hat that covered his face. Struggling to remain calm, she blinked hard and squinted into the dark. This didn't feel like her other experiences of death-echo synaesthesia. The silhouette bent closer and a deep growling voice whispered in her ear, 'I know who you are. I will save you from the demon.' A chill ran down her spine. No death echo had ever addressed her before. The apparition moved nearer and she saw the glint of a hypodermic needle, and a large knife in the man's belt.

She opened her mouth to scream but a huge hand clamped over her face. 'Quiet,' the figure hissed, moving the hypodermic so close she could see droplets on the needle tip. Suddenly, she felt the needle pierce the skin of her arm and she twisted her body away, slipping off the side of the bed, escaping his grip.

She could already feel the effects of whatever he had injected into her. Her body was no longer hers: her limbs and vocal cords no longer obeyed her commands. She tried screaming for help but only a mewing sound came from her lips. When she tried to crawl to the door she barely moved. Still conscious, she saw the intruder wedge a chair under the door handle, jamming it shut, then he bent and swung her over his shoulder as easily as if she were a doll. Unable to scream or struggle, she felt as if she was outside her body, looking down on her inert self—a silent, helpless witness to her own abduction. He carried her to the open window where she could feel the cool breeze and see the moon in the star-filled night sky. The beauty of the scene made her predicament seem even more surreal. Who was he? Why was he here? What did he want with her? She heard banging and her name being called. There was a crash of rending wood. Someone was kicking at the jammed door. *Thank God*. She didn't want to die. Not before she had at least discovered her real name.

The intruder hesitated and reached for his knife. Suddenly, the door broke open. A figure rushed in and struck her abductor with such force that he dropped her to the floor. The fall pushed the air from her lungs, making her gasp for breath. The intruder quickly regained his poise and lunged with his knife. Rotating his body with balletic grace, her rescuer avoided the blow before unleashing a kick that slammed her abductor against the window. For a moment the two figures squared off against each other and all she could hear was the sound of their laboured breathing. Then the intruder snorted with disgust, exited the window and was gone.

Only when her saviour shouted at an orderly to call the police and bent down to check her injuries did she realize it was Nathan Fox. When he discovered she couldn't move or speak he gently picked her up off the floor and laid her on the bed. 'You're safe now,' he said. 'I'm pretty sure he injected you with ketamine. The effects should wear off soon.'

The next hour was a blur of doctors, nurses and police. As soon as the police arrived to examine the scene she was moved to another room. Professor Fullelove and Detective Karl Jordache, the cop she remembered from the night of the fire, both came to check on her. Fullelove told her that fortunately her attacker had managed to inject only a small amount of ketamine. Jordache reassured her that the man would be found and a twenty-four-hour watch put on her room. Despite all the assurances, however, she only felt safe again when the feeling returned to her arms and she could embrace Fox. The surprising hardness of his body and strength of his arms comforted her more than any words. Slowly he disengaged, laid her back on the bed and gave her a glass of water. Her parched mouth felt like she had been sucking cotton wool. She explained to the police everything that had happened, including what the intruder had said to her.

'Can you remember the *exact* words he used?' said Jordache.

'Yes. "I know who you are. I will save you from the demon.'"

'You must have got a good look at him, Nathan. You fought him,' said Jordache.

'Not really. It was too dark, the moon was behind him and his hat obscured his face.' He rubbed his leg. 'He's goddamned big, though, and as strong as an ox. I detected a faint smell.'

'So did I,' Jane Doe said.

Jordache turned to her. 'What sort of smell?'

'Like dead flesh.'

'What about his face, Jane? Did *you* see what he looked like?'

'I only got a glimpse. I couldn't give you much detail.'

'Did you recognize him from anywhere?'

Something about the way both Jordache and Fox were studying her made her pause. She thought of the shadowy pursuer in her nightmares and shivered. 'You're looking at me like I should have done. Why?'

Fox and Jordache exchanged a glance, then the detective handed Fox a thin brown envelope. 'Not now, Karl,' Fox said. 'It can wait till the morning. She's still my patient and she should get some rest.'

'What can wait till the morning?' she said. Fox frowned. 'Tell me,' she insisted. 'What's going on?'

'Tell her,' said Jordache. She heard someone calling the detective. 'I'll be outside if you need me.'

Fox waited for Jordache to leave then sat by her bed. 'It's about the intruder . . .'

The attack had so shaken her that she felt a strange relief when he told her about the three murders and their connection to her. At least it explained why the man had singled her out. Sort of.

133

'You sure it's the same man?' she asked, when Fox had finished.

'He spoke about "saving you from the demon", which is similar language to that used in messages at the crime scenes. The ketamine he injected you with is a signature of two of the killings. From the little I saw and felt, he was big enough to fit a vague description the police got from a storekeeper on the fringes of Old Town. And his smell fits some of the witness statements. So, yes, I'd say it was the same man.'

'He stapled *my* newspaper photograph to the faces of his victims?'

'Yes.'

'He said he knows who I am. You think he really knows me? Knows who I was?'

Fox shrugged. 'Possibly, but it's just as likely he became fixated on your avenging angel persona. Frankly, the way he attacked you while insisting he was trying to save you points to him being delusional. So, my guess is he doesn't really know you at all. But I could be wrong.'

'The police have any idea who he is?'

'Like I said, they have a vague description, but nothing concrete yet.' He paused. 'The police are worried he'll kill again and are desperate for leads. I've explained your amnesia to them but Jordache wants to interview you about the homicides, to see if it triggers anything. He believes you might be key to finding this man, especially after what just happened. I said I'd talk you through the homicides. You OK with that?'

'Yes.' She wanted to find the killer as much as the police did, especially as he might be the only link to her past.

'Jordache gave me pictures of the victims and some crime scene photos to show you to see if anything registers.' Fox pulled a sheaf of photographs from the brown envelope and laid them on the table: the victims face up; the crime scene pictures face down.

'I don't recognize any of the victims.'

He nodded like he didn't expect anything else. 'Look at the crime scene pictures. But be warned. They're not pretty.'

She turned the pictures over and flicked through them. The photographs were graphic but after her death-echo synaesthesia these mute, static, odourless images of bloody mutilated corpses held no fears. Even the severed head didn't faze her, although it troubled her to see her photograph stapled to the victims' faces. She coolly studied each picture and read the marker pen messages, noticing the similarity to the language used by the intruder, but she felt no connection to what she was seeing. 'I'm sorry. These pictures mean nothing to me.'

'I didn't think they would,' Fox said quietly. He paused and looked at her. 'There is another way you could find out more about the homicides and the killer.'

She understood immediately. 'I'd have to visit the actual crime scenes. But it must be just you and me. No one else, not even the police, must know about my . . .'

'Your gift?'

'No one. You must never tell *anyone*.' She trusted Fox but there could be no misunderstanding about this. 'If you do decide to tell someone, even for the most noble medical reason, then I'll deny it. And without my testimony no one will believe you.'

He nodded slowly. 'No one, not even Jordache, will come inside when we walk the crime scenes.'

She glanced back at the graphic photographs and felt suddenly nauseous. 'What about the bodies? The head and . . .?'

'Don't worry. They'll all have been removed.'

She made a decision, excitement overruling fear. 'Let's do it.'

CHAPTER TWENTY-TWO

They arrived at the first crime scene a little after nine o'clock the next morning.

When Fox had told Jordache he wanted to walk the crimes scenes with Jane Doe, the detective had protested, 'I meant show her the photographs of the victims and the message, Nathan. Not walk the goddamned crime scene. There's nothing there except blood and shit.'

'The place might be relevant and it gives context to the photographs and messages. You're the one who insisted on jogging Jane Doe's memory, Karl, not me. If you think she knows the killer or the victims then we either do this properly or we don't do it at all.'

'Then why can't I walk the scene with you?'

'Because you'll cramp her style and you agreed to let me handle this my way, without asking questions.'

Jordache and his team waited outside while Fox and Jane Doe entered the derelict apartment block alone. Fox watched his patient constantly, still shocked by last night's intrusion into her room at Tranquil Waters, determined to extricate her from the scene if it proved too much. This promised to be Jane Doe's toughest test. Even Fox could sense a disturbing atmosphere here. Leading her silently past the elevator and into the stairwell, the smell of urine, viscera and blood was stronger than he remembered. The body had been removed but a strip of white tape outlined where it had lain. 'You OK, Jane?' She nodded silently, seemingly overwhelmed by her surroundings. 'Want me to brief you on what the police think happened?'

'No. Let me see it for myself.' Looking pale but focused, she stepped into the area where the body had lain. She leaned forward and when she touched the wall she exhaled loudly, as if winded by the impact of what she was experiencing.

'What is it?' He stepped closer but she raised a hand and waved him back.

'Later,' she said, not looking at him. 'I'll tell you later.' For a long while she stayed there, bent almost double, then she slowly straightened and began ascending the stairs. She went to the top of the first flight and turned to him. 'You sure the victim was a man?'

'Yes,' he said, surprised. Jane Doe had seen the crime scene pictures. She knew that all the victims were men. 'The killer dressed him in female underwear but the victim was a man.'

She stared intently down the stairs for a long while, seeing something he couldn't, then shook her head in confusion. 'It doesn't make sense,' she said to herself, stepping back and closing her eyes. When she opened them again she gasped. 'Ohh,' she said, experiencing a sudden epiphany. She scampered quickly down the stairs, as if following a falling object, and crouched over the taped outline

137

of where the corpse had lain. As she stared down she began nodding to herself. The fear had gone from her face, replaced with intense concentration. 'That's strange.'

'What?'

'I need to see the next crime scene. Can we go there now?'

'You got anything yet, Nathan?' Jordache hissed as they arrived at the deserted warehouse where the second victim had been dispatched.

Fox was as much in the dark as the detective. 'Not yet,' he said, lifting up the crime scene tape for Jane Doe to pass. 'Not yet.' Fox no longer led but followed her to the crime scene. Her newfound confidence impressed but also unnerved him. When they were alone in the warehouse she walked straight to the tape marking where the body had lain, dropped to her knees and pressed her palm against the floor—not tentatively but firmly, *expertly*. Now the fear was under control she seemed to be mastering her gift. It occurred to Fox then that she was the perfect crime scene investigator. Trained CSIs had to study the evidence to extrapolate what had happened but she could viscerally relive the crime from the victim's point of view—again and again. She stood up abruptly and frowned. Looking anxious but in command of her feelings, she stared down at the tape and kept shaking her head. 'Why do that? Why?'

'Why do what?'

She looked up, startled, as if she had forgotten Fox was there. 'I need to see the third murder scene.'

'Then will you tell me what's going on?'

'First I've got to check out something. Something

weird.'

By the time they arrived at the final crime scene, Jordache was bristling with impatience. 'Speak to me, Nathan. Does she remember anything or not?'

'Later,' Fox reassured him. 'After we've seen all the murders, I'll tell you everything.' He hoped that whatever Jane Doe had discovered would be worth the wait. As soon as she walked into the hotel room where the last victim had been decapitated, her face drained of colour and her newfound confidence deserted her. This had been the most traumatic murder and, as she placed her hand on the wall, Fox could tell it was taking all her strength to remain emotionally detached from what she was seeing and not run from the room. 'This is hideous. This is hideous,' she kept saying, again and again. She stared into the bloodstained but empty wardrobe, then walked into the bathroom. 'How could anyone do this? Who was she?'

'She?' Fox said aloud. 'There were no women involved in any of the homicides.'

'Yes there were,' she said quietly. 'There were women involved in all three.' She slumped on the bed, exhausted. 'My photograph may have been stapled over the victims' faces but I'm not the only link between the three killings. I'm not even the main one.'

'Really? What is?'

'Each murder happened before.'

'Happened before? What do you mean?'

She looked down and shielded her eyes with her hands, like a child watching a frightening movie. 'I can't stay in this room any longer. I can't concentrate.' She began rocking from side to side. 'Don't take me back to Tranquil Waters. Take me somewhere without any memories. Take me somewhere safe.'

Fox took her hand and helped her from the bed. 'Come with me.'

CHAPTER TWENTY-THREE

Jane Doe kept close to Nathan Fox as he led her away from the last crime scene. When he helped her into his car, Detective Karl Jordache scowled. 'Why can't you debrief her here? At least tell me whether she remembers anything or not.'

Fox gunned the engine and lowered his voice. 'It's complicated, Karl. As soon as I've got anything concrete I'll call you. I promise.'

'But what about keeping her safe from whoever did all this?'

'I'll take care of her.'

'Yeah, right.' Jordache swore quietly and ordered two of his policemen to follow their car. Driving away from the crime scene, the cops in the lone police car didn't realize that they too were being followed. Fox said nothing as he drove and Jane Doe was grateful for the time to order her thoughts and recover from her ordeal. Reliving the gruesome crimes had made her aware of how close she had come to being one of the killer's hapless victims, and how lucky she was that Fox had intervened when he did. Despite the horror of the crime scenes, however, she was surprised and encouraged by how well she'd coped. Only a few days ago she would have been unable to remain at any of the places for even a few seconds—especially

140

the scene of the horrific beheading. She hadn't passively endured them either: she had actively probed each scene for clues. Not only had she stared into the dark heart of her deepest fears and not blinked, she had seen something that could help solve the case.

The car slowed and she felt herself stiffen as they approached a circular tower block. 'What is this place?' she asked.

He turned into the underground car park. 'It's my home. You don't like it?'

'The apartment block's shape reminds me of my nightmares.'

'Thanks.' He smiled and patted her arm. 'My aunt hates it too but north-west Portland is a good location, and the apartment suits me fine. It should suit you too. It's a new-build with few "memories" to distract you. You've no reason to be scared.' He got out, led her to the elevator and pushed the top button.

When he brought her into his apartment the interior surprised her. It was as striking as the block's exterior was bland. Comfortable Italian furniture and rich Persian and Afghan rugs softened the minimalist white walls, downlighters and stripped wooden floors. Much of the walls was glass, affording sweeping views over Portland and along the river. Quirky, colourful artworks covered the remainder of the walls, alongside shelves crammed with books. A framed collage of photographs dominated one corner. Fox was right about the archaeosonics. She sensed no bad echoes here. The place calmed her, made her feel safe. 'The view of the block's pretty dull,' he said. 'But the views from it are great.'

141

'I like the décor.'

He smiled. 'You sound surprised. What were you expecting?'

'No. No. It's just that you're a psychiatrist and reveal so little of yourself . . .' Embarrassed, she turned to the open-plan, well-equipped kitchen and pointed to the glass-fronted drinks fridge. It contained some wine but was dominated by rows and rows of bottled beers. 'You like your beer.'

'Want to try one?'

'OK.' The idea of alcohol appealed. It would be her first taste since losing her memory, assuming she had drunk before then. He took out a bottle, poured it into a glass and handed it to her. It was a golden cloudy colour and when she put it to her lips it tasted sweet. 'I like it.'

He smiled. 'Most people don't know that Oregon's one of the beer capitals of the world. 'Take a seat and let's talk about what you experienced back there. You seemed to cope with it better than before, as if you're getting to grips with your death-echo synaesthesia. You said the homicides had happened before?' He took out his notebook and pen. 'Tell me what you meant.'

She sat on the couch. 'They were copycat killings. Each murder copied an earlier one committed in precisely the same place years before. Remember my first room in Tranquil Waters, when I saw two death echoes: the hanging man and the man cutting his wrists?'

'The hanging man who died earlier was fainter than the other guy.'

She nodded. 'It was the same at the three crime scenes. I experienced the death echoes of the three men who were killed but also three fainter

142

signatures of women who had been murdered before, in exactly the same place and almost exactly the same way.' She swallowed hard. 'The only difference I sensed was that all the women had been raped before they were killed. Apart from that, it was like one murder had been written over the other.' As she described each murder he noted every detail down.

'You're saying the killer choreographed his murders to fit with the earlier deaths?'

'Exactly. Each male victim was even dressed like the earlier female victim: the first died in underwear, the second a blue dress, and the third was naked.'

He laid a crime scene photograph of one of the corpses on the coffee table. 'What about the "*Serve the demon, save the angel*" messages written in coloured marker pens?'

'They must have happened after the victims' deaths because I didn't experience them in the death echoes. I did see a picture of my face in the first murder, though. I think my photograph in the newspaper was one of the last things the victim saw.'

'What about the killer? Or killers?'

'That's the odd thing. The male victims all resembled the killers of the earlier, female victims. It was like someone knew what they'd done and was punishing them by killing them in exactly the same way as they'd killed the women.'

'Are you're saying that the male victims of the current homicides were the perpetrators of the original ones?'

'Yes. They looked a lot younger in the earlier death echoes but I'm sure they were the same men.'

'What about the man who killed them? Did you see him?'

She looked down suddenly, frightened. 'Yes. It was the same man who attacked me in my room.'

'You sure?'

'I'm sure.'

Fox's phone rang. It was Jordache. He put it on speaker. 'You got anything yet?' said the detective.

'I might have,' said Fox, glancing at Jane Doe, 'but I need your people to check something first. It's going to sound a little strange so hold the questions. You ready? You might want to write this down.'

'Shoot.'

He scanned his notes. 'Check if there've been any prior *female* homicides at the three crime scenes. Go back at least thirty years and compare the MOs against these three homicides. Concentrate on unsolved cold cases. Then pull out the mugshots of anyone suspected of the earlier female homicides and compare them with our male victims.'

'Why?'

'Check it out. You'll see why.'

'What about Jane Doe? What's this got to do with her?'

'Come on, Karl, I said hold the questions.'

Fox heard a frustrated groan. 'I'm a detective, Nathan, it's what I do.'

As Fox hung up Jane Doe rose from the couch, too tense and wired to sit still. Seeking distraction, she glanced around Fox's apartment until she spied a cardboard box overflowing with childhood memorabilia, including a cricket bat, a baseball catcher's mitt, notebooks and stacks of faded photographs. Fox saw where she was looking and smiled self-consciously. 'Ignore those. I've been meaning to throw that box away for years.'

She picked up a creased, faded photo of Fox as a boy with his family. 'How did you lose your parents and sister?'

'They were in the wrong place at the wrong time, shot dead by two men holding up a gas station.'

'That's awful. Where were you?'

'I was with them. But somehow I wasn't hurt. Not a scratch.' He frowned. 'I don't know why. I can't remember.'

She nodded slowly. 'Is that why you became a psychiatrist?'

'I think I went into medicine because my father had been a doctor in England and I wanted to follow in his footsteps. I don't really know why I chose psychiatry.' He shrugged. 'Perhaps I did hope it would help me make sense of what happened.'

'Has it?'

He sighed. 'I'm working on it.' She felt a sudden urge to comfort him, like he had comforted her, but didn't know how. Then she remembered the drive back from his aunt's. 'I noticed you slowed down by the gas station on the way back from seeing Samantha. Was that the—?'

'Yes it was,' he said quickly. The tight expression on his face told her to drop the subject but she couldn't. Not yet. She could help him, she realized, repay some of the debt she owed him. 'I could go back there for you and see if—'

'No,' he interrupted sharply, panic flashing in his eyes. 'This isn't about me. I'm not the one with the problem.'

'I'm sorry, I only wanted to help. I didn't mean

to . . .' She tailed off, afraid to jeopardize her relationship with the one friend she had in the entire world. Fox had not only dragged her from the depths of despair but also saved her life.

'It's OK. I'm sorry,' he said quickly, regaining control. 'I overreacted.' There was an awkward silence, then he checked his watch. 'We'd better go.'

She felt a stab of panic. 'Do I have to go back to Tranquil Waters?' After her ordeal last night and visiting the intruder's grisly crime scenes today she was in no hurry to return to her room.

'You'll have police protection.'

'I don't care, I don't think I can sleep there tonight.'

'I understand but you can't stay here. I'm your doctor.' He made two calls. When he told her what he had arranged she breathed a sigh of relief. 'You should feel safer there.'

'I will. Thank you. You sure it's OK? I don't want to impose.'

'I'm sure,' he said softly. His smile reassured her but as they left the apartment she saw his smile fade and sensed Fox wrap an invisible cloak around himself, forming a barrier she would never breach. She remembered the photograph of the fierce little boy in the karate uniform, standing apart from the others. *Never let them get too close. Never lose control.*

CHAPTER TWENTY-FOUR

As Fox drove Jane Doe away from his apartment, neither they nor their police detail noticed the anonymous white van parked across the street. The driver inside seethed with rage as he watched them pass, his ire aimed at both Fox and himself.

Why hadn't he just tranquillized her, like he had the others? Why had he hesitated? Why had he needed to talk to her? His delay had allowed that meddling fool to come to her aid and complicate matters. He could have been caught and then everything would have been lost. His hesitation had not only alerted her to his presence but the police would undoubtedly increase security. Getting to her now would be significantly more difficult.

As he pulled away and followed the Porsche his phone rang. The ringtone caused waves of purple and red to shimmer before his eyes. He considered not answering but knew it was futile. He slowed the vehicle and picked up. 'Hello?'

'Where are you?' demanded the familiar voice. 'Have you found her yet? Is she with you?'

'No. No. But I'm close.'

'How close?'

As he watched the Porsche stop at the lights he became aware of his shirt sticking to his skin, drenched with sweat. 'Very close. I've seen her. I know where she is.'

'So why haven't you done what I asked?' the voice snarled. 'Are you going to fail me again?'

'No. No.' His temples ached from the pressure in his head. 'I'll have her within a day,' he said.

'Good. I'm in Portland. We can meet.'

He froze. 'You're in the city? How long have you been here?'

'Long enough to see the news reports and know you've been lying to me. You of all people should know not to hide things from me. They say the authorities have had her for days.' He spoke slowly as if to a slow child, his voice thick with anger. 'Why didn't you tell me she'd been found?'

'She has no memory. She's told them nothing.'

'That's not the point. What have you been doing out here among the children of men? Have you been drawing attention to yourself? To us?'

'No, no. I've been finding out exactly where she is,' he said quickly. 'I went to get her last night.'

'So why haven't you got her?'

'There was a problem.'

'What problem?'

He explained what had happened. 'It was dark. Nobody saw me.'

'Can't you do anything right?' the voice hissed. 'You should have told me where she was and let me handle it. Listen very carefully, there can't be any more mistakes or misunderstandings. This is what I want you to do.'

As he heard his orders he tried to protest. 'But I'm so close. I just need a little more time.'

'There is no more time,' said the voice. Then the phone went dead.

As he watched the Porsche pull away from the lights he could taste the acrid taint of failure and frustration on his tongue. Dr Fox believed he was his patient's protector and helper, but he was wrong. His interference last night had only sealed her fate. For a second he hesitated, unsure what

148

to do, but he knew he had no choice. Whatever his orders were, he had one last chance to finish this and he had to take it.

He pushed his foot down on the accelerator and followed the psychiatrist's car.

CHAPTER TWENTY-FIVE

When Fox had called his aunt and told her about last night's attack, she had not only agreed Jane Doe could stay with her but insisted on it. As he drove up to the house he saw a police squad car parked on the kerb outside. After a brief complaint about moving the security detail from Tranquil Waters, Jordache had acknowledged that Jane Doe might be safer staying somewhere the killer didn't know and sent two uniformed officers over from the clinic with a bag of her personal effects.

Samantha was waiting by the front door and as Fox parked his car she hurried over and greeted Jane with a hug. Before Fox had turned off the engine both women had disappeared into the house. Following them inside, he found Samantha settling Jane into what had been his old bedroom and winced at the old baseball bat and tennis racket in the corner and the high school pennants, Stanford class photos and other paraphernalia of his youth that bedecked the walls. Perhaps this hadn't been such a good idea. After the awkward exchange in his apartment, when Jane Doe had offered to go back to the scene of his family's murder and fill in the missing minutes that had changed his life, he was reluctant to expose any more of his personal life.

He realized, however, that as Jane Doe helped Samantha put fresh sheets on the bed she was oblivious to his old room and the mementoes of his youth. Relaxed and smiling, she appeared totally secure in Samantha's presence, all trace of her earlier panic gone. Judging by the maternal way his aunt clucked over her, Samantha was equally delighted to have company and someone to look after. He felt suddenly foolish. 'Everything OK?' he said, more gruffly than he intended.

'We're just fine,' said Samantha. 'Aren't we, Jane?'

Jane smiled. 'Very much so.'

'You want to stay for dinner, Nathan?'

'No thanks, I'd better get going but if you need me for anything . . .'

'Don't worry about us,' said Samantha. 'We've got two policemen outside. Relax, go.'

'I'll check on you both in the morning.'

Samantha walked over and kissed him on the cheek. 'You do that, darling. Good night.'

As he left the house, Fox approached the two uniforms standing by the squad car. Jordache had reassured him that the killer had no way of knowing Jane Doe was here or Fox wouldn't have risked endangering Samantha, but he still wasn't taking any chances. 'Jane Doe's staying with my aunt tonight so you take good care of them both. OK?'

'Don't worry, Doc,' said the taller cop, walking to the back yard. 'I'm taking the rear.'

'And I'm staying right here,' said the shorter cop, a neat black guy with a serious face. 'No one's getting into that house unless they come through us.'

The man in the anonymous white vehicle parked across the street watched the doctor talk to the policemen and then drive away. Despite the air-conditioning he dripped with nervous sweat and his smell filled the car. He had seen his target— the woman they called Jane Doe—enter the house with the old lady and it appeared they were the only ones inside. The urge to act was overwhelming but he had to wait for the right moment. He watched as the policeman patrolled the front of the house for the first hour then retired to his car and drank coffee from a flask. It was clear from his relaxed body language that the officer didn't expect trouble. Why should he? He had no reason to suspect that the doctor and his patient had been followed here.

Waiting till it was dark, he accessed Google Earth on his cell phone and studied the layout of the neighbourhood. Then he drove the van round the block and parked on the street behind the house. A welcoming fresh breeze cooled his face as he got out and checked his bearings. The houses on this street backed on to a narrow public access path, which separated their rear gardens from those on the old lady's street. Darting down a side alley, he found the path and walked down it until he reached the back of the old lady's house. The narrow wooden gate to her garden was bolted at the top but by reaching over he easily pulled back the bolt. Peering through the gap he could see extensive lawns, a summerhouse and the other policeman sitting on a bench by a pair of glazed folding doors that led into the main house. Like his colleague the cop looked relaxed, settled for the night. Through the glazed doors he saw the old lady enter the kitchen with his target. He bit his lip and told himself to be patient.

He stood in the shadows until shortly before eleven, when the folding doors opened and the old lady gave the policeman a cup of coffee, before returning inside and disappearing from the kitchen. A few minutes later a light went on upstairs and he saw both women clearly in the window as they drew the curtains.

A radio crackled and the cop put down his coffee. 'Everything's fine here. They've just gone up to bed. How about you?' A laugh. 'You better not fall asleep. Yeah, I'll check you out in an hour.' The cop replaced his radio, stood up and did a cursory scan around the garden. Then he walked past the summerhouse, towards the gate and the darkest part. After another quick look round, the policeman turned his back, unzipped his fly, closed his eyes and began pissing loudly against a tree.

The right moment had presented itself.

Pulling a syringe from his bag, the watcher slipped the latch and pushed open the gate.

*   *   *

Unlike the terrifying death echoes Jane Doe had experienced at today's crime scenes, the archaeosonics in Fox's old room were reassuringly benign. She wasn't sure if it was Fox's innocent childhood souvenirs on the walls or Samantha's maternal presence, which pervaded the entire house, but she felt secure and calm. As she prepared for bed she looked around the walls, breathed in the smell of beeswax polish and freshly laundered sheets, and imagined the young Nathan Fox sleeping here, cocooned by the love of his aunt and uncle. When she rediscovered her own family she hoped she had an aunt, or even a mother, like Samantha.

Earlier, Samantha had served simple but delicious pasta and salad, which they had eaten in the kitchen with a bottle of Italian red wine. As they talked Jane Doe had felt her anxieties fall away. It had been wonderful not talking about herself. Although they had briefly discussed last night's intrusion and the murders, they had talked mainly about Samantha's late husband and Fox, who she clearly loved with a savage pride.

There was a knock at the door. 'You need anything?' Samantha asked.

'No. You've been very generous. Thanks for letting me stay. It's just for one night, I promise.'

Samantha ruffled her hair. 'Don't worry. It's nice to have the company. I'm just going to lock up downstairs then I'm off to bed. Sleep well.' The door closed and as she lay on the bed she heard Samantha's receding footsteps. Resting her head on the pillow she instantly felt herself falling asleep.

Crash.

She jolted awake, unaware how much time had passed. The noise had been close. Disoriented, she wondered if it had been real or in her dreams. Then a high-pitched alarm sounded, causing an array of psychedelic colours to spike before her eyes. She sat up, suddenly alert, a cold feeling in her stomach. Within moments she became aware of distant police sirens and the cop downstairs banging on the front door, shouting: 'Open the door. Get out of there. He's inside. He's in there.' She sprang from the bed and ran to the bedroom door. It was solid wood and there was a strong lock but she no longer cared about her own safety. All she could think about was Samantha. By coming here she had put Fox's aunt at risk and would never be able to forgive herself if anything happened to her. She opened the door.

Moments earlier

Dispatching the cop took seconds. The man was still pissing, his flow uninterrupted, as he collapsed to the ground. The intruder replaced the empty syringe in his bag, then, using his sleeved arm, pushed the handle on the folding doors. They weren't locked and opened easily. Exhilarated, he stole silently into the house and walked up the main stairs without encountering anyone. When he reached the landing he heard a door opening ahead and a soft voice: '. . . company. I'm just going to lock up downstairs then I'm off to bed. Sleep well.' It was the old lady.

He stepped into a dark doorway to his right. The light from the landing revealed a study crammed with history books and display cases. He heard the old lady approaching and backed further into the gloom. Her footsteps came closer until she passed the open door. As he watched her walk out of sight he sensed something solid behind him. Reaching down, he realized it was a desk. As his knuckles brushed the surface, the back of his hand touched a large, flat stone.

His reaction was instant and involuntary. He jumped, as if electrocuted, pushed the stone away from him and sent it crashing to the floor. Scrabbling to regain his equilibrium, he heard the footsteps return and saw the old lady reappear in the doorway. She looked small and frail. Dazed, he pulled out his knife but she made no attempt to run away or turn on the light. Instead she reached for something unseen on the landing wall.

'You shouldn't be in there,' she said, firmly. 'That's my husband's office. I think it's best you leave now.' Her tone added to his confusion. She sounded angry more than frightened and remarkably calm—much calmer than he felt. She stepped away from the door and gestured to the stairs. 'I'm pushing the panic button now. I suggest you go before the police come.'

He heard her backing away, towards the end of the landing, as the alarm sounded. Its piercing wail intensified his disorientation. Still reeling from the earlier shock, his head began to ache. He needed time to concentrate. He had to think. He couldn't make another mistake.

'Samantha!' The unseen cry cut through the fog and restored his focus. *She* was here. He was so close he could taste it on his tongue. He would end this now.

*   *   *

Jane Doe's first reaction when she opened the bedroom door and saw Fox's aunt backing down the landing towards her was relief. She was unharmed.

'Samantha!'

'Go back to your bedroom, Jane,' said Samantha, darting an anxious look over her shoulder. 'Our guest's just leaving.' She pointed to a dark doorway

155

on her left and Jane realized the intruder was in there. *He* was in there.

Instinct took over and Jane leapt at Samantha. Grabbing her arm she dragged her down the landing and bundled her into the bedroom. As she slammed the door shut behind them, she fleetingly saw the intruder—the man she had glimpsed in the crime scene death echoes—rush out of the study and storm down the landing towards her. Heart pounding and hands shaking, she turned the key in the lock, seconds before he threw himself against the door. The wood was solid but the juddering impact was so strong she feared it wouldn't hold. Without speaking, she and Samantha reached for a heavy chest of drawers by the window. As they pushed it against the door he threw himself at it again.

'What do you want with her?' Samantha shouted as the wood bowed and creaked. Jane Doe thought she heard him say something but two gunshots from downstairs drowned it out as the policeman tried to shoot open the lock to the front door. 'The officer will be through the front door soon and he's armed. Go. Leave us alone.'

Jane Doe pushed open the window but it was too high to offer any escape. A juddering impact smashed the door, splitting one of the panels, pushing back the chest of drawers. Frantically she searched for a weapon. Fox's old tennis racket was too light. The baseball bat was better. Wielding it like an axe, she found it felt strangely familiar in her hands.

The scream of fast-approaching sirens rose above the din. 'Listen! More police are coming,' said Samantha. 'They'll be here any minute.' Jane

Doe heard panting on the other side of the door. As she gripped the baseball bat and braced herself for another impact there was a rending crash downstairs. The intruder swore under his breath then ran, his heavy footsteps clattering along the landing and down the stairs. Jane Doe embraced Samantha and they held each other close as more shouts and gunshots rang out. Then it went quiet, including the alarm and sirens, and all she could hear was the beating of her own heart.

CHAPTER TWENTY-SIX

The next morning, when Fox entered the homicide incident room of the Central Precinct headquarters, he had calmed down enough to greet Jordache and his team with a brisk nod. He sat at the narrow conference table with two of Jordache's detectives: Phil Kostakis, who Fox had worked with before, and Dennis Allen, a wiry guy with a receding chin and wispy goatee. Jordache eyed him warily and handed him a cup of coffee as a peace offering. There was a pile of dog-eared manila folders on the table beside them, each filled with papers.

'Sorry, Nathan. We screwed up.'

Fox nodded and took the coffee. 'We both screwed up, Karl. At least no one was badly hurt. What are you doing to catch the bastard?'

Last night he had been less civil and understanding. After rushing round to Samantha's house, he had yelled at the police chief for allowing the killer to get so close to his aunt and his patient. Jordache had admitted his people had made mistakes and had since doubled the protection detail, but once his rage had cooled Fox acknowledged that much of the blame was his own: he must have led the killer to Samantha's house. Although neither woman had been harmed, Fox now felt a personal stake in catching the killer.

Jordache was no less motivated. Not only had the killer drugged one of his officers, he had humiliated Portland's Finest. Last night's attack on Jane Doe hadn't been foiled by his men but by Fox's aunt, a little old lady. Unfortunately, Samantha hadn't been able to see the killer's face and no usable fingerprints had been found in the house, but Jordache's team had been busy. They had checked out what Fox had told them after visiting the crime scenes with Jane Doe yesterday and a pattern was emerging.

A frantic search through old case files had confirmed that prior homicides with identical MOs had indeed been committed at each of the three crime scenes. Each of these prior victims, however, had been female and all had been raped before being murdered. The most recent was eleven years ago, the oldest almost a quarter of a century ago. The female victims had each been dressed and killed in exactly the same manner as their later male counterparts. All these prior homicides were so-called 'cold cases': unsolved old crimes.

Jordache didn't sit at the table. Instead he paced the room like a lion in a cage. 'How the hell did Jane Doe know about the prior crimes?'

'She didn't know,' Fox said, careful to protect Jane Doe's secret. 'It was a hunch.'

'Some hunch,' said Kostakis, rising from his chair. He picked up one of the manila folders from the table and walked over to a large whiteboard on the main wall of the homicide incident room. The board had been divided into three sections, one for each crime scene. The sections were subdivided into a grid of five columns: 'victim', 'suspect/perp', 'location', 'MO', 'time/date'; and two rows: 'current case', 'prior case'. Kostakis pointed to the first section on the board. 'The prior homicide in the first cold case file was at the exact same location as Vince Vega's murder, in the stairwell of the abandoned apartment block.' He opened the manila folder. 'When I studied the file I discovered something interesting.' Kostakis took a photo of a woman from the folder and attached it to the 'victim' column. 'The victim was a hooker called Nancy Luce. There wasn't enough solid evidence to convict but guess who the main suspect was?'

'Vince Vega,' Fox said, as Kostakis took another photo out of the folder and placed Vega's mugshot in the suspect column.

'It gets more interesting when you check out the list of suspects for the two other crime scenes,' said Jordache. 'In each case the victim of the later homicide was a suspect for the earlier one.' Jordache stopped his pacing and slapped his palm against the whiteboard. 'The pattern's pretty clear.'

'It seems we've got a vigilante on some kind of divine mission,' Kostakis said, holding up a photo of one of the marker pen messages. 'He sees himself as an avenging angel meting out justice to the demons in the world.'

'But why now?' said Allen, stroking his goatee. 'These are old crimes. And why the connection to Jane Doe?'

'Perhaps she's his inspiration—and the trigger,'

159

said Fox. 'He reads her story plastered all over the press, sees her as this avenging angel stepping into hell to save those girls from the Russian traffickers and becomes obsessed with her. He *thinks* he knows her and wants to match her deeds so he targets the suspects of similar unsolved crimes: rape-homicides.'

'That would explain why he drugged the cop last night but didn't kill him,' said Kostakis, nodding.

'The killer doesn't actually know Jane Doe?' Jordache said. 'He knows her image in the press but not *her*?'

'It looks that way,' said Fox.

'What did he want with her last night and the night before?' said Kostakis.

'I'm not sure,' said Fox. 'But we have to assume he's dangerous. Obsession can flip from love to hate in an instant for no rational reason.'

Jordache frowned. 'If his kills are virtual duplicates of the earlier crimes, how did he find out about the prior murders? How did he know the details of the victims, the MO of the crimes and the prime suspects?'

Allen tapped the pile of manila folders on the table. 'He's got to have access to files like these.'

'A lot of this stuff's available on the web if you know where to look,' said Kostakis, 'but it's more likely he had some inside knowledge. Which probably means he is or was involved in law enforcement or journalism. In the past he may even have known one or all of the earlier victims, and had dealings with Vince Vega or Kovacs or Paz. We could start with journalists and PIs who fit the physical description we got.'

'We've got to be careful with this, Phil,' said

160

Jordache. 'If we're right, then we've got to include serving police officers and ex-cops as suspects, especially those in homicide and vice.' He turned to Fox. 'What do you think, Nathan? You think this stacks up? You think the profile makes sense?'

Fox nodded cautiously. Given the little they knew, it made as much sense as anything else. 'There probably is no real connection between the killer and Jane Doe. And since the suspect had to have access to details of the past murders, it's a good idea to focus on journalists and law enforcement professionals. I'd also include administrative staff and third parties involved in processing crime pictures and managing files. It might be worth spotlighting men with a past grievance or trauma which could have fuelled a need for violent justice and revenge.'

Fox's phone rang and he grabbed it from his pocket, concerned it might be from Samantha or Jane Doe. 'Excuse me, Karl, I'd better get this.' He picked up. 'Fox.'

'Dr Fox, it's Professor Fullelove. You need to come back immediately.' She sounded unusually breathless and excited.

'Why? What's happened, Professor?'

When she told him, he sat back in his chair and let the news sink in for a moment. 'I'll be right over.' He put the phone back in his pocket and stood up. 'Sorry, Karl, but I've got to go.'

'What's up?' said Jordache. 'Is there a problem?'

'Not a problem.'

'What then?'

'We've got a walk-in at the clinic asking about Jane Doe. He says he knows her. Says he knows who Jane Doe is.'

CHAPTER TWENTY-SEVEN

When Fox got back to the clinic he saw two police cars from the increased security detail parked in the driveway. After last night's incident Jane Doe had felt so guilty about endangering Samantha she had insisted on returning to Tranquil Waters. Fox drove to the staff car park and entered the clinic by the side entrance. He found Professor Fullelove hovering by his office. He had never seen her look so flustered.

'He's in reception,' she said without any preamble. 'He wants no media coverage and won't give his name or say anything until he talks to Jane's doctor and the person in charge here. We can interview him in one of the conference rooms. I suggest we only inform her once we've checked him out.'

'Fine. I'll get her updated medical file.' He had already briefed Fullelove on Jane Doe's total synaesthesia, explaining that it—rather than psychosis—was responsible for her hallucinations. He had, however, omitted any mention of her death-echo synaesthesia. Jane had insisted that that was kept strictly off the record.

'Does her file contain any identifying features not released to the media?'

He reached for the folder in the cabinet by his desk. 'Yep. She has a birthmark on her left scapula.'

'Good. Let's go.'

He felt a surge of excitement that the mystery of Jane's identity was about to be solved. He had so many questions to ask about her background, especially how it might explain her unique synaesthesia. As they approached reception he noticed Professor Fullelove smooth her skirt, adjust her hair and slow her usual brisk walk to a hip-swaying stroll. A young nurse walked past and did exactly the same. Both performed these unconscious subtle gestures immediately they spied the stranger standing by the reception desk. Fox saw others whispering and throwing glances at the visitor. The object of their attention radiated a still calm, apparently oblivious to the excitement rippling around him.

Sexual charisma, from the Greek *kharisma*, meaning 'gift from god', is an elusive and indefinable thing. One of Nathan Fox's colleagues at Stanford had once attempted the impossible task of defining it for his PhD thesis. He had interviewed scores of high-profile movie stars, politicians and successful businesspeople but discovered that although all had seemed attractive, magnetic and charming, less than a handful had possessed genuine charisma in person. The rest were so disappointing he had abandoned his PhD. 'Essentially, charisma's as rare as genius,' he'd concluded. 'You've either got it or you ain't. And if you've gotta ask, then you ain't got it.'

Although he was probably in his fifties and his face was too craggy to be conventionally handsome, the visitor clearly had whatever that elusive quality was. Dressed in black trousers, white collarless shirt and a long blue linen jacket, the man was about six feet tall, a few inches shorter than Fox, and lean, with a light tan, piercing blue-green eyes and striking cheekbones. His shoulder-

163

length silver-grey hair was as thick and sleek as an animal's pelt. As he directed his smile at Fullelove and shook her hand the redoubtable professor almost blushed. When he extended his hand and turned those piercing eyes on him, even Fox felt his power. 'A pleasure to meet you, Dr Fox.' He spoke quietly with the deep timbre of someone who is accustomed to being heard—and obeyed—without raising his voice.

'Our primary concern is Jane Doe's welfare,' Professor Fullelove said after they had settled in the conference room. 'She has no memory of anything or anybody and we need to determine you're genuine.'

'I understand,' the man said softly.

'What's your name?' Fox asked.

'Regan Delaney.'

'You have any identification?'

Fox saw the muscles clench in the man's jaw. He was clearly unaccustomed to having his word questioned. 'It's complicated. I've lived off the grid for some years and I doubt any government agency has any recent record of me.' He smiled so disarmingly that Fox found himself smiling with him. 'My birth family were horse breeders in northern California but that was many years ago, before I founded our settlement here in Oregon. My people live in the wilderness, away from the corruptions of the cities. We make no apology for avoiding the intrusions of the modern world— or the attentions of the government. We're self-sufficient, keep ourselves to ourselves and cause no harm to others. All we ask is that the rest of the world shows us the same consideration.'

'What sort of settlement is it?' asked Fullelove.

The man reached for an amulet hanging from his neck by a silver cord. It appeared to have been fashioned from a single piece of stone in the shape of an ankh: an ancient cross topped with an oval loop instead of a vertical bar. The loop was filled with a large amethyst. 'We are a religious community.'

Fox found himself staring at the amulet, remembering a muscled forearm and the tattoo of a cobra coiled around a similar strange-shaped cross. His collar felt suddenly tight and he was aware of beads of sweat forming on his forehead. 'You're a cult?' he said.

Delaney smiled. 'That's such an emotive term, Dr Fox. You know what they say: if you believe in it, it's a religion; if you don't, it's a sect; and if you fear or hate it, it's a cult. We prefer to see ourselves as a family.'

That didn't reassure Fox. Charles Manson had called his cult the Family and that hadn't ended well. He thought of his parents and sister and the two cult members who had killed them, and of the patients he had treated because of their damaging involvement with cults, and he immediately disliked and distrusted Regan Delaney. He tried, however, to remain objective. Her being a cult member helped explain the enigma of Jane Doe: why she appeared on no database and why, despite the media coverage, it had taken so long for her people to find her.

'Can you please tell us some more about your religious community?' said Fullelove. 'To help understand and protect our patient we need to discover as much as we can about her background, especially if you intend to return her to a cult.

165

What's the name of your community?'

'If you think it's important, we call ourselves the Indigo Family.'

'What are your beliefs?' asked Fullelove.

A shrug. 'It's difficult to explain personal beliefs without exposing them to ridicule. Suffice to say we're concerned with seeing beyond the material constraints of the human world, with harnessing and harmonizing our physical and psychic senses to glimpse the spiritual realm. We seek to be at one with the universe by going beyond the human to experience the divine.'

Fox listened but made no comment. Delaney's mystic nonsense fitted the formula for most New Age cults: cherry-pick the appealing aspects of Eastern religion, apply some Western concepts, add a dash of magic, then stir. His scepticism was tempered by his knowledge of Jane Doe's death-echo synaesthesia. 'How did you find out Jane Doe was here?'

Delaney placed both hands on the table and clasped them in front of him. 'I venture into what you call civilization from time to time. I saw the news reports.'

'Can you prove you know her?' said Professor Fullelove. 'Are you aware of any identifying features?'

A nod. 'She has a birthmark on her back, on her left shoulder blade.'

Fullelove reached for Jane Doe's medical file but Fox already knew the answer. 'She does have a mark on her left scapula,' Fox said. 'Anything else you can tell us about her?'

'She has the *mothú*.'

'The what?' said Fullelove.

'The *mothú*. The sense. The third eye.'

'I'm still not following you,' Fullelove said.

'You probably prefer to call it synaesthesia.'

'Are you aware she has *total* synaesthesia, Mr Delaney?' said Fox. 'This is incredibly rare, probably unique.'

'The *mothú* in all its forms is an uncommon and misunderstood gift,' Delaney said matter-of-factly. He stared at Fox. 'But then you must know that, Dr Fox. I see you have it, too.'

Fullelove's eyes widened. 'How do you know that?'

'He has an indigo aura. It's obvious. To me, at least.'

It was Fox's turn to scrutinize the visitor. He burned to ask him about Jane Doe's death-echo synaesthesia. 'Anything you can tell us about my patient's unique synaesthesia could prove beneficial . . .'

'Beneficial to who, Dr Fox?' countered Delaney with a half-smile. 'To her? Or to you and your research?'

Fox frowned but kept his voice even. 'To her, of course. Particularly in understanding her hallucinations.'

For the first time Delaney paused. 'Hallucinations?'

'Yes. Dr Fox is helping her gain some detachment and manage her fear,' said Fullelove.

'We'll help her back at the settlement,' said Delaney. 'My people can clear her chakras and—'

'Her chakras?' interrupted Fox. 'Jane Doe needs *proper* treatment.'

Delaney laughed. 'Psychiatry is no more proper or effective than the ancient medicine we use.

167

Chakras have been around for thousands of years. Psychiatry is in its infancy. You psychiatrists can't even fully explain how most of your new miracle drugs work.'

'You can't compare—'

'Is she physically recovered?'

'Yes,' said Fox.

'Is she mentally sound, apart from her memory loss?'

'I believe so, but—'

'Can you cure her amnesia, Dr Fox?'

'Not directly, no, but we can help treat it. If you tell us why you think she went missing we might uncover the stresses that triggered her fugue state. Something apparently frightened her. Do you know what it might have been? Do you know why she might have been trying to escape the cult?'

Delaney shook his head. 'She wasn't escaping anything. She's no longer a child and, like all my people, she's free to come and go as she pleases.' He sat back in his chair and crossed his arms. 'I'm the reason she left.'

'Why?'

'She'd say I neglected her, didn't pay her the attention she thought she deserved. So she ran away, hoping I'd come after her.' He sighed. 'So here I am. It's hard to be a good parent, sometimes, especially when *everyone* regards you as their father.'

'You regard yourself as her parent because you're the father of the cult?' said Fullelove. 'The father of the Indigo Family?'

'Yes. But I'm also her blood father. She's my daughter.'

Fox scoured his face for a likeness. The greying

Delaney had once been dark but Jane Doe was fair. 'Would you be prepared to take a DNA test?' he asked.

'Is that necessary, Professor?' the visitor asked, turning the full beam of his charm on Fullelove. She blinked and then turned to Fox. From her doe-eyed expression it was obvious she didn't doubt the man's sincerity. Fox felt differently.

'Professor, my patient's making good progress but she's still very vulnerable,' said Fox. 'Without documentation I feel a paternity test is crucial.' He turned back to Delaney. 'Even if the test is positive she still has to agree to see you. She has full-blown retrograde amnesia with no recollection of her past life so it's extremely unlikely she'll know who you are.'

Delaney's jaw clenched again, but the smile didn't waver. 'Give me any test you think necessary. Just let me see my daughter.'

CHAPTER TWENTY-EIGHT

After taking a saliva swab from Delaney's mouth, Fox escorted the visitor back to reception. On the way, he made a detour past the room in which Jane Doe had sensed the two suicides on the first day. It was still unoccupied so he opened the door and led Delaney inside. 'This is the kind of room Jane Doe's in now.'

'I don't doubt the standard of care here, Dr Fox. I just want to see my daughter.' As Delaney stepped through the doorway and looked round the room, Fox watched him closely. Delaney peered into

169

the adjoining private bathroom and, as his hands brushed the walls, Fox thought he saw Delaney momentarily narrow his eyes. Then the moment passed. If the man possessed the same death-echo synaesthesia as the woman he claimed as his daughter, then it didn't affect him in the same way. He certainly didn't seem frightened of it. Fox waited a moment longer then escorted him back to reception.

After taking Delaney's cell phone number and arranging to call when the results of the paternity test came through in a few hours, Fox returned to his office. As he sat at his desk he tried to forget about Jane Doe and concentrate on the other case files piled up in front of him. Assuming the results came back positive, he would alert Jane Doe that her father had arrived and, depending on what she decided to do, she could soon be out of his life. No longer his patient. No longer his concern.

Simple.

Except it wasn't simple. Jane Doe was unlike any other patient he had ever treated; he couldn't just let her go. He still had too many unanswered questions. Not just about her symptoms and death-echo synaesthesia but also about Delaney, his cult and the details of what had caused Jane Doe to run away.

Sitting at his computer, Fox Googled one of the terms Delaney had used to describe synaesthesia: *mothú*. He discovered that it was an Irish Celtic noun meaning 'sense'. What else had he called it? *The third eye*. Fox had heard the expression before, through his karate sensei, and understood vaguely that it was an Eastern term for second sight or the sixth sense. The definition he found on the web was fuller:

The third eye (also known as the inner eye) is a mystical and esoteric concept referring in part to the ajna (brow) chakra in certain Eastern and Western spiritual traditions. It is also spoken of as the gate that leads within to inner realms and spaces of higher consciousness. In New Age spirituality, the third eye may symbolize a state of enlightenment and is often associated with visions, clairvoyance, precognition and out-of-body experiences. People who have allegedly developed the capacity to use their third eye are sometimes known as Seers.

The mention of chakras made Fox cast his mind back to his years as a curious medical student. According to traditional Indian medicine, chakras were centres of physical and psychic energy found in the body and its spiritual counterpart, the 'astral body'. Chakras acted as circular portals through which the universal life force could enter and exit. This chimed with his aunt's theory that death echoes were caused by an explosive exodus of energy at life's end.

Chakras had been around for thousands of years but like other ancient belief systems had no scientific evidence to support their existence or therapeutic value. New Age practitioners claimed that they worked by interacting with the body's ductless endocrine glands and lymphatic system, feeding in positive bio energies and disposing of negative ones. They stressed that the location of the seven major chakras along the spinal cord coincided, approximately, with the various organs

171

of the endocrine system as well as the main ganglia of the central nervous system.

Symbolized by individual crystals and stylized lotus flowers, each chakra corresponded with one of the seven colours of the visible light spectrum of the rainbow. Chakras governed specific mental, physical, emotional and spiritual qualities and their spiritual importance increased the higher up the spinal column they were located. The lowest, located between the genitals and the anus, was red, symbolized by a lotus flower with four petals and associated with physical sexuality, emotional security and spiritual survival. The highest, located on the crown of the head, was violet, symbolized by a lotus flower with a thousand petals and associated with pure consciousness, inner wisdom and the death of the physical body. The theory was that harmonizing and clearing the chakras led to total physical, emotional, mental and spiritual health. Fox noted that the sixth chakra, the so-called third eye located between the eyebrows, was indigo in colour and guessed this was how Delaney's cult had got its name. He Googled 'Indigo Family' but found nothing.

Fox now turned his attention to Delaney. Remembering that his birth family were horse breeders in northern California, Fox entered 'Delaney horse breeders northern California' into the search engine and got an immediate hit: the Delaney Stud Farm near Sacramento. He clicked on the website and discovered that the Delaney family came from generations of horse breeders who had emigrated from Ireland in the early 1900s and founded a business in California, breeding and trading thoroughbreds. Fox rang the number on the contact page and a woman answered. 'Delaney Stud Farm. How can I help you?'

'I'm calling to see if you know of a Regan Delaney?'

There was a pause, then a clearing of the throat. 'Regan Delaney is no longer associated with the family business and hasn't been for many years. The Delaney Stud can take no responsibility for any issues you might have with him.' Fox explained that he had no issues with Regan Delaney but was a psychiatrist who needed some background information on him in order to help a patient. There was another pause. 'His brother is away on business, Dr Fox. Give me your contact number and I'll get him to call you.'

The reaction to Regan Delaney's name disconcerted and intrigued Fox enough to make him search the web for more information on the family. After almost an hour he had discovered that the son of the founder of the American business had died fifteen years ago, leading to a very public legal schism. Fox could find few details of the schism except that one of the two main beneficiaries of the will had stripped his share of the inheritance out of the business. Lawsuits followed, involving charges and counter-charges of insanity and bringing the family business into disrepute. What happened to the heir who took out his assets wasn't recorded but the original business almost went bankrupt. Only now was it back on an even footing.

Guiltily, Fox realized that his desire to delve into Jane Doe's background had as much to do with his own need to find out about Delaney and his cult as it did with concern for her welfare. What's

173

more, his little fishing expedition had raised more questions than it had answered. As Fox pondered this and determined to put his patient's happiness and wellbeing before his own prejudice, there was a knock on the door.

CHAPTER TWENTY-NINE

Jane Doe couldn't believe the news when Fox told her about her father. When the psychiatrist had said there was something he needed to tell her, she'd guessed it might be about last night or Samantha or a new development with the killer. Never in her wildest dreams did she think it would be this.

'Are you sure?'

'Positive. The DNA test was conclusive. You have a clear genetic link.'

Jane Doe had assumed that being found again—by her own father, no less—would make her feel ecstatic. At last she could rediscover her identity and once again be the person she was supposed to be. Strangely, however, her immediate reaction when Fox told her the news was panic. As desperate as she was to be reunited with her father, he now represented the unknown. In the last few days Fox had become more familiar to her than any forgotten family. 'What's his name?'

'Regan Delaney.'

She repeated the name slowly to herself, tasting every syllable. It worried her that his name tasted bitter on her tongue. 'What's he like?'

'Meet him and decide for yourself.'

'But what if I don't recognize him? What if I

174

don't remember him?'

'You probably *won't* recognize him. You don't yet recognize yourself.'

'What if I don't like him?'

'Then you don't like him. There's no law that says daughters have to like their fathers.' He smiled. 'You're not a minor. He can't make you do anything you don't want to. Meet him, see what you think and how you feel, then decide what you want to do.' Fox held out his hand to her, as he had on the day they first met. 'Come, let me take you to him.'

She met him in the conference room. He was alone and Jane Doe's first impression when Regan Delaney stood to greet her was how striking he looked. Surely she should remember a father as impressive as this—and yet he was a total stranger. He stepped forward and took her shaking hands in his. 'Sorcha, you were lost but now are found.'

'Sorcha,' she repeated slowly. She pronounced it as he did—*Sorraca*—and the taste of strawberries exploded on her tongue. She had liked the taste of 'Jane' but this was better, much better. 'Is Sorcha my name?'

A nod. 'It's Irish. It means radiant light.' He moved closer to embrace her and she became hyper-aware of his every detail: his smell; his voice; the lines on his face; the way his eyes creased when he smiled. She realized she was searching desperately for anything about him that she remembered. How could this striking man, her own father, be such a stranger to her? Then she remembered the night of the fire, when she had first spied her reflection in a mirror and not recognized her own face. Delaney turned to Fox.

175

'Could you leave us for a moment?'

Fox glanced at her and she nodded. 'I'll be in my office if you need me.'

'Please sit, Sorcha,' Delaney said, after Fox had left. 'What can I tell you? What do you want to know?'

She sat facing him, mesmerized by his eyes, which seemed to draw her in and make the rest of the world fade out of focus. 'Tell me everything,' she said, as questions tumbled out of her mouth. 'Where do I come from? How old am I? What's my family like? Do I have any brothers or sisters? Where's my mother?'

He smiled and raised his hands. 'Slow down. There's no rush.' For the next half-hour, Delaney explained about the Indigo Family, their home—a private Eden deep in the Oregon wilderness—and how its members strived to explore all their senses in order to reach beyond the physical and become one with the spiritual and universal. He spoke with such passion about the beauty of the land and of the family's beliefs that she found herself falling under his spell. Whenever she asked detailed questions, however, he would tell her to wait until she returned to the bosom of the family, 'when everything will be answered'. The more he talked about exploring the limits of the senses, the more her own synaesthesia made sense. 'Where do I get it from?'

'From both your mother and me,' he said. 'She's passed to the other realm now but your mother first showed me the path and introduced me to the Indigo Family.'

'What was she like?'

'Beautiful, like you. She too was fair. You're

176

a younger version of her.' He reached for the locket round Sorcha's neck. Her right hand sprang up defensively but he gently pushed it away and opened the locket. 'This was hers. Your mother wore it always. Until she passed.' He showed Sorcha the photograph inside. 'This is you as a baby. She loved you very much.'

Sorcha took the silver heart from him and looked again at the picture—at the stranger she had once been—and thought of the mother who had loved her. If the locket had been important to her before, it was now precious beyond words. 'Why did I leave the Indigo Family?'

'I don't know. You were always headstrong. I think I neglected you and you ran away to teach me a lesson.' His voice became serious. 'I read in the newspapers about what you did for those girls. Tell me what else has happened to you. Dr Fox says you've been having hallucinations.'

Delaney had Fox's gift for listening and she found herself telling him everything: her amnesia, her hallucinations and the killer who had stapled her newspaper photograph to three murder victims, tried to abduct her from her room and attacked her last night. As he listened, the expression on his face changed—sympathetic when she spoke of her amnesia and hallucinations, angry when she told him about the killer—but he never interrupted.

Finally, for no other reason than it seemed natural to, she told him about her death-echo synaesthesia. As she spoke, she studied his face but he betrayed neither surprise nor scepticism. He just nodded understandingly. He seemed to know her better than she knew herself and she realized, suddenly, that he probably did. 'Who else knows about this?' he asked.

'Dr Fox, but he's promised to keep it off the record. I don't want to be treated as a freak.'

'Do you trust Dr Fox to keep his counsel?'

'Completely.'

He smiled and patted her on the shoulder. 'Don't be frightened of this. Embrace it. The *mothú* in all its shapes and forms has been around for centuries, nurtured as a gift that makes us special, chosen. All those with the *mothú* possess the third eye, and have the potential to see beyond the normal realm. And your *mothú* is unusually strong. When you return home all will become clearer. You won't feel an outsider among the Indigo Family because most have some form of the *mothú*. There your gift will be understood, cherished and nurtured. Only we can fully appreciate you.' He paused and smiled at her. 'They're eagerly awaiting word of you and are expecting me to bring you back. We must return as soon as possible.'

The thought of leaving Tranquil Waters and Fox snapped her back to reality and sent a surge of panic coursing through her. 'But I need time. Dr Fox is treating me.'

He nodded slowly and smiled. 'I understand why you're nervous but there's nothing for you here. Dr Fox doesn't really care for you, Sorcha— not like your family. He's only interested in your condition. You're a puzzle to him. Nothing more. My understanding of retrograde amnesia is that your memory could come back at any time, with or without Dr Fox's treatment. There's little modern medicine can do to discover your lost identity, apart from reassuring you that you're safe and finding ways to stimulate your memory.' He took her hand

178

and squeezed it. 'Surely the best way of doing that is to return to the place you've lived in all your life and be reunited with your family? We can teach you more about your powers than any psychiatrist.' His face hardened. 'And now I know there's a dangerous killer who means you harm, you *must* come home.'

She still felt anxious about leaving with this stranger. 'But . . .'

Delaney put a finger over her lips. 'Don't worry. Everything will be all right.' He looked into her eyes and flashed a paternal smile, which stirred within her a deep sense of longing—and belonging. 'You're my daughter, Sorcha. You belong with me. You belong with your family.'

Staring at her father, she noticed his aura for the first time and realized it was subtly different to any she had seen before.

CHAPTER THIRTY

For a few hours Fox put Jane Doe—or Sorcha as he would have to learn to call her—out of his mind and concentrated on his other patients. Later, however, as he prepared to leave for the day, he found his thoughts returning to her; he wondered how her meeting with her father had gone and what she intended to do about his reappearance in her life. When he had expressed concern about his patient returning to a cult, Professor Fullelove had dismissed his fears, believing it was in Jane's best interests to be reunited with her father and return to whatever her old life was. There was no

179

medical reason to keep her at the clinic and after the recent abduction attempts it would be safer for her and everyone else at Tranquil Waters if she left. Fox told himself that whatever happened was out of his hands but the thought of his vulnerable patient leaving before he had fathomed her intriguing gifts frustrated him, and the idea of her returning to a cult alarmed him.

He went to look for her in her room. She wasn't there so he checked the television lounge, the indoor swimming pool area and the art therapy studio. Although she wasn't in any of these places, he was surprised by how many fellow residents knew her. 'Try the physical therapy room, Doctor. Jane likes her exercise.'

When he checked the gym and asked the orderly supervising the exercise machines, one of the residents checked her watch. 'Knowing Jane, she'll be on the running trail about now. She says it helps clear her mind.'

Knowing Jane. The phrase provoked a smile. The resident and the others he had encountered clearly had no problems with Jane Doe's identity. As he wandered outside, the lawns and the small lake were bathed in golden evening light.

'Dr Fox.' The familiar voice made him turn towards the setting sun. For a moment the low angle of the light blinded him. Then he blinked and saw Jane Doe running towards him with effortless graceful strides. Two officers were shadowing her from a discreet distance. Both were panting hard. Watching her, he registered the curve of Jane's neck, the shape of her profile and the way the sun caught her hair. As she got closer, her luminous green eyes drew his attention. When she slowed and fell into step beside him she was breathing harder than usual and her skin seemed to glow. Despite her exertion, she exuded a clean, fragrant scent of soap and musk. 'How's Samantha?'

'She's fine. How did it go with your father, Jane?'

She smiled. 'The name's Sorcha.'

'I'm sorry. I've only known you as Jane and it's hard to change.'

'It's OK. You can call me whatever you like.' She reached out and touched his arm. The fleeting contact was like an electric shock, raising the hairs on his arms, inflaming his skin. In that instant, senses ambushed and defences breached, he saw her for the first time not as a patient but as a woman in her physical prime. 'Can I talk to you about my dad?'

He took a breath and composed himself. 'Of course you can.' He led her down to the lake as the two cops watched from a distance. 'So what did you think of him?'

'It's bizarre but he seems to know everything about me, all my hopes and fears. He always says just the right thing to reassure or inspire me. I like him.'

'He's pretty charismatic. Did he talk about the cult?'

She nodded. 'He made it sound kind of cool and the whole Indigo Family thing made me feel better about my synaesthesia. Apparently many of the cult members have some form of it. The *mothú* is kind of their thing.' Fox listened carefully. Despite his distrust of Delaney's cult he would have loved to interview its members. They would make a fascinating research group for better understanding synaesthesia in all its various forms. Sorcha paused.

181

'I told him about my death-echo synaesthesia.'

'Really?' At the lake's edge she sat on a small bench and he sat beside her. 'Why?'

'I don't know really. Something about him, the way he listened, made me want to tell him everything.'

'What did he say?'

'He told me not to be afraid of my gift and that the family would help me appreciate and develop it.' She frowned and gazed out at the still water. 'You think I should go back with him?'

'What I think is unimportant. This is about what *you* want. Anyway, you haven't got to decide now.'

'I do. He wants to take me back tomorrow.'

Fox felt a sudden stab of panic. 'Tomorrow?'

'He says my family's waiting.' She sighed. 'It's all a bit sudden and I'm not sure I'm ready to go yet. That's what I wanted to talk to you about.'

'Can't you ask your father to wait a few days?'

'I did, but he was pretty adamant. He's convinced you've done all you can for me and sees no reason for me to stay here any longer than I have to. Especially now he knows there's a killer in the city obsessed with me. He thinks I'll be safer with his people and the sooner I leave Portland the better.'

'So what are you going to do, Jane—I mean, Sorcha?'

'I'm not going to let some sick killer decide for me, that's for sure. His fixation with me has got nothing to do with how I spend the rest of my life.' She sighed. 'It should be simple. I assumed I'd want to go home and find out more about myself—or the person I once was—but suddenly I don't see it as a return home. Portland seems more like home to me now. I know you better than I know my family, and

I trust you.' She turned and looked into his eyes. 'What do *you* think I should do? What do you want me to do, Nathan?'

'I want what's best for you.'

'What's that? It's not like my father lives across town so I can drop by, check out my old home and come away if I feel like it. Once I return to my wilderness family I doubt I'll be able to come back to the city any time soon. Tell me what to do. You know me better than I know myself. I'll do whatever you say.' She looked into his eyes with the same need and hunger she had displayed the first time they'd met. Back then he would happily have told her to go. But now he realized he didn't want her to leave. Not because she was an intriguing mystery or because he didn't want her to return to her father's cult but because, for the first time, for whatever reason, he had met someone he wanted to keep in his life. 'What should I do, Nathan? Do I stay or do I go?'

It was an impossible question for Fox to answer. Personally, he wanted to tell her to stay and go nowhere near her father's cult. Professionally, he knew he couldn't allow his personal prejudices and feelings to compromise her future. Whatever emotions she stirred in him, she was still his patient. Nothing more. Nothing less.

*   *   *

Sitting next to the psychiatrist, watching the sunset, Sorcha was no less torn. She envied Fox the memories and relationships that enriched his life: his professional career; the affection he and his aunt shared for each other; the karate trophies;

even the photographs of his murdered family. Good and bad, they all informed Fox of his identity and anchored his place in the world. If she returned home with Regan Delaney, her own memories and relationships could eventually be restored to her—along with a deeper understanding of her synaesthesia. Her father clearly *wanted* her. He had come for her and was committed to her return. By going back with him she would belong with someone again. She had assumed that rediscovering her past self was what she wanted more than anything in the entire world but it wasn't that simple any more. Her father was a stranger to her and although she desperately wanted to rediscover her place in the world, she couldn't escape the fact that she didn't want to leave. Specifically, she didn't want to leave Fox. 'Do I stay or do I go?'

Fox said nothing for a while. 'This isn't a medical decision . . . Sorcha. Clinically there's little reason for you to stay at Tranquil Waters much longer. Despite your amnesia your brain scans show no physiological abnormalities. You sleep without medication; you have no symptoms of clinical depression. Your eating's OK and you're physically fine. I'd be discharging you soon, anyway, because it's important you get on with your life in the real world. The real question is whether you want to return to your old life with your father and his cult, or start a new life with support here in Portland?'

'What do *you* think I should do, Nathan?' she pressed.

'It doesn't matter what I think. Only you can know whether you need to resolve your past before you decide your future. You wouldn't be human if you didn't want to find out where you came from

184

and who you were. In your position I'd probably want to learn as much as possible about the person I once was before I embarked on the rest of my life.'

'You want me to go back?'

'I don't *want* you to go back,' he said, gently. 'As your psychiatrist, I'd have liked more time to help you understand your synaesthesia but, aside from your amnesia, you're perfectly healthy. This isn't a medical choice. It's a life choice. One you've got to make yourself. It's *your* past and it's *your* future.'

As she looked down at the lake's still waters, the depth of her disappointment shocked her. She suddenly realized that, however much she wanted to go home, she would have stayed if he had asked her to. How foolish could she have been? Whatever she thought she felt for Fox, she realized that her father was right. Fox saw her primarily as a patient. The only reason he wanted her to stay was to investigate her unique synaesthesia. She might be an interesting case but she was kidding herself if she thought she could ever mean anything more to Nathan *'never let them get too close'* Fox. Like her father had said: she belonged with her own.

'You're right. I must decide. And I think I should go home.' She searched his face for a reaction but aside from a small nod he gave nothing away. 'I want to thank you, though, for everything. I wish I could do something to repay you and Samantha for all your help and kindness.' She paused. 'The offer to go to the Chevron garage and find out what happened still stands.'

Fox shook his head. 'Thanks. But no thanks.' He reached into his jacket. 'You can do one thing for me, though.' He retrieved a sleek black phone from his pocket. 'You can take this as a parting gift. It's got all my numbers programmed in. If you need me for any reason, whenever or wherever, just call me.'

'I can't take this.'

'Don't worry, it's not my work phone. I only bought it because I like gadgets and wanted a separate phone without any sensitive patient data on it. The truth is I hardly use it. Take it. Put it in your pocket. Seriously, call me whenever you want.'

'As my psychiatrist?'

He shook his head. 'I'll no longer be your psychiatrist. Just call me if you need me—or want to talk about anything.' He smiled and gestured to the watching police. 'It'll be dark soon and they're getting jumpy. We'd better go back.'

She rose from the bench and followed him towards the lights of the clinic. 'Yes. I suppose it is time to go back.'

CHAPTER THIRTY-ONE

Regan Delaney returned to Tranquil Waters the next morning. After a number of formalities, including an interview with the police, his daughter was released to him just before eleven o'clock. The clinic had assured Delaney that his privacy would be respected and the media would be told only that she had left the clinic and returned to her family.

As Sorcha Delaney said her goodbyes and thanked all those who had treated her, the sombre mood was reflected by a grey sky, dark with low cloud. Delaney, however, felt anything but sombre. When his daughter sat beside him in the red Toyota

Landcruiser and the door slammed shut behind her, he experienced a triumphant rush of excitement. He wouldn't admit to relief, however, because that would mean acknowledging the possibility of Sorcha deciding not to return with him. Men seldom rejected him. Women never.

He frowned when he watched her wave to Dr Fox. Although the psychiatrist had never let his professional manner slip, Delaney sensed both the man's distrust of him and the mutual attachment between Fox and Sorcha. Once Delaney drove his daughter into the wilderness their bond couldn't threaten his plans, but it still rankled. She had even insisted on taking time out to say goodbye to Fox's aunt. As he pulled away from the clinic, he watched Fox waving in the rear-view mirror and frowned at the memory of their last exchange. Though he had thanked and praised Fox effusively for helping his daughter, the psychiatrist had coolly held his gaze, impervious to his charm offensive. 'It was a pleasure,' he had replied. 'Just make sure *you* look after her now.'

Had the self-righteous quack been preaching to him? Or, worse, had he been threatening him?

Either possibility sparked a surge of anger within Delaney, which he quickly suppressed. Anger was unnecessary. He had his prize. He glanced at Sorcha, marvelling at how he—the Seer—had been blind to her value. He kept his eyes on her for as long as he could, expecting her to turn and meet his gaze, but she ignored him, focusing on the sleek black phone Fox had given her. The way she held it, as if it were some kind of talisman, pricked his pride. It symbolized her lack of total commitment to him.

'Are you happy, Sorcha?'

She nodded but still kept her eyes on the damned phone.

Softening his voice, he purged it of anger. 'Look at me. You're returning home to where you belong. To where you're valued.'

She turned to him and managed a small smile. 'I know.'

'You don't need these people. We'll help you explore your gift better than any psychiatrist. He doesn't really care for you. Not like your family does.' He gently took the phone from her and turned it off. Then he opened the window. 'Perhaps it's time to throw away these meaningless distractions.'

'No.' She reached out and grabbed it back. 'It's not meaningless. It's a gift.' She touched her locket. 'One of the few things in this world I know to be mine.'

'But it's useless. Where we're going cell phones don't work.'

'I don't care. He gave it to me.'

He tried one more time. 'To discover new lands, Sorcha, you must lose sight of the shore.'

She held the phone to her chest. 'I'm not trying to discover new lands, Father. I'm trying to reclaim old ones.'

Both lapsed into silence and as Delaney turned east towards Highway 84, neither he nor his daughter noticed the anonymous white four-wheel drive following three cars behind.

*　　　*　　　*

Neither Professor Fullelove nor Chief of Detectives

Jordache had expressed any qualms about releasing Fox's patient to her father and his cult. Not only was it Sorcha's legal decision to leave the clinic but Fullelove had been visibly relieved to surrender responsibility for her. After ruling Delaney out as a suspect—he didn't fit the description of the killer and had been out of town for the murders—Jordache had been similarly relaxed about Sorcha leaving with her father. From a police perspective the only practical reason for her to stay was to act as bait, but that was neither ethical nor practical given her father's insistence on leaving Portland with his daughter. Moving Sorcha out of harm's way freed up the officers on her security detail and gave him one less thing to worry about.

Fox, however, couldn't shake off the disquiet he had felt ever since Sorcha's father had arrived to claim her. He had no evidence against Delaney and his Indigo Family and knew his hatred of cults was born of what had happened to his family and his experience with a few patients. Nevertheless, as he watched the car drive away, he found it hard to maintain his precious detachment. Not only was he ambushed by loss, an emotion to which he had strived to become immune, but also he feared he had somehow failed to protect her. *I did the right thing*, he told himself. *She was my patient and I put her needs first.* Still, the knowledge that he could have kept her from leaving tormented him. When she had asked him if she should stay he could have convinced her to start a new life in Portland. But he hadn't.

He stifled the sudden urge to call the phone he had given her. What would he say? As he pondered this, his BlackBerry began ringing. Perhaps she had changed her mind? Perhaps she wanted to come back? He reached for the BlackBerry and checked the display but the call wasn't from his iPhone.

He picked up. 'Fox.'

'Dr Nathan Fox?'

'Yes.'

'My name's Connor Delaney. My secretary said you'd called. How can I help you?'

'Thanks for getting back to me, Mr Delaney.' The bird had flown: Regan Delaney's Toyota Landcruiser was long gone. Whatever Connor Delaney had to tell him now was academic. 'I was calling on behalf of a patient of mine, about your brother, but—'

'What's he done now?'

'Nothing. I was just hoping to find out a bit more about him, that's all, discover what sort of person he is. And to ask what you know about his cult.'

He heard a groan, then a humourless laugh. 'Regan and his goddamn Indigo Family. Short answer is, don't let your patient anywhere near him or his cult.'

'Why?'

Connor must have detected the alarm in his voice because he stopped laughing. 'You really want to know about Regan and his cult?'

Fox took a deep breath. 'Yes.'

'You're in Portland, right? You can be at the stud in less than two hours. Jump on a plane to Sacramento and I'll tell you all about the cult and *exactly* what kind of person my poisonous, egotistical, psychotic brother is.'

190

CHAPTER THIRTY-TWO

Father and daughter drove for hours, heading east along Highway 84. Leaving civilization far behind, Sorcha soon found herself in deep wilderness, amid forest-clad mountains, rushing rivers and waterfalls. The only evidence of man was the ribbon of tarmac they drove on. As she stared at the panoramic vista, the road ahead seemed as unknowable as her future and the road behind as empty as her past. And yet the land was somehow familiar and comforting to her in a way the city had never been. For the first time since she had lost herself she had a sense of coming home.

Her father turned off the main highway and took increasingly smaller roads until they came to a place where the tarmac stopped. Named, appropriately, Road's End, it boasted a solitary gas pump, a run-down diner, a grocery store and not much else. They stopped for petrol and a bathroom break, and filled up with coffee and burgers. The few people they encountered didn't smile or greet them. Just watched them warily, especially her father. 'Do they know you?' she asked.

'My people do business here occasionally,' he said. 'Barter mostly.'

'They don't seem very friendly.'

'People always fear what they don't understand.' He got back in the Toyota, engaged the four-wheel drive, and turned off the tarmac on to a barely discernible earth track, which snaked its way through sloping sunlit meadows until it disappeared into a dark forest. He turned on the headlights.

191

'This is best done on horseback but the four-by-four can handle it.'

As her father drove deep into the forest, the large vehicle barely squeezing through the gaps, he seemed to follow an invisible track that threaded through the dense trees. Eventually, approaching seven o'clock in the evening, the car emerged into lush pasture, bordered by a rushing stream, which the last rays of the setting sun transformed, as if by some magical alchemy, into gold. Ahead was a painted metal sign: *Private Property. Keep Out.*

'It's beautiful,' she said. 'Is this land yours?'

'It's ours, all of it. As far as the eye can see.' He smiled and checked his watch. 'We need to keep going if we want to get home before dark.' He gunned the accelerator. 'Sunset's in less than two hours.'

Within the hour they arrived at a small rise that looked down upon the settlement. Seeing it in the glow of twilight made her sigh with pleasure, although she had no recollection of ever having been here before. Why would she have ever left such a place? Contained in a natural bowl, bounded at the front by the bend of the river and at the back by a densely wooded rise, the cluster of wooden barns and cabins and single white stone tower seemed to emerge organically from the terrain as if planted there. Although her father's dominion stretched to thousands of acres, this was its heart. The place was every inch the Eden her father had described back at Tranquil Waters. As they descended into the bowl they passed a field of ripening corn and a large orchard. Ahead she could see neat lawns, crop fields and pastures teeming with cows and sheep. At first she thought a wooden paddock fence marked the perimeter of the settlement, until she realized it corralled a herd of beautiful horses. There was no continuous fence round the settlement: the bend of the river at the front and the dense forest at the rear acted as natural boundaries. A bridge was the only visible way in and out. There was a gate across it and a gatehouse. The gate was open but a large sign informed trespassers to get off the land or risk being shot.

As they approached, she found her eyes drawn away from the gilded setting to the large crowd gathered by the bridge. It seemed as if the entire population of the settlement—at least two hundred people—had come to greet her. All wore simple clothes in a variety of faded colours but a few, including the two guards manning the gatehouse, wore conspicuously bright purple-indigo tunics over their clothes. The disproportionately large number of women and children in the crowd surprised her. As the Toyota drove closer she could see their faces, excited and expectant. 'You've got quite a reception committee,' Delaney said, smiling.

Over the bridge, he stopped the car and helped her out. People began calling her name: 'Sorcha. Sorcha.' The passion of their welcome unnerved her. Most of the crowd, with a few exceptions, possessed an aura of deep blue or indigo. And each sported a matching coloured spot on their forehead. They all seemed to know her but when she searched their faces she saw only strangers. Any sense of familiarity and homecoming she had felt when leaving the city evaporated and she suddenly wished Fox was by her side.

As she followed her father through the crowd, it

193

was clear that they were devoted to him. All bowed to him and tapped their foreheads in greeting. Some reached out to touch his arm or shoulder. All referred to him as the Seer. She noticed the corralled horses running in frantic circles as if catching the excited mood and the spectacle triggered a memory. She looked up at the round, windowless tower which dominated the settlement and stopped walking. Just below its conical slate roof, embedded in the white walls, a large mosaic eye of purple-blue crystals stared down at her. Her mouth dried and her chest tightened. The circling horses, the high tower and the giant eye were the stuff of her nightmares. She had definitely been to this Eden before. Suddenly, despite her unease, she felt tantalizingly close to remembering all that had happened here. As the crowd surrounded her, trapping her, she turned to see the indigo-clad guards close the gate bridge behind her. Nervously she scanned the dizzying, claustrophobic whirl of faces, half expecting to see the demonic pursuer of her nightmares. As she stepped out of the sun's dying rays and into the shadow of the looming tower, she pointed upwards. 'I remember that.'

Delaney's eyes narrowed. 'What? The tower?'

'Yes. And the eye.' She could hear her voice trembling but wasn't sure if it was excitement or fear.

'I told you you'd remember things,' he soothed, taking her hand. 'I'll explain everything later. Now, come with me.' Trestle tables, laden with drink and food, had been arrayed in rows outside one of the great barns, and a whole pig was roasting on a spit over an open fire. Her father led her to the main table where three women in indigo robes

194

greeted them. One was heavily pregnant and another carried a newborn baby. All were smiling at her but she also detected scrutiny in their eyes. The youngest, the blonde, dipped a finger in a pot of dye and pressed it to her father's forehead. The mark it left was a different colour from any of the other dots. Then, using the same dye, she pressed her finger to Sorcha's forehead. As everyone sat at the tables her father smiled at her. 'It must seem a bit overwhelming but everyone wants to celebrate your homecoming.' Then he stood, raised his hands and projected his voice over the crowd. 'On this beautiful evening, days from Esbat, we welcome back our precious daughter, Sorcha. Her ordeal among the sub-indigos has stolen her memory, but we must give thanks that she has returned safely to us from the children of men. Soon we fast for Esbat but tonight we celebrate . . .'

Delaney spoke as if life outside the settlement was a perilous place for the Indigo Family. Watching their rapt, smiling faces, it was obvious they worshipped him. Their unquestioning devotion made Sorcha feel uncomfortable, especially when they glanced at her with the same hungry expectancy. As she looked around she noticed an attractive older woman with an indigo dot on her forehead, long plaited greying hair, hoop earrings and large glasses, sitting on one of the outlying tables. Unlike the others, she didn't appear transfixed by her father. Instead she smiled warmly at Sorcha and, when she caught her eye, gave a little wave. Sorcha didn't recognize her but the woman's natural gesture and smile made her feel like she knew her. Then Delaney stopped speaking, the food was served and Sorcha was enveloped in a flurry of activity.

As Sorcha thought of the woman and wondered who she was, she didn't notice another pair of eyes staring at her. The large man stood alone, concealed behind the slaughterhouse on the edge of the settlement. Behind him was an anonymous white four-wheel drive. Unlike the others, his face expressed no joy or excitement at Sorcha's return. His unblinking eyes were as cold as those of a predator watching its prey.

CHAPTER THIRTY-THREE

Connor Delaney's call so alarmed Nathan Fox that he cancelled his afternoon appointments and caught the first plane to Sacramento in northern California. After the hour-and-a-half flight he arrived at the Delaney Stud Farm at 2.40 p.m. Located only twenty minutes from the airport, the manicured lush grasslands, white paddock fences and clapboard stable blocks seemed a million miles away from the bustle and noise of the Californian capital. Gleaming chestnut horses cantering in front of the main house completed the idyllic scene.

Despite the obvious beauty of his property, Connor Delaney's worried eyes expressed no pleasure when he surveyed it. He seemed to see only the peeling paint and other signs of neglect that years of financial woe had forced upon him. After a brisk greeting, the horse breeder led Fox to the veranda of the big house and pointed to the neighbouring golf and country club. 'That's new. All that land once belonged to the family until Regan took out his inheritance and almost bankrupted me,' he said bitterly. 'I had to sell off prime land just to survive.'

Like a smudged version of his attractive, charismatic younger brother, Connor Delaney was shorter and heavier, with thinning hair. He was more serious and anxious, too. As a psychiatrist, Fox had come across his type often: the dull but dutiful older son who obeyed the rules and put in the hard work, only to see a charming but feckless younger sibling flout every rule and steal all the prizes. Connor pointed to the paddock. 'You ride, Dr Fox?'

'I learned as a child.'

'I've got two horses saddled up. We could talk and ride.'

Fox laughed. 'As long as they're good-natured. I haven't ridden in a while.'

Connor smiled and something about the way his mouth moved reminded Fox of Sorcha. 'Don't worry, old Stan's not got an ornery bone in his body. We'll just walk them, stretch their legs.' Connor led him to the stables and within minutes Fox was riding a bay gelding out into the paddock. He had only ever been a competent rider but it felt surprisingly good to be on horseback again, especially in this setting. Connor rode beside him. 'So tell me. What's your patient got to do with Regan?'

Fox hesitated, not wanting to say too much. 'We were treating her for amnesia. Your brother recognized her and came to take her home.'

'Back to his cult?'

'Yes.'

Connor frowned. 'The only reason Regan came

197

for her was because he needed her for his Great Work.'

'Great Work?'

'It's what he calls his insane, all-consuming project. The Great Work was a term used in European medieval alchemy to refer to the successful transmutation of base metal into gold. It also had a spiritual meaning: converting base humans into something more divine, free from the constraints of the material world and closer to gods. I don't know the details of Regan's Great Work but I know it involves the *mothú*.' Connor leaned back in his saddle, warming to his theme. 'To understand my brother and his cult you've first got to understand our family history and his obsession with the Delaney *mothú*.'

'There's a long history of synaesthesia in your family?'

His host smiled. 'Synaesthesia? I forgot that's what you shrinks call it. Yeah, we've got history, centuries of it. We come from an old line of Irish Travellers, or Pavees, as we prefer to call ourselves. The Delaneys are one of the oldest families on the road. We travelled the length and breadth of Ireland before crossing to England and eventually America. Unlike the thieves and con artists that give Pavees a bad name, we've always taken pride in earning an honest wage through our skill with horses, for which Buffers—non-Travellers—pay handsomely.

'Initially we trained, treated and bred horses for the gentry but soon we became breeders in our own right, focusing on thoroughbreds. We know all about bloodlines and selective breeding because for centuries we've practised it on our own family. My ancestors believed superstitiously that the Delaneys' identity and success lay in the *mothú*, the sense—what you call synaesthesia. It's been in the family for generations and not just by accident. We actively sought out partners who had synaesthesia, marrying cousins and sometimes even closer family members in order to keep the *mothú* within the bloodline. The superstition was so strong it didn't matter which kind of synaesthesia we had and it didn't really matter if it helped with horses or business. The *mothú* was seen as a special badge of birth that gave us status within the family.

'Almost a hundred years ago my grandfather, Seamus, broke away from the British and Irish Delaneys and came to America with a string of thoroughbred stallions and brood mares. He moved here to California and set up business. His family—he had three daughters and one son, my father—still kept itself to itself and observed the traditions but over time things changed. As the family became more successful they became more embedded in Buffer society. First they travelled, taking their horses and expertise to wherever the work was, then they rented a spread and people began to come to them, and finally they bought this land and settled down. My grandfather and then my father realized that to build on their success they had to network, become more mainstream and fit in. We were all sent to the best Buffer schools and almost overnight the *mothú*, the backbone of our family tradition, went from being seen as a prized gift and badge of honour to an embarrassment, a superstitious quirk we were all happy to dispense with. All except for Regan, of course. He wasn't happy at all.'

199

'Why not?'

'Like most Delaneys, I inherited a basic form of synaesthesia: grapheme-colour. I see letters and numbers as colours. It doesn't really affect my life and I don't regard it as particularly significant. Regan was very different, though. He claimed to have every form of synaesthesia you can think of—and some you can't.'

'Can you give me examples?'

'Sure. I don't know the scientific names for them all but he claimed to see letters as colours, feel what others were feeling, see auras . . .' Connor proceeded to list all the forms Sorcha had exhibited in Fox's first session. 'Like I said. He claimed to have every sort you can imagine.'

'You sound like you didn't believe him?'

'You could never be sure what to believe with Regan. The family were kind of embarrassed because if he did have a freak form of the *mothú* it would almost certainly be a genetic mutation due to the generations of inbreeding. Unsurprisingly, he supported the traditional family view that the *mothú* marked him out as special, which of course meant he was *really* special, unique.

'His conviction was reinforced by the fact that everything came easy to him: he was beautiful, bright, charming and doted on—however he behaved. When he was younger he used to bring rocks and bricks and chunks of rubble home and make them into weird sculptures and mosaics. Never explained why. When he got older he had his pick of women and screwed around like it was going out of fashion. I can't recall one woman who refused him. Part of his bizarre courting ritual was to make extreme claims about his *mothú*.'

200

'Such as?'

Connor frowned and shook his head. 'You really want to know all this stuff?'

'Please.'

'When he reached puberty he claimed that every time he had an orgasm he had an out-of-body experience. He believed his soul literally left his body. Said he could sense things beyond the physical world, beyond the veil dividing life and death.'

Fox had read that synaesthetes made up a high proportion of those claiming to have out-of-body experiences. 'Were any of his claims ever tested?'

Connor Delaney grimaced. 'No. The guy's an egotistical liar with no conscience. He'd say and do anything to promote himself and get what he wants. He only got his veterinary qualifications, which were important to the family business, to please Dad.'

'What did your father think of him?'

'He thought the sun shone out of his ass,' Connor spat. 'In Dad's eyes, Regan could do no wrong. Then one day a horse Regan was treating kicked him in the head. He recovered but constantly complained of splitting headaches and became increasingly obsessed with sex and death and, of course, his goddamn *mothú*. He began reading books on the occult and world religions, searching for anything that reinforced his convictions. He spent hours poring over the Old Testament. Ever heard of the Nephilim?'

'No.'

'The Nephilim appear in the Old Testament, in both Genesis and Numbers. According to the Bible, angels known as the Grigori were sent down

201

to earth to watch men. In time these "sons of gods" saw how beautiful the "daughters of men" were and mated with them, injecting their divine blood into the human gene pool. The progeny of these couplings were the Nephilim, hybrid beings with superhuman senses and powers, and Regan became convinced that the *mothú* in all its forms was some kind of angelic trait, a throwback to these angel–human crossbreeds and a vestige of divine power. Basically, anyone with the *mothú* was a descendant of the Nephilim and had divine blood in their veins. Everyone else was just a base human. Of course, Regan, with his extreme synaesthesia, saw himself as purer than most—a throwback to the original fallen Grigori rather than the half-breed Nephilim. He wanted the family to reinstate the importance of the *mothú* but none of us took him seriously. Then he met Aurora, who had just returned from India, her head filled with New Age nonsense. Aurora claimed to be a healer and she took Regan very seriously. She reinforced and validated every fantasy he had about himself.'

'How?'

'Aurora was part of a New Age commune that called itself the Indigo Family. Many of them had followed the hippy trail to India and been influenced by Eastern mystics and gurus. Aurora introduced Regan to chakras, the third eye and all these other New Age concepts. He claimed she cured his headaches using crystals. Aurora was an emotion-colour synaesthete who saw auras and she believed Regan's aura was unique. When she took him to meet the rest of the Indigo Family, most of whom were fellow synaesthetes, they embraced him too. Apparently synaesthetes have an aura which ranges from turquoise through blue to purple-indigo, hence the cult's name, whereas non-synaesthetes, or sub-synaesthetes as Regan liked to call them, have auras at the "lower" end of the colour spectrum: from red, through orange and yellow, to green. To show their particular aura many cult members painted a coloured spot here like the Hindus do.' Connor pressed a finger to the middle of his forehead, leaving a white mark. 'Something to do with the sixth chakra or the third eye, which they believe helps them see into the spiritual realm. Like I said, most in the cult had blue or indigo auras but Aurora said that Regan's was even purer, higher up the spiritual spectrum, beyond indigo. Whatever the hell that means.'

Fox nodded. 'I guess she confirmed your brother's belief that his synaesthesia was a kind of superpower.'

'Totally. The cult's and his belief systems aligned perfectly.' Connor laughed humourlessly. 'This was where the madness really got serious. The Indigo Family reinforced all his prejudices and self-delusions, removing any vestigial constraints. Within months, although he still spent time on the family business, he was the cult's leader in all but name. Then the suicides happened.'

'What suicides?'

'About ten members of the Indigo Family were found dead in a stone barn on the commune. The details of their deaths were mysterious and suicide was suspected but two other family members told the police they saw Regan lead them into the barn and then come out alone. When the police came for him, he later bragged that the cops had to fight off half the commune to get to him.'

'What happened?'

'The two witnesses vanished and the cops released him a few days later due to lack of evidence. The commune welcomed him back like a persecuted messiah. It was clear he'd found his place in the world. Soon after that they started calling him the Seer.'

'The Seer?'

'Something to do with the third eye. He was always exaggerating what he could see, boasting about his powers.' Connor sneered when he said 'powers'.

Fox thought of Sorcha's gift. 'I know many of the visual aspects of synaesthesia, such as seeing colours, can *seem* like hallucinations but did he ever claim to see anything significantly out of the ordinary which you thought might be genuine?'

Connor Delaney looked like he was about to laugh. Then he stopped himself and turned back to the house, which was now some distance away. 'There was one time,' he said quietly. 'Come with me. I want to show you something.' He kicked his horse's flanks and broke into a canter. Fox followed.

Back in the house Connor led Fox upstairs to a large bedroom. 'Our father died in this room,' Connor said. 'He'd been ill for some weeks and died in great pain. Only I was with him when he passed but after his body had been moved Regan insisted on sitting in here for hours on end. When I asked why, he told me he was reliving our father's death—even though he hadn't been here when it happened. He believed that if he relived the experience enough times he'd see where his spirit had gone. See beyond the veil. He took the

204

headboard for a keepsake. Said it made him feel closer to Dad. What freaked me out at the time, though, was he told me exactly how he'd died. Details only I knew. Details I'd told no one about.'

Fox said nothing but the story made him wonder if Regan Delaney shared his daughter's death-echo synaesthesia. If so, why hadn't he reacted when Fox had showed him into Sorcha's original room at Tranquil Waters?

Connor continued, 'Two days later the will was read. Our father was an old-time patriarch and left little to our female cousins. The bulk of his inheritance went to Regan and me, half each—even though I was the oldest and had done most to build the business. Regan immediately demanded his share in cash because he wanted to buy up a large chunk of Oregon wilderness so he could lead his cult—what he now called his *real* family—to a new promised land.'

'Do you know where in Oregon he set up his cult?'

'I've got geographical coordinates in the legal files but it's in the middle of nowhere. I told him his plans would bankrupt the family business but he didn't care. Eventually, to keep the business I had to sell land and horses and take out a crippling loan to pay off Regan's share. The pressure made my wife leave me. My brother walked away with millions and took three of my best thoroughbreds. He even stole the Delaney family Bible, which contains the family tree and had been handed down to the first-born male for centuries.'

'Why take horses if he wanted out of the business?'

'He thought the purity of their bloodline

205

mirrored his own. Ninety-five per cent of the hundreds of thousands of thoroughbreds on earth come from *one* foundation stallion in England, back in the late seventeenth century. The other five per cent come from two other stallions in England. Every thoroughbred in the entire world comes from the loins of three stallions.' Connor Delaney shook his head. 'I don't blame the Indigo Family for all this, though. In fact I almost feel sorry for them. Cults are often accused of brainwashing their members and hijacking their lives. But my brother did the hijacking. He took a commune of harmless hippies and misfits who dabbled in crystals, wore colourful tie-dyed clothes and wanted to heal the world and turned them into a hardcore cult focused on achieving his Great Work. The last time I saw them, just before they went off to Oregon, they'd already become a pretty strict, well-organized community—a sort of Rainbow Amish.'

'What exactly do you think your brother's Great Work is?'

Connor shrugged. 'I can't say for sure.' Then his eyes narrowed. 'But I can tell you one thing. It'll be hugely ambitious and he'll be totally ruthless. You must understand that my brother doesn't just believe he and his Indigo Family are descended from fallen angels who bred with humans. He wants to *recreate* the golden age when these ancestors of his—these most pure of thoroughbreds— once walked the earth.' Shaking his head at the preposterousness of what he was saying, Connor led Fox out of the bedroom and back towards the stairs. He smiled. 'It's funny you being a psychiatrist because it's felt like therapy getting all this shit off my chest.'

206

Fox wasn't sure how he felt about his visit. He had learned that Regan Delaney was selfish, obsessive and delusional and that the Indigo Family was as dysfunctional as any cult Fox had encountered, but he had no reason to believe Sorcha was in any immediate danger—or any proof. Professionally, he had discovered how his erstwhile patient might have come by her rare gift. It appeared to be a strange genetic inheritance, a freak mutation in her bloodline resulting from centuries of Delaney family inbreeding.

Approaching the stairs, they passed another room. Fox glanced inside and saw a child's bed and a cluster of pink toys. 'That's my daughter's room,' Connor said proudly. 'She'll be five next year. She's out with the horses and can already ride better than me.' He smiled. 'It's funny. I never had any children with my first wife but my second's given me two. Perhaps, by breaking up my first marriage, my brother did me a favour after all.'

Fox was no longer listening. He was staring at the wooden letters pinned to the door, which spelled 'Angela'. 'You buy those letters or make them?' he asked, taking a photo with his cell phone.

'I made them,' said Connor. 'Angela's my daughter's name. Why? You want to know why I coloured the letters that way?'

A chill ran down Fox's spine. 'No,' he said, more calmly than he felt, wondering how he could have missed the connection. 'You've already told me why.' He checked his watch then shook Connor Delaney's hand. 'Thank you for everything, but I'm afraid I have to leave now.'

'Why?'

'I need to get back to Portland and if I run I can

catch the five p.m. flight.'

As he left the house and jumped into the waiting cab he punched a number into his BlackBerry. He was trying to call Sorcha and warn her but the iPhone he had given her wasn't answering. *Shit.* He left a voicemail, telling her to call him urgently, then phoned Jordache. The detective was busy but his assistant promised to courier the crime scene photographs to Fox's apartment that night. Fox checked his watch again and willed the cab to reach the airport in time. If the photographs confirmed his suspicions then Sorcha faced a far more dangerous threat than a delusional father.

PART 3
The Great Work

CHAPTER THIRTY-FOUR

At midnight, the excitement of Sorcha's homecoming had subsided and the settlement was quiet. His exhausted daughter was asleep in her room, but Regan Delaney was too preoccupied to retire. He stepped out into the night to wander his domain.

As he walked among the silent wooden cabins within which his followers slumbered he looked up at the night sky. In a few days the silver moon would be full and Esbat would be upon them. Despite the mild air, the sense of anticipation caused goosebumps to erupt on his arm. Passing a sign forbidding entry into the forest on the rise behind the settlement, he breathed in the smell of the giant sequoia redwoods. The forest was quiet except for the occasional cry of lovesick owls. He smiled up at the massive trees, standing like silent sentinels guarding his settlement and his secrets. Even the tower's giant eye, gleaming in the moonlight, could not see into their depths.

Back inside his private quarters, he went to his concealed room and checked the closed-circuit monitors, toggling through the cameras secreted in various sites around the settlement. He saw two Watchers patrolling the bridge but most of the screens showed his people asleep in their beds. Usually he searched for forbidden activity so he could publicly shame the wrongdoer and reinforce his people's belief that he, the Seer, saw everything. Tonight, however, he selected the room in which his daughter lay sleeping. Because of the low light

211

the black and white image was grainy but when he zoomed in on her face he could still make out her features. He remembered the day she was born and how he had stared into her eyes, wondering what they had seen before coming into existence and what they would see after she died. As he studied her face now, he smiled. He had reclaimed her just in time, days away from taking the Great Work to the next stage. Then the lens zoomed out and the excited glow of anticipation curdled in his belly.

Someone was standing at the foot of Sorcha's bed, watching her sleep. Disbelief paralysed Delaney for some seconds. How could an intruder be in Sorcha's room? What was he doing there? How dare anyone steal into his private chambers? As he zoomed in on the intruder, fury replaced shock and he ran to Sorcha's room.

*   *   *

Exhausted, Sorcha lay on her bed, in deep sleep. Again the nightmares visited her but tonight the circling horses, the eye staring down at her from the looming tower and the shadowy figure chasing her seemed even more real and frightening.

Suddenly, something sensed in the real world pierced her dreams and dragged her from the depths of her unconscious. As she surfaced she became aware of a mounting, suffocating dread pressing down on her chest. The terror of waking was so great that she would have preferred to return to her familiar nightmares.

As her eyes flickered open she heard herself cry out. A figure was standing by her bed, bending over her, reaching out his hand but in her half-asleep state she couldn't move away. She flinched as he touched her brow and stroked her forehead.

'Relax. It's only me,' the figure said.

As her eyes focused she recognized her father. A warm wave of relief flooded over her. She was home, back with her family. She sighed and felt herself descend into deep sleep once more. As she lost consciousness she didn't register the anger and concern on her father's face or the trace odour hanging in the still air like the smell of death.

CHAPTER THIRTY-FIVE

When Fox returned to his apartment that evening the photographs of the three crime scenes were waiting for him. As he laid them on the dining table he ignored the mutilated victims and focused on the blow-ups of the killer's messages:

SERVE THE DEMON
SAVE THE ANGEL

Ignoring what the messages might mean, Fox compared the coloured letters on the crime photographs with those on his cell phone. The colours Connor Delaney had used to spell the word 'Angela' on his daughter's bedroom door corresponded almost exactly with the marker pen letters that spelled the word 'Angel' in the crime scene photographs. In all pictures, the A's were red, the N's blue, the E's green and the L's differing shades of yellow. Even the G's were similar brown tones. Fox knew why Connor Delaney had chosen

213

the colours: he had grapheme-colour synaesthesia and saw individual letters as a particular shade. But why had the killer assigned the same colours to identical letters? Was it a coincidence?

Fox retrieved the notes he had made the day he'd first discovered Sorcha's synaesthesia. What had she said when he had shown her the letter A? *'You've written it in black ink but everyone knows A's are red . . . E's are olive green.'* Grapheme-colour synaesthetes often ascribed similar colours to the same letters, which indicated that not only were Sorcha and Connor Delaney synaesthetes but the killer was, too. Did that mean the killer knew Sorcha and was part of her past?

He needed to speak off the record with someone about this to check his thinking before he went official. Fullelove already thought he was spending too much time on an ex-patient so he doubted she would be too receptive, and he would have to get his facts straight before he spoke to Jordache. Whatever his facts were. He packed up all the photos, files and notes and picked up his car keys. Within half an hour he was at Samantha's. There was a squad car outside but otherwise no sign of the recent attack. The front door had been repaired and when she opened it she showed no ill effects. 'What are you doing here, Nathan? Not checking on me again, I hope. I can look after myself.'

He smiled. 'You've proved that. I need your help. It concerns Sorcha.'

'Well, in that case come in.' She escorted Fox into the kitchen and poured him a glass of wine.

'Have you got any beer?'

She grimaced. 'You know I only serve proper drink in this house. This is a very good Sauvignon

214

Blanc. All the way from New Zealand.'

He smiled and took the glass. 'Thank you.'

'So what's this about Sorcha? When she said goodbye to me, by the way, I got the distinct impression she didn't want to go.' She raised an eyebrow. 'And I don't think I've ever seen you so . . .' she paused, searching for the word, '. . . engaged by someone. I'm surprised you let her go.'

He frowned. 'She was my patient. I did what I thought was right for her.'

'Nathan, my dear, you might understand the human mind but it appears you still have a lot to learn about the human heart.' She sipped her wine. 'Why are you concerned about her now she's out of harm's way?'

'Because I'm not sure she is out of harm's way.'

'Why?'

He laid out his files and photographs on the kitchen table and told her about what Connor Delaney had said about Regan Delaney, the cult and their obsession with the third eye. 'We all assumed the killer didn't know Sorcha personally but was fixated on her public persona. The cops were happy for her to leave Portland and return to some remote cult because they figured she'd be safer there, out of the way. But what if the killer *does* know her? What if he is or was part of the cult?' Fox showed Samantha the picture on his cell phone and explained his theory of the coloured letters. 'The colours of the letters at *all* the crimes correspond exactly with the ones used by Connor Delaney. And with the letters Sorcha mentioned.'

She frowned. 'Matching colours might mean the killer's got synaesthesia. But even if he does have it, it doesn't automatically follow he's a member of the

215

cult.' She paused. 'Nathan, I know what you think about cults and why. But I've dealt with a few New Age cranks in my time—you wouldn't believe the New Age gurus and mystics who've jumped on to the quantum physics bandwagon to give credibility to their theories about the duality of the body and soul—and Regan Delaney's cult doesn't sound any more sinister than the rest.

'He's certainly not the first person to interpret synaesthesia as a spiritual or psychic gift, either. Back in the seventies, a synaesthete and self-styled psychic parapsychologist coined the phrase "Indigo Children" to describe kids with indigo auras who allegedly possessed supernatural traits and abilities, including telepathy. Despite widespread scepticism from the medical and scientific community, many parents, particularly of difficult children, were only too happy to have their little darlings classified as Indigo Children because it implied they were special. Later, of course, most of the children were diagnosed as having nothing more glamorous than attention deficit disorder, or being plain spoilt.

'My point is, Nathan, Sorcha's probably fine where she is, whatever the cult's obsession with indigo auras, the sixth chakra or the third eye.' She tapped her forehead as she said 'third eye', leaving a white mark, just as Connor Delaney had in Sacramento. The gesture sparked a tantalizing connection in Fox's mind. He picked up the pile of crime scene photos on the table and began shuffling them like a deck of cards until he found himself staring at a graphic close-up of the severed head from the third crime scene. His aunt turned pale when she saw the image.

'I'm sorry,' he said, quickly concealing the

picture from her. He had seen enough, however, to bring the connection into cold, sharp focus. *How could he have been so blind?* He riffled through the photos, focusing on pictures of the other victims. 'But the killer can't have known . . .?' he started to say, before the connection led to another chilling insight.

'What is it?' said Samantha.

'I think the killer's definitely connected to Sorcha. Even more closely than I feared.'

'Why?'

He explained his insight and waited for Samantha to pick it to pieces. But she didn't. 'You could be right. If you are, it would explain something that happened the other night.'

'What do you mean?'

'Come.' She led him to Howard's study. 'The intruder was hiding in here when I walked past. I only knew he was in here because he knocked something over and made a loud noise. I should have been the one in shock when I confronted him but he seemed even more stunned than me. I found this on the floor after he'd gone.' She picked up the Mayan sacrificial stone from Howard's desk. It was broken in two. 'His fingerprints aren't on it but that doesn't mean he didn't touch it.'

Fox understood immediately. It confirmed his theory. He reached for the phone and dialled Karl Jordache's number.

'What are you going to do?'

'Try to convince the police that ghosts exist.'

CHAPTER THIRTY-SIX

Fox knew it was going to be tough to win over Jordache. Like all good detectives, Jordache believed in one thing only: hard evidence. The next morning, however, when they met in the homicide incident room deep in the warren of corridors that made up Portland's Central Precinct police headquarters, Fox realized it was going to be tougher than he had thought. The exhausted detective seemed more irritated at being called away from whatever he had been doing than interested in what Fox had to say.

'You got a *new* theory?' Jordache sighed, gesturing to the notes and crime scene photographs plastered over one wall of the incident room. 'We've been up all night pursuing the last one.'

'I think I've found a link between the killer and my patient. And a link to the cult she's returned to.'

Jordache sighed. 'Nathan, it's not like you to get so involved with an ex-patient. We've talked about this. She's not your concern any more. She's history. Let it go.'

'You don't want to hear my theory?'

Jordache rubbed his eyes. 'We've already—' He stopped and collected himself. 'Sorry, Nathan, it's been a long night. Go ahead. Your hunches are always worth listening to.'

'This isn't a hunch.' Fox walked over to the crime scene pictures on the wall and explained about his visit to Connor Delaney, the cult and the matching coloured letters in the messages.

'Aren't you taking this synaesthesia thing a little

218

far?' said Jordache.

'It shows a connection. It proves the killer had synaesthesia like Sorcha and was probably—'

'It's just coloured letters, Nathan. It *proves* nothing. It's circumstantial at best.'

Fox pointed to the crime scene pictures showing Sorcha's portrait stapled to the victims' faces. 'Look where the staple is in Sorcha's picture . . .' he indicated each of the victims, '. . . in *all* the crime scenes. And look where the staple is in each of the victims.' Fox tapped his forehead. 'It's in the exact same place as the sixth chakra, the third eye.' He pointed at a close-up. 'If you look closely you can see a trace of marker pen around the staple in the newspaper. The killer drew a dot on Sorcha's picture, on her forehead, before gunning in the staple—the same dot that members of the Indigo Family wear. The killer's either a member or an ex-member of the cult and he definitely knows Sorcha.'

Jordache shifted uncomfortably in his chair. 'For argument's sake let's say you're right and the killer does have synaesthesia like Sorcha. And let's say he is or was a member of this cult. These were copycat killings. Forget motive for a moment. How would a member of a remote cult have known about the prior murders that took place at each crime scene?'

Fox paused. He had promised Sorcha he would keep her death-echo synaesthesia a secret, but could see no other way of convincing Jordache that her life may be in danger. 'There is one explanation. Bear with me here.' As Fox explained his aunt's theory of archaeosonics and his discovery of Sorcha's unique synaesthesia, he could see the detective becoming more and more incredulous.

'Let me get this straight, Nathan. You're saying somehow people's death throes are recorded in the subatomic fabric of the building in which they died and that Sorcha's rare form of synaesthesia lets her play back these stored memories and relive their deaths?'

Fox tried to ignore the scepticism in Jordache's voice. 'I know it sounds crazy but that's how I knew about the prior murders. Sorcha told me after visiting the three crime scenes.'

'She *sensed* them?'

'She saw, heard, smelt and felt them. And I believe the killer did too. He's not just a member of the cult, he also shares her death-echo synaesthesia. When he was in my uncle's office he touched and broke a sacrificial stone used by the ancient Maya, a stone literally soaked in the blood of countless sacrificial victims. I think he sensed something from that stone so unexpected, visceral and shocking that he involuntarily knocked it off the desk and alerted my aunt.'

'A sacrificial stone? Are you kidding me? What was his motive for killing the three men?'

'I'm not sure. He obviously doesn't share Sorcha's natural fear and revulsion for death echoes so I'm guessing he's psychotic. I think they excite him and he uses them not only to relive the murders but also to replicate them with a twist.'

'If he gets off on these death echoes then how come the sacrificial stone shocked him?'

'Because it was so intense and unexpected.'

Jordache groaned. 'What does your Professor Fullelove say about this . . . death-echo synaesthesia?'

'She doesn't know about it.'

220

'How come?'

'Sorcha wanted to keep it confidential.'

'I bet she did. Listen to yourself, Nathan. With the greatest of respect, if I told you what you've just told me, without any real proof or a corroborating witness, would you believe me? Even if I did believe you, what can I do about it? Rush out to this cult in the middle of nowhere and do what exactly? No judge in their right mind's going to give me a search warrant based on sacrificial stones, a crazy theory of archaeosonics and a diagnosis of an entirely new condition . . . death-echo synaesthesia.' He crossed his arms and shook his head. He looked sad and tired. 'Hell, I'm no great fan of cults but where's your goddamned perspective gone? I warned you Jane Doe would get under your skin but come on, this sounds like you're making up reasons to worry about her. She's gone now. She's no longer your concern.'

'She could be in danger, Karl. The killer could be the reason she ran away from the cult in the first place. And now she's returned . . .'

'She's not in danger from the killer. Trust me.'

'How can you be so sure?'

Jordache sighed. 'Because I think we've got him already.'

'You're kidding.'

'That's what we've been working on all night. We unearthed a few suspects that fit our profile but one guy ticks *all* the boxes.' Jordache gave a tired smile. 'He's still in one of the interview rooms.'

'Can I see him?'

'Sure. See if you can ID him. I know your aunt didn't see him the other night and you didn't get a great look at him at Tranquil Waters, but you did

221

fight him.' He led Fox down the corridor and into a viewing room. Through a one-way mirror Fox could see Kostakis interviewing a man. 'Recognize him?'

The man was big enough to be the intruder Fox had fought with but triggered no recognition. 'No.'

'His voice?'

'I didn't hear him speak. You sure it's him?'

'Pretty sure. He's a journalist called Frank Johanssen. Used to be the senior crime reporter for the *Oregonian* but had a breakdown after his wife was raped and murdered in Old Town a few years ago. Claimed the police knew who killed her but wouldn't act because of lack of proof. He's now freelance and writes mainly about how the justice system failed him but he still has links with local police and has good knowledge of the underworld. He knows most of the major players in Old Town from back in the day and has access to all the information required to have committed the copycat killings.'

It was Fox's turn to be sceptical. 'The victims were cut up pretty good for a journalist.'

'Johanssen knows how to use a knife. His old man was a butcher in Salem and Johanssen used to help him out when going through college. He has motive, too. He says Jane Doe inspired him to act: to go through the old files, clean up Old Town and mete out some biblical justice.'

'Has he confessed?'

'Kind of. Didn't say much until Kostakis went through each crime in detail. Then he smiled and said they weren't crimes at all, but acts of justice. He doesn't even want a lawyer with him. Says there's no point because the justice system is full of shit anyway.'

Fox stared at the man, struggling to see a connection between the person behind the glass talking with Kostakis and the one he had confronted in the dark. He wished Sorcha were here now because she might be able to recognize him from the death echoes at the crime scenes. Not that Jordache would believe her. 'Does he have that rancid smell?'

'No. But that doesn't mean anything. He might have just needed a shower.'

'Why did he attack Sorcha if she was such an inspiration?'

'Not sure yet but we're working on a theory that he meant her no harm. That he just wanted to meet her, connect with her.'

'I fought the bastard, Karl. It wasn't a social call. He had a knife. He poisoned her, for Christ's sake. Two nights ago he poisoned one of your cops.'

Jordache led him back to the incident room. 'He *tranquillized* them, Nathan. There's a difference. Anyway, it makes a lot more sense than your archaeo-goddamn-sonics.'

In the incident room Fox noticed a file open on the main table. It contained a photo of the suspect. 'What if you've got the wrong man?'

A shrug. 'Ever since we've had him in our sights the killings have stopped.'

'Perhaps they stopped because the killer's followed Sorcha back to the cult?'

'Drop it, Nathan. You can't just make up stuff because you don't like cults.' Jordache groaned. 'I'm too tired for this shit. All the evidence points to this guy being a shoo-in. And that's good enough for me.' Fox realized that Jordache wasn't going to change his mind. And if the detective—his friend—

223

didn't buy his story then no one would. Fox was on his own. He handed Jordache a notebook and Samantha's paper on archaeosonics. As Jordache flicked through them, Nathan slipped the suspect's photograph into his pocket. 'What the hell are these, Nathan?'

'The notebook records all the death echoes Sorcha sensed at the crime scenes. It covers the earlier murders as well as the recent ones. Read it. Some of the details might surprise you.'

Jordache sighed. 'And this?'

'That paper explains the scientific theory behind what I've been trying to tell you. When you find out you've got the wrong man you might want to read it, too. Call my aunt about anything you don't understand. She'll be expecting your call.' He turned and walked away.

'You're going after Sorcha, aren't you?' Jordache called after him. 'Goddamnit, Nathan, what the hell's wrong with you? Leave it alone. Not every cult's evil. Don't do this, Nathan. Listen to me. This is none of your goddamn business. It doesn't have anything to do with what happened to your folks . . .'

Even when Fox could no longer hear Jordache, he could hear his sensei's voice echoing in his ears: *maintain control, keep your distance*. But it was too late. He had already got too close and couldn't leave it alone. Exiting the police building, he recalled Sorcha telling him about her nightmares and knew with a certainty he couldn't explain to Jordache—or to himself—that the killer was closing in with the same relentless inevitability as the pursuer in her dreams. Sorcha was now at her most vulnerable: alone in a remote cult, with no memory of her past to guide her, dependent on a family of strangers. As Fox climbed into the car he caught his reflection in the rear-view mirror, staring back at him, challenging him:

Who will Sorcha turn to when the killer comes for her?

Who can she trust to help and protect her?

Who, if not you?

CHAPTER THIRTY-SEVEN

Sorcha woke at dawn, roused by the rising sun filtering through the slats in the wooden shutters. During last night's homecoming feast, her father had introduced her to the three women in the indigo robes, referring to them as his Wives. After the feast, they had drawn Sorcha a bath and shown her to her room. She had been asleep by ten o'clock. Her sleep had been restless and filled with dark dreams, but when she awoke, she realized there were no death echoes in the room—not even white noise. Only the sound of birdsong and lowing cows disturbed the silence. She reached under her pillow and turned on the phone Fox had given her. As her father had said, there was no signal. She suddenly wished Fox was here. Every new discovery she had made since losing her memory she had made with him, but now she was on her own.

She got out of bed and pulled back the shutters. The first thing she saw was the tower from her dreams etched against the cloudless sky. In the bright morning sun its staring eye appeared less sinister and gave her hope that soon she would rediscover her past life. Looking out on the other cabins and barns she could see people going about their chores. Two women ambled out of a cowshed, weighed down by pails of milk, laughing in the golden light.

What had caused her to leave this idyllic place?

As the morning light flooded the bare bedroom she searched it for traces of the person she had once been. But there were few clues. No posters or pictures adorned the walls, just a mirror and a large bronze ankh above the bed. On the table by the window were a brush and some basic toiletries and in the small bookcase in the corner a few old paperback novels. The one thing that caught her eye was a faded photograph in a wooden frame, sitting on the top shelf. The woman smiling at the camera looked familiar. When Sorcha moved closer she realized the woman looked like her. She was holding a baby: the baby in her locket. Sorcha touched her mother's face and smiled. The woman was no longer alive and Sorcha couldn't remember her, but just seeing her mother holding her infant self validated her existence and anchored her place in the world.

In the adjoining bathroom she put the soap and shampoo to her nose, but nothing triggered her memory. After showering she found fresh clothes laid out on the chair by the foot of her bed. The handmade, hand-dyed garments—underwear, jeans, cotton T-shirt and sweater—were clean but worn. Judging from their perfect fit she realized they must be her old clothes, and the thought comforted her. Looking at herself in the mirror she wished she could inhabit her old identity and memories with the same ease.

As she opened her bedroom door and stepped

barefoot into the corridor she heard voices. Walking towards them she came to a half-open door and was about to knock when she spied Regan Delaney lying naked on his back. Maria, the pregnant redhead, straddled him, full breasts swaying above his face. The blonde lay beside him, caressing his inner thigh. The third woman sat on the edge of the bed, nursing her newborn with one heavy breast, while stroking Delaney's forehead. All the women were naked, whispering chants of encouragement as they stared devotedly at Delaney's face.

Transfixed by the rhythm of the women's writhing bodies, Sorcha stared in horror at the tableau, the urgency of their whispers increasing with the quickening tempo of their movements. Suddenly, Delaney groaned and thrust his hips upwards. As he reached orgasm, his eyes opened and, as if in a trance, his pupils rolled back in his head, leaving only the whites visible. The women stared at him the whole time, eyes wide with rapture. 'What can you see? Tell us what you see,' the redhead pleaded, breathlessly, thighs shaking with exertion.

As they listened for his answer the young blonde turned to the door. Showing no embarrassment, she smiled at Sorcha: a knowing, self-satisfied smile. As if icy water had been splashed over her, Sorcha instantly regained control over her body, recoiled and ran as fast as she could down the corridor. Finding herself in the main chamber, surrounded by bookshelves, she tried to calm herself and purge the images from her head. For the first time she was grateful for her amnesia because, mercifully, it had felt like she had witnessed a stranger copulating, rather than her father.

'Good morning, Sorcha.' She swivelled round to see him walking towards her. He wore a long black robe and was smiling. If he was aware of what she had just witnessed, he gave no sign. 'Sleep OK?'

'Yes, thank you.' She had wanted to ask him about her mother but now couldn't find the words. Feeling herself redden she turned to the wall and found herself staring at a six-foot-high tapestry of overlapping twin figures, one bold, the other its pale shadow. The legs and arms of both figures were stretched out as if performing a star jump. Seven wheel-like vortices ran up each of their spines, reflecting the seven colours of the rainbow, from red at the base to violet on the crown of the head. The sixth, indigo vortex in the brow was shaped like an eye. Each vortex was linked to its twin by a silver thread—except for the top one. The thicker thread connecting the seventh, violet vortices on the crown of the heads was a braided cord. The face on each figure was a stylized likeness of Delaney.

'Do you know what that tapestry represents?' he asked.

She looked closer, grateful for something to focus on. 'No. Should I?'

'The bold figure represents our carnal body and the shadow figure its spiritual counterpart, the so-called astral body—what some religions call the soul. The vortices running down the spine represent the seven major chakras. These link the two bodies and are the key portals for receiving, storing and expressing the life force vital for their wellbeing. Each chakra has a designated role in governing a particular physical, mental, emotional and spiritual

228

aspect of our life.'

He pointed to the base of the spine. 'The vortices at the lower end of the spine are the animal chakras and deal with our most basic needs.' He pointed to the red vortex. 'The first, near the anus, sexual organs and the adrenal medulla—responsible for the fight-or-flight reflex—is called Muladhara, the root or base chakra. Physically it governs sexuality, mentally it governs stability, emotionally it governs sensuality, and spiritually it governs our sense of security.' He pointed to the orange vortex. 'The second, in the sacrum near the testes and ovaries, is the sacral chakra, Svadhisthana. Physically this governs reproduction, mentally creativity, emotionally joy and spiritually enthusiasm.'

He pointed to the torso. 'The middle chakras are known as the human chakras and deal with our more complex and advanced needs.' He pointed to the green vortex in the chest, between the yellow in the abdomen and the light blue in the throat. 'This, for example, is Anahata, the heart chakra. It's physically responsible for circulation, mentally passion, emotionally unconditional love and spiritually devotion.'

'The most advanced chakras of all, however, are above the neck. These are what we in the Indigo Family focus on. These are the divine chakras.' He pointed to the stylized indigo eye on the man's forehead. 'The brow chakra, Ajna, is linked to the pineal gland, which Descartes believed was the location of the human soul. It produces the melatonin that regulates sleep and waking. This, the sixth chakra, is usually deep blue or indigo and is often called the third eye because it governs our intuition, unconscious and the balancing of

229

our spiritual and base selves. Like a sixth sense, it acts as a lens into the other realm. Meditation can be used to access and develop this chakra but we synaesthetes are genetically predisposed to use this sixth sense automatically.'

'What's the top chakra, the violet one? What does that represent?'

'The seventh or crown chakra is the most important of all. The sixth chakra allows one to glimpse the immortal, eternal and infinite. But the seventh chakra allows one to become all-knowing, like a god. The crown chakra is the major portal through which all energy is channelled and dispersed to the other chakras. Sometimes called the God Source, it's related to pure consciousness and is strongly associated with death. Located at the top centre of the head, in the exact same place as the soft spot on a newborn baby's head, it's the portal through which all our life energy flows in at birth and out at death. If the sixth chakra is the eye or lens into the spirit world then the violet crown chakra is the doorway.'

He pointed to the tapestry. 'Note the thicker silver cord linking the bold and shadow figures. What people term out-of-body or near-death experiences, we call astral travelling, whereby we inhabit our astral body and leave our carnal shell. When this happens the astral body remains tethered to its physical self by the silver cord linked to the crown chakra. This is our lifeline to our carnal body just as our umbilical cord was our lifeline to our mother's body before birth. Once it's broken we can never return to our body and we physically die.'

'You believe all this?'

'I *know* all this. Chakras date back more than four thousand years and the silver cord is mentioned in the Old Testament of the Bible, in Ecclesiastes.' He paused, gave her a knowing smile and gestured back to his bedroom. 'What you witnessed back there wasn't just me having sex. At the peak of physical ecstasy I leave my physical body and become one with the spiritual. The French are right when they call it *le petit mort*. It *is* a little death, a glimpse into eternity.' He laughed at her blushes. 'Don't be embarrassed about what you saw. It's only natural.'

Mortified, she stared fixedly at the tapestry. He spoke with such conviction it was hard to evaluate what he was saying rationally. His talk of life energy leaving the body at death was bizarrely reminiscent of Samantha's theory of archaeosonics. 'Did *I* believe in this before I lost my memory?'

'*All* the Indigo Family knows this to be true. How else do you explain your gifts? Unlike most people out there in the world, with auras at the bottom of the chakra scale, most Indigo Family members are blue or higher and possess some synergistic extra sense.' He pointed at the dot on her forehead, then at the one on his. '*Our* auras are higher still. We go beyond indigo. Our gifts and potential are exceptional.' He smiled. 'Yours even more than mine.'

She was about to broach the subject of her mother when the blonde suddenly appeared and whispered urgently in Delaney's ear, causing his face to darken with anger. He fingered the amethyst set in the ankh hanging around his neck. 'Are you sure, Zara?' he said. His frown intensified as he listened to her whispered response. 'Sorry,

231

Sorcha, I must go. I'll leave you in Zara's capable hands.' Showered and dressed in her indigo robe, Zara looked even younger than when she'd been in bed with her father. Sorcha suppressed a shudder, trying to purge the image from her head. 'Make Sorcha breakfast, Zara, then show her around,' Delaney said. He glanced meaningfully at the blonde. 'As we discussed.'

She nodded. 'I understand.' As Delaney hurried away, Zara turned to Sorcha and smiled. Despite her youth it was a knowing, patronizing smile. 'I realize you can't remember anything but before you left we were friends.'

Sorcha looked hard at the girl, trying to recognize her. 'Good friends?'

'*Best* friends.'

Sorcha smiled blankly at the stranger. If she had hoped that returning here would instantly ignite old memories, she had been mistaken. If anything, watching her father have sex, hearing him talk about his beliefs, and discovering that this strange child-woman had once been her best friend made her feel even further away from the person she had once been.

CHAPTER THIRTY-EIGHT

Unlike at Tranquil Waters where nobody had known her, everyone in the settlement treated Sorcha with a disconcerting blend of reverence, familiarity and expectancy. It was unnerving being in a place where everyone knew her better than she knew herself. Even the disciplined schoolchildren meditating in neat rows greeted her as if she were a celebrity.

'Why are they meditating?' Sorcha asked Zara as the young blonde showed her round.

'They're learning to focus their energy through their chakras. If they balance and clear the chakras, energy can flow freely between their physical and astral bodies. You used to understand this better than anyone.'

They passed a circle of women sitting in the shade of a large tree. Deva sat in the middle, cradling her baby. Sorcha watched as she kissed the infant then laid it on the ground, stood and walked out of the circle. Immediately she left, the others closed the circle, took the baby in their arms and dabbed an indigo dot on its forehead. 'What's happening there?'

'All neonates are born pale indigo and remain so for the first month. Then they become the colour they're destined to be. The Seer's Wives can only keep their babies for this crucial first month. Then, once the infant's colour becomes apparent, they must surrender their baby to the other mothers in the settlement, or surrender their position as one of his Wives.'

'Why?'

'The Seer's Wives must be totally dedicated to him. Nothing can be allowed to distract them.'

Sorcha watched Deva walk away. She didn't look back at her child. Her face was devoid of any expression. 'It's very cruel. She must be devastated?'

Zara frowned. 'Why? Deva's proud that her baby's a true indigo and, although the others will look after the child, she'll see it whenever she wants to. We're all family here.'

'Was my mother one of the Seer's Wives?'

'Yes.'

'Was I given away?'

'No.'

'Why not?'

'You weren't born an indigo.'

Sorcha frowned. 'You said all children were born indigo.'

'Unless they're beyond indigo.' She pointed to the dot on Sorcha's forehead. 'You were born a violet. Very rare.'

Passing the corral, Sorcha was drawn to the horses. A beautiful chestnut stallion came over and nuzzled her hand. Sorcha felt an immediate bond. 'Can I ride?'

Zara laughed. 'Of course you can. You're an excellent rider. You love horses. You love everything about this place. I still can't understand why you left. The Seer has such plans for you.' Her incredulous tone made it clear to Sorcha that the girl thought that by leaving she had been both ungrateful and unfathomably stupid. Zara strode on and beckoned her to follow. 'Come, let me show you the Great Hall where everyone gathers for meditation and family meetings.'

Sorcha followed her to a vast barn in the centre of the settlement. Painted on each of the large double doors were the same twin figures depicted on the tapestry in her father's quarters, complete with the seven coloured chakras running up their spines. The hall was abuzz with people preparing chairs and tables, and arranging flowers. She noticed children helping. Unlike the children in the school, who were all indigo, they were a selection of

234

what her father had called 'the lower colours'.

'Why aren't they in school with the others?'

Zara frowned at the question, like the answer was obvious. 'They're more useful here.' Then she smiled, as if remembering that Sorcha no longer knew the most simple and obvious things. 'Don't feel sorry for sub-indigos. We treat them well, much better than their kind treat us outside the settlement. Out there sub-indigos are in the majority and because they fear us they try to destroy us.'

'Why do you say that?'

Zara sighed as if talking to a slow child. '*Everyone* knows it. The Seer told us. Why else would he create this retreat? So our kind can develop our gifts safely and get ready to take our place in the world.'

As Sorcha processed this she watched the activity around her. 'What's everyone doing?'

'Preparing for Esbat.' Zara sighed again. 'I suppose you don't remember that either? Esbat's the monthly gathering that occurs every full moon when the veil between the sensory and the spiritual world is thinnest. First we fast, then we meditate, focusing our life energy on reaching beyond our base physical senses to experience the spiritual. Finally, we feast and celebrate until our physical hunger is sated. Each Esbat the Seer selects two members to wear the white robe and assist his Great Work. It's always been a sacred time but this Esbat will be even more special than usual.'

'Why?'

'Because *you* have returned.' In Zara's eyes and tone Sorcha detected jealousy. 'The Seer values you above all of us. He says that with you by his side he can now move closer to completing the Great Work.'

'The Great Work?'

'The Seer's lifelong quest to reach beyond the physical world and discover the path to the spiritual realm. He's already helped many to travel to the astral plane and soon—' Zara stopped abruptly and looked down as if she'd already said too much. 'Only the Seer can tell you about the Great Work. All will become clear on Esbat.' As Zara led her around the hall, everyone stopped what they were doing and turned to her. 'Do you like it?' Zara asked, pointing to a ten-foot-tall floral display above the raised dais at the far end of the hall: two pillars of violet flowers met in an arch of white and yellow blooms.

'It's beautiful,' said Sorcha. 'Does it represent something?'

Before Zara could reply, the woman with plaited greying hair and hoop earrings Sorcha had noticed at the welcoming feast the previous night stepped forward and embraced her. 'Sorcha, I'm so glad to see you again.' She smelled of lavender and had an indigo spot on her forehead but didn't wear one of the indigo tunics or robes that appeared to indicate a position of power and trust.

'Remember what the Seer told us, Eve,' Zara said curtly, trying to pull her away. 'She's lost her memory. She doesn't know who you are.'

Ignoring Zara, the woman embraced Sorcha tighter and looked deep into her eyes. 'My name's Eve. I knew your mother from the old days, when the Indigo Family lived in California. We were friends.' She pressed her face so close that the steel of her hoop earrings felt cold against Sorcha's

236

cheek. Then, so quickly and quietly that Sorcha wasn't even sure she had heard her, the woman whispered urgently in her ear: 'Be careful. Trust no one.' Then the woman stepped back as if nothing had happened. 'Welcome back.'

Before Sorcha could respond, Zara was pulling her away from the woman. 'Come,' she said. 'Let's get some air.' As she led her out Zara turned to her. 'You should steer clear of Eve. She likes to stir up trouble.'

Sorcha turned back to the woman. 'Who is she?'

'Eve's one of the original members of the Indigo Family. The old ones think they're special because they were members before the Seer came,' Zara said. 'They mutter how everything was better in the old days. But it wasn't. They're confused and forget their place.'

Eve didn't look or sound confused, thought Sorcha, wondering what to make of the woman's whispered warning. Why should she be careful? Who should she not trust? As she left the barn she saw men erecting an avenue of torches on each side of the path leading to the looming tower. She headed towards it.

'Where are you going?' Zara demanded.

Sorcha pointed upwards. 'The tower's one of the few things I can remember. Where's the entrance?'

'There are two. One's at the end of this path, the other's in the enclosed walkway connecting the tower with the Seer's quarters. Both are locked. You can only enter the Observatory by permission of the Seer and only a select few are summoned.' From the pride in Zara's voice she had clearly been one of the few. Sorcha suspected that she too had been inside, at least once in the past.

'The Observatory?'

'It's where the Seer labours on the Great Work.'

'How? What's inside?'

Zara unconsciously stroked her belly and a secret smile creased her lips. 'No one's allowed to speak of what they experience in there.'

It was becoming evident to Sorcha that it wasn't only her memories that were being withheld from her. She needed some time on her own to think through what to do—and to consider Eve's warning. At that moment a bell rang. With Pavlovian immediacy everyone stopped what they were doing and moved towards a large barn behind the Great Hall. 'Lunchtime,' said Zara. 'Come, let's go to the refectory.'

'It's OK. I'm not hungry.'

Zara frowned. 'But it's the lunch bell. You have to have lunch when the bell rings.'

'You go, Zara. Thanks for all your help, but I think I'll wander round by myself for a while.' Without waiting for a response, she veered off the path towards the looming trees covering the rise at the back of the settlement. She came to a large wooden shed, slightly removed from the rest of the buildings, and detected a cloying, oddly familiar smell. There was sawdust and blood on the stone path leading to the door and through one of the windows she glimpsed carcasses hanging on hooks. It was evidently a slaughterhouse and the buzzing of flies caused splashes of yellow and red to shimmer before her eyes. She put a hand over her mouth and walked quickly on until she passed a sign forbidding entry into the forest. She considered ignoring it but saw Zara coming after her and headed back towards the bridge. It would feel good to get out of the settlement for a while. Spying Zara out of the corner of her eye she walked faster. Before Sorcha could step on the bridge, however, one of the indigo-clad men from the gatehouse blocked her path.

'I'm sorry, but the Seer wants you to stay within the settlement until after Esbat.'

'Why?'

'For your own safety.'

'My safety? I don't understand.'

'Come,' said Zara, breathlessly, gripping her arm and leading her back. 'The Seer is not to be questioned.'

'I'm going to damn well question him,' Sorcha said. She pulled her arm out of Zara's grip and headed off in the direction of his quarters. 'I'm going to ask him what the hell's going on.'

'But he's the Seer.'

'He's also my father.'

'He's father to us all.'

She shuddered when she thought of what Zara and the other two women had been doing with Delaney earlier. 'Please, Zara, go and have lunch and leave me alone for a while.'

'But I'm supposed to stay with you all day.'

'Do you want me to tell the Seer that you've been unhelpful?'

A mix of fear and anger flickered in Zara's blank eyes and Sorcha felt a cruel satisfaction. She was beginning to think that maybe there was no mystery about why she'd left the settlement. Maybe she'd just got sick of the stifling rules and everyone's unquestioning obedience to her father. Maybe that was why Eve, her mother's friend, had warned her to trust no one. As she entered

Delaney's cabin, she glanced back and saw Zara still standing by the bridge. Inside, she could find no sign of her father. She considered waiting in her room but was too restless. Beyond the bedrooms she found a long corridor with a single door at the far end. She walked towards it and tried the handle. The door was locked with an electronic keypad and she assumed she was in the enclosed walkway connecting her father's cabin to the Observatory.

Going out the main door of the cabin, she saw that her assumption was correct and headed for the stone tower. Up close, looking up the windowless white walls was like looking up a sheer cliff face. With its staring eye the structure resembled an oversized lighthouse or a storage silo but there was no crane, or access, except the two doors on the ground floor. The Observatory, as Zara had called it, looked eerily familiar to Sorcha and she wondered what its real function could be.

Walking around the base she discovered the second door, also locked with an electronic keypad. Embedded in its dark wood was another mosaic. Unlike the eye at the top of the tower, this was small, circular and fashioned from rough fragments of plaster, amethyst, brick and concrete. Intrigued, she brushed her fingers over the embedded pieces. Instantly, she pulled her hand away, as if needle-sharp splinters had impaled her fingers. Since arriving at the settlement she had sensed nothing unusual but touching those fragments of embedded rubble felt like she had been exposed to the splintered shards of numerous death echoes. Even as she wondered what the mosaic pieces could be, the experience strengthened her conviction that the tower was key to unlocking her own memories.

240

She pressed a hand to the tower's stone walls but detected nothing. Then she registered a sound. Someone was walking towards the door, towards her.

Panicked, she retreated around the curve of the wall, away from the footsteps. Even though she had done nothing wrong she was nervous of being discovered snooping around the forbidden tower. As she listened to her heart thumping in her chest, watching colours dance before her eyes, she realized she'd only been back a day and was already intimidated by the place and its rules. Pressing herself against the wall, she heard someone push four buttons on the keypad. Each pushed button made a unique tone, which flashed a distinctive colour before her eyes. She heard the door open and was curious who could be missing lunch and entering the secret observatory. Thinking it might be her father she peered around the wall, ready to confront him. But the door was already closing, hiding whoever had stepped inside.

As she stepped away from the tower a hand grabbed her shoulder and pulled her back. Panicked, she turned and saw Eve pressed against the wall, holding a finger to her lips. 'Sssh. If we're seen talking together it could put us both in danger. Be careful, Sorcha. Nothing is what it seems.'

'I don't understand,' Sorcha hissed, heart pumping in her chest. 'What do you mean?'

'We can't talk here. Not now. The Seer has ears and eyes everywhere. Be outside the Great Hall at midnight and I'll tell you everything I know. I must go to lunch now before I'm missed. Wait five minutes before you follow me.'

Then she was gone.

Sorcha stood frozen for some moments, glancing nervously around the deserted settlement, paranoid that she was being watched. Her mouth felt dry and her hands were shaking. She had returned here because she thought it was safe, her home, but now everything about this idyllic place had taken on a new, sinister cast. Unnerved, she hurried back to her room, closed the door and collapsed on the bed. As she lay there she looked out at the looming tower, then at the picture of her mother, and wished Nathan Fox was here to guide her. Suddenly, she was no longer scared of whether her memory would return but of what she might remember when it did.

CHAPTER THIRTY-NINE

Where the hell is it?' Nathan Fox cursed in the gloom as he checked the coordinates on his hand-held Global Positioning System. Although they matched the coordinates Connor Delaney had emailed him earlier, there was no sign of Regan Delaney's settlement. In the gathering dusk there was no sign of anything much—except trees. Connor had warned him that his brother's domain was extensive and the coordinates for the settlement might not be precise but Fox had assumed they would get him closer than this.

Leaving Portland early this morning, armed with the coordinates, a satellite GPS and a map downloaded from Google Earth, Fox had reassured Samantha it would take him only a couple of days to find the cult, alert Sorcha about the killer, and then return—hopefully with her. Although he had briefed his aunt to tell Jordache to send out a search party if he wasn't back after the weekend, he had felt confident. Even after Jordache had warned him against going and Professor Fullelove had admonished him for being unprofessional and taking unplanned leave. He didn't feel confident now, though. His phone had stopped working hours ago and he was stuck in a forest of giant sequoias, in the middle of the night with only the cry of owls for company. He felt tired, lost and hungry. And every muscle in his thighs and buttocks ached.

His car had got him as far as the tiny town of Road's End, where the road had literally ended. The townspeople had warned him to stay clear of the Indigo Family: 'People go missing round those parts.' Taking his car as security, they had loaned him a horse, a black gelding, complete with a saddlebag of basic supplies and a hunting rifle, which fitted snugly in the saddle holster. Fox soon discovered that his mount, unlike the calm horse he had ridden at Connor Delaney's, was easily startled and as temperamental as a Ferrari.

Following the GPS on the roads was one thing but off-road was a different story. Regardless of the GPS instructions, he could only go where the terrain—and the horse—let him, which was rarely in a straight line. Gripping tightly, he had crossed rivers, traversed ravines and cut through forests to get here. But *here* wasn't yet where he wanted to be. And it was getting dark.

The skittish horse seemed even more jumpy in the forest and Fox shared his unease. He unconsciously touched the butt of the hunting rifle, reassured by its presence. In the fading light there was something prehistoric about the monumental ferns and massive trees that made him feel an unwelcome interloper. It also reminded Fox of the first time he had seen giant sequoias in Oregon, the day his parents and sister had been murdered. His greatest unease, however, derived from being lost. The coordinates Connor Delaney had given him covered such a wide area, he began to fear that he would never find not only the settlement but also the way out of the damn forest.

'At least it isn't raining,' he muttered as he reached a wide, circular clearing. Ahead, hidden among the ferns, was a small wooden hut, which encouraged him to think he was getting close. In this wilderness it could only belong to Delaney or his people. Perhaps it was a hunting base. Suddenly, the horse reared up. As Fox calmed the spooked animal he looked down. The earth was softer and more churned up than elsewhere in the forest, and Fox assumed the horse had momentarily lost its footing.

Stiff and aching, he dismounted and tied the horse to a tree. He tried the hut door but it was locked. Looking up beyond the looming trees he saw the first stars appear in the evening sky. It would be dark soon so he decided to pitch camp for the night. He fed and watered the horse, heated some stew and beans on a small Primus stove, then rolled out his sleeping bag on the soft ground. As he manoeuvred his aching body into the bag the forest was surprisingly noisy and he feared he wouldn't sleep. He looked up at the moon. Almost full, it seemed to hang in the night sky like an overripe fruit.

He wondered what reception he'd get tomorrow,

assuming he found Sorcha. He had no desire to visit Delaney and his cult tomorrow, let alone appear uninvited and without warning. He did, however, find the prospect of shaking up the self-absorbed Delaney and his people by telling them they had a killer in their midst perversely satisfying. Before he could ponder this more, his exhausted body overruled his racing mind and he fell fast asleep.

CHAPTER FORTY

That night, the Wives served Sorcha and her father a sumptuous supper in his private quarters. As they poured purple-red wine into Sorcha's glass and filled her plate with roast chicken, potatoes, zucchini and beans—all from the settlement, her father assured her—she sensed the Wives watching her. Their constant scrutiny heightened her unease. Was she among friends and family or supping with her enemies? Eve had told her to trust no one but did that include her own father and his women? The wine tasted richer and headier than the red she had drunk at Samantha's. As she sipped it she welcomed its calming effect. 'Tell me about my mother.'

Delaney looked up from his food. Zara leaned towards him. 'Eve approached Sorcha and made a nuisance of herself. She told Sorcha she was a friend of Aurora.'

'She didn't make a nuisance of herself,' Sorcha said. 'She greeted me.'

'Zara, you're being disrespectful,' Delaney scolded the blonde, who reddened. 'Eve has been with the family from the beginning. She was one

245

of the pioneers.' He turned to Sorcha. 'Eve was indeed a good friend of your mother's. She and Aurora were with the Indigo Family back in the old days, in California.'

'Before you joined?'

He nodded. 'It was Aurora who introduced me to the family. Your mother changed my life. She revealed to me my potential and my destiny. And when I brought the family to Oregon she was by my side. My strongest ally.'

'What was she like?'

He smiled. 'Very like you. Brave, gifted and beautiful.' He looked suddenly wistful. 'And headstrong.' He sipped his wine and gestured to her locket. 'She always kept you close to her heart, Sorcha. Never left your side when you were a child. Wouldn't let any of the others care for you. She was protective right up to the end.'

'How did she die?'

'An aneurysm. It was very sudden.' He frowned, as if unaccustomed to questions, picked up the earthenware carafe and poured her more wine. 'What did you see today, Sorcha?'

'Not much. I wasn't allowed to leave the settlement.'

He smiled. 'It's for your safety, Sorcha. I lost you once. I don't want to lose you again. Things will be different after Esbat.'

'What the hell is this Esbat everyone keeps talking about?'

'You'll experience it for yourself in two days' time. Did you see anything that jogged your memory today?' He turned to Zara. 'You did show her round the settlement?'

'I tried,' Zara said defensively. 'Until she insisted

on looking around by herself.'

'I seem to remember the tower,' Sorcha said, sipping more wine. 'I don't know why but I feel it's key to regaining my memory. What happens inside? What function does it serve for the Great Work?' She sensed the women stiffen.

'The Great Work?' said Delaney, glancing at Zara. 'What have you told her of the Great Work?'

'She told me nothing,' said Sorcha. 'She said I had to ask the Seer. You.'

Delaney nodded. 'It's better I show you rather than tell you.'

'When?'

'When the time's right, Sorcha,' chided Zara.

Sorcha ignored her. 'Will you at least tell me how it concerns me?'

Delaney smiled. 'It concerns us all.'

'You're very inquisitive,' said Maria, the pregnant redhead, pointedly.

'You should know better than to question the Seer,' said Deva. The brunette had made no mention of her baby since surrendering it that morning.

Delaney smiled at his Wives. 'It's all right. Sorcha has no memory. She needs to ask her questions.' He turned to her. 'Be patient, Sorcha. I promise everything will become clearer on Esbat. It's only two days away.'

As the evening wore on, any further questions were parried with the same promise that all would be revealed on Esbat. After supper, Sorcha excused herself and went to her room. The wine had made her drowsy but she made herself stay awake by walking around the room, waiting for the others to retire. When it was quiet she climbed out of her bedroom window and made her way to the Great Hall. The moon was almost full and the clear night sky so luminous with stars that she kept to the shadows. She reached the main doors of the hall twelve minutes before her midnight rendezvous with Eve. She could see light in the gatehouse by the bridge but otherwise the deserted settlement appeared to be asleep. She was anxious about what Eve might tell her but as she waited in the balmy air her drowsiness overcame her nerves. Sitting on the soft grass, she leaned back against the wall and allowed her eyes to close.

She woke with a start, mouth dry, head aching. Eve was standing over her, shaking her gently. 'Sorry I'm late,' she whispered, 'but I wanted to be sure I wasn't followed. Come.' She pulled Sorcha gently to her feet and led her to the edge of the forest at the back of the settlement. When they were obscured by foliage she sat down on the grass. 'This will do. The Seer has eyes everywhere but we should be hidden from your father and his Purple Powers here.'

'Purple Powers?'

'It's what us old-timers call the Seer's inner circle—his so-called Watchers. The ones who wear the purple robes and tunics, the high-level pure indigos who are totally devoted to the Seer.'

'I thought everyone here was devoted to my father.'

'They are. They *worship* him. But the Purple Powers are his eyes and ears.'

Sorcha saw that Eve's aura was pure indigo. 'Your aura's high level and you're a senior member of the family. Why aren't you a Watcher?'

She laughed without humour. 'Me a Purple

Power? I ask too many questions.' She felt in her pockets and extracted a small colour photograph. 'First of all, let me show you this. It's a picture of your mother and you. Take it. I have a copy.' As Sorcha stared at the smiling woman in the picture, noting the eyes, cheekbones and hair, the oddly familiar face stirred a deep sadness within her. 'I took it a few days after the Indigo Family moved here. She was very happy then.'

'What was she like?'

'What I remember most about her was how full of life she was. She always saw the best in people.' Her voice hardened and she checked her watch. 'Sorcha, we haven't much time and you need to understand what you've come back to. In the past you've always been happy here but things changed recently and just before you left something happened that made you run away.'

'What?'

'I don't know. You couldn't tell me. You were too upset and there wasn't time.' She pointed to the tower. 'I've been concerned for some time about the darker aspects of the Seer's Great Work and on the day you fled I saw you running out of there, very upset. Something happened in there that made you run. Something that frightened you.'

'What exactly is his Great Work?'

A sigh. 'It's hard to define. It's been evolving over time, becoming ever more ambitious. Before Aurora introduced your father to the Indigo Family, all we wanted was a place where indigos could gather, explore their sensory gifts and use their third eye to get in touch with their spiritual side. But after the Seer joined he took control and pushed the boundaries. He wanted us to recapture

249

the golden age of our ancestors, the Nephilim, the fallen angels. From the beginning, he lay with all the purest indigo women. He once told Aurora that he loved her above all others but needed to breed a race of angels that could straddle this world and the next. You may have noticed how many of the children resemble him.'

'What did my mother think of this?'

'Aurora fought him at first but after you were born she had complications and bore no more healthy children. Aurora decided then it would be selfish not to allow the Seer to further his divine bloodline. She worshipped your father. She believed totally in his ability to leave his body and contact the other side. She thought he was a throwback to the Grigori—the watcher angels who slept with human women and created the Nephilim. So she accepted his other Wives and consoled herself that she was supporting him while he led us on a great journey.

'When he first moved us to Oregon, we were all excited to be in this beautiful and bountiful place. He had led us to a promised land in this world and we believed he would soon lead us to one in the next. He provided the funds that allowed us all to build the settlement. When he began building his tower, however, he brought everything in from outside: craftsmen, stone and special materials. He told no one what it was for. Only that it would assist his Great Work, help him peer through the veil and observe the other side. We discovered whatever we could by watching its construction.'

'What did you find out?'

'Not a lot. It has several floors, no windows and a spiral staircase running up the centre. The walls are constructed of two layers. The outer skin is basic stone, the inner wall inlaid with amethyst shipped in from Brazil. And there's a layer of what looks like black rubber between them.'

'Rubber?'

'I don't know what it's for. Insulation? Damp? He called it his observatory and as it grew ever higher, so his own presence loomed larger over us. He introduced stricter rules. He began segregating sub-indigos from indigos, and adopting customs from other religions. He forbade entry into the forest. He introduced the Watchers, robes and a hierarchy. He made everything more ritualized. Esbat was once just a feast night for drawing down the moon, celebrated by Wiccans, but he made it into a formal ceremony, in which two white-robed assistants called Pathfinders were selected to accompany him to the tower and help him contact the other side. He became obsessed with astral travelling—out-of-body experiences—and contacting the spiritual realm.'

'How did my mother feel about this, since she'd invited him into the Indigo Family?'

'At first, she had no problem with him reforming the family. We needed leadership and he gave it. But when the tower was complete, he became more autocratic and secretive and your mother grew increasingly concerned about what the tower was for. She never doubted his powers but began to doubt his motives. She researched the Grigori and the Nephilim and discovered that many sources regarded them as being not so much benign angels as fierce demons. Your mother became worried about what the Seer was doing in there. Especially when some of the Pathfinders summoned to the

251

tower didn't return.'

'What happened to them?'

A shrug. 'He says some left the commune on a mission for the Great Work. He claims to have guided others to the spiritual realm where they chose to remain.'

Sorcha remembered Zara saying something similar. 'What do you mean, guided them to the spiritual realm?'

'The Seer believes his astral body—what some call the soul—can leave its physical shell. Anchored to his physical body by the silver cord attached to his crown chakra, he can travel the astral plane in search of the spiritual realm. He claims to be able to take those less gifted with him. And if they choose to sever the silver cord and stay in the astral plane, then so be it. It's a great honour and privilege to be chosen. Each Esbat everyone desperately wants to be summoned to the tower. Those that are selected and return are forbidden to talk of what they experience there.' Eve sighed. 'Sadly, just after your mother expressed her concerns to me, she got ill.'

'My father said she had an aneurysm.'

'He told me that, too. He said she got ill so he took her to the tower to guide her to the other side. I never saw her again. Her death worried me, for many reasons, but I *really* began to worry when your father started involving *you* in his Great Work. Until recently you were left alone but your mother always worried that your father would involve you sooner or later.'

'Why?'

Eve smiled and stroked Sorcha's hair. 'Because you're special—*really* special. I have your mother's

252

gift for seeing auras but you have *all* the gifts of the third eye. Your father's aura is violet with an indigo tinge—almost unique—but yours is purer still: violet with a white border.'

'White?'

'If you combine the major colours you get white light. A pure white aura is the purest of all. Some call it the divine aura—a halo. Although the Seer sired a number of children with other pure indigos, Aurora was the only woman who produced a violet for him and survived the birth. He tried many more times with her but after her first pregnancy—which produced you—all her other babies were stillborn. In the past his focus on the Great Work has been elsewhere but recently he's become convinced you're the key to completing it.'

'Why?'

Eve shook her head. 'All I know is that something about your father's work, and your role in it, made you leave—made you run for your life. You may have lost your memory but whatever frightened you then hasn't gone away. In fact I think it's going to happen at Esbat, the day after tomorrow.'

'So what do I do?'

'You have two choices. One, you confront your father. Make him tell you what he's doing. His whole authority and status as the Seer is based on his aura. Yours is purer than his. You have the power to challenge him.' She paused. 'Two, you leave again. Get away from here, as far as you can, and never come back. Whichever you choose, I'll support and help you.' Sorcha heard a noise, which made Eve start like a panicked deer and stand up. 'It'll be dawn soon. I must get back.' She bent and

253

kissed Sorcha on the cheek. 'If you do confront your father, ask him about Kaidan.'

'Who?'

'His mother died in childbirth but he's the only other violet your father sired. Aurora said the Seer always saw Kaidan as the key to creating his brave new world. Ask your father why he's suddenly shifted his attention from Kaidan to you. What's changed? I must go.' Eve patted her shoulder then hurried into the night.

'Wait,' Sorcha hissed. As she watched Eve disappear, her mind raced with questions. Why had she run away before? Should she run away again? Or should she stay and confront her father? And who the hell was Kaidan? God, she wished Nathan Fox was here now to help her decide the best thing to do.

CHAPTER FORTY-ONE

Eve hurried back to her cabin, anxious not to be seen. The Seer and his Watchers had already marked her out as a troublemaker and she didn't know how they would react if they knew she had been talking with Sorcha. Seeing Aurora's daughter again had filled her with both fear and hope: fear that Sorcha might be in danger, and hope that in coming back here with no preconceptions, free of her father's brainwashing, she would see the Indigo Family for what it was. As Eve reached for the door of her cabin she allowed herself to feel optimistic. If Sorcha stayed and confronted her father, then her gifts and courage could change things, help restore the family to its original, simpler values.

Suddenly, a figure appeared out of the shadows and stepped in front of her. When the moonlight revealed his face Eve froze. She started to speak: 'What are you—?' Before she could say more he clamped a hand over her mouth and she felt a needle prick her arm. Her legs buckled beneath her and as she fell, he threw her over his shoulder. She tried to struggle and cry for help but the only muscle in her body that appeared to be working was the heart beating frantically in her breast. As he carried her away from the cabin into the shadows, she tried to regain her bearings, wondering where he was taking her. Her panic swelled as he changed direction and carried her towards the looming tower, its conical helm silhouetted against the moon like a black spearhead aimed at heaven.

*   *   *

Making her way back to her cabin, Sorcha had got as far as the Great Hall when two Watchers appeared from the gatehouse by the bridge and began walking towards her. She stopped in the shadows, holding her breath, aware that dawn was coming and it was getting lighter. When they turned and walked back to the bridge, she waited for them to re-enter the gatehouse. Just as she was about to break cover and run across the moonlit ground she heard someone coming from the cabins to her left. Holding her breath, she pressed herself flat against the timber walls and peered round the corner of the Great Hall. A man passed within yards of her. He was carrying something large over his right shoulder. At first she thought it was a sack or a rug. Then he stepped into the moonlight and she realized it was a body.

As she released her breath, she detected a faint malodour in the night air, then it was gone. Blood pounding in her temples, Sorcha peered closer. A woman was slung over his shoulder, two limp arms hanging down. Even before she saw the face and hoop earrings she knew it was Eve. Her eyes stared blankly at Sorcha. Dismissing all previous thoughts of fleeing to her cabin, Sorcha followed the man round the wall of the Great Hall, careful to stay concealed. When he turned out of sight, she ran and peered round the corner, almost tripping over the steps to the main doors. Ahead she could see the meandering path and knew instinctively where he was heading. Moving as quietly and inconspicuously as possible, she followed. When he reached the tower he stopped and laid Eve on the ground. Pausing by the door, he turned his head to look behind him and she saw his face in the moonlight. The shock was so great she had to press a hand over her mouth to stop herself crying out. She had to be mistaken. It couldn't be *him*.

How could the intruder who had tried to abduct her in Portland be here? Why was the killer she had glimpsed in the death echoes of the three crime scenes taking Eve to the locked Observatory? She remembered back to the night at Tranquil Waters, when he had slung *her* over his shoulder, as drugged and helpless as Eve. Fox had saved her then. But he wasn't here to help her now.

Sorcha considered running to her father for help. He controlled this place. He could stop this happening. But there wasn't time. She searched the ground beneath the trees and picked up a sturdy

256

branch, then broke cover and ran to the tower. As the man concentrated on the keypad she raised the branch and struck him as hard as she could over the head. 'Leave her alone,' she shouted. The wood snapped like tinder on his skull and the man turned to her, surprised but unhurt. He rubbed his head and frowned. Then he pushed her to the ground and jumped on her, winding her. His smell filled her nostrils. She punched and kicked him but he was too strong. 'Help,' she cried. 'Help.'

As if in response to her cries, she heard a harsh voice bark, 'Get off her.' Then a stinging smack as a riding crop swished through the air and struck her attacker across the back. It came down again two more times. 'Get off her.' The guttural voice was so thick with fury she didn't recognize it at first. Then she looked up and saw the Seer standing over her, raining blows down on her attacker. He had at least four Watchers with him. 'Get him off her and bring him inside. Bring Eve in too.' Relief and gratitude flooded through her as her father reached down and pulled her to her feet. He had saved her. She was safe. She tried to thank him but he turned away, scowling.

The Watchers took them into the Seer's private quarters. They laid Eve on the couch in the main chamber and Sorcha held her hand, wondering how long it would take for the drug to wear off. The Watchers left the killer standing by the tapestry. He looked even larger in the confines of the room. 'Leave us,' said the Seer.

'But he's dangerous,' she said as the Watchers left. 'He's a murderer.'

Ignoring her, Delaney focused on the big man. 'What the *fuck* were you doing?' he snarled. There

257

was a sudden flurry of movement as his arm lashed out with the riding crop again. The man showed no pain as he parried the blow with his palms.

'You haven't hit me since I was a child,' he said, impassively.

'You haven't disobeyed me since you were a child,' spat her father. 'Can't you do anything right? I expressly ordered you not to do anything in the city that could bring the children of men back here, but still you disobeyed me. First you killed those men. Why? For a cheap thrill? Then you tried to reclaim Sorcha by force. *Twice*. Now you do this. You were supposed to be discreet, damnit. Esbat is only a day away. You know nothing must jeopardize the Great Work.'

'Nothing *will*,' the big man said. 'As always, I've done this only because you demanded it of me. Everything is in place for the Great Work. I didn't know Sorcha had seen me with Eve until she attacked me. I had to defend myself.'

Sorcha stared at Delaney, too stunned to process what she was hearing. 'You know him?' she demanded, hating the tremor in her voice. When she had first lost her memory she had felt alone and abandoned but this betrayal by her own father, the one man she thought she could trust, was worse. 'He's the killer who murdered those men in Portland and tried to abduct me—and you *know* him?'

Delaney frowned. 'Of course I know him,' he said. 'So do you. He was supposed to keep a low profile until after Esbat but Eve forgot the golden rule—loyalty to the family—and had to be dealt with.'

She looked down at Eve's motionless body and

258

blank eyes. 'What are you going to do to her?'

'Don't worry about her. If Kaidan had been more discreet we wouldn't be having this conversation.'

'Kaidan?' Sorcha said. It was the name Eve had mentioned.

A cruel smile curled her father's lips. 'You won't remember, of course, but Kaidan's your half-brother.'

Sorcha's rage turned to horror. 'He's a killer. How can he be my half-brother?' A cold realization swept through her. 'Is he why I ran away?'

'Kaidan wasn't meant to kill anyone. He was only supposed to find you.'

'He tried to kill me.'

Kaidan shook his head. 'Not true. If I'd wanted to kill you, you'd be dead.' He turned back to Delaney. 'You have no cause to be angry. Now you've got Sorcha back you can use her to take your Great Work to the next stage.'

'Use me for what?' Sorcha demanded. She turned to the exit and saw the three Wives blocking the doorway. 'What did you bring me back for? Why do you need me?'

Her father frowned, eyes cold and dismissive. 'Stop asking stupid questions, Sorcha. We all have sacrifices to make and a destiny to fulfil. You ran from yours once. You won't do it again.' He turned back to her half-brother, who was heading for the door. 'Don't walk out on me, Kaidan. I haven't finished with you yet.'

'Haven't you?' Kaidan retorted. 'Sorcha's the important one now, the *special* one. Well, you've got her back. Nothing stands in your way. Don't worry, I'll still do my duty at Esbat.'

'Will you?' Delaney taunted him. 'You failed last

time. How do I know you'll succeed this time?'

For the first time Kaidan's cold eyes flashed with anger. 'I've always done everything you've asked of me. I've only ever failed you *once*. It won't happen again.' At that moment, the dawn light seeping in through the windows caught Kaidan's profile and Sorcha noticed his aura for the first time. Though similar to the Wives', his hue went beyond indigo. She had seen only one other aura like it: her father's—*their* father's.

As the gravity of her predicament sank in, she felt nauseous. One thing was clear: her father hadn't brought her back out of love. She had a futile urge to pick up Eve, push past Kaidan and the Wives and flee, when a man appeared in the doorway.

'I must speak to the Seer,' the Watcher said, breathlessly.

'What is it?' said Delaney.

'You have a visitor.'

Delaney glared accusingly at Kaidan. 'Who have you brought here?'

The Watcher glanced at Sorcha. 'His name's Fox. Dr Nathan Fox. He says it's about her.'

Sorcha's heart soared. Fox had travelled through the wilderness to find her. She was no longer alone. Then she saw the look on her father's face and her elation evaporated.

'What happens now?' said Kaidan.

'I'll tell you *exactly* what happens now.' Her father looked at the Watcher. 'Where's Dr Fox?'

'In the gatehouse.'

'Keep him there. Make him welcome. Tell him I'll be with him shortly.' When the Watcher left, Delaney went to a drawer by the bookcase, pulled out a silver cord with a knot tied in the middle and glanced at the Wives. 'Hold her.' The three women pulled Sorcha away from the couch. Zara clawed at Sorcha's locket, popping open the clasp on the silver chain.

'Give it back to me,' Sorcha demanded. 'That's mine.'

Delaney took the locket from Zara and handed it to Kaidan. 'Put it in the tower for safekeeping.' A cruel smile curled his lips. 'Return it to her mother.'

Sorcha didn't understand. 'She's still in the tower?'

'Your mother will *always* be in the tower.' Delaney laughed, as if at a private joke. 'Don't worry. You'll get your precious locket back after Esbat. If you behave.' Delaney bent down to the helpless Eve, looped the cord around her neck and placed the knot over her windpipe. Staring at Sorcha, eyes cold as the dead, he tightened the garrotte. 'Understand one thing, daughter of mine, I cannot and will not allow anyone to threaten the family or the Great Work.' Sorcha watched the muscles and sinews move in her father's wrists as he pulled the garrotte tighter around Eve's neck, crushing the larynx. Despite the paralysing drug, Eve's legs began to twitch. Her bloodshot eyes bulged in their sockets, her tongue protruded from her mouth and her face turned puce. Horrified, Sorcha tried to run to her but the Wives restrained her, their fingers digging into her arms. 'To protect the family and stop this fool doctor meddling in our business, you will do exactly as I say, Sorcha,' her father said with chilling calm. He pulled the garrotte one last time and Eve stopped twitching. 'Do you understand me?'

Sorcha nodded, not trusting herself to speak.

CHAPTER FORTY-TWO

Two hours earlier

Fox woke before dawn, his body stiff and aching. The soil in the forest clearing, which had seemed so soft and welcoming when he had fallen asleep, had compressed overnight, giving no support to his back or protection from the hard rocks beneath. He felt like he had slept only a few minutes but when he checked his watch, hours had passed. After making some breakfast, he intended to investigate the hut and clearing, but the dawn light was poor, and the horse was evidently spooked by the place and desperate to leave.

When the rising sun revealed a trail through the trees, Fox grimaced with pain, remounted and followed the meandering path downhill. After a few hundred yards he turned a corner and, suddenly, below him through the trees he saw buildings. He reached into the saddlebag and extracted a pair of binoculars. Despite the gloom, the settlement looked larger and more organized than he was expecting, a proper village rather than some hippy commune. Delaney's cult was clearly prosperous and thriving. Though the settlement itself was contained between the forest and the bend of the river its footprint spread further: the flat valley over the river was covered with a patchwork quilt of crop fields and orchards. Watching smoke rise from the cabin chimneys and people emerge to start their daily chores was like witnessing a scene from a bygone century. The only incongruous objects were a large modern generator and a round tower, which, with its conical slate roof and white walls, looked like something from a fairy tale.

He was tempted to continue on the direct path down from the forest and enter the back of the settlement but decided it would be prudent to enter via the main gate and introduce himself. Downstream, the river narrowed and he could see a ford where he could cross, ride round and go in over the bridge. The detour wasn't long and when he saw the signs warning that trespassers would be shot, he was glad he'd taken it. As he approached the bridge two men stepped into his path. Both had indigo dots on their foreheads and wore indigo tunics over their jeans.

'This is private property. Who are you?' said the first man, raising his rifle.

'My name's Fox. Dr Nathan Fox.'

'Get off the horse.'

As Fox dismounted the second man peered at him. 'He's a pure indigo. He's one of us,' the man said, lowering his rifle. 'What are you doing here, brother?'

'I need to speak to Regan Delaney.' Both men looked at him blankly. 'The Seer?' Their faces instantly changed. His horse was led away to be fed and watered and Fox found himself sitting in the gatehouse with a mug of coffee in his hands. After more than an hour's wait he was summoned to a large log cabin next to the tower and ushered into an impressive chamber filled with books. A large tapestry inspired by Leonardo da Vinci's Vitruvian man hung by the fireplace; the coloured chakras

263

running up the spine reminded Fox of diagrams he had seen at medical school. Glancing at the books, he noted that their subjects and titles chimed with what Connor Delaney had told him about his brother. Tomes on religion, science and New Age beliefs dominated. There was even one entitled *Magnum Opus*—the Great Work. Regan Delaney might be deluded but he did his research.

'Dr Fox, what a surprise,' said a familiar voice. Delaney wore a black tunic over dark trousers and sported a violet dot on his forehead. 'Welcome to the Indigo Family. I'm sorry to keep you waiting but you've come at a busy time. Can I get you a coffee or anything?' He extended his hand.

Fox shook it. 'No thank you.'

Delaney gestured to the couch by the fireplace. 'Please, sit.'

'No thanks, I came to speak with Sorcha.'

'Why? She's not your patient any more.'

'I came to warn her. I believe she's in danger.'

The welcoming smile remained on Delaney's face but his hand reached for the ankh around his neck and clutched it tight. 'In danger? From who?'

'The killer in Portland. The one who stapled Sorcha's picture to his victims' faces.'

'The police told me the killer had nothing to do with her.'

'They were mistaken.' Fox told Delaney about his trip to Connor and his insight into the coloured letters on the killer's messages. Then Fox told him about the killer's apparent fixation on both Sorcha and the third eye. Finally, he told him about the sacrificial stone and related his theory that the killer not only shared Sorcha's synaesthesia but also her rare death echo variant. 'I think he knows

Sorcha and is or was a member of your Indigo Family. He may even be here now.'

Delaney frowned. 'This sounds like a police matter. Why aren't they here?'

'They already have a suspect and when I explained my theory, especially about death-echo synaesthesia—'

'They didn't believe you?'

'No.'

'Yet you still came all this way alone to warn Sorcha. I'm impressed with your dedication.' Delaney thought for a moment. 'You visited my brother. Why? To learn more about me and the Indigo Family?'

'Yes.'

'No doubt you were curious to know if Sorcha was returning to a good home.' A teasing smile crossed Delaney's lips. 'You sure you haven't come here now simply to satisfy your curiosity, and see Sorcha again?'

'Like I said. I came to warn her.'

'That there's a killer in our midst?' Delaney sighed. 'Dr Fox, I'm sure you're mistaken. I can't think of a single disaffected member who's left the Indigo Family since we moved here over fifteen years ago. And, apart from Sorcha and me, nobody's set foot outside the settlement in the last few months. Whoever killed those men in Portland had nothing to do with us. To be frank, Dr Fox, I'm more concerned about your arrival upsetting and disturbing Sorcha, just as she's settling down and reclaiming her life. She's perfectly safe here. No family member would wish Sorcha harm.'

'How can you be so sure?'

'She's too important.'

She's too important? It was a strange phrase for a father to use about his daughter. 'She's too important to what? The Great Work? Perhaps one of your people wants to sabotage the Great Work by harming Sorcha?'

Delaney raised an eyebrow. 'You *have* been talking to Connor. That's ridiculous. No one here would want to undermine the Great Work. I'm sorry, but I have to agree with the police. I'm afraid you've had a wasted journey. Sorcha's perfectly safe here. And perfectly happy.'

'What about the killer's death-echo synaesthesia? That can't be a coincidence.'

'There's no proof the killer has any form of the *mothú*, let alone what you call death-echo synaesthesia.'

Fox remembered Connor telling him how his brother had lingered in the bedroom where their father had died. 'What about you, Mr Delaney? Do you share your daughter's death-echo synaesthesia?'

Delaney frowned and again clutched at the amulet around his neck. 'You're not accusing *me* of being the killer, are you?'

Fox noted that Delaney didn't answer his question. 'I just want to speak with Sorcha about my concerns. Let her decide.'

Delaney studied him a moment, then nodded. 'Very well. After you've come all this way the very least we can do is allay your fears.' He headed for the door. 'Come, I'll show you the settlement on the way. Whatever my brother's told you, I want you to see for yourself that Sorcha's in the bosom of her family and safe. All I ask is that you promise to leave after you've spoken with her.'

'And if she chooses to leave with me?'

'Why would she want to leave? Will she be any safer with you?' Delaney smiled. 'It's more likely *you*'ll want to stay with us, Dr Fox. After all, you're one of us, an indigo.'

As he followed Delaney outside, the morning sun was already shining down on the settlement. Seeing it bathed in golden light, Fox had to admit it was hard to imagine evil lurking in this bustling, idyllic retreat from the world. Everyone they passed greeted Delaney with genuine awe and reverence. However deluded he might be, his subjects didn't appear fearful or downtrodden. 'Why is the Great Work so secret?'

'It's not so much secret as private—and sacred.'

'Can you tell me what it is?'

'It's more than just one thing. The Great Work involves a number of stages.' Delaney pointed at the corral. 'Connor must have told you about the horses, the thoroughbreds.'

'Yes.'

'Well, a key part of the Great Work has always been nurturing and perfecting human thoroughbreds.'

'You mean synaesthetes?'

A nod. 'Turquoises, blues, indigos and beyond. From the very beginning, before I joined them, the family have been nurturing those with heightened, synergistic senses. People like you, Dr Fox. When I joined, however, I immediately realized we had to take it further. The world's in a mess because its dominant species is a mess. To protect the future we must look to the past. We need to reach beyond the physical preoccupations and limitations of our base humanity—and rediscover our primal link

267

with the divine.'

Fox frowned. 'Isn't that what all religions try to do?'

'I'm not talking about prayer and some vague promise of an afterlife. I'm talking about using our sensory gifts to explore and inhabit the spiritual realm, now—in my lifetime. In *our* lifetime.'

'Why's Sorcha so important to this?'

'You know how special she is, Dr Fox. You know what she's capable of. She's about as pure a thoroughbred as you can get. Her retrograde amnesia also serves as a powerful metaphor for the Indigo Family. Did my brother tell you about the Nephilim—the progeny of fallen angels and humans—and that all indigos are descended from these hybrids?'

'Connor told me of your beliefs. Yes.'

'Just as Sorcha has lost her memory and forgotten her identity, so most indigos have forgotten theirs. They've forgotten that they're the descendants of angels, with divine blood running in their veins. Only by restoring this genetic memory and lost identity, and accepting that they're *more* than human, can they realize their full potential. Not only to make this world fit for angels, but also to shake off their earthly shackles and regain their connection with the spirit world.'

Fox didn't challenge Delaney's convictions—and delusions. Not only would it be pointless, he saw no reason to antagonize his host and jeopardize his mission. As they passed the tower he noticed the large eye. Glancing back at the horses he remembered what Sorcha had told him of her nightmares. Had her subconscious remembered this place in her dreams? If so, why had it terrified her? 'What's the tower for?'

'It's an observatory.'

Fox looked up at the windowless structure and assumed he was joking. 'A what?'

'A *spiritual* observatory. It helps me look beyond the veil dividing the physical and spirit realms. Its lens doesn't look outward to the stars but inward to the soul.'

'How does it work?'

Delaney shook his head. 'Only the chosen can enter and I doubt *you* would see anything of interest inside.'

As they approached the Great Hall, Fox noticed people engaged in feverish preparations. 'What are they doing?'

Delaney led him through the doors into the building. 'Getting everything ready for tomorrow's feast of Esbat.'

'I thought Esbat was a Wicca ceremony for witches?' One of Fox's patients had been obsessed with the occult and often talked of Esbat.

'It is. We borrow practices from all spiritual traditions. Esbat is the time when we concentrate all our senses—physical and spiritual—to look beyond the veil that separates the human world from the divine. We all passed through this veil once, when we were born, and we'll pass through it again when we die. But in our lives most can't remember what we experienced before birth or predict what we'll experience after death.'

'And you believe your observatory can help you see beyond the veil during your lifetime?'

A smile. 'Once we master control of our astral bodies we cannot only see beyond the veil but pass through it and visit the other side.' Delaney

269

expressed himself with such conviction that Fox could only nod in acknowledgement.

As he considered his response, Fox glanced around the Great Hall. The soaring space seemed even larger because of two large glass panels in the roof, which revealed the blue vaulted sky and allowed light to flood the hall. Standing by the raised dais were three striking women in exquisite indigo gowns. Evidently preparing for tomorrow night's ceremony, the trio were attending to a fourth woman. Fox watched, entranced, as they decorated her hair with violets and white lilies and fussed over her dazzling white robe. When they stepped back to reveal the creature in all her glory, her ethereal beauty made even their considerable charms seem ordinary.

'Look who's come to check up on you, Sorcha,' Delaney said. 'I told him he's got nothing to worry about, but Dr Fox wanted to see for himself.'

'Hello, Sorcha.' As Fox stepped forward to greet her she took a step away from him. His heart fell when he saw the fear in her eyes. After all they had been through together it hurt him to think that Delaney could be right and *he* might now be the cause of her anxiety. For the first time Fox doubted whether he should have come.

CHAPTER FORTY-THREE

Sorcha's first reaction on seeing Nathan Fox was fear—for him. She was still trying to absorb her discovery about Kaidan and her father's clinical dispatch of Eve, and it took all her self-control not to run to Fox and warn him about the danger he had stumbled into. She restrained herself. Her father had made it chillingly clear what would happen to the psychiatrist if she did.

'Hello, Dr Fox.' She kept her voice formal and made no attempt to introduce him to the others. She was acutely aware of Delaney watching her, along with the Wives, who had stayed by her side ever since Fox's arrival, wrapping her in the white robes before marching her over to the Great Hall. Kaidan had disappeared with Eve's body and Sorcha's precious locket. It took all her concentration not to reach automatically for the missing silver heart. She felt naked without it. 'What brings you here?' She tried not to think about her father's plans for her and focused instead on reassuring this most perceptive of men that she was fine and that he should leave as soon as possible. The least she could do, after all he had done for her, not just in Portland but in coming here, was to steer him away.

Fox glanced at the Wives, then at Delaney. 'May I speak with Sorcha alone, in private?'

'As you wish,' said Delaney.

Sorcha led Fox out of the hall to a copse of trees near the tower. Within the copse was a shaded bench. Fox waited for her to sit then sat beside her. Though the place seemed private, Delaney had warned her that he had ears and eyes everywhere, and she had no reason to doubt him.

'How are you feeling, Sorcha?' Fox asked softly.

She had forgotten how reassuring his voice was. 'Fine. You didn't need to come all this way to check on me. How's Samantha?'

'She's good. She asked after you. Has your

271

memory returned at all?'

'Not yet but each day feels better. Coming back here was definitely the right thing for me to do.'

'Have you experienced any more death echoes?'

'No.' She pointed back to the hall. 'As you can see, I'm happy and busy. We're preparing for Esbat and I have a starring role in the festivities.'

'That's good.' His blue eyes searched hers. 'You haven't felt threatened by anything or anyone since you returned?'

'No. Compared to Portland this place feels very safe.'

He nodded. 'You've no worries about the cult or your father's beliefs? Nothing you find uncomfortable?'

'No. I'm happy here. Why?'

'You seem a little nervous.'

She looked away, afraid her eyes betrayed her. She had to convince Fox she was fine and make him leave. 'To be honest, it's *you* that's making me nervous,' she said. 'This place is full of everything I want to remember. You remind me of all the bad things that happened in Portland. All the things I want to forget.'

'I'm sorry,' he said, softly. 'That wasn't my intention.'

'What was your intention? Why did you come?'

'I was concerned about you.' She listened as he explained his theory. 'The coloured letters in the messages indicate the killer has grapheme-colour synaesthesia. I think he also shares your death-echo synaesthesia, but unlike you the death echoes don't repulse him. They excite him. I think that's why he committed copycat killings—to recreate and intensify the death echoes of the original crimes.

272

I came because I suspect he's one of the Indigo Family and wishes you harm. I don't think you're safe here.'

As she listened, she squirmed inside. Everything he said, every deduction he had made was chillingly accurate and yet she couldn't say a word. She couldn't tell him that if the killer shared her death-echo synaesthesia then it was because he was her half-brother. Or that her father was aware of the crimes. 'You've told Detective Jordache all this?'

A pause. 'Yes.'

'You promised you'd tell no one about my death-echo synaesthesia.'

'I was worried about you.'

She pretended to be angry but she didn't care any more. She only cared that he had come. And now she had to make him leave. 'Does he share your concerns about the killer?'

'Not exactly. He found some of my theory a little hard to swallow.'

She imagined Fox trying in vain to explain death-echo synaesthesia to the sceptical police. And yet, despite his famous detachment, Fox had still come all this way to warn her. On his own. 'So this is just *your* theory. The police don't think I'm in danger at all.'

Fox reached into his jacket and pulled out a photo of a large, heavyset man. 'Do you recognize him?'

'Who is he?'

'The prime suspect the police have in custody. Look closely at his face. Is he the man who tried to abduct you from your room at Tranquil Waters or the killer you sensed in the crime scene death

273

echoes in Portland?'

Sorcha didn't need to look at the picture to know he wasn't the killer. Kaidan was. 'I barely saw the man who tried to abduct me and only glimpsed the killer in the death echoes.' She pointed at the picture. 'It could be him though.'

'Really?' Fox looked crestfallen, like a gambler who has played his trump card only to see it beaten. 'I was sure you'd say he wasn't the guy. I was sure the killer was still at large. That's why I came to warn you.'

She stoked the hurt and rage she felt for her father and directed it at Fox. 'The last time we spoke you said I should return home and rediscover my past. I've done that and so far I'm doing fine. Now, just as I'm settling back into my old life, you come out here and tell me to be scared of something the police have already taken care of. What do you want me to do, Nathan? Leave my family—the one place I feel safe—and come back to Portland with you? You're a psychiatrist, not a bodyguard. Why should I be any safer with you? At least my father and his people can protect me here. Why would I want to go back to Portland anyway? What do I have back there? Nothing, except bad memories.'

Fox didn't respond, just sat back and watched the people bustling in the sunshine, preparing for Esbat. His face was hard to read. He turned to her again and frowned. 'Where's your locket?'

'It's back in my room. I took it off to try on my robes.'

'You never took it off back in Portland.'

'Like I said, I feel more confident here. I don't need to wear it all the time.'

274

He leaned in close and whispered, 'You sure everything's OK, Sorcha?'

When she looked into those concerned blue eyes she almost lost her resolve. 'I'm fine, Dr Fox, really. I'm grateful for all you've done for me but now I think you should go home, stop worrying and let me get on with rediscovering the rest of my life.'

He maintained eye contact for a while longer, then gave a small nod. 'Very well. I'm sorry if I've upset you.' He stood up, rested a hand on her shoulder, then walked away.

CHAPTER FORTY-FOUR

How could he have been so unprofessional and so wrong? As Fox rode away from the settlement he didn't look back. He kept thinking about the wisdom of Sensei Daichi's words: *Never let them get too close. Never lose control.* By abandoning that code and allowing Sorcha to get under his skin he had compromised both his judgement and his perspective. His elaborate theory about the killer being part of the cult now appeared to be a circumstantial house of cards. Had Jordache been right? Because of what had happened to his family, had he projected his hatred of cults on to Delaney's and made the evidence fit his prejudice? If so, how did he let that happen? He was supposed to be a psychiatrist, for Christ's sake. For all he knew, the man Jordache had in custody probably was the killer and Sorcha was in no danger at all.

Delaney had invited him to stay for lunch but Fox left as soon as he could. He didn't want to cause Sorcha any more distress and wanted to get back to Road's End early enough to reclaim his car and get home that night. After accepting food, water and directions he had climbed back on the horse and set off. Delaney had instructed him to cross the bridge and ride through the woods on the far side of the valley but the skittish animal seemed intent on going back the way they had come. Fox didn't fight him. Downriver, he crossed the shallow ford and soon found his way back to the path above the settlement. After checking his GPS, he patted the animal's flank and re-entered the forbidden forest.

He was lost in his thoughts, still trying to work out how he could have got it so wrong, when he heard someone coughing. He reined the horse in and listened. The coughing was coming from ahead—and above. Reaching for the binoculars, he trained them on one of the towering giant sequoias. At least fifty feet up its massive trunk, a man was descending in a makeshift timber lift. He was big, wore gloves and carried a burlap sack. As Fox followed the lift's descent to the ground, he noticed a horse tethered to a wooden hut and realized it was the same clearing where he had spent last night.

The man got off the lift, took a shovel from the shed, walked to the centre of the clearing and began digging into the soft earth, a few yards from where Fox had lain in his sleeping bag. The man didn't dig very deep before he turned his back to Fox and emptied the sack's contents into the hole. After refilling the hole, he threw the shovel, gloves and sack into the hut and locked the door—all with the casual efficiency of someone putting out the weekly garbage. Something about the man's size and the way he moved seemed tantalizingly familiar. Fox waited for him to mount his horse and ride away in the direction of the settlement, then edged into the clearing.

Intrigued why anyone would bring something down from a high tree and then bury it, Fox dismounted and walked to the centre of the clearing. Getting down on his knees he scooped the soft earth out of the hole. The first object he uncovered was a bone, so small he assumed it was part of the earth. More digging revealed a larger bone, then a skull. Fox didn't need medical training to know it was human. He dug faster, bare hands scrabbling at the earth, revealing more bones: a femur; a humerus; a full set of phalanges from a left foot. All were clean of any soft tissue. As he removed the bones he discovered more underneath, and then more beneath them: too many to have come from one sack. He excavated wider and discovered yet more bones. All human. To his horror, he realized they were of varying sizes. There were large male adult femurs, an adult female pelvis, and bones so small they could only belong to children. The unformed sutures on two tiny skulls told him they were from newborns. Both were clearly deformed.

He straightened up, light-headed, chest tight. What was this place? Stepping back, he took in the circular clearing. Walking from one side to the other, he kicked the ground, feeling the hardness of the earth beneath his feet. Wherever it felt unusually soft, he kicked away a patch of topsoil to reveal more bones. From its centre, he estimated that the shallow grave extended six feet in every

277

direction, forming a circle twelve foot in diameter. He shuddered. No wonder he had woken in pain this morning: he had slept on a bed of human bones, covered with only a loose layer of soft earth.

This place had to belong to the settlement. This was Delaney's private land and there were no other humans for miles around. As he stared down at the discarded bones he remembered how the man had unceremoniously dumped the contents of the sack into the pit. If this was the Indigo Family's graveyard, then they had little respect for their dead. Fox looked up at the towering redwoods. What had the bones been doing up there? He wandered over to the tree from which the man had descended and found the rudimentary lift: an open timber frame with a three-foot-square base. Looking up, he saw a channel had been cut through the branches to accommodate its ascent. Beside it, a series of ladder rungs had been nailed strategically to the massive trunk, presumably as a back-up. From what he could see, the contraption relied on a complex system of weights, ropes and pulleys, none of which inspired much confidence. Hanging from a cable in the lift was a metal control box with two arrow-shaped buttons.

He swallowed hard. Ever since he was a child he had had a fear of heights and this promised to match his worst nightmares. He had to see what was up there, though. Taking a deep breath, he stepped into the lift and pressed the 'up' arrow. He heard a low hum, then the rope above jerked into life and the platform began to rise. As the lift ascended, his grip tightened on the wooden frame. The urge to press the 'down' button was almost overwhelming. He turned towards the trunk, studying its soft,

278

spongy red bark so as to avoid looking out and down. As he rose higher, the breeze blowing through the trees became stronger. Though it was fresh, he smelt something foul in the air.

He looked up. There was a thick branch to his right then, directly above, a platform extended from the trunk. As the lift passed the branch and rose through an opening in the platform, Fox realized that, except for branch tips from neighbouring trees, there was only blue sky above. The top of the tree had been lopped off. The lift stopped level with the platform, a few feet below the top. Fox stepped out, grateful for the rickety rail round the platform's edge, and risked a glance down. As he glimpsed the ground he gasped. He estimated he was at least a hundred feet up.

He detected the bad smell again, then two crows flapped past and alighted on the sawn-off treetop, a few feet above him. Turkey vultures circled the sky above. With the aid of two steps and a handrail, he climbed tentatively on to the flat, sawn-off crown of the trunk. The treetop was about ten foot in diameter with a wooden deck attached to one side, extending the area an additional five feet. There were no railings and the panoramic vista across the roof of the forest was breathtaking.

Fox wasn't looking at the view, though, or even thinking about his vertigo. His total focus was on what lay at his feet.

CHAPTER FORTY-FIVE

Watching Fox leave had been heartbreaking. Sorcha had felt as if all her hopes were leaving with him. As she wondered what lay in store for her, she consoled herself that at least he was safe.

'You did well, Sorcha,' her father said, after Fox had gone. 'Remember, you're one of the family and we look after our own.' As Delaney walked away he turned to the Wives. 'Keep an eye on her.'

Sorcha ignored them and as soon as the lunch bell rang walked briskly towards the refectory, immersing herself in the crowd hurrying to lunch.

'Wait,' said Zara as she and the others followed.

Sorcha didn't look back. She allowed the crowd to sweep her along, carrying her away from the Wives. They tried to keep up but the crowd pulled them further apart. Just before she entered the large barn, she turned and pointed to the small block of restrooms at the back of the refectory. Zara's face lit up with relief and she nodded when she realized where Sorcha was heading.

Knowing she had only a few minutes, Sorcha hurried into the women's block and locked herself in one of the restrooms. The six-foot by four-foot room had a toilet and a basin. The walls went all the way to the ceiling but the door stopped inches from the floor, leaving a gap. She pulled off her white robe, revealing jeans and T-shirt, and hung it on the door hook, arranging it so the hem was not only visible through the gap but also obstructed prying eyes. Then she stepped on to the toilet and tried to pull open the narrow window, but it had been bolted so it would only open an inch. Frantic, she searched the small room. In the cupboard under the sink she found two rolls of toilet paper, a can of Lysol and a metal nail file. Looking at the window, she realized the file wouldn't help dislodge the bolt and even if it could the window was probably too narrow to squeeze through. Then she felt the floor move under her right foot. Bending down, she noticed that two floorboards by the basin, secured with two screws, were loose. She managed to unscrew them with the tip of the nail file, and then pull up the boards. The space was tight but she squeezed herself down the hole.

'You OK in there?' she heard Zara say outside the door.

'Leave me alone. I've got cramps. I'll need a few minutes.'

'It's just nerves,' Zara said. 'You don't need to be anxious about Esbat. It's going to be fine. We'll all help you.'

Easy for you to say, you witch, Sorcha thought, as she eased herself as quietly as she could through the floor. In the space beneath, she crawled on her belly until she emerged from under the back of the block. Her first impulse on finding herself outside was to run for the forest. But what then? Delaney's land was in the middle of the wilderness and stretched for miles. She had no food, directions or transport and her father would send people after her. She felt the back pocket of her jeans, where she had put the iPhone Fox had given her. If she managed to reach civilization and get a signal she could summon Fox. But she would still be lost from herself—with no memory of her true identity and past. If she left now she might never know what

281

her father's Great Work entailed and the part she was expected to play in it. She might never know the reason why she had originally fled, or what had happened to her mother. She reached for the locket round her neck, feeling its loss as keenly as a missing limb. Her father had told Kaidan to return the locket to her mother in the tower. When Sorcha had asked if she was still in there the Seer had laughed: 'Your mother will *always* be in the tower.'

What did he mean by that? What had happened to her?

She had to find out, Sorcha realized, and she had to get her locket back before she left this place. But how? As the last chimes of the lunch bell caused colours to dance before her eyes an idea came to her. It could work. Everyone would be at lunch for at least an hour. Filled with fresh purpose, she felt her fear subside. Sticking close to buildings, trees and any cover she could find, she moved quickly across the deserted settlement. Leaving the harsh glare of sunlight, she stepped into the shadow of the tower.

CHAPTER FORTY-SIX

The three human corpses lying at Fox's feet were in various stages of decomposition. Taking a handkerchief from his pocket he covered his mouth and nose. Two of the bodies were male adults: one in an advanced state of putrefaction, the other virtually a skeleton. The body attracting the birds, however, was that of a middle-aged woman, naked except for a pair of hoop earrings. She was freshly dead and Fox realized that the man had probably removed the bones from the platform and buried them to make space for her. The weathered treetop, encrusted with bird droppings, was stained black with old blood and viscera. Stifling the urge to gag, he walked to the edge, turned into the breeze and gulped fresh air.

In the valley below, he could see Delaney's settlement in the distance nestled neatly in the bend of the river. A bell began ringing and ant-like figures started moving towards the refectory. Fox realized it must be lunch. As he watched the Indigo Family obediently heed its Pavlovian call, he realized they would know nothing of the corpses discarded in the forbidden woods. The exposed bodies and buried bones reminded Fox of what an Indian patient had once told him about the way the Parsi people dealt with their dead. As Zoroastrians, Parsis believed that the body was impure and shouldn't be allowed to pollute the earth after death through burial or cremation. Instead, the deceased were brought to a ceremonial 'tower of silence', traditionally located on an elevated mountain plateau, and left exposed to the animals and elements. When the bones had been picked clean and then dried and bleached by the sun, they were buried in pits of lime. Delaney's cult, which indiscriminately borrowed from various spiritual traditions ranging from Christianity to witchcraft, appeared to have adopted elements of the Parsi way of death. Unlike the Parsi ritual, however, there was nothing spiritual or ceremonial about the way these bodies were served up on this grisly bird table, or the way the bones were dumped in the landfill site below. A society can be judged by the way it deals with its dead and, despite Delaney's obsession with all things spiritual, certain members of his cult appeared to have nothing but contempt for their dead.

Two large vultures settled on the woman's body and he kicked them away. As they retreated he noticed something that made him kneel and take a closer look at her corpse. The stiffness of the body and the tight grimace on the face were typical of rigor mortis. Rigor—when the adenosine triphosphate that enables energy to flow to the muscles drains from the body—normally sets in a couple of hours after death and lasts up to eighteen hours. This told Fox that the woman had died any time from yesterday evening to early this morning. What interested him more, however, was the bruising around her neck. He had seen the familiar pattern before, at several crime scenes. The woman had been fatally strangled with a ligature. Suddenly, he was less concerned about how Delaney and his cult dealt with the dead and more with how they treated the living.

Looking out towards the settlement, Fox used his binoculars to search for the large man who had buried the bones, wondering again why he had seemed familiar. Could he be the same man he'd confronted in the dark at Tranquil Waters? Fox searched the path leading out of the forest but couldn't see any sign of him. He then scanned the deserted settlement. A sudden flash of movement made him shift his gaze towards a small outhouse attached to the back of the refectory. He steadied the binoculars and tightened the focus. A figure was climbing out from under the crawl space. It looked like Sorcha. She was in jeans and T-shirt. No sign of the white robes she'd worn earlier.

What was she doing?

He watched as she got to her feet, crept along the back of the building and peered round the corner, checking the path was clear. He had been right. She *was* in trouble. Mesmerized, he watched her turn to the forest, the obvious escape route, and for a second he thought she was going to make a dash for it. Then she checked herself and instead began moving in the opposite direction: towards the tower.

Why?

Another movement caught Fox's eye and he realized someone else was watching Sorcha. The big man was leaving the cover of the forest and riding down the path into the settlement. The man slowed behind a tree, then dismounted and moved stealthily around the perimeter towards Sorcha, following her every move, a lion stalking its prey.

Forgetting the corpses and his vertigo, Fox jumped down on to the platform below, stepped into the lift and urgently pressed the 'down' button.

CHAPTER FORTY-SEVEN

As Sorcha crossed the deserted settlement, her mouth felt dry and her palms damp. The sound of her pumping heart made flashes of colour dance before her eyes. She again considered running to the forest but knew escape would be futile on foot. She looked over at the horses. Zara had said she was a good rider but she would have to ride bareback and the guards in the gatehouse would stop her

285

before she got out of the corral, let alone crossed the bridge. Her attention was drawn inexorably back to the tower as if her mother's locket were calling her. She wasn't sure what scared her more: discovering something so shocking it brought all her memories flooding back, or discovering nothing. She quickened her step, keen to get inside before Zara and the others noticed she was gone. She almost smiled when she realized it would be the last place they would look.

As she reached the tower, she detected a movement in her peripheral vision. Then a familiar malodour tainted the air. She turned just as Kaidan's massive frame appeared round the curve of the tower. Before she could react, he grabbed her with his left hand and slammed her so hard against the wall the force expelled the breath from her lungs. In his right hand he carried a rifle.

'What are you doing here, sister?' he hissed. 'Why aren't you running away, back to your precious doctor?'

'I want my locket back,' she rasped.

He glanced up at the tower. 'You want to go inside?' The smile left his face, replaced by a contemptuous scowl. He patted the wall. 'What makes you think you can handle what's in here when you couldn't handle it before? What's changed?'

As Sorcha caught her breath she studied the face of the killer she had run from in her nightmares and glimpsed in death echoes. Delaney had said she and Kaidan were half-siblings but she could see little likeness. His build was bigger and heavier, and his eyes and facial expression were coldly blank, as if all humanity had fled. Confronting her nightmare

286

in the flesh was strangely liberating. After the terror and confusion she had endured over the last few weeks, she realized there was nothing more to fear. She leaned forward until her face was inches from his. 'I don't know what's changed because I can't remember what happened the last time I was here. I'm guessing I saw something unspeakable and I need to find out what it was so I can reclaim my memory. Did it involve my mother, or the Great Work, or you, Kaidan? If it involved you I'm not surprised I ran away, knowing what you did in Portland.' She spat at him. 'You may be my half-brother but you're sick.'

Something flickered in those dead eyes as he wiped her spit from his face. 'Don't judge me. You know nothing about me.' He spread his arms, indicating the deserted settlement. 'You've lived all your life in these sunlit fields with the other indigo cattle, in perfect ignorant bliss, free of any responsibilities.' He jabbed his own chest. 'I've lived only in the shadows. You've no idea what the Seer's asked of me, the sacrifices I've made to help the Great Work. It may be an honour and a privilege but you wouldn't believe the things I've seen. The things I've done.'

'You didn't have to do them. You always had a choice.'

Kaidan's dead eyes sparked into life and his face coloured. 'You still don't understand. This is our destiny. *Your* destiny. I've proved I'll do almost anything to fulfil his dream but because I failed him once he now doubts me. You've done nothing but he now thinks you're as important as me.' He shook his head in disbelief. 'You return with no memory, the slate wiped clean, and he believes you're ready

287

to participate in the Great Work. Even though you ran away the very first time you were tested. Have you any idea what's expected of you? How far he wants you to go? How far he *needs* you to go?' He sighed, leaned the rifle against the wall and grabbed her in his arms. She tried to break free of his grip but he was too strong and pulled her towards the door.

'Get your goddamn hands off me.'

'You want to see in the tower? You want your precious locket back? You want to know what happened to your mother? You want to know why you ran away? Come on. I'll show you everything.'

Gripped in his arms, squeezed against his hard body, inhaling his smell, she was suddenly overcome by an indistinct but powerful sense memory. She couldn't remember the event, only the visceral terror and revulsion it had invoked, but she instinctively knew it had involved Kaidan. *What had happened in there? What was he going to show her?* Her newfound fearlessness gave way to panic. It was one thing to steal into the tower alone. It was something else entirely to be dragged in by a killer. She fought harder but his large arms only tightened their grip around her body. Controlling her panic she focused all her efforts on the middle finger of his right hand. Closing her eyes, she snapped it back with all her force. The instant he cried out and loosened his grip she swivelled and kneed him as hard as she could in the groin. As he bent double she reached for the rifle and, holding it by the barrel, brought the stock crashing down on his head.

She didn't watch him fall or check he was down. She just ran as fast as her legs would carry her towards the forest, desperate to get as far away from Kaidan as possible. She looked back only after she had climbed the rise at the rear of the settlement and reached the first sequoia. To her surprise and relief, he was still down, out cold. She quickly scanned the deserted settlement below but couldn't see anyone raising the alarm or chasing her. Zara and the others could appear at any moment, however, so she carried on into the forest, not knowing what to do or where to go. Her mouth was parched. She would have to find water soon and then food. In the green shade of the looming sequoias, she shivered at the thought of spending the night out here in only a T-shirt and jeans. She couldn't even think about how she was going to negotiate her way through the countless, seemingly identical redwoods and find civilization. Or what she would do if she did.

A sudden noise startled her. Someone was coming down the path on horseback. Fast. She ran for cover into a bank of ferns. She could use a horse. She raised the rifle and automatically released the catch. She had no conscious recall of firing a gun before, but some part of her evidently remembered how to handle a hunting rifle. As she pushed it to her shoulder, pressed her cheek against the stock and placed her finger on the trigger, the weapon felt familiar and oddly comforting in her hands.

The rider suddenly stopped, yards from where she was standing, reached for a pair of binoculars and scanned the settlement below. She ran on to the path, heart pounding, rifle trained on his head. 'Get off the horse.' It was only when he lowered the binoculars that she recognized him. 'Nathan! I thought you'd gone! What are you doing here?'

'As it happens, I was rushing back to rescue you. But it looks like you're doing pretty well on your own.' He pointed to the rifle. 'Mind putting that down?'

She quickly lowered the weapon and replaced the safety. 'I might not need rescuing but you could give me a drink.'

He passed her a flask of water and scanned the settlement again. 'You're not rescued yet. Jump on the horse. I want to get out of here before your delightful family discovers you're missing.'

She took a slug of the water, slipped her rifle into the saddle holster, then took his extended hand and pulled herself up behind him on the horse. As Fox kicked the horse's flanks and galloped into the forest, she wrapped her arms tight around him, inhaling his clean, musky smell, allowing it to purge Kaidan's stench from her nostrils.

CHAPTER FORTY-EIGHT

Walking among his people as they ate lunch in the refectory, Delaney soaked up their devotion and fed off their excitement. This was their last major meal before the Esbat fast began at sunset tonight; it would end with the feast tomorrow evening. As he stopped to speak with members of his flock he kept thinking about Sorcha and what was planned for tomorrow night. The anticipation thrilled him but also made him more apprehensive than he liked to admit. He found himself looking for his daughter but could see only Maria and Deva on the top table.

'Where's Sorcha?'

'In the bathroom,' Maria said.

'Zara's with her,' said Deva.

He frowned, a small alarm bell ringing in the back of his mind, and walked out of the refectory. Maria and Deva looked at each other, then followed. When he reached the restroom block he found Zara knocking on one of the doors. 'Sorcha, speak to me. Are you OK? Answer me.'

Delaney strode over. 'How long's she been in there?'

Zara shrugged nervously. 'I don't know. Fifteen, twenty minutes? She's got cramps. She wanted some time.'

Delaney frowned. 'You left her alone?'

'I've been waiting out here. She can't get out.'

'Have you looked under the door?'

'Her robe's covering the gap.'

He pushed past her and banged on the door. 'Sorcha, it's me. Let me in.' He waited a beat then kicked the door hard. It took two kicks to break it down. When he saw the missing floorboards his heart skipped. Zara visibly wilted. 'Cramps? You stupid bitch. She's gone.'

'She won't get far,' a voice growled behind him.

He turned as Kaidan appeared. The side of his head was swollen and bloody. 'What do you mean?'

'She has no horse, food or drink. Only a rifle.'

'Where the hell did she get a rifle?'

'She took mine. I caught her by the tower but she . . .'

'You let her get away again?' Delaney couldn't believe it. It was as if Kaidan was doing this on purpose.

Kaidan pointed to his head. 'I didn't *let* her.'

291

'How long's she been gone?'

'A few minutes. The Watchers in the gatehouse saw no one go over the bridge or enter the corral so she must have gone into the forest. I've got the Watchers mounted up to help me look. We'll get her back. She hasn't got a horse and won't get far on foot.'

'You saw her by the tower?'

'Yes.'

'Why didn't she run straight from here into the forest or cross the river?'

'She wanted her locket back. She asked about her mother, the Great Work and what made her run away last time,' said Kaidan. 'I think she believes the answers to all her questions are inside the tower—and all her lost memories.'

Delaney nodded slowly. Perhaps all was not lost. 'Go, take the Watchers and search the forest.'

'You want me to saddle up a horse for you?' said Kaidan.

His father considered for a moment. He wanted to play back CCTV camera footage from the hard drive, see if it shed more light on what had happened and where she had gone. He had no cameras in the forest, though. 'No. I'll stay here. In case she comes back.'

'Comes back?' said Zara. 'Why would she come back?'

'Because she knows she won't get far by herself.' He thought of the locket and her mother. 'More than that, she's not only running away from me, the settlement and her fears—she's also running away from her past. From herself. And that's not easy to do. Not easy at all.'

Fox had been riding for some minutes when he abruptly reined in the horse.

'What are you doing?' Sorcha asked.

Fox dismounted. 'This won't take long. We've got a little while before they discover you've gone and when they do they'll assume you're on foot and won't have got this far.'

'Why here?' she asked, noticing the small hut.

He walked to the centre of the clearing. 'I need to show you something before we head off. I want another witness to this.' He bent down and began digging with his hands, scooping away the soft earth.

Sorcha gasped in shock when his digging revealed a skull and bones. 'What is this place?' she said.

'It's where your Indigo Family disposes of its dead. I saw the big guy you knocked out burying something here. When I dug around I found loads of human bones: adults, children and babies. Deformed babies.' Sorcha remembered Eve telling her how Delaney had tried for more violet children with Aurora but all had been stillborn. Fox pointed up at one of the trees. 'He brought the bones down from up there.' He told her about the platform on the roof of the forest where bodies were placed to be picked clean by the birds. He walked a few feet across the clearing and dug another small hole, revealing more bones. 'This whole area is a shallow bone pit.'

'But there are so many bodies. How can so many people from the settlement have died in the last few years?'

293

'I don't think they all just died. It looks like some were murdered. Possibly in some kind of ritual. One of the fresh bodies I saw up there had been strangled with a ligature.' Sorcha shuddered when he told her about the hoop earrings on the female body. As she looked down on the bones discarded in this unmarked pit a heavy guilt pressed down on her. And shame. At this moment she wished she were still Jane Doe, with no knowledge of her past life or her family and its terrible legacy.

'I need to tell you something, Nathan.'

He looked at her. 'Yes?'

'The man I fought just now, the man you saw burying the bones, was the killer in Portland.' Fox nodded like he'd guessed that already. She swallowed hard and continued, 'He's also my half-brother.'

As Fox absorbed what she'd said she searched his face for shock or disgust but saw no sign of either, only a quizzical frown. 'Do you know why he killed them?'

'No, but my father knew about the killings. He strangled Eve. It was her body you found up there. I saw him do it. My family professes to be descended from angels but they're demons. *We* are demons.' She pointed down at the bone pit. 'My family's responsible for this.'

Fox placed a hand on her arm. 'You aren't, though.'

She shrugged his hand away. 'How do you know? How do *I* know? I can't remember anything. Perhaps I knew about all this. Perhaps I was part of it before I ran away. If I didn't know about it I should have. Something terrible happened in that tower that changed my life. Something I desperately need to remember. I might not *want* to remember it but I *need* to. I have no memory, no identity, nothing. The only family I have left appear to be monsters. I need to know if I'm like them.'

'You're *not* like them.'

'How do you know?'

'Because I know you.'

'How can you say that? *I* don't know me. I've no idea who I was or who I am.' Needing to make some connection with the dead and perform some penance, she bent down to the pit and reached for an adult skull. She hoped the intensity of its death echo might somehow purge her guilt and shame. But the echo was faint, as if its life energy had departed at the time of death, leaving only a vestigial trace in the desiccated bone. 'Why do this? Why kill these people? How can this possibly help my father's Great Work?'

She sensed Fox kneeling down beside her. 'I don't know,' he said gently. 'But we'll find out. Come, it's getting late and we need to tell Jordache about this.'

'About what? He didn't believe you before, why should he believe you now?'

Fox took the skull from her, returned it to the pit and replaced the soil. 'We'll tell him about this place.'

'Jordache will say it's a private graveyard. And if we tell him about Kaidan we can't prove my half-brother was the killer or that he was even in Portland. I saw him in my death echoes but that's legally irrelevant. Besides, even if Jordache does believe us, by the time he brings the police back here my father and Kaidan will have realized I got away and removed any incriminating evidence.' She thought of her mother and a surge of panic gripped her. 'My locket's in the tower. I must get it back.'

'We'll get it when we return with Jordache and his men.'

'It might not be there then.'

'It's just a locket, Sorcha,' he said gently.

She shook her head angrily. Why didn't he understand? 'It's not just a locket. It's my past. It's my mother. It's all I have. It's who I was and who I am. I *have* to get it back.' She took a deep breath, trying to stay calm. 'I need to get into the tower. Now. Not just to get the locket but also to find out what happened to my mother and uncover the truth about the Great Work before the Seer has a chance to dismantle or hide what he's been doing in there. What he's *still* doing in there.'

'It's too dangerous, Sorcha. Let the police handle this. I came here to take you to safety.'

'There's no such thing. I'll never have safety. Not until I know why I originally ran away.' She pointed down at the bones in the earth. 'I don't *deserve* safety until I know why my father and half-brother are doing this and what my role in it was. Once I'm inside the tower I hope I'll recover my memories. It's the one place that contains all the answers: to my past, my mother's fate, my father's Great Work and the part he wants me to play in it.'

'Your identity isn't defined by your past or your memories, Sorcha, and certainly not by what your family may have done,' Fox said quietly. 'What defines you is what you do and the choices you make *now*. You decide who you are. You and fate determine your future. No one else does.'

'In that case I *choose* to go back into the tower. I'll hide until it gets dark and then go in.'

Fox shook his head. 'I didn't come all this way just to watch you walk back into the dragon's lair.'

'You haven't got to come with me, Nathan,' she snapped. 'You prefer *avoiding* the place that changed *your* life, and putting your head in the sand might work for you. But not for me.'

Fox glared back at her and for a while neither spoke.

She softened her voice. 'Please, Nathan. I *need* to walk back into the dragon's lair, if only to discover if I'm one of the dragons. It's not just about the locket.' She reached into her jeans back pocket and pulled out the iPhone Fox had given her. 'This has got a camera. I'll take pictures of what I find, show them to Jordache and then we'll have all the proof we need.'

Fox said nothing for a moment, then he sighed. 'How are we going to get in? The tower's locked.'

'We?'

'Of course. I didn't come all this way for the fun of it. How are *we* going to get back in there?'

She smiled. 'I think I know a way.'

CHAPTER FORTY-NINE

That evening it began raining hard. In the forest, the trees provided some shelter from the summer storm but the temperature dropped rapidly. Fox gave Sorcha his fleece and waterproof jacket and donned the oilskin provided in the saddlebag. As Fox had expected, the riders searching for Sorcha had assumed she was on foot and confined their efforts to the area near the settlement. It had been relatively easy to keep out of their way and now the rain made it easier. The downpour washed away their tracks and drowned out their sound, and as night fell they could see the searchers' sputtering torches illuminating the forest.

As Fox and Sorcha rode from one sheltered vantage point to another, they pooled their information, but it didn't help them divine the true nature of Delaney's Great Work or Sorcha's role within it. In the moments of silence Fox found himself reflecting on their earlier exchange. Sorcha's adamant decision to return to the tower to recover her locket and confront her past had forced Fox to re-examine his own reluctance to re-enter the Chevron garage where his family had been murdered.

The longer they waited, the more he hoped Sorcha might still change her mind and return to civilization with him. Whatever her doubts about herself, Fox was convinced Sorcha had had nothing to do with her father's and half-brother's crimes. The fact that she had risked her life to enter the basement of the Russian Mafia's house in Portland to break out the caged girls told him all he needed to know about her character and values. He suspected, however, that nothing was going to convince her to come back with him now. Especially when he watched the sodden, torch-bearing riders return to the settlement. 'Why've they given up so quickly?' he whispered in the dark. 'If you're so damn important to your father, why aren't they out searching all night?'

Sorcha shrugged. 'They can't see much in this rain and it's dark and cold. If they think I'm on foot with no food or proper clothing they probably

298

assume I'll have to stop and find shelter for the night. They can track me better tomorrow.'

They waited another hour, until they were certain the riders had gone, then moved close enough to look down on the settlement. By midnight the last of the lights had dimmed from the windows, save a lone glow in the gatehouse by the bridge. Fox glanced at Sorcha. 'Ready?'

She nodded, lips trembling with cold. 'Ready.'

In a dense part of the forest, sheltered and screened by massive ferns, they tethered the horse to a tree. Near the bone pit, it was far enough from the settlement to avoid attracting attention but close enough for them to get back and ride away. 'Let's keep this simple,' whispered Fox as they headed down the path to the settlement, shielding their rifles from the rain. 'We get inside the tower, find your locket, photograph any evidence of your father's Great Work and then get out. *Whatever* else we find, we don't hang about. We get out of here and let Jordache handle the rest. OK?'

Sorcha nodded but didn't look at him. Just stared ahead into the dark. As they carried on in silence, all he could hear was the falling rain and the squelch of their wet footsteps in the soft, waterlogged earth. When they reached the settlement the rain suddenly stopped and the moon appeared through the storm clouds. Although it wouldn't be full until tomorrow, it looked plump and round and Fox felt more conscious of its unblinking scrutiny than that of the sinister eye on the tower. When Sorcha made a move he held her back. Only after the clouds again obscured the moon's gaze did he release her arm and follow her across the dark settlement to the door of the tower.

'Put your ear against it and listen for any movement inside,' Fox said.

Sorcha shook her head. 'You do it,' she hissed. 'I'm not touching that door.'

'Why not?'

She pointed to the mosaic of embedded rubble fragments. 'Those stones are toxic.'

'What do you mean?'

'Each one must have come from a place of death. When I touched them yesterday, I got a jumble of echoes.' Fox remembered Connor telling him how his brother Regan used to collect random pieces of rubble to fashion into odd sculptures and mosaics. Perhaps they weren't so random. He put his ear to the door and listened. 'It sounds quiet inside.' Then he turned to her and asked the question she hadn't answered till now. 'How are we going to get in?'

*   *   *

Sorcha didn't answer because, despite all her bravado about returning to the tower, she wasn't yet sure her plan was going to work. The idea had come to her only a few hours earlier, when she had 'seen' the sound of the lunch bell as a cascade of colours. She studied the keypad: twelve keys configured in three columns and four rows. Those on the top three rows were marked 1 to 9, those on the bottom 0 * #. Ignoring the markings, she closed her eyes and systematically pressed each individual key, listening to the unique sound it made—and the colour it flashed up in her mind's eye. As each colour appeared she compared it to those she had 'seen' when overhearing the code being entered yesterday.

300

'Good idea. Visual memory is more precise than aural,' she heard Fox say when he realized what she was doing. It took her less than twenty seconds to match the colours to the correct combination of keys and unlock the door. 'Impressive,' said Fox.

She shrugged. 'If I've got this goddamn *móthu* I may as well use it.'

Fox waited, allowing her to lead the way, but she hung back, suddenly nervous, so he stepped confidently into the dark interior. It impressed her that, although he refused to enter the garage where his family had died, he had the courage to lead her, without any hesitation, into a place of genuine danger.

As she followed him inside, the door closed behind her, engulfing them in total darkness. Immediately she sensed something in the building. It was an indistinct distant murmuring but it filled her with dread and made the fine hairs on her forearm stand on end. Thankfully, an automatic sensor turned on a series of concealed lamps, bathing the interior in a low atmospheric light. They were in the base of the round tower. The walls were rough stone and the floor tiled with slate. A faint smell of pine disinfectant hung in the air. A thick pillar stood in the centre of the circular chamber with two partitions extending to the external wall, creating an internal pie slice of a room. The door to this section was closed. A second door in the outside wall evidently connected directly to Delaney's quarters. In the central pillar was another door, which presumably led to the stairs. The door had been painted with the now-familiar Vitruvian man, complete with its shadow twin and chakras up the spine.

'Recognize any of this?' whispered Fox.

She pointed to the Vitruvian man. 'That's on the doors of the Great Hall and on a tapestry in my father's quarters. But nothing else is familiar.'

Fox tried the door in the partition wall but it was locked. Sorcha reached for a small keypad, tried the same code she had used earlier and the door opened. Inside was an Aladdin's cave of high-tech equipment and a large safe. There was no sign of her locket. One wall was covered with monitors displaying images from various closed-circuit television cameras around the settlement. This was clearly where Delaney spied on his flock. 'When he told me he had eyes and ears everywhere he wasn't lying,' she said.

'Perhaps this is why he calls his tower the Observatory,' Fox said, taking pictures with his BlackBerry. 'His cynical way of controlling his flock and convincing them of his spiritual gift—his third eye.' Sorcha sensed relief in Fox's voice. 'Perhaps this is all there is?'

Sorcha knew differently and felt herself drawn to the door in the central pillar. Close up, the painting of the Vitruvian twins was subtly different to the similar images she had seen earlier. The coloured chakras running up the spine, which had been depicted as spiral vortices, were stylized lotus flowers here. The biggest difference, though, was how the physical body and its spiritual twin had been inverted. In the other images the physical body had been painted in bold colour, with the astral spirit body a ghosted shadow in the background. In this image, the spirit body had become the vibrant, dominant entity and the physical body the pale shadow.

302

Leaving Fox alone, she opened the door and stepped on to the stone steps of a spiral staircase, which led up into the dark. The sense of muted whispers was stronger here—louder. She swallowed hard and vaguely heard Fox calling after her, telling her to wait, but the tower's siren call was too strong. Ignoring Fox, she climbed the dark stairs, triggering sensors that turned on soft lights as she ascended.

Arriving at the first landing she didn't register the details of her physical surroundings. She was almost swamped by the echoes now bombarding her senses. What was this place? What had happened here? She tried to remember what Fox had taught her and let the various visions, smells and sounds flow past her. But this was much more intense than anything she had experienced at Tranquil Waters, or at the crime scenes.

She entered a room on her right and then immediately stepped out again, careful to stay away from the walls, fearful that if she touched anything she would be overwhelmed. As she hurried back to the stairs, every room she glanced in was physically empty—and yet brimming with menace. On the stairs, every step that took her higher ratcheted up her dread, but she couldn't stop. Like a shark, she had to keep moving or die. Breathing hard, she climbed to the next level, then the next. As if she were running an invisible gauntlet, the sensory onslaught intensified the higher she rose, forcing her to move still faster.

Regardless of the level, every empty room she glanced in looked the same but felt totally distinct. As she hurried up the tower she realized she was in one of her recurring nightmares: running through a deserted hotel filled with vacant rooms, occupied only by the ghosts of the dead. She tried to reach back to other memories, from before her amnesia, to the day she had fled this place. She sensed them hiding in the recesses of her mind, still too frightened to break cover and make themselves known to her.

Running past a room on the sixth level she suddenly stopped dead. For a second she didn't know why. Then she saw the locket hanging casually on the door handle like a *Do Not Disturb* sign. She replaced it around her neck and held it tightly, as if to ward off the ghosts swirling around her. Taking a deep breath, she entered the empty room and pressed her hand hard against the wall. As soon as her flesh touched the stone she cried out like an animal in pain. The experience was so intense and visceral that any attempts to distance herself from the images, sounds and smells were futile. Holding her hand against the stone made her doubt all that Fox and his aunt had told her. This was no neutral echo or residual imprint but a soul in torment—a soul she knew. As if in a trance she reached into her pocket and found the photo Eve had given her of her mother. She didn't need it to match her mother to the death echo, though, because Aurora's face looked just like her own. Even more shocking, Sorcha didn't see only her mother in the death echo. She also saw her father. How could Delaney have done this to a woman he professed to love? Then she remembered what he had done to Eve and knew the answer.

As well as the death echo other fragments of memory surfaced, broken and disjointed like the shards of a shattered mirror. She sensed that something else had happened in this death chamber, something as disturbing as the murder of her mother. She pulled her hand from the wall, ran back to the stairs and climbed higher.

CHAPTER FIFTY

Moments earlier

Where the hell was she? Why hadn't Sorcha waited for him? As Fox stepped into the central stairwell, flickering lights revealed a spiral staircase that snaked its way up into the tower. This was the only way up and down. If Delaney came in while they were up the tower they would be trapped like rats. 'Sorcha,' he hissed. 'Where are you?'

When she didn't reply he cursed under his breath, checked the safety catch on the rifle and followed her up the stone steps. Reaching the first level, he stepped into a circular landing surrounded by bright red doors. All were open and as he glanced into the rooms radiating out from the centre he noticed they were totally empty—devoid of any furnishings or décor. Except one: a wetroom complete with shower, basin and toilet. In an alcove by the bathroom was a pile of mattresses, cushions and pillows covered in immaculate white linen. On the top pillow lay a small noose and a cord with a knot in its middle, both of braided silver silk.

'Sorcha? Sorcha, where are you?' Still no reply. As he moved back to the stairwell he noticed on the pale stone floor an image of Leonardo's Vitruvian man inlaid with amethyst. At the base of the man's spine, the site of the first chakra, a lotus symbol had been set with a red gemstone—a triangle within a square within a circle surrounded by four lotus petals:

Pausing to review the claustrophobic rooms, Fox registered the pattern on the walls. In the low light, it resembled natural marbling but when he looked closer he noticed plaques of polished amethyst embedded in the pale stone. Veins of the same amethyst ran like violet blood vessels through the walls, connecting the plaques. The positioning of the concealed lamps gave each room the semblance of a small private gallery with each plaque a work of art. He noticed that some of the plaques were blank, but most featured four lines of chiselled text. The top line was a series of numbers in the form of a date; the second a word—Neonate, Child or Adult; the third a single letter—M or F. The last line featured the same symbol as that on the Vitruvian man. Although they contained no names, the plaques were evidently memorials of some kind.

The next level had an identical layout: rooms radiating from a central circular landing, an amethyst Vitruvian man inlaid in the floor, a single bathroom, a pile of immaculate white mattresses and cushions with a silver cord and noose on the top pillow. The doors on this floor, however, were orange. As was the gemstone symbol on the site of the second chakra on the Vitruvian man's lower spine—a spiral circle surrounded by six lotus petals:

The same symbol featured on the engraved plaques in the rooms. He called Sorcha's name but when she didn't reply he climbed higher. Again, the next level had an identical layout but with yellow doors and a different symbol on the plaques. In the middle of the man's spine was a yellow circle containing a triangle and surrounded by ten lotus petals:

Each floor appeared to have a different colour and symbol, corresponding to the chakras. The next level had green doors with the symbol of a green circle containing a six-pointed star and surrounded by twelve lotus petals. The level above had blue doors and the lotus symbol, on the Vitruvian men's throat, of a blue circle, containing a smaller circle within a triangle, surrounded by sixteen lotus petals. Fox had reached the fifth chakra and as he ascended his unease intensified.

A sudden cry from above fractured the silence. 'Sorcha!' he shouted, abandoning all attempts to keep quiet. Gripping his rifle tighter, he hurried up the stairs to the next level, where all the doors were dark indigo and the Vitruvian man's forehead bore a symbol—a triangle within a circle flanked by two large lotus petals—designed to resemble a stylized eye. This was the level of the sixth chakra, the so-called third eye. Glancing into the rooms, looking for Sorcha, Fox noticed most of the plaques were blank, which surprised him. If these were memorials to the Indigo Family's dead then he would have thought there would be *more* indigo plaques, not fewer. On one wall he could see a faint ghost of the embedded dark blue crystals that formed the mosaic eye on the tower's external wall. He was almost at the top but there was still no sign of Sorcha.

He ascended higher until he came to a violet door, emblazoned with another Vitruvian man. On the crown of the man's head was the symbol of a circular lotus flower with a thousand petals:

He had reached the seventh level, the highest chakra, the top of the tower. Opening the door, he ascended more steps through an opening in the floor above and found himself standing in the centre of a large circular chamber. The light was softer than on the lower floors and his eyes took a moment to grow accustomed to the strange glow. Above, he could see the vaulted underside of the conical roof. Underfoot, a giant version of the circular lotus symbol on the door covered much of the pale stone floor. Fashioned from polished amethyst, some of the petals had been patterned with a network of decorative holes through which he could glimpse the level below. The light from the lower level shone up through the gemstone, casting a violet glow around the chamber. A spider's web of glowing amethyst radiated out from the symbol, connecting it to the walls.

To his left, a bed-sized amethyst plinth, covered with white cushions, seemed to have grown out of the symbol. A silver cord and small noose lay on one of the cushions, like chocolates on a turned-down hotel bed. To his right was a white concave table, above which a large mirror and lens descended from the ceiling. Fox realized the room was a camera obscura. During the day, a lens in the roof would reflect light into the darkened room, projecting real-time images of the settlement on to the white table, allowing Delaney to look down on his subjects: a godlike observer of his domain.

He heard someone speak: 'Who am I?' The voice sounded so flat and detached it took him a second to realize it was Sorcha's. 'Only a demon could have done this. And if my father's a demon, then what does that make me?' Fox stepped round the plinth and saw her on the floor, head down, poring over a simple black accountant's ledger. He moved closer. She was sitting in the thin strip of pale stone between the symbol on the floor and the wall, feet tucked in as if to avoid the amethyst inlay. Her rifle lay on the floor beside her, next to an ancient leather-bound Bible. Fox wondered if it was the family Bible Regan Delaney had stolen from his brother. She was clutching her locket. 'You found it, Sorcha.' She said nothing. 'You OK?' She didn't respond and he stepped closer. 'What is it, Sorcha? Talk to me. Has anything triggered your memory?' She still didn't reply. 'I'm sorry we haven't found any evidence. But at least you found the locket. Come on, we've got to go.'

309

'I can't,' she said. She raised her head and he saw her haunted eyes and ashen face. She looked as terrified now as on the first day they'd met.

'What is it? What's wrong?' He glanced around the chamber. 'This tower's creepy but I've checked every level. There's nothing in here.' Something about the way she looked at him caused the hairs to rise on the back of his neck. 'Is there?'

'Yes, there is,' she said in the same chilling monotone she had used on that first day at Tranquil Waters. 'I haven't recovered *my* memory yet but this place is filled with other people's memories.'

'Whose?'

She placed the black ledger on the floor, careful not to touch the amethyst, and pushed it to Fox. 'Theirs.'

Putting his rifle down, he picked up the book and opened it. Every line of almost every page was filled with names, followed by notations which echoed those he had seen on the plaques below: a date; age description (Neonate, Child or Adult); gender (Male or Female); a coloured dot. As Fox flicked through the pages it was evident that the earlier entries contained predominantly red, orange, yellow and green dots: the lower chakras. Only the latter pages had blue dots and a few indigo, including one entry with the name Aurora. The name of Sorcha's mother. He felt suddenly cold. 'What do you see in this tower, Sorcha? What can you *feel*?'

She pointed to the ledger. 'All of them. Their bones may be in the pit in the forest but their dying echoes are in here. This tower is infested with ghosts. Including my mother's.'

A shiver ran through Fox. Perhaps it was his

imagination, or his own mirror-touch synaesthesia, but at that moment, looking into her eyes, he felt what she was feeling and sensed the ghostly echoes all around him. 'Let's go,' he said, reaching for her. 'Let's get out of here, now.'

'I can't,' she said again. She pointed down at the floor, to the solid expanse of inlaid amethyst that surrounded the exit. 'I can't walk across that again. I can't touch the violet.'

'Why not?' Fox sensed a movement behind him and the cloying smell of death. Something hard, like the barrel of a gun, prodded his back. His heart skipped and he reached for the rifle on the floor.

'She can't touch the violet gemstone on the floor because it's where the dead live,' said an unseen voice. 'Leave the rifle where it is, Dr Fox, and I'll explain everything.'

CHAPTER FIFTY-ONE

I hoped Sorcha might be drawn to the tower, like a moth to a flame,' said Delaney, 'but I didn't expect you to be here, Dr Fox.' He gestured to Kaidan, who held his pistol against Fox's back. 'I'd introduce you to my son, Dr Fox, but I believe you've already had dealings with each other in Portland.'

At that moment the Wives arrived in the chamber and stood in the centre of the amethyst lotus flower. They had been following, the heavily pregnant Maria slowing them down on the stairs. Zara stepped forward and picked up Fox's rifle. 'Pass me mine,' Kaidan said, pointing to the weapon on the floor beside Sorcha. Putting his

311

pistol in his belt, Kaidan stood back and levelled the rifle at Fox.

Zara moved towards Sorcha's locket but Delaney stopped her. 'Let her keep it,' he said. 'It doesn't matter now.'

'How could you have created this place?' Sorcha said, tears of anger in her eyes. 'How could my own father be so evil? I know what you did to my mother.' She shot a look at her half-brother and Delaney noticed Kaidan avert his gaze as if ashamed. This angered him. He saw Fox notice it too. Sorcha pointed down at the amethyst lotus flower, which covered most of the floor. 'How can this be any part of the Great Work? What's "great" about this?'

Delaney shook his head impatiently. Why couldn't she see the genius of what he had done? 'You of all people must understand this tower's power.' He spread his arms as if to embrace an unseen crowd. '*They* understood. All of them realized it was a privilege. They *begged* to participate in the Great Work. And, in due course, so will you.'

Fox helped Sorcha to her feet then turned to Delaney. If he was scared he didn't show it. 'What is this place?' he said.

Delaney picked up the family Bible from the floor near Sorcha and placed it carefully back on the amethyst plinth. 'I told you earlier. This tower's my observatory.' He tapped the concave surface of the white table. 'I use the camera obscura to look down upon my people going about their everyday lives on earth. But the main purpose of this place is to observe and experiment with astral bodies. What some call the soul or the spirit, and what you rather unimaginatively call . . .' He paused, searching for the right phrase.

'Death echoes?' said Fox.

'Yes. Echoes. The word's wrong but if it helps you to understand . . .'

'You have the same synaesthesia as me?' said Sorcha.

'Where do you think you and Kaidan got it from? Yours is more evolved, though. I can observe and sense death echoes but you can actually *feel* and *empathize* with them, walk in their shoes.'

'How long have you known you had it?' Fox said.

'Ever since I can remember. As a child I used to wander the streets near where my folks lived, seeking out places which resonated with what you call death echoes: abandoned buildings, hospitals, residential homes for the elderly, crime and accident scenes reported on the news.'

'Didn't they frighten you?' said Sorcha.

He smiled at the question. 'No, they excited me. They offered a glimpse beyond the mortal world. I used to collect souvenirs from the scenes, a piece of the wall or another part of the surrounding fabric, and make them into sculptures.'

'Like the mosaic on the door to this tower?'

'Exactly.' He clutched the ankh around his neck, warming to his theme. 'Each piece only contains a fragment of its death echo but put together they create a pleasing chorus. But I always wanted more. That's why I built this tower. Over the years I learned the key factors for creating the most resonant echo—the most defined imprint.'

He raised four fingers and counted them down. 'Number one, how recent the death. Number two, how violent and traumatic. Three, how close the

313

dying subject was to the imprinted material. Four, the material's composition. Composition is crucial. Some woods and bone imprint poorly and many man-made plastics and rubbers don't imprint at all. Natural stones, crystals and minerals imprint best but some work significantly better than others. A few can even conduct the absorbed imprint in the same way copper conducts electricity—allowing the echo to travel a considerable distance away from the place of death. I used all this knowledge to build my tower,' he said proudly. 'The outer shell is local stone. Then in the middle there's an insulating layer of rubber, which contains and concentrates the echoes within the tower. The inner wall is the most important, though. It's constructed of stone veined with an interconnecting network of amethyst.'

Fox looked at the violet gemstone on the floor and in the wall. 'Why amethyst?'

'Many reasons. It's tough: seven on the Mohs scale of mineral hardness. Diamond, the hardest, is ten. Amethyst is cheap too; there are vast deposits in Brazil. The main reasons for choosing amethyst, however, are that the violet gemstone is the colour of death, it corresponds to the seventh chakra and gives the most defined imprint.' Delaney pointed to the ankh around his neck. 'This contains an amethyst taken from a section of the headboard above my father's deathbed. The headboard only contained a few decorative inlays of the gemstone but its imprint of my father's death was deeper and more resonant than in the surrounding wall. It's also an excellent conductor for channelling the echoes.'

He reached out and patted the black ledger in

Fox's hand. 'Every one of the souls listed in there is in my collection.' He turned to his son. 'We started at the bottom with the reds and the other animal chakras, didn't we, Kaidan? Then we began working our way up.' Kaidan didn't respond but Delaney didn't care. He was enjoying explaining his work. 'As well as colour, we've experimented with age and gender, to see which subjects reveal the clearest path to the infinite. Our hypothesis is that the higher up the chakra scale, the better the subject.'

He watched Fox flick through the ledger, scanning the names, struggling to understand the enormity of his vision. 'You're saying that each of the people listed in this book was murdered next to one of the plaques in the walls?' said Fox. 'Just to imprint their individual death echo and add it to your collection?'

'They weren't murdered. They contributed gladly to the Great Work. Most pleaded with me to sacrifice their worthless physical shell for a glimpse of the infinite. Now, by touching a plaque I can experience that individual's dying imprint. But the Great Work is about more than just collecting death echoes.'

'And this?' Sorcha said, tentatively reaching down to the violet lotus symbol on the floor. As soon as she touched the amethyst she pulled back her hand as if scalded. 'What madness made you do this?'

Delaney frowned, unaccustomed to being challenged or questioned. He would have to make them appreciate and acknowledge the genius of what he had done. 'It's not madness. It's very simple.' He pointed at the white concave table

315

on which images from the camera obscura were projected by day. 'That's for observing the living.' His foot tapped the amethyst flower on the floor. 'This is for communing with the dead. This is my chorus of lost souls, my symphony of the dead and my inspiration for continuing with the Great Work. Death echoes diminish the further they travel from their source but, as I said, amethyst is an excellent conductor. The network of amethyst in the walls connects the individual plaques and then channels each death echo up the tower.

'Like veins carrying blood to the heart, every death echo flows into this amethyst lotus flower beneath our feet, the symbol of Sahasrara, the crown chakra of pure consciousness: the God Source. This symbol resonates with the faint but combined death throes of all the imprinted souls in this tower.' Delaney bent down, as if in prayer, placed his cheek flat against the polished gemstone and closed his eyes. For a moment he said nothing, just allowed the intense visions, smells and sounds to swirl around him. 'This, Dr Fox, is why Sorcha can't touch the violet. To me, this amethyst beneath our feet is a heavenly choir of the dying. Touching it makes my heart soar, makes me feel alive and validates my mission. To her, though, it's a sea of damned souls. She's so sensitive to their cries she fears that if she stands on it she will drown in their suffering. I envy the connection she feels.'

Fox stared down at the polished amethyst as if trying to see the ghosts in its shimmering reflective surface. 'What do you hope to achieve by capturing all these death echoes?'

'To follow their path and see beyond the veil. To regain my rightful, divine inheritance. Isn't it

316

obvious? And this is just the start. A small part of the Great Work.'

'But these are nothing more than imprinted echoes,' said Fox. 'Residual memories of a spent life force. You only sense them because of your rare synaesthesia. They can tell you no more about the afterlife than a spent match can tell you about fire. You're not a god. There's no magic here. How many people have to die before you understand that?'

Delaney couldn't believe it. The man still didn't understand. 'Don't be so obtuse. These are much more than echoes: they're spiritual footprints, a trail left by the departing astral body. A trail we can follow.'

'How can you know that?'

How can I know that? Had the psychiatrist not been listening? Did the man not understand that he was the Seer? Delaney's veneer of civility suddenly deserted him. 'How *dare* you fucking question me? How dare you doubt me? What do you know of this? Have *you* studied the phenomenon? Have *you* experienced it? Of course you haven't. *I* have.'

Fox still wouldn't back down. 'Whatever it is, your Great Work's over,' he said. 'When the police come looking for me—'

'They'll find nothing,' Delaney snarled. 'You were never here.' He indicated Kaidan. 'The police didn't think the killer was linked to us before, why should they think he is now? Not only have they no proof Kaidan was ever in Portland, they don't even know of his existence. And the police won't find anything to interest them in here. A silk garrotte is used for every sacrifice, which leaves no blood or mess, no trace at all.'

317

'What about the bone pit in the forest?'

Delaney thought for a second, absorbing the fact that Fox had found the burial ground. 'What about it? It's simply an unconventional burial site on private property—an offering back to nature of our discarded bodies. Assuming the authorities do find it, Kaidan will have already removed anything remotely incriminating. If I were you, Dr Fox, I'd worry less about dismissing the Great Work and more about what's going to happen to you.' He turned to his daughter. 'What do *you* think, Sorcha? Will you kneel on the lotus flower, touch the amethyst and then tell me they're nothing more than empty echoes or dumb imprints?' Sorcha didn't move. 'I thought not.' He turned to the Wives. 'Enough of this. Take her away.'

* * *

While listening to Delaney talk about his precious tower and Great Work, Fox had been studying the man, trying to understand better who he was dealing with. Throughout his career Fox had interviewed numerous patients and criminals with every form of psychosis and neurosis, but the ruthlessness of Delaney's psychopathy and scope of his megalomania were in a different league. Not only could the man not comprehend why anyone would be horrified by his Great Work, he demanded adoration for its brilliant vision and execution.

Fox's main focus had been on Kaidan, however. He'd been waiting for when the big man might lower his guard—and rifle. That moment came when Delaney ordered the Wives to take Sorcha away. As the Wives approached, both Regan

318

Delaney and Kaidan shifted their attention for an instant, and Fox took his chance. He lashed out with a straight punch to Kaidan's solar plexus, then he turned and hit him hard, aiming for the larynx with the point of his elbow. But Kaidan twisted as he fell, protecting his throat. Fox reached for the rifle, but before he could wrest it from Kaidan's fingers Delaney was upon him. He was strong and it took Fox precious seconds to fend him off by slamming the heel of his hand into Delaney's face with a satisfying crunch. By then Kaidan had recovered enough to ram the rifle barrel into Fox's gut and then slam the stock against his back. Fox's legs buckled beneath him and he fell to his knees, winded. As Kaidan stood over him and raised his rifle butt Fox tried to catch his breath and defend himself. Then Sorcha stepped on to the amethyst and threw herself at her half-brother.

'Leave him alone.'

'You're on the amethyst, Sorcha,' said Delaney, spitting blood from his mouth. 'You care that much for Dr Fox?'

She ignored Delaney and bent down to Fox. 'I'm so sorry, Nathan,' she said. 'For getting you into this.'

'It's OK,' he wheezed. As the Wives pulled her away he tried to rise to his feet, but Kaidan hit him again. 'Where are you taking her?' Fox demanded. 'What are you going to do with her?'

Delaney bent down so his face was inches from Fox's. His skin was white with anger. 'That doesn't concern you any more.' He revealed a syringe in his right hand and injected the contents into Fox's shoulder. The instant he felt the jab Fox knew it was ketamine. He could feel the numbness running

319

like ice through his veins. He tried to fight the drug but knew it was futile. His head fell to the floor and before his face lost all feeling the polished amethyst felt cool against his cheek. He had fallen on one of the areas patterned with holes and as he lay there he glimpsed the Wives dragging Sorcha down the staircase. 'Nathan, Nathan,' she kept calling up to him. But he couldn't reply.

'Dr Fox, you should never have got involved with my daughter,' said Delaney, taking the small silk noose, which Fox now realized was a hand tie, and securing his right wrist to the amethyst plinth. His voice sounded far away. 'You should never have come here.' At that moment, if Fox could have spoken, he would have agreed with him. Delaney walked towards the stairs. 'Come, Kaidan. We must prepare for tomorrow.'

'What about him?'

'He's not going anywhere. Let him get to know the other ghosts.' Fox heard the violet door close but could still hear Sorcha calling his name. 'Help them keep her quiet,' said Delaney, sending Kaidan ahead. As Fox lay immobile, he noticed the plaques on the walls around him. All were blank. Delaney had no violet death echoes in his collection. Was this why Sorcha was so important to his Great Work? Were they both to be sacrificed at Esbat so they could join Delaney's chorus of the dying?

Suddenly, the lamps went out, leaving him paralysed and in virtual darkness. Only a dim light from the level below shone through the holes in the glowing amethyst. He no longer had any sense of his body and wondered how much ketamine Delaney had given him. Large enough doses could cut you off from your surroundings and sense of self. Drug users called it the K-hole. As well as making it impossible to move or talk it could also make swallowing or breathing difficult.

He thought of the other lost souls trapped in the tower and suddenly felt very alone. It would be days before his aunt alerted Jordache that he hadn't returned and even then the detective would have no reason to suspect the worst. It could be a week before Jordache came looking for him, if he came at all. By then Fox could be nothing more than an imprinted memory, his dying moments recorded in the walls of the tower. Trying to keep at bay the echoes in the dark, he peered through the holes carved in the floor, and focused on the weak light below.

Suddenly, he saw two figures. For a second he feared they might be ghosts, then realized they were Delaney and the heavily pregnant Maria. For some reason they hadn't yet gone down with the others. As he listened to their whispers he was glad they were still there, perversely grateful for any human presence.

Then he saw what they were doing and wished he could turn away.

CHAPTER FIFTY-TWO

As Regan Delaney stood on the indigo level and watched Kaidan help the others escort Sorcha down the tower, he could taste the blood from his split lip. Who the hell did Fox think he was? How dare he come here to his domain and question the greatness of what he had achieved? Did he not have the vision to appreciate he was on the brink of something truly miraculous?

'Relax,' Maria soothed beside him. 'He's not worthy of your anger. He cannot understand what you're trying to do. He knows nothing.'

Fox had dismissed his project before he had explained the final stages and the ultimate objective of the Great Work. Delaney couldn't remember the last time someone had challenged him—let alone questioned the Great Work to which he had dedicated his life. How dare Fox claim the astral imprints were just echoes? What did he know of such matters? He was a quack. Maria was right: the man knew nothing. But he would learn soon enough.

The cause of his tension wasn't just Fox, though, it was the prospect of tomorrow night. Maria stroked his arm, sensing his apprehension. 'Everything's in place,' she said. 'After Esbat tomorrow night, your Great Work will be one step closer to completion.' She moved her hand to his crotch and began caressing him through the cloth. 'Nothing will go wrong. All of us will help. You are our Seer.'

She led him into one of the rooms and pressed his hand against one of the engraved amethyst plaques. Instantly, intense images, sounds and smells flooded his senses. Despite his anger and tension, he felt himself become aroused. He considered getting the cushions from the alcove but his need was too urgent. Keeping his hand pressed against the amethyst, he turned Maria to the wall and hitched up her robe. As he mounted her he felt for her distended belly. The child in her womb—his child—would be born any day now and he wondered if, after all these years, it would be another violet. As his pleasure intensified, he smiled. After tomorrow night it wouldn't matter if the child were born with a violet aura or not. Quickening his thrusts he pressed his palm harder against the wall plaque. Maria turned to look over her shoulder, cheeks red with exertion. 'I want to see your face,' she panted. 'I need to see your face.'

He groaned, pushed back his head and stared blindly at the ceiling. As he reached orgasm his eyes rolled in their sockets until only the whites were showing. For a few ecstatic seconds he was a god unconstrained by earthly bonds. He felt his spirit self depart his physical body, travel the astral plane and commune with the echoes around him. He sensed his pure consciousness merge with the astral signature imprinted on the amethyst plaque beneath his hand—the imprint of Aurora, the indigo mother of his violet Sorcha—and for a tantalizing moment, was convinced he was about to accompany her on her journey to the other side: to death. Then, knees trembling, forehead glazed with sweat, he was back in the physical world, returned to his mortal body. If while travelling the astral plane the invisible silver cord linking his two selves were severed, then his spirit would be free to follow Aurora all the way. But if that happened his physical body would die and he would never be able to return. To succeed in the Great Work he needed to straddle both worlds—the living and the dead. In time though, with Sorcha's help, that would happen. He was sure of it.

'What did you see?' Maria asked. 'What did you see?'

He smiled, brimming with renewed confidence.

323

'The future,' he said. 'I saw the future.'

CHAPTER FIFTY-THREE

Sorcha fought with all her strength but Kaidan and the remaining Wives were too powerful. After they bundled her into her room and locked the door and shutters, she collapsed on the bed, exhausted, holding her locket.

She was glad to have it back but Fox had been right. They should have gone back to get Jordache and the police when they'd had the chance. All she had achieved by entering the tower was to confirm how truly diabolical her family were. She had known Kaidan was a murderer from his handiwork in Portland. But her father was far worse. He had not only murdered Eve and ordered the murders of all the lost souls in the tower but he had killed her mother with his bare hands. When Sorcha had relived her mother's dying moments it had been almost too much to bear. Not only had she felt Aurora's pain and terror as if it were her own but she had seen her father's face, as close as a lover, staring into her eyes as he'd tightened the silk garrotte round her neck. She would never forget the excitement on her father's face as he'd squeezed out her mother's last breath.

She tried to calm herself and process what had happened. If she was going to be any use to Fox and herself, she needed to regain the equilibrium and distance the psychiatrist had taught her. However vivid the images, smells and sounds in the tower, however much they terrified her when she inhabited the victims' pain and suffering, she had to remember that they were just residual memories of terrible events. If her father chose to believe they were the victims' sentient souls, cursed to relive their deaths again and again, it was because he wanted to commune with the dying and follow their path to the other side. To maintain her sanity, she had to remember—and trust in—what Fox's aunt had told her: death echoes were nothing more than the light from dead stars. They were the vapour trails of souls long gone, harmless and no longer in pain.

She had hoped that entering the tower would help her recover her own memories but it had triggered only tantalizing glimpses of her past. Beyond the death echoes, she sensed something more recent had happened in the room where her mother had died, something involving Kaidan and herself. She couldn't bring it into focus, though, and memory flashes of Kaidan and her as children further confused her already hazy recall. She could remember fighting with him in the tower as if her life depended on it and feeling intense fear and revulsion when she had fled down the stairs. But she also remembered them both as children, bonded by their colour and branded the violet twins. She could recall him stroking her hair and her dressing the wounds on his shoulders after their father beat him. Like reflections in the shards of a shattered mirror, these partial recollections proved more disorienting than her earlier amnesia, without pattern or order.

As she tried to reassemble the fragments, she wondered what her father wanted with her. Did he intend to sacrifice her and enshrine her death echo in the tower because he believed her violet aura might better illuminate the path to the other side? Or did he have something else planned for her? She couldn't believe that his Great Work culminated in collecting death echoes. It seemed too petty, like a cruel child hoarding dead beetles. Her father had to be aiming for something more ambitious.

The sound of the door opening made her rise from the bed. Zara and Deva appeared with a bowl of steaming soup. She found it surreal that they could hold her captive, prepare her for who knows what horrors lay in store, and yet bring her soup. It smelt like chicken. 'Where's Dr Fox? Is he OK?'

'He's sleeping in the tower. You'll see him tomorrow,' said Deva. 'Now drink this. It'll soothe you.'

'I don't want soup. I can't eat after what's just happened.'

'You must drink it. It contains a sedative to help you sleep. If you don't have the soup we'll have to inject you. Trust me, this is more pleasant.'

'Zara, how can you be with my father and serve him after all he's done?'

The blonde smiled. 'He's a god. It's not our place to question him. Everything he does, he does for the Great Work, which benefits us all. We must all play our part.'

Deva nodded. 'To be summoned to the tower on the night of Esbat is a great honour and privilege.'

'But I don't want the honour.'

'Of course you do,' Deva said. 'Everyone wants to be chosen. You'll feel differently tomorrow.'

'Don't be frightened,' said Zara. 'We know what it means. It's special. You're lucky. Not only will the Seer be there when it happens—we all will.'

She smiled her infuriating, patronizing smile. 'We'll make it easier for you. Now drink your soup.'

Sorcha grabbed the steaming bowl and threw it against the wall. 'There's no way I'm going to be complicit in this. Whatever it is.' She stepped close to Zara. 'Listen to me. I don't want this. It's not an honour or a privilege. This is wrong. This is against my will. Do you understand?'

'We understand completely,' said Deva, behind her. As Sorcha turned she felt the needle pierce her right buttock. Then Zara and Deva were bundling her into bed, clucking soothing platitudes as if placating a truculent child.

Both the Wives and the room seemed to retreat as if Sorcha were being pulled back into a deep hole. Before she lost consciousness she registered the door opening and her father sitting on the bed. He was smiling and stroking her face. 'Get some sleep,' he said from some faraway place. 'Tomorrow will be challenging but worth the sacrifice because something miraculous will come of it.'

*   *   *

After Regan Delaney and Maria had left, all the lamps had automatically switched off, plunging the tower into total darkness, leaving Fox with the persistent image of Delaney's sightless eyeballs staring up at him. He remembered Connor telling him how his brother claimed to have an out-of-body experience when he reached orgasm, but what disturbed Fox more was that Delaney had been touching one of the plaques when it happened. It was almost as if he believed his disembodied spirit could commune with the echoes of the dead.

327

Fox regarded himself as a rational man but he understood better than most the dark, illogical turns the human mind could take. That night, lying paralysed in the tower, Fox wasn't sure what he knew or believed any more. The ketamine hadn't rendered him unconscious but hyper-conscious, as if he had become nothing but a mind with no body. Deprived of all sensory stimuli, he could feel nothing, see nothing, and hear nothing. Even the amethyst pressing against his nose had no smell. Nevertheless, he sensed the constant presence of others crowding around him in the dark. Whether it was the drug, sensory deprivation or just his imagination fuelled by what he knew had happened in the tower, Fox constantly heard whispers, glimpsed shadows and detected bizarre smells in the pitch black. The idea of being surrounded by the dead unnerved him until he thought of his parents and sister and imagined their ghosts protecting him.

As he lay there willing the effects of the drug to fade, he went over everything he had learned since first meeting Sorcha, searching for anything that might give him leverage over Delaney. He reviewed his first sessions with Sorcha, his meeting with Connor Delaney and his subsequent interactions with his brother—everything he had learned up till tonight. The discipline kept his mind active and staved off fear but it also confirmed the seriousness of his predicament. Over time, he began to feel sensation returning to his body and his mind drifting towards sleep. Part of him craved the escape of unconsciousness but another part needed to stay awake and plan. As he slipped towards sleep he recalled what Sorcha had told him

328

about the tense relationship between Kaidan and his father and he wondered how best to exploit it. As he pondered this he thought of the three grisly killings in Portland. Sorcha had said that Delaney had known about the murders but hadn't approved of them. That meant they had nothing to do with the Great Work. Kaidan had carried them out on his own against the Seer's express orders.

Why?

Fox had assumed Kaidan was simply getting his kicks in the Big City, sating his psychopathic hunger for killing in a target-rich environment. But something Sorcha had mentioned in the forest and something Fox had seen earlier tonight told him that the killings might have been more an act of rebellion. The more he thought about them, the more key he believed them to be. If he could understand the motivation behind his crimes, he could understand Kaidan. And if he could understand Kaidan he could influence him. As he struggled to stay awake, his mind wandered back to the crime scenes in Portland. His last conscious image before sleep claimed him was of a severed head in a bloodstained wardrobe. But it wasn't the head or the blood that occupied his thoughts; it was the photograph of Sorcha stapled to the corpse's forehead and the cryptic message written over her face in coloured letters:

SERVE THE DEMON
SAVE THE ANGEL

CHAPTER FIFTY-FOUR

Some hours earlier. Portland

As she did most evenings, after returning home from the university, Samantha Quail brewed herself a pot of her late husband's favourite tea: Twining's Assam. She had only recently stopped automatically putting out a second cup for him. Even as she glanced in the fridge and considered supper, she realized she was still thinking about what Howard and Nathan might like, rather than what appealed to her. Whatever she told Nathan, she still missed Howard more than she cared to admit, particularly in the evenings when the big house seemed so quiet and empty. She missed Nathan, too, although he had only been away for a couple of days.

The sound of the bell made her close the fridge and hurry to the door. She hoped it might be Nathan, returned from seeking Sorcha in the wilderness, but it wasn't. 'Hello, Samantha. Can we talk?' She had known Detective Jordache for years, ever since the fateful day he had led her nephew out of the garage in which her sister, brother-in-law and niece had been brutally murdered. This evening he looked uncomfortable, almost as uncomfortable as the night Sorcha had stayed with her and Jordache's men had failed to stop the killer getting into her house. As well as a notebook, she noticed he was carrying her paper on archaeosonics under one arm.

'Come in.' She went to the kitchen, finished pouring her tea, then made Jordache a black

330

espresso the way she knew he liked it.

'It's about Nathan.' He took the coffee and thanked her. 'You know the three homicides he was helping us with?'

She nodded. 'He said you might pop round to ask a few questions once you'd had a chance to think things through. He also said you didn't believe his theory about the killer and Sorcha.'

Jordache sat beside her at the kitchen table, placed the documents in front of him and took another sip of coffee. 'What Nathan said was pretty hard to believe.' A shrug. 'But we've just lost our prime suspect: a head case who tried to take credit for the homicides until we discovered he was with his sister in Seattle on the night of the first killing. So we're back to square one.' He paused. 'And . . .'

'And what?'

Jordache picked up the notebook. 'Nathan made detailed notes in here about what Sorcha told him she "sensed" at the three crime scenes: both the prior murders and the recent ones. The prior ones can be explained because most of the details were in old police records.'

She laughed drily. 'Come on, Karl. How could Sorcha have known what was in police records? She has no memory of her life before a couple of weeks ago and afterwards she was stuck in Tranquil Waters.'

Jordache grimaced and raised a hand. 'I know. I know. The point is: they happened years ago and records exist so it would be *possible* for her to learn the details. But the new killings are much harder to explain away. Sorcha told Nathan stuff—like how one of the victims was stabbed—which she couldn't have known.'

'So how do you explain it, Karl?'

'I can't.' He tapped Samantha's paper. 'Is this how *you* explain it? With ghosts?'

'They're not ghosts. They're recordings, burned into the fabric of a building. Archaeosonics is unproven but the evidence is growing.' She summarized the key points of her thesis just as she had for Sorcha when they had first met. 'Crucially, Sorcha's unique synaesthesia enables her to play back these imprinted dying moments.'

He frowned. 'Her death-echo synaesthesia?'

'That's what Nathan calls it because she appears to experience a building's archaeosonics through the prism of her five senses—creating a sixth. Did Nathan tell you about the envelope experiment he conducted at Tranquil Waters?'

'No,' said Jordache. 'I'm afraid I wasn't at my most receptive or open-minded when we last spoke.' She told Jordache about the experiment and her subsequent discussion with Fox and Sorcha. 'So you believe her gift is possible?' he asked.

She nodded. 'Quantum physics says it's not only possible but probable. Especially as nothing else explains her visions or sensory hallucinations.'

'Could anyone else possess this death-echo synaesthesia?'

'I don't see why Sorcha should be unique. As you know, Nathan was convinced the killer had the same synaesthesia and was a member of her father's cult. That's why he went off to warn her.'

'I thought he was just hung up on Delaney's cult because of what happened to his folks. He shouldn't have gone by himself. I told him not to go.'

She raised an eyebrow. 'You gave him no

choice.'

'When do you expect him back?'

'He said I should call you if he hadn't returned by the end of the week. Tell you to go get him.' She felt a cold shiver. 'Karl, you think Nathan's in real danger?'

'Possibly. I don't know,' Jordache said, a little too quickly. 'I need to know more about Regan Delaney's cult. Did Nathan tell you anything about it?'

'Only a little. If you want more, you should go see his brother, Connor Delaney, in Sacramento.' She got up anxiously. 'Nathan left me his number.' As she pressed it into his hand she locked eyes with Jordache. 'He's your friend, Karl. If he is in danger, then bring him back safely to me. Like you did once before.'

CHAPTER FIFTY-FIVE

Sorcha slept in deathly oblivion until her nightmares returned. She woke before dawn, in a cold sweat. The sedative had made her mouth feel dry and her temples ache but the confusion in her head troubled her more. In her dreams she had again been running from a demonic pursuer through a deserted hotel of empty rooms, occupied only by the ghosts of the dead. It was obvious now that the hotel of the dead was the tower and her demonic pursuer was Kaidan. She was running from him because of something specific that had happened.

But what?

Had he attacked her? Was he jealous of her

because she had usurped his place in their father's Great Work? If so, why did her father need her now? Kaidan had obviously borne the burden of their father's expectations for most of his life so what had happened to make her more important? Had the Great Work changed? Had something happened between Kaidan and Delaney? Or had something changed with her?

Rubbing her eyes with frustration, she sensed she held the answers to all these questions within her, if only she could remember them. She was aware of her lost memories hovering on the cusp of her consciousness, tantalizingly fragmented and unfocused, and realized she was running out of time. Soon it would be dawn, and then Esbat, with all it threatened, would be upon her.

PART 4
Beyond Indigo

CHAPTER FIFTY-SIX

The pain in Nathan Fox's bound wrist woke him, accompanied by the throb in his skull, and the ache in his back and gut from where Kaidan had hit him with the rifle. The pain at least welcomed him back to his body and told him that the numbing paralysis from the ketamine had passed. He rolled over in the dark to get more comfortable on the polished amethyst floor. Relaxing his hand, he tried to loosen the garrotte-like grip of the silk noose around his wrist but the more he picked at it the tighter it became.

Unsure if it was night or day, he noticed a pinprick of light coming through the top of the conical ceiling and realized the chamber wasn't as dark as before. He rose to his knees and looked across at the concave table. Its white surface was alive, illuminated with moving images projected from a lens at the top of the tower's conical roof. It appeared to be just after dawn but as the lens rotated there was enough daylight for it to project a clear and detailed panorama of the surrounding settlement into the camera obscura.

As he watched the Indigo Family emerge from their cabins and go about their business he saw many head for the Great Hall, no doubt to complete the preparations for Esbat. A rush of anxiety made him stand and stretch his muscles. The sudden movement triggered the lamps. The light was low but after his night of darkness Fox welcomed it like the sun.

On the amethyst plinth, next to the black ledger,

337

Fox noticed the leather-bound family Bible Regan had stolen from Connor. Flicking through its ancient yellowed pages he was surprised to see how many had been defaced with red ink. Words and chapters had been ringed and underlined, like a student's notes in a thumbed school text. In Ecclesiastes 12:6 the words *before the silver cord is broken* had been underlined three times. And every mention of the Grigori or the Nephilim in the books of Genesis and Numbers had been ringed in red.

At the front of the Bible was a thick concertina of pages which, when unfolded, revealed a lovingly illustrated family tree scribed with beautiful calligraphy. The tree went back centuries, to when the Delaneys first appeared in Ireland. Two things stood out. The first was that all the men's names were written in bold capitals, the women's in regular lower case. The second was that most of the names had an asterisk by them, which, according to a legend at the top of the first page, meant they possessed the *mothú*. Seeing how many people had inherited the family trait and how far back it went helped Fox understand how important this had once been to the Delaneys. Some of the lines in the tree were drawn ambiguously, indicating that on more than one occasion close family members had married each other to keep the *mothú* alive. He unfolded more pages until he found Regan Delaney's name.

He heard a door opening and footsteps on the stairs. His heart jumped. They were coming for him. Kaidan appeared through the opening in the centre of the lotus symbol and stepped into the room. Two men in indigo tunics were with him.

338

When Kaidan saw the Bible he strode over and took it from Fox. 'I was just looking at your family history and couldn't help noticing how patriarchal it is,' Fox said.

'This is none of your business,' Kaidan growled, replacing the Bible on the plinth.

'The women appear to be there only to make up the numbers,' Fox said, 'which is strange, given the importance your father and his ancestors placed on the *mothú*. Did you know synaesthesia tends to be passed down through the female line?'

Kaidan ignored him, pulled a large knife from a sheath on his belt and cut the silk tie on Fox's wrist, releasing him from the plinth. He then looped another silk tie around both hands and tightened it. Close up, beneath the smell of soap and shampoo, Fox smelt a subtle malodour. Though Kaidan had just showered he still carried the smell of death about him. Medical examiners, who dealt with death daily, had told Fox they sometimes had to shower two or three times to purge the smell from their skin but Fox surmised that Kaidan probably had a mild form of trimethylaminuria, a rare metabolic disorder that most commonly caused sufferers to excrete the smell of fish or, in some cases, decay.

'I understand why your father valued you more than your half-sister, Kaidan, because you were the first-born male and she was just a worthless girl. But I don't understand what happened to make her so important now. What did you do wrong? What changed your father's mind about her?'

Kaidan turned to the men. 'Take him,' he barked.

The men pulled him up by the silk tie around his

wrists and dragged him to the stairs. Kaidan led the way. 'Where are you taking me?' Fox said.

'To the preparation suite,' said Kaidan. 'So you can ready yourself for tonight.' Something flickered in his cold eyes. 'You should feel honoured. The Seer's chosen you to be one of the two Pathfinders selected every Esbat.'

'What about Sorcha?'

'She'll be joining you.'

'And you? Do you still have a role in the Seer's Magnum Opus?'

A half-smile curled his lips but didn't reach his eyes. 'Oh yes. I still have a role.' The men dragged Fox down the stairs, out of the tower and across the still-quiet settlement to a cabin beyond the Great Hall. The preparation suite consisted of a small room with a prayer mat on the floor, a bathroom and an adjoining larger room with a couch, table and chairs. The table was generously laden with food and drink. Two sticks of incense burned by the window, which was covered with a wrought-iron grille. Kaidan pulled out his knife again and cut Fox's silk hand ties. 'Use the bathroom, make yourself comfortable. The others are fasting until the feast tonight but you won't be eating then so take whatever you like now.'

'Why won't I be eating tonight?'

'Pathfinders don't take part in the feast.'

Fox rubbed his wrists. 'Is this my last supper?'

Kaidan ignored the question. 'All Pathfinders are brought here, isolated from the others, provided with peace and quiet and all physical comforts. Consider it an opportunity to prepare and purify yourself for Esbat.' Kaidan told the two Watchers to stand guard outside. As soon as they had closed and locked the door Kaidan raised the knife and held the blade close to Fox's face. For the first time his eyes betrayed the white heat of his anger. 'Don't you dare disrespect me in front of the Watchers,' he seethed. 'Sorcha has *not* become more important than me. We're both equally important.'

Fox couldn't help wondering if the blade inches from his right eye was the same one that had severed the man's head in Portland but he kept his voice calm, adopting the tone he used with all his patients—and murder suspects. He had to engage him if he wanted to probe the killings in Portland. 'I understand,' he said. 'It must be very difficult.'

Kaidan pushed the knife closer. 'How can you possibly understand? I did everything the Seer asked of me. I've only ever failed him once—and tonight I'll put that right.'

'I understand you've devoted your whole life to your father's goal, done terrible things in his name, made unimaginable sacrifices and surrendered all your own hopes and dreams to his. So it must be devastating to have him now throw all that dedication and loyalty back in your face just when the project is reaching its climax. Turning to your sister for help when she doesn't even want any part of the Great Work.'

Kaidan blinked, taken aback by Fox's assessment. 'He still needs me to play my part.'

'I'm sure he does. But why do you obey him?'

'He's the Seer,' Kaidan said.

'Sorcha told me your aura's as pure as his, if not purer. Surely your power's equal to his? You're obviously angry with him. Why do you take it?'

Kaidan looked at him as if he was speaking a foreign language. 'He's my father. He's the Seer,' he said again. '*Everyone* obeys him.'

'That's not true,' Fox said softly. 'You disobeyed him when you killed those three men in Portland. Why? At first I thought it might be just for the sadistic thrill but it was more than that, wasn't it?'

Kaidan narrowed his eyes. 'They were nothing to me.'

'Then why make the killings so elaborate? Why target rapists and murderers and then kill them the same way they killed their victims? And why did you staple a picture of Sorcha to their faces and leave a cryptic message? What does "*Serve the demon, save the angel*" mean, Kaidan? Were you talking about the demon in you or is the demon someone else . . .?'

Kaidan stepped back, still brandishing the knife. The confused look on his face told Fox that the young man was so conflicted he probably didn't know himself why he had done what he had done—not consciously, anyway.

'What's going to happen to Sorcha, Kaidan? Are we both to be killed and added to your father's collection?'

Kaidan smiled coldly. 'You still don't get it, do you? To my father, killing the children of men is no different to slaughtering cattle but Sorcha's not a daughter of man. She's *his* daughter. She's special.' He walked to the door. 'She's been touched with the divine.' As he spoke of his sister, Kaidan's harsh tone softened and Fox detected wistfulness, even affection in his voice. He recalled Kaidan's evident shame when Sorcha had accused Delaney of killing her mother. In his experience true psychopaths were incapable of shame. Then he remembered the Mayan sacrificial stone in his uncle Howard's study. When Kaidan had touched it he would have experienced the intense death echoes of countless sacrificial victims, women whose hearts had been pulled out of their chests still beating. Perhaps it wasn't simply the shock of the unexpected that had made Kaidan knock it to the floor. Perhaps the imprints in the stone had repelled and horrified him, as they would do any sane human being. If so, then there might still be the dying embers of a conscience within him.

'When you said you've only failed the Seer once, did your failure involve Sorcha? Was it something you didn't—or couldn't—do?'

Kaidan sheathed the knife and turned to leave. 'Stop trying to get inside my head. What happened in Portland is unimportant. It's in the past. Only the future matters, and Sorcha and I are *both* the future. She and I are the only violets my father produced and without more violets there'll be no Great Work.' He stood by the door and looked Fox in the eye. 'You're a shrink so you think you understand the human mind. But to understand my father you've got to look beyond the petty concerns of the children of men and strive to know the mind of God.' Kaidan knocked on the door and waited for the Watchers to unlock it. 'You can't begin to imagine what he's planned for Sorcha,' he said as the door opened. He paused before closing the door behind him. 'And me.'

But when Fox glanced through the window at the thoroughbred horses running round the corral and considered the Delaney family Bible he *could* imagine what the Seer had planned. In his time as a clinical and forensic psychiatrist Fox had been exposed to many terrible things but the dawning

343

realization of what awaited Sorcha made him shudder.

CHAPTER FIFTY-SEVEN

Talking to Fox about the killings in Portland had confused Kaidan and given him a headache. What the hell was the shrink talking about? He hadn't selected his victims or the way he'd killed them for any specific reason. They had been nothing more than impulsive acts to help ease the tension in his head.

Hadn't they?

He rubbed his temples and cursed Fox. The first kill had certainly been a spontaneous impulse he had felt compelled to act on. But the other two? Had he really sought those victims out? Had he selected them? All he knew with any certainty was that the temporary peace he had gained from killing them had soon dissipated. That was why he'd put the Portland killings behind him once he had returned to the settlement. He had told himself—and kept telling himself—that it was easier to obey his father and accept his destiny than it was to question it. If the Seer wanted to involve Sorcha in his plans then so be it. All their lives Kaidan had borne the searing heat of his father's relentless scrutiny alone. It was time Sorcha played her part and shared the burden. Whatever had happened, whatever his father's reasons, Kaidan knew he was still key to the Great Work. The Seer still needed both of them—Sorcha *and* him—to take it to the next level.

344

Nevertheless, Fox had stirred up all of his old unresolved emotions. However much he wanted to dismiss the psychiatrist's words, Fox had perfectly articulated his anger at being sidelined by the Seer after sacrificing everything to the Great Work. The shrink seemed to understand him better than his own father did—better perhaps than he understood himself. Kaidan had always believed it was a great honour and privilege to execute his father's plan. Being the Seer's son and right-hand man had not only defined his life but also justified everything his father had demanded of him. Every deed for the Seer, no matter how steeped in blood, served a higher purpose which transcended banal morality. Moreover, Kaidan was his heir, the future. So to be told that his half-sister, who had done and sacrificed nothing, was suddenly the Seer's shining new hope for the Great Work was hard to bear.

As Kaidan made his way to his father's quarters, he wrestled with his confused feelings. He felt angry and bitter, but not with Sorcha. How could he be angry with his half-sister when she wanted no part in their father's work? All he knew with any certainty was that he needed to speak with her before tonight.

*　　　*　　　*

By the time Kaidan entered her room, Sorcha was trying to reconcile the jigsaw of her shattered memories and half-remembered flashes of her half-brother as a child with the killer he had become. She turned to look at him. 'Kaidan, were we close as children?'

He sat on the chair by the bed with his hands on

his knees. 'They say we were born within hours of each other. After my mother died of pre-eclampsia your mother nursed me as her own. She was the only mother I knew. They called us the violet twins.'

She tried to imagine this killer as an innocent child. 'Did we look out for each other?'

Kaidan nodded. 'We used to hide together from our father when he was in one of his rages. And you dressed my wounds when he beat me.'

'Did he beat you a lot?'

A shrug. 'The Seer has very high expectations.'

'What about my mother—*our* mother? Did she protect you?'

'I think she tried but she had her hands full protecting you. And there wasn't much she could do. Our father's the Seer. Everyone worships him. No one defies the Seer.' He frowned, remembering something. 'Apart from you. You were fearless. You sometimes protected me.' A smile creased his lips and for a moment Kaidan looked almost animated. 'One time I had a nosebleed over one of the Seer's books so you cut your finger and told him you'd got the pages bloody. You knew he'd beat me for it but figured he'd leave you alone.'

'Why?'

'You were invisible. You were a girl. He never asked anything of you. I think that's why you defied him. To get his attention. As I grew up, our mother spent time with you, while the Seer focused on me. I was his great hope. The violet son. The future.'

She remembered the death echo in the tower and shuddered. 'Why did he kill our mother, Kaidan?'

He looked down. 'You'll have to ask him.'

'What happened, Kaidan? How did that child

I'm remembering become a killer? What happened to you?'

He stiffened and crossed his arms. 'I did my duty. That's what happened. Everything I've done has been for the Great Work.'

'For the Seer?'

'Of course, whatever he asked of me.'

'What about me?' A shiver of fear ran through her. 'Was I involved in the killings?'

He looked at her for a long while. Then he shook his head. 'No.' She felt her shoulders sag, relieved to absolve her past self of her family's monstrous sins. 'You were lucky,' Kaidan said. 'As a girl you had it easy. I was the one he moulded. I was the one he put to work in the slaughterhouse when I was seven to harden me up. I was the one he forced to kill a man when I'd barely turned twelve. From you he expected nothing. Until now.'

'Did I *know* about the killings?'

Again he paused. And again he shook his head. 'No one, except the Seer's inner circle, knows about the sacrifices in the tower. You only found out about them on the day you ran away.'

'Is that why I ran away?' She studied his face and tried to read his blank eyes. 'Or did something else happen?'

He looked down at his feet and clasped his hands together. 'That won't happen again. I've promised the Seer I won't fail this time. Tonight I'll do my duty.'

Fear surged through her. 'Do what duty? Kill me? Is that why my father's involving me now? Because he needs a violet death echo?'

He looked up at her and a spark flared in his blank eyes—a spark she couldn't read. 'It's strange.

347

Dr Fox thought the same thing but I'd never kill you, Sorcha. I couldn't. The Seer has other plans for you.' He paused. 'For us.'

Something about the way he said it and the way he looked at her heightened her unease. 'What about Nathan? What's going to happen to him?'

'Why? What's he to you?'

'I owe him everything.'

Kaidan's eyes narrowed. He looked almost jealous. 'Does he know how you feel about him? It's obvious he cares for you.'

'Why's it obvious he cares for me?' she said, before she could stop herself.

'Because he came for you. Because he's risked his life for you,' Kaidan said, his unblinking eyes studying her. 'Because he's going to die for you.'

CHAPTER FIFTY-EIGHT

Chief of Detectives Karl Jordache didn't like things he couldn't understand. He had become a detective to solve crimes and eliminate reasonable doubt. However, since reading Nathan Fox's clinically detailed notes on Sorcha's death-echo synaesthesia and Professor Samantha Quail's paper on archaeosonics, he had been neck-deep in doubt— reasonable and unreasonable. Talking with Fox's aunt yesterday had only increased his concern that Fox could be right about the killer being part of the Indigo Family and spiked his guilt for letting his friend go alone into the remote unknown, without back-up.

This morning he had been tied up in meetings

with the district attorney but at lunch he had flown out to the stud farm in Sacramento to talk with Connor Delaney about his brother's cult. Now, as he stood in the main house watching Connor's daughter riding one of the horses in the paddock he remembered the pathologist's reports on the first and last victims. Both bodies contained traces of ketamine: an anaesthetic drug popular in veterinary medicine, particularly for tranquillizing horses.

'You ever use ketamine on the horses?'

'We used to,' said Connor. 'Now it's mainly Rompun.'

'You said your brother was a trained veterinarian, who also breeds horses in his cult.'

'Yes.'

'So he'd know how to get hold of ketamine and how best to use it?'

'Sure he would,' Connor Delaney said. 'What's this about? Dr Fox said my brother had come to reclaim a patient from his cult. Said she'd got amnesia or something and wanted to make sure she'd be safe going back with him. He didn't say anything about ketamine.'

'Did he ask you about your brother's synaesthesia?'

'I told him the *mothú* has been in our family for centuries and my brother's got a pretty intense form of it—in fact he claimed to have most forms of it. That's why the Indigo Family embraced him and made him their leader. Where are you going with this?'

Jordache told him about the murders. 'Dr Fox believed that whoever committed the murders also had a pretty intense form of synaesthesia and was part of the cult.'

349

Connor looked horrified. 'You think my brother had something to do with them?'

'He wasn't in Portland when the homicides were committed. But someone from his cult—someone with a rare form of synaesthesia and access to ketamine—may have been. Fox was concerned the killer was after his patient who was also very synaesthesic.' He paused. 'Did he tell you who she was?'

'No.'

'Sorcha was Regan's daughter. Your niece.'

Connor opened his mouth in shock. 'His daughter? How old?'

'Young. Early twenties tops.'

'You say she's very synaesthesic.'

'Very, according to Fox.'

Connor thought for a moment. 'She could be one of the violet twins. I remember seeing them once, towards the end of our legal battle with Regan. Aurora claimed both had auras even purer than their father.'

'Twins?'

'They were actually half-brother and half-sister born at about the same time. Something happened to the boy's mother and Aurora sort of adopted him. The girl was a real sweetie, although Regan seemed only to notice the boy, who he shouted at a lot. Strange kid, big for his age and clumsy. Oh yeah, he had some sort of problem. What did Aurora call it? Some long medical name beginning with a T. Whatever, it made the poor bastard smell funny.'

Jordache leaned forward. 'Smell of what?'

'Weird, like something had died.' Jordache's surprise must have shown on his face because

Connor frowned. 'What is it?'

'Witnesses said the killer smelt of death.'

Connor said nothing for a moment, then muttered a heartfelt 'Shit' and went into the kitchen. He returned with a calendar. 'What was Sorcha doing in Portland? Had she run away from the cult?'

'That's what Fox was trying to find out.'

'But Regan came for her? Wanted her back?'

'Of course. She was his daughter.'

Connor shook his head and studied the calendar. 'You don't know my brother. He doesn't think like you or me. The only reason he'd have left the safety of his settlement and come to Portland to reclaim her was if she—or her aura—were valuable to him and his Great Work.'

'His what?'

Connor didn't answer, just looked up from the calendar and gazed out at his young daughter riding one of the beautiful horses in the paddock. She waved at them and both men waved back. Connor's face was pale. 'Shit,' he said again.

'What?'

'If you want to protect my niece and help Dr Fox, it's not just her half-brother you need to worry about. Tonight's a full moon, what Regan's cult calls Esbat. If I'm right—and I hope to God I'm not—then you've got till midnight, the witching hour, to save them both.' He checked his watch. 'That only leaves a few hours.'

'What do you hope you're not right about?'

When Connor told him, Jordache's first reaction was disbelief. 'You've got to be kidding?'

'Like I said, I hope I'm wrong.'

Jordache thought of Sorcha, not much older

351

than his own daughters, and how he had dismissed Fox's fears, letting his friend go after her alone and unprotected. Fox wasn't even a cop, for Christ's sake, just a goddamn shrink. What chance did he have against a killer? Jordache felt sick. As he picked up his phone and rushed out to the car he hoped Connor Delaney was wrong. God, he hoped he was wrong.

CHAPTER FIFTY-NINE

Fox knew he had nothing to lose when Kaidan returned to the preparation suite and placed a pile of items on the table. For the last few hours he had tried not to think about what Regan Delaney had in store for Sorcha and him tonight. In particular he'd tried not to think of the silver silk wrist ties and braided cords—which he now realized were garrottes—strewn casually on the piles of white linen in the tower.

Instead he had tried to focus on his last conversation with Kaidan and review all he could remember of the killings in Portland. Just as it was all beginning to fall into place, Kaidan had brought in the pile of items. It wasn't the bag of toiletries and towel, the worn but freshly laundered thick white robe or the scuffed sandals that confirmed his worst fears, but the strange headpiece designed to cover the mouth and the band of silk that Fox suspected was a gag. He could sense he was now on Death Row, hours from his execution. As Kaidan laid the paraphernalia on the table he quickly slipped the headpiece and gag into his pocket as if he hadn't intended Fox to see them yet. He pointed at the toiletries and robe. 'You need to shower and wear these for the ceremony.'

Fox couldn't help staring at Kaidan's pocket. 'Why?'

'It's what the Pathfinders willingly wear,' Kaidan said as if speaking to a difficult child.

'They willingly wear a gag?'

A shrug. 'Even the most devoted can sometimes lose their nerve. A gag protects their dignity by guaranteeing they don't disgrace themselves should their resolve falter.'

'Do the Indigo Family know the Pathfinders are gagged?'

'If you can't or won't wear what's required, the Watchers and Wives will *help* you. They appreciate what a great honour it is and envy the opportunity you've been given.'

'If any of them want to take my place, they're more than welcome to it.'

'They haven't been chosen,' Kaidan said. 'It's not their time.'

Fox patted the pile. 'I'll prepare myself but I want to talk about you first.' Kaidan stiffened. 'I know what you were trying to do in Portland. I know what *"Serve the demon, save the angel"* means.'

He shook his head. 'That's in the past.'

'But it could affect your future—and Sorcha's.'

'I don't care,' said Kaidan. But he made no attempt to leave so Fox tried to do what he'd done many times before: explain to a killer why he had killed. Only this time Fox's own life depended on it.

'When did your father start brutalizing you? I'm guessing you were just a boy. He did a good job. He conditioned you to obey him totally. How many people have you killed for him in the tower?' Kaidan said nothing, just stared back. 'You've lost count, I guess. Judging from the bones in the forest and the ledger, it's included men, women and children. You've always rationalized these terrible deeds, of course, telling yourself they were for a greater good. For the Seer and the Great Work.

'Then your father began to involve Sorcha and you hated that. It confused you and made you feel worthless. You thought you felt bad because your father had undervalued your contribution and your sacrifice. And I thought that too, at first. I thought you hated Sorcha, were jealous of her, and wanted to kill her so you could retake your place at the centre of the Seer's plans. But now I realize that wasn't true. That wasn't true at all.'

Keeping his eyes locked on Kaidan's, Fox did something he had never done with the killers he had confronted in the past. He stepped closer to his subject, until he was only inches away. 'The thing is,' Fox continued, 'your father's a natural psychopath—on the Hare psychopathy checklist, I'm guessing he'd get close to a perfect score—but I don't believe you are. When you thought what you were doing was for some pseudo-divine purpose you could just about rationalize it, but when it affected those you cared about it tortured you. I saw you exhibit shame when Sorcha accused your father of killing her mother. I'm guessing Sorcha's mother had been like a mother to you, too. And when Sorcha got involved in the Great Work you found it even harder to accept. Not because she was usurping your position with your father but because you didn't want her to go through what you had.

354

Your problem, though you can't consciously admit it to yourself, is not that you hate Sorcha but that you *love* her.'

Kaidan turned away. 'You're so full of shit.'

As he turned, Fox reached for the knife in his belt. Kaidan tried to stop him but Fox was too quick. When the big man lunged, Fox used Kaidan's own impetus to roll him on his back and push the knife up under his groin. 'That's why you couldn't do what your father ordered you to do on the day she fled,' Fox continued, barely missing a beat. 'And that's why you killed those men in Portland.'

'I don't have to listen to this bullshit.'

Fox pushed the blade harder against Kaidan's groin. 'Yes, you do. If I twist the knife to the right I'll cut your femoral artery and you'll bleed to death in seconds. If I twist it to the left I'll cut off your balls.' Kaidan scowled, face blank and eyes dead, but said nothing so Fox continued, 'When Sorcha fled you begged your father to let you search for her—to find her and put right your failure. But when you got to Portland something happened while you were searching for Sorcha. Something which distracted you. A super-synaesthete like you must have found the city a sensory rollercoaster, especially coming from this place. I'm guessing you were drawn to the seedier part of town, seeking out the most violent death echoes. Old Town must be infested with them. Am I right?'

Kaidan twisted suddenly and tried to throw him, but he was too clumsy and slow. Fox easily rode the move and kept the knife blade pressed against Kaidan's groin. 'Where did you chance upon Vince Vega, your first victim? Was it walking down the street? In a hotel? In a bar? You recognized him

355

from one of the death echoes, didn't you? You knew what Vega had done and made a connection with your father and with Sorcha.'

Kaidan's eyes widened in disbelief. 'It was in a bar. When I was watching Sorcha on the news,' he said, before he could stop himself.

Fox nodded, trying not to betray relief that his hunch had been correct. 'You not only compared Vega with your father. You contrasted him with Sorcha, who had saved those girls from the Russians and would be at your father's mercy as soon as you delivered her to him. You couldn't defy the Seer directly but by punishing Vega you could feel like you were rebelling against the Seer and siding with Sorcha. Defying your father—if only in the guise of Vega—and avenging his victims made you feel good about yourself for the first time since you were a child. After killing Vega you sought out other men like him, rapists and murderers of women, in the target-rich hunting ground of Old Town. They all became surrogates for your father. When you killed them—in the same way they'd killed their victims—you were punishing your father, protecting Sorcha and avenging her mother. You saw the killers as your father and the victims as Sorcha; that's why you stapled her photograph over their faces.

'Despite your unquestioning loyalty to the Seer and despite all his talk of the Indigo Family's genetic links to angels, you subconsciously believe he's a demon. The message you left at every crime scene expressed this inner conflict, your dilemma. Should you serve your father or save Sorcha? You knew you couldn't do both. I now think you broke into both the clinic and my aunt's house because,

356

in some half-assed way, you were trying to save her. You knew your father was coming to reclaim Sorcha and wanted to take her somewhere safe, somewhere he could never find her—or you.'

Kaidan glared at him but said nothing.

'I know what your father wanted you to do when you failed him, Kaidan. And I think he wants you to do it again tonight. But you didn't fail. Don't you understand that? By defying him you succeeded. Your better nature won. Whatever you've done in the past, Kaidan, you can still become the person you want to be. You are the choices you make now, *today*. You didn't want to hurt your half-sister because you couldn't. You won't accept it but . . .'

'But *what*?' snarled Kaidan. 'I love her? I don't love her. *You* do.'

It was a schoolboy's retort but it stopped Fox short for a moment. In the silence he became aware of muted sounds outside: birdsong, excited laughter and horses neighing. He pushed his face close to Kaidan's. 'The important thing is, Kaidan, you have the power to defy your father and stop this madness,' he said. 'You don't have to serve the demon any more. You can save the angel. And by saving her you can save yourself.'

Fox saw something spark in the man's eyes, a glimmer of understanding. Kaidan opened his mouth and was about to speak when the door opened and the two Watchers stepped into the cabin. As they raised their rifles and aimed at Fox, Kaidan smiled at him. 'What are you going to do now?' Fox detected sadness in his smile. Then Kaidan stopped smiling. 'Do it. Use the knife. Sever the artery or cut off my balls. Either way you'll solve your precious Sorcha's little problem. Or haven't *you* got the balls?'

It would be so easy: one flick of his wrist and the man would bleed to death. But it wasn't easy. Not for Fox.

Like a wild animal, Kaidan instantly sensed his hesitation. Scowling in disgust he grabbed at Fox's knife hand. 'You're so fucking weak. Get him off me,' he shouted to the Watchers, who cudgelled Fox with their rifles until he dropped the knife. Kaidan got to his feet, picked up the blade and checked his groin. Looking down at Fox he frowned. 'You should have done it. Killing a man gets easier after the first one. Trust me.' He turned to leave.

'Save the angel, Kaidan,' Fox shouted after him. 'Don't serve the demon. There'll be no turning back if you obey the Seer this time. You'll destroy the one person you love and be enslaved to your father for ever. Whatever he's made you do in the past he can't make you do this. He can't make you inseminate your own sister.'

At that moment the Wives appeared in the doorway, blocking Kaidan's exit. Sorcha was with them. Shock and horror were etched on her pale face.

CHAPTER SIXTY

Inseminate your own sister. Sorcha's mind froze as she tried to process Fox's words. She couldn't, wouldn't believe them. But as Kaidan tried to push past her, more wreckage of her memory surfaced. She remembered the weight of his body pressing down on her, the smell of his sweat, the redness of his face as he tore at her clothes. Then she remembered running away, down the stairs, out of the tower.

What had happened?

'What did you do the day I left?' she said, grabbing her half-brother's shoulder. 'What happened in the tower?' He avoided her gaze and tried to push past, but she clung on. 'What did you do to me?'

'Nothing. I did nothing. Nothing happened.'

'What about tonight?' she said.

Kaidan pulled her hand from his shoulder. 'Try to understand something, Sorcha,' he hissed. 'This isn't just your sacrifice. It's mine too. I don't choose to do this but we *both* have to play our part in the Great Work now.'

'This isn't for any great work,' she said. 'This is for our sick father. Nothing more. Nothing less.' She slapped him as hard as she could across the face. Kaidan didn't flinch. Just turned and strode away.

The Wives pushed the Watchers after him. 'Go. Leave us. We must prepare them.'

Fox shepherded Sorcha into the small prayer room and blocked the doorway. 'How can you stand by and let this happen?' he shouted at the Wives as they tried to follow. 'How can you possibly justify incest?'

'That has no meaning here,' said Maria, holding her pregnant belly. 'The Indigo Family are all descended from angels and share the same bloodline. We're related to each other. We're *all* part of one family.'

'Let us past,' said Zara, carrying the piles of

359

clothes.

'We have to prepare you for Esbat,' said Deva. 'You both need to be prepared.'

'Enough of this preparation bullshit!' Fox roared at them. 'Whatever robes you wear and whatever rituals you make up you'll never "prepare" me to be murdered or Sorcha to be raped by her own half-brother.' He grabbed the robes and toiletries. 'Leave everything with us. We'll prepare ourselves. Now go and leave us alone.'

'But . . .'

He slammed the door in their faces.

'Why's he doing this?' Sorcha said, still in shock. 'Why does my father want this?'

'Because Kaidan and you are the only two violets he's produced and he needs more. He's tried to produce other violets but failed. I guess he hopes you'll produce not only more violets but purer ones, with even closer genetic ties to the fallen angels he believes you're descended from.'

She remembered Eve telling her that although Aurora had been the only indigo to provide a violet heir and survive she hadn't been able to produce any more. So that was why the Seer had turned his attention to her. She was the only viable brood mare for the violet stallion, her half-brother. Sorcha shuddered. 'But what then? Are we supposed to start a whole new bloodline? It's madness.'

'There's a good chance Kaidan won't do it,' Fox said. 'After talking with him I don't think he'll go through with it. He still cares for you.'

'Cares for me? How can you say that? He tried to rape me.'

'He didn't do it, though. Couldn't do it. He told me it was the first and only time he's failed your

360

father. That says something.'

Looking at Fox, she marvelled at the calm way he talked of Kaidan as if he were merely a difficult patient. She wanted to believe Fox was right and that her brother wouldn't do this. 'So there's hope?'

'There is for you,' he said, examining the thick white robes the Wives had left for them. 'Kaidan didn't follow through before so he may not follow through again. There's less hope for me.'

'Why?'

'Because Kaidan's never failed to kill before. But I'm not going down without a fight.' He put down the robes, picked up one of the stools in the corner and pointed to the door. 'Try and keep that closed for as long as you can.' He raised the stool above his head, then threw it against the window, smashing the glass.

'What are you doing, Nathan? We can't escape. There's a grille over the window.'

'I'm not trying to escape. Not yet.'

'Then what are you doing?' she asked as she heard footsteps running towards the door.

He moved towards the shattered window. 'Getting us some insurance.'

*   *   *

When Kaidan arrived in the Great Hall the preparations were virtually complete. Although the Indigo Family ate their everyday meals in the refectory, at Esbat all children under puberty were fed early and settled in the cabins before the adults gathered in the Great Hall to celebrate the rite and break their fast. The centre of the large space had been cleared and the wooden floor covered with prayer mats. Around the perimeter of the room were rows of long trestle tables laid with platters, goblets and cutlery and loaded with tureens of food and flasks of wine. At the end of the hall was a raised dais of two tiers. A large table, with three throne-like chairs at one end, dominated the first tier. Arrangements of flowers decorated the tables and walls. The most elaborate arrangement, an arch of violets crowned with white lilies, adorned the top tier of the dais.

The Seer stood by the top table straightening the large tapestry of the Vitruvian man hanging on the wall. When Kaidan saw his father he thought of what Fox had told him. The psychiatrist had talked a lot of bullshit but he was right about one thing: Kaidan did have a superior aura to his father and needed to command his respect. The thought of confronting him now, however, made his heart race. With anybody else he could be ruthless and fearless but with the Seer he was still an insecure child, desperate for approval. He watched his father pick up a flask and gesture to one of the helpers. 'Have the herb bags been placed in the wine?'

The man bowed and touched his forehead. 'Yes, Seer.'

'Good.' Looking around the hall, the Seer's eyes rested on the elaborate flower arrangement on the top tier of the dais and he smiled. Then he saw his son and beckoned him over. 'Not long now, Kaidan. Everything's in place.'

'I need to talk to you about tonight.'

'I need to talk to you, too. Come, walk with me.'

Outside, the sun was setting. The sky was clear and the moon would soon appear above the sequoias. Kaidan could feel the anticipation in the air as his father led him to a quiet part of the settlement, near the forbidden forest. Excited groups of cult members bowed and tapped their foreheads in greeting when they passed. 'What do you want to talk to me about?' the Seer asked.

'It's about Sorcha.' As he took a deep breath and braced himself for his father's rage, Kaidan nervously reached for his knife. He almost wished Fox had used the blade on him. It would have made things so much simpler. If his father refused to listen to him now he might still threaten to use the knife on himself. 'I don't want to do it tonight. I'm *not* doing it tonight.'

The Seer studied him for a moment but remained calm. 'Why not?'

'I've done everything else you've asked of me. Everything. This is one thing I won't do. I can't do.'

His father narrowed his eyes. 'You're worried you *can't* do it—or you *won't* do it? There are ways to help you get it done.'

'I won't do it. If what I've done for you and the Great Work has meant anything, then I beg you not to ask me to do this. Ask anything else of me, but not this.'

The Seer was still calm. 'Why are you so against it? Why make your stand on this small thing?'

'Sorcha's my half-sister.'

'So? She's a high-level violet and we're all family here. Throughout history divine lineages have kept their bloodlines pure this way: the Greek gods, Hawaiian royalty and the Egyptian pharaohs all practised it. Tutankhamun's parents were brother and sister. It has an honourable and proven history. The Delaneys themselves married within the family to keep the *mothú* bloodline strong.' He pointed to the thoroughbred horses in the paddock. 'It works. Every one of the hundreds of thousands of thoroughbreds in the world is descended from just three stallions and seventy-four foundation mares. And they're perfect—the best and most valuable racehorses in the world.'

Kaidan shook his head. 'There must be another way. If you let Sorcha lie with a pure indigo she may produce violets. Dr Fox said that the *mothú* is passed down by the female line.'

The first flash of anger lit up the Seer's eyes. 'Dr Fox? You've been listening to Dr Fox?'

'My decision has nothing to do with Dr Fox,' he said hurriedly. 'I just don't want to do this. It feels wrong to me.'

'I never said it would be easy, Kaidan. But we all have to make sacrifices.'

'I know, but I feel I've proved myself already. And I'm sure there must be another way.'

The Seer turned to look at the sunset and again Kaidan fingered the sharp blade of his knife, preparing for the onslaught. But still his father's voice was calm and reasonable. 'Do you feel I don't appreciate you enough, Kaidan? Do you feel I haven't given you credit for all you've done so far?'

'It's not that. I just don't . . .'

The Seer nodded as if in understanding. 'Perhaps you're right about Sorcha.'

Kaidan could barely believe his ears. 'What are you saying?'

'I've noticed you've lost your focus since returning from Portland. I think by shifting my attention on to Sorcha I've confused you, made you less committed to our goal.'

'No, no. I'm still committed.'

The Seer nodded. 'I'm glad to hear that, Kaidan, because I need you. I can't do this without you.' He reached out and patted his son's shoulder: something Kaidan couldn't remember him ever doing. 'You're more than my son, Kaidan. You're my right-hand man. My successor. But I understand this might have been a mistake. Ever since I focused on Sorcha, things haven't been right between us. Perhaps this is a step too far for you.'

Still wary, Kaidan waited for the backlash. 'You have no problem with me not going through with this tonight?'

The Seer sighed. 'I can't force you to do it.' He turned to Kaidan and looked him in the eye. 'All I ask is your full support with everything else I may need you to do. Whatever I ask, whatever I decide, you mustn't object to it. You understand?'

Kaidan nodded enthusiastically, feeling more valued and appreciated than he could remember. Fox had been right. He did have power and he could command respect. His commitment to the Great Work had been refreshed. 'I understand. I'll do whatever you want. Anything at all.' The Seer smiled at him. 'Maria's almost due,' Kaidan said, desperate to please his father. 'Perhaps *she*'ll provide a violet.'

'Perhaps.' The Seer moved away, facing the sunset. 'Now I must go and prepare.'

Taking his hand off the knife, still not quite believing how painless it had been, Kaidan asked again, 'So will you forgive me for tonight?'

The Seer turned back to him and shrugged. 'Like you said, I'll have to find another way.'

CHAPTER SIXTY-ONE

The brain has a region called the parietal lobe, which establishes our sense of space and time. By detecting where our body physically ends and the larger world begins, it anchors us in the real world. Research has shown that intense prayer or meditation can shut the region down, disabling the anchor and replacing our sense of self with a sense of oneness with the cosmos or God. Fox had read d'Aquili and Newberg's research but had never seen the power of meditation demonstrated so conclusively as he did now in the Great Hall.

Fox and Sorcha sat at the top table on the first tier of the raised dais. The Wives and Kaidan sat with them. Arrayed in rows before them, the adults of the Indigo Family sat cross-legged on prayer mats. All wore coloured robes and each had a tilak on their forehead that matched the colour of their aura: most were indigo, like those on the Wives' foreheads. Kaidan sported a violet tilak and a violet robe. Sorcha and Fox's tilaks were violet and indigo respectively but their robes were as white as sacrificial lambs. Both wore a white headpiece that revealed their eyes, nose and forehead but covered their gagged mouth. Their bound hands were secured to the table.

When they had been dragged—bound and gagged—to the Great Hall both had tried to appeal for help but it soon became clear that nobody was going to stop Esbat running its course. The cult members apparently regarded Pathfinders with awe and envy and couldn't understand why anyone might not want to touch the infinite. On entering the hall the members had drunk wine from the surrounding tables but left the food untouched. Now, they sat on the floor, eyes closed, deep in trance, listening spellbound to their leader.

The Seer stood on the dais before them, wearing a violet robe fringed with gilt and sporting a violet tilak on his forehead. He had shaved his head, revealing tattoos on his pale scalp that echoed the lotus symbols on the Vitruvian man in the tower: on the crown of his head was the violet lotus flower of the seventh chakra; on the back of his head, at the level of the tilak, was an indigo eye, symbolizing the sixth chakra; and on the back of his neck the blue symbol of the fifth chakra. The lights dimmed as the Seer spoke and his voice had a hypnotic quality. 'You must each strive to reach beyond the mortal and touch the divine. Look inside yourself to create a link between your physical body and your spirit being.' Standing with his legs apart, he slipped the robe from his shoulders and stretched out his arms. Wearing only a loincloth, his lean and muscular body resembled the Vitruvian man on the tapestry behind him. The coloured tattoos on the back of his head continued down his spine, the seven lotus symbols corresponding to each of the seven chakras.

'Start at the base of your spine and focus on Muladhara, the red vortex of the first chakra, which governs spiritual security,' he intoned. 'Visualize a silver thread and mentally pass it through the chakra and connect it to the chakra's twin in your spirit body. Now move up the spine, feel it tingle as you access Svadhisthana, the orange sacral chakra. Unlock the enthusiasm it governs as you pass another silver thread through it to form a link with its spiritual twin. Now travel to your solar plexus and in your mind's eye pass a thread through Manipura, the yellow chakra. As you connect with its spirit twin, feed off the growth it governs. Now travel up to the heart to Anahata, the green chakra . . .'

As Delaney spoke, Fox could see the cult members swaying as one, mentally trying to leave their physical bodies and connect with something bigger than themselves. He bet that if their brains were scanned now their parietal lobes would show little or no activity. Fasting, which made you light-headed, undoubtedly helped the effect and he wondered if there was also something in the wine they had drunk. Whatever it was, it had worked because, aside from Sorcha and himself, not one person had their eyes open or fidgeted in their seats.

'. . . Pass a silver thread through Vishuddha, the blue throat chakra, and connect with its spiritual twin,' Delaney continued. 'Now we come to the brow of the head, to Ajna, the sixth chakra. This is the indigo chakra, the third eye. Visualize it as a lens through which you can see your spirit self in its entirety, free of all physical constraints. Pass a thread through the chakra, make the link with its spiritual twin and prepare yourself to travel beyond indigo.

'Gather up all the threads connecting the six chakras and braid them into a cord. Now follow this cord through the seventh chakra, Sahasrara, the violet chakra in the crown of your head. This cord will lead you out of your physical body to your spirit self and be your link back. Let all other connections slip away. Leave your physical body behind and trust in this one silver cord. On this night of Esbat, when the moon is full and the veil between this world and the spirit realm is thinnest, be at one with your mind, and the universe. Free yourself to wander the astral plane and access the infinite.'

Apart from Delaney's hypnotic voice, Fox could hear no other sound. He looked up at the glass panels in the roof. The full moon appeared like a vast pearlescent disc, still rising in the clear night sky. He turned to Sorcha who was glancing nervously at Kaidan, sitting with his head down and eyes closed. If he hadn't been tied to the table Fox felt they could have walked out unnoticed by everyone, except Delaney. Fox sensed that the Seer, despite his theatrics, was very awake and very aware.

Suddenly, Delaney clapped his hands and the trance was broken. His people stirred as if from a deep sleep. Then the hall filled with excited chattering and a buzz of anticipation. 'Let us break our fast and satisfy the hunger of our physical bodies.' Delaney donned his robe and pointed to the laden tables around the hall. Everyone rushed to them and pounced on the food.

Under the unblinking gaze of the full moon, the next two hours passed in a blur of bacchanalian excess. At times, as the Indigo Family gorged themselves on food and drink, their feasting sounded more like a raging battle than a banquet. Delaney, however, ate little and drank only water from his goblet. When the platters had been stripped of food and the flasks emptied of wine, the sated cult members turned again to their Seer as he rose to address them. 'In the past, most

Pathfinders have been sub-indigos but tonight we are fortunate.' He turned to Fox. 'This Esbat is rare. Not only do we have an indigo to light our path to the other side . . .' Two Watchers freed Fox from the table, though his hands were still bound together, and forced him to his feet. 'But we also have a violet—a pure violet—who will do so much more for our kind.' The Wives freed Sorcha from the table and made her stand. Everyone began cheering.

'Just as Sorcha lost her memory and forgot her identity, so most of us in the Indigo Family had forgotten ours. We had forgotten that we are descended from fallen angels, with divine blood flowing in our veins. Only by restoring this genetic memory, and accepting we're more than human, can we reclaim *our* lost identity and realize our full potential. Only then can we shake off our earthly shackles and truly regain our connection with the spirit world. To reclaim our inheritance and restore our bloodline to its original purity will require sacrifice. From us all.'

Delaney glanced at Kaidan, then at Sorcha. 'Tonight, Sorcha will make this sacrifice and lead us down the path to purity.' The Wives led her to the top tier of the dais and stood her beneath the arch of violets topped with lilies. In her white robe, she resembled an expectant bride. 'Tonight, two violets will unite to try and create the purest aura of all: the halo of divine white.' Sorcha's face had paled to the colour of her robe. She looked pleadingly at Kaidan, and Fox saw him shake his head as if to reassure her. 'But one sacrifice isn't enough,' said Delaney. 'For this to happen, one other sacrifice is necessary.' Delaney glanced at his son and Fox saw

370

anger flash in Kaidan's eyes.

Why?

Fox knew Kaidan didn't want to go ahead with the incest but why the sudden anger? Had he secured an agreement from Delaney not to do it, only to have his father renege at the last minute? Like everyone else, Fox could only watch, mesmerized, wondering how Kaidan would respond. Then something happened that not only shocked Fox, but also visibly surprised Kaidan. Regan Delaney turned, stepped up on to the next tier and in a perverse parody of a marriage ceremony stood beside his daughter under the arch of violets. 'Tonight,' he said, 'to guarantee the purity of the bloodline for future generations, *I* too will make the sacrifice.'

CHAPTER SIXTY-TWO

Sorcha was still numb with shock and disbelief as the Wives, Kaidan and the Watchers dragged her and Fox out of the Great Hall towards the tower. When she met Fox's eye she could see he was equally surprised. This neither of them had expected.

Despite it being almost midnight the path to the tower was brightly lit, both from the torches along the way and from the full moon's silver light. She scanned the faces lining the path, searching for help, hoping to see shock, horror or compassion, but all she saw was excitement and wonder. They wanted this. They evidently found nothing abhorrent in the Seer sleeping with his daughter.

371

As father to the Indigo Family, he was father to them all and if he thought it best to make this sacrifice for them, then they should be grateful for his humility and selflessness.

As they entered the tower, Delaney turned back to the Indigo Family. 'It's almost the witching hour,' he told them. 'Do not waste this fertile time.' Then he closed the door on the restless crowd. As he led them up the stairs the Seer made no allowance for Maria, who was close to giving birth and clutched her pregnant belly in discomfort. After the first few steps, Fox slipped and fell. Sorcha winced as she watched him roll down the stairs, feeling every knock on her own body. Luckily his hands had been bound in front of him so he could use them to protect his face, but it had clearly hurt. He made no sound but lay curled in the foetal position, his head in his hands, rocking. She tried to go to him but the Wives held her back. When Kaidan pulled him to his feet, however, Fox didn't look hurt and there was a renewed fire in his eyes.

The shock of her father's declaration must have breached the blockage in her memory because as she continued up the stairs she remembered her naïve thrill at being summoned to the tower for the first time, on the day she had fled the settlement. She recalled the Seer leading her up the stairs, watching her closely, studying her reaction to the death echoes, his excitement increasing as hers turned to horror. On the indigo level he had led her into the room where her mother had died—not from illness as her father had told her, but by his hand.

She recalled his words as clearly as if he was uttering them now: 'Your mother was an exceptional woman, Sorcha, and I owe her a great deal, but she refused to understand what I was trying to achieve in this tower. She threatened to go to the authorities unless I stopped doing what I was doing, and, of course, I couldn't allow that. I couldn't let anyone threaten the Great Work, not even Aurora. I'm showing you this, Sorcha, because I want you to understand what's expected of you. In the past I've asked nothing of you but I now need you to take your place alongside Kaidan and contribute to the Great Work.'

Kaidan had appeared then and she remembered her father holding her down and ordering her half-brother to 'Do it. Do it, quickly.' The memories surfaced faster now, like scenes from a film: feeling Kaidan lying on her, heavy and panting; herself kicking and screaming as she fought against her father's grip; Kaidan suddenly pulling back; their father turning on him and beating him; fleeing from the tower, pursued by Kaidan; running into Eve who helped her escape.

Now as she retraced her steps up the tower she wished she had listened to Fox. In the top chamber, the amethyst plinth had been made up into a bed of immaculate white linen. A ring of candles surrounded the glowing amethyst symbol on the floor. Smoke curled in the soft violet light and the smell of incense hung in the air. She noticed silk nooses like the one binding her wrists attached to each corner of the plinth and her anxiety surged. As if on hot coals she ran across the glowing amethyst until she was on plain stone, desperate to distance herself from the death echoes and that bed. Fox followed and stood beside her, shoulder to shoulder. The Seer gestured to Zara to remove

373

their gags. As soon as Sorcha could speak, she turned to her father: 'You can't do this.'

Delaney turned to the Wives and the Watchers. 'Go down to the bottom and wait,' he told them. 'I'll call you when we're ready.' When they had gone he turned back to her. 'I don't *want* to do this, Sorcha. But it's the only way to take the Great Work to the next stage.' He spoke so sincerely that for a second she allowed herself to think he had misgivings and genuinely didn't want to do it.

'I'm your daughter,' she said. Now her memory was returning she recognized Delaney as her father, rather than a stranger, making the prospect of incest even more repugnant.

'It's wrong,' said Fox. 'You cannot do this.'

'How can purifying a bloodline be wrong?' Delaney said, picking up the family Bible from the white table and opening it on the family tree. 'We Delaneys did it in the past and have successfully kept the *mothú* in our bloodline for centuries.'

Fox shook his head. 'That doesn't make it right. Even if you ignore the morality of it, this will do the opposite of what you're trying to achieve. This will *weaken* your bloodline. This makes no sense.'

Delaney frowned. 'If you bred thoroughbred horses you'd understand.'

'I do understand,' said Fox. 'Inbreeding has made thoroughbreds brilliant at one thing: running fast. But they're riddled with other problems directly linked to their inbreeding. Many have small hearts or are prone to breaking bones and bleeding lungs. This is insane.'

'Did you know about this, Kaidan?' Sorcha said, vainly willing her tormentor to become a protector. 'Do you agree with this?'

Kaidan wouldn't meet her eye but turned to the Seer. 'When did you decide to do this? Today? Or have you planned it for some time?'

A cruel smile curled Delaney's lips. 'Don't question me, Kaidan. You should feel grateful. You didn't have the courage or the commitment to do this so I'm having to. You said you'd support me in anything I decided to do, so long as I released you from doing *this*. Remember?' Kaidan nodded, subdued. 'Then let *me* decide what's best for the Great Work.'

'But why?' Sorcha cried. 'I don't understand. What good can this do?'

Delaney sighed and smiled patiently at her. 'On the day you left I was glad Kaidan failed because I finally realized how important you were. With you, I could complete the final part of the Great Work, which has many stages. The first was simply to nurture indigos and appreciate our special heritage. The second was to study the souls of the dead, which is why I built this tower. I can't connect like you do, Sorcha, because your *mothú* has evolved more than mine. You merge with the souls and feel what they're feeling—but I still sense them. The third was to practise projecting my astral self from my physical body. In the tower, when I have sex and reach orgasm my spirit leaves my body and dances with the souls trapped in here. For a few fleeting moments, I throw off my earthly bonds and become pure spirit. I become an angel again, a god.'

'Bullshit,' said Fox. 'You might *feel* like that's what's happening, and you might *want* it to happen, but it's not. Don't you understand? It's just your synaesthesia. You aren't really leaving your body, you just *feel* like you are. It's a neurological trick

375

of the mind. You aren't communing with spirits or ghosts because there are no ghosts, only echoes. This tower is nothing more than a jukebox of memories which, because of your synaesthesia, only you, Sorcha and Kaidan can play. Sorcha feels the echoes more than you because she has empathy. There's only one reason you can't feel the death echoes. You have no empathy. You're a psychopath.'

The muscles clenched in Delaney's jaw. 'Dr Fox, you know nothing about this. You've never experienced what I've experienced. Before you met Sorcha you didn't even know what a death echo was, so please don't presume to lecture me on what is and isn't real. You'll find out soon enough whether this tower contains the souls of the dying or just their memories—when I add *you* to my jukebox.' He spat out the last word and turned back to Sorcha. 'Sorcha, these first three stages are but building blocks for the fourth, which is the ultimate aim of the Great Work. And for this I need you.'

'What is the fourth stage?' she asked, feeling sick. She glanced at Kaidan and Fox and could see both were listening intently.

'The fourth stage is to reclaim our divine legacy as descendants of the Grigori and the Nephilim, and become gods again. The ultimate aim of the Great Work is to transcend death and become immortal.'

'How?'

'By reattaching the ageless astral body, the soul, to a new physical vessel.'

As she looked into her father's eyes she could see that he totally and utterly believed in what he was saying. 'How?' she said again.

'The transmigration of souls works best with unborn babies and babies less than a month old, neonates. They're ideal because their physical bodies and brains are so flexible and receptive. As Dr Fox no doubt knows, all newborns have synaesthesia, the *mothú*, for the first month of their lives, until their brains develop. This means that every baby is born an indigo. The only exceptions are those born beyond indigo. You and Kaidan were both born violet—as was I. The point is, there's a window of time, from when a baby is in the womb to one month after its birth, when it's an empty vessel, a receptive shell. The physical body's connection with its astral twin is still flexible, the silver cord is not fixed. There's a hole in their crown chakra—the anterior fontanelle. You feel it as the soft spot on the top of a baby's head. This is the portal.'

He smiled. 'Although I can project my astral body at the moment of orgasm, it's only fleeting.' He pointed to himself. 'Because of the silver cord attached to my physical body I must always return to it. If I'm to lead our people into the future and reclaim our divine inheritance I must transcend my ageing physical body. But when I cut the silver cord and reattach it to a brand new physical body it must be to the right one—a purer one.'

Sorcha's mouth felt so dry she could hardly speak. 'What are you saying?'

'Our progeny will be the perfect physical vessel. Your physical body already contains fifty per cent of my DNA. Our child would contain seventy-five per cent. If you gave birth to a boy, I would have one month in which to take over the body.'

'How the hell would you do that?' said Fox. His

377

face no longer showed anger, just incredulity.

'When my astral self leaves my physical body at the moment of orgasm I'll arrange for my physical self to die. This will sever the silver cord, freeing me from my old body. I can then enter the crown chakra of the unborn baby or neonate and reattach my cord to this new vessel. I will be reincarnated.'

'You really believe this?' said Sorcha. 'You would kill yourself in order to be born again?'

'Of course. In order to be born again you have first to die. If you gave birth to a boy I could astral-project into him and be reborn.'

She shook her head in disbelief. 'You're saying I would give birth to you—my own father?'

'Yes.' He smiled. 'If you gave birth to a girl I could take it even further. I'm not yet sixty, I could wait till our daughter reached puberty, then inseminate *her*. The child she gave birth to would be made up of eighty-seven-point-five per cent of my DNA. I would be astral-projecting into a vessel that to all intents and purposes was a purer, better version of myself. Just as Sorcha is purer than me, then this offspring will be purer than her—beyond indigo, beyond violet. Pure white. A god.'

'And that god will be you?' said Fox.

'Yes.'

'How do you even know Sorcha's fertile tonight?'

'This is only the first impregnation. We may need more. But this is the most fertile time for all the women in the settlement. Because of their constant close proximity to each other, all the women in the settlement eventually synchronize their cycles so they ovulate at the full moon. If Sorcha had been away for more than a month it might have changed, but she hasn't.'

Sorcha swallowed. She knew he was right and that made her feel worse. It was like he had already taken control of her body. 'So the Great Work has got nothing to do with the Indigo Family. You took over this whole cult and built this damn tower just to create a new vessel for you? Just so you could live for ever?'

Delaney frowned, angry that she and Fox didn't understand. 'No. I'm doing this for them, for my people. I'm simply leading the way. I'm the pioneer, nothing more. Because of my work all the Indigo Family will one day be masters of their spiritual selves. They'll become like the angels they're descended from: immortal. We'll *all* be immortal. I'm merely the leader, taking the first step, making the initial sacrifice.'

'But it's all fantasy,' said Sorcha. 'You *must* see that.'

'Haven't you been listening to me?' Delaney said. 'We all have to make sacrifices, Sorcha— even you. This is the only way ahead. By securing my immortality I can rekindle the Indigo Family's divine heritage and secure its future.'

Fox stepped forward and tried one last time. 'Don't do this, Regan. If only because it won't work. It can't work. You're basing everything—the belief that you're descended from gods, the cult, the Great Work, the killings, incest—all of it, on a rare sensory anomaly, synaesthesia. There's no substance to any of it. When you arrange for your body to die you *will* die. Your soul won't inhabit your child. You will die. You will be no more. This is pointless and moronic.'

'Pointless and moronic?' Delaney scowled at Fox, his face puce with rage. 'I'm sick of your certainties, Dr Fox. I hoped you could at least appreciate what I was trying to achieve. I wanted you to understand. But I can see you're too stupid. I don't care what you think—any of you—because tonight you'll see I'm right.' He nodded to Kaidan. 'Call the others up. It's time.'

When Kaidan left, Delaney turned back to Fox. 'Let me explain what's going to happen to you. Tonight, we'll both project on to the astral plane: you through death, me through sex. You'll be taken to one of the indigo rooms where a plaque's been allocated to you. There you'll be strangled with a silk garrotte. It'll be slow and painful, I'm afraid. A traumatic death is necessary to make a strong imprint. Some of our early attempts were poor because my devoted followers died too willingly and painlessly. The very first pioneers, in California, took their own lives—so eagerly and happily that they left virtually no imprint at all.' He tapped the large lotus symbol on the floor beneath his feet. 'After your physical body has died, your astral body, the freshest imprint in the tower, will flow up the amethyst to this symbol of Sahasrara, the seventh chakra, where you'll join all the other souls. At midnight—the witching hour—I will lie with Sorcha here on the amethyst plinth. As I impregnate her and leave my body I will find you. We will dance, you and I, the dance of death. But unlike you, Dr Fox, I will return to the living.'

CHAPTER SIXTY-THREE

As Kaidan approached, Sorcha moved closer to Fox. 'I'm so sorry I got you into this,' she whispered, voice cracking with emotion. 'I'm so sorry I didn't listen to you.'

'Don't worry about me,' he said. 'Everything I did I chose to do. I wouldn't have done anything differently.' As Kaidan and the two Watchers pulled him away he said, 'Don't give up hope.'

Fox didn't struggle or protest when they led him away. There was little point: they were too many and there was nothing more to say. He caught Sorcha's eye as the Wives closed in on her. 'It'll be all right,' he mouthed. She bravely nodded but he could see from the terror in her eyes that she didn't believe what he was saying. He wasn't sure he believed it either. Nevertheless, he felt strangely calm. As they led him down the stairs he could feel the shard of glass he had taken from the smashed window hidden in the hem of his robes. He glanced down at the tie binding his wrists and hoped that when he had fallen on the stairs and used the shard to cut the silk rope he had cut enough strands.

When they reached the indigo level, he turned to Kaidan. 'Are you going to do it?'

'Yes.'

He nodded. 'I'm glad.'

A frown. 'Why?'

'I want to look into your eyes when I die, Kaidan. It'll help knowing that even though I'm being murdered, it's by someone whose life is even more screwed up than mine. I want to watch you squirm when you think about what you're letting your father do up there. Christ, Kaidan, I understand why you killed those men in Portland. I really do. They were murderers and rapists—just like your father. A part of you was rebelling, punishing him and avenging the women you care about in your life. I can even understand you killing me. I mean nothing to you. But I can't fathom why you'd let your father do what he's going to do to Sorcha.'

Saying nothing, Kaidan led him into one of the rooms. The amethyst plaque on the wall in front of Fox had already been engraved with the date, M for male and A for adult. An eye-shaped lotus symbol indicated his indigo status. He wondered if his name had already been written in the black ledger. As he looked around the dimly lit empty space he felt a surge of anger. What a depressing place to die, just to serve a psychopath's delusional belief system. How pathetic and pointless.

One of the Watchers passed Kaidan a silk garrotte. 'Shall we hold him?'

Kaidan shook his head. 'It's OK. Dr Fox is as good as dead. Go up now and tell the Seer it's done. Then go down to the base of the tower. The Seer will want some privacy. I'll join you when I'm finished here.' Kaidan stared at Fox as he waited for the Watchers to leave. 'You only want to save Sorcha so you can have her for yourself.'

As Fox looked into the killer's eyes he thought of his parents and his sister and how they had died just as senselessly as he was about to. Thinking of them stoked his rage and helped focus his mind. At this moment anger was so much more useful than paralysing fear. 'I admit I have feelings for Sorcha,' Fox said. 'Why can't you? It's not too late,

Kaidan. I know the pain you're in, the conflict you feel, but you can still choose a different path. Your father doesn't care for you or any of his so-called Indigo Family. He only cares for himself. You're nothing to him, Kaidan, and never have been. He only needs you now to do his killing. You'll never be his heir because he intends to become his own heir. His obsession with the Nephilim and the Grigori has got nothing to do with spirituality or showing people the way to a better place. For all his talk about leadership and sacrifice, he is motivated solely by the oldest and most selfish instinct of all— to perpetuate himself, to cheat death and become immortal.'

With practised ease Kaidan wound the garrotte around his wrists and pulled it taut. 'Turn to the wall.'

Fox didn't move. 'You know what I'm saying is true.' He heard Sorcha cry out above and kept his eyes fixed on Kaidan's, trying to access any last vestige of conscience the man might have. 'You can still save the angel, Kaidan. At this moment, whatever you did in the past doesn't matter. All that matters, all that defines you, is what you do *now*. You can choose to be either a victim of your past or the hero of your future. You decide what happens now—no one else. Do what you want with me, but save your sister. Not for me but for you. If you kill me you'll lose no sleep but if you let your father destroy Sorcha—the angel you love, the only pure thing in your life—you'll regret it for the rest of your days. Trust me on this one thing.'

Suddenly, Kaidan smiled. It was a rueful, gentle smile that changed his face completely. For the first time Fox saw a resemblance to Sorcha and glimpsed the man he might have become. In that small expression of humanity, however, Fox also realized there was going to be no reprieve for him or Sorcha. 'I've gone too far and my hands are too covered in blood to save the angel now,' Kaidan said.

'It's *never* too late,' said Fox.

'I fear it is for me. And for you,' said Kaidan. 'I've no choice but to serve the demon because I've become one myself.' As he stepped forward and raised the garrotte, his smile faded and the humanity left his eyes. 'For what it's worth, I'm sorry.' Watching Kaidan pull his arms apart to tighten the garrotte, Fox tried to pull his own hands apart. But the silk tie wouldn't break. He hadn't cut enough of the strands.

CHAPTER SIXTY-FOUR

Sorcha cried out and fought with what strength remained but with her hands tied it was impossible. 'We want to help you. Let us help you,' the Wives soothed as they dragged her towards the bed. She almost welcomed the rush of death echoes that engulfed her as her feet touched the lotus symbol on the floor. The terrifying visions of souls being strangled, their cries of torment and the sense of dread emanating from the amethyst at least distracted her from her own fate.

First, the Wives placed her right foot into one of the loops and tied her ankle to the plinth, then they looped her left. Once both ankles were secured they cut the tie on her wrists and bound each hand separately so she lay on her back, spreadeagled like the Vitruvian man. Zara and Deva began loosening Sorcha's white robe, opening the front and rolling it back. Then they cut away her underwear so the lower part of her body was totally naked and exposed. All the time the Seer watched with a detached, inscrutable look on his face. She pulled against the ties, but the more she struggled, the more the silk bit into her flesh. She looked at Zara, suddenly remembering her from a more innocent time, from before she had known what her father's Great Work really entailed.

'Help me,' she screamed at her. 'We were friends once. I remember now. Don't let this happen. He's my father, Zara. This is wrong.'

'The Seer is father to all the Indigo Family. He's a father to us all,' Zara said, replacing her gag and tightening it. 'Now be silent.'

'Calm yourself,' said Deva, stroking her forehead. 'The Seer's very skilled. Don't fight him. Surrender to him, enjoy it.'

One of the Watchers suddenly appeared in the room, touched his forehead and addressed the Seer. 'Kaidan instructed me to tell you it's done. Dr Fox is dead.'

Her father nodded slowly, savouring the news. 'Good. Now leave us.'

The shocking, final realization that Nathan was gone brought tears of disbelief and despair to Sorcha's eyes. She suddenly realized how much he had meant to her. Up till now she had harboured the faint hope that, as they had once helped each other as children, Kaidan might somehow help her and spare Fox. But it was not to be. Fox was dead. Hope was dead. All was lost.

385

When the Watcher left, the heavily pregnant Maria began to disrobe the Seer and Sorcha saw the tattoos on his taut, muscular back. She looked away when Maria removed his loincloth, still not believing this could be happening—still unable to accept what he was going to do. 'How can we help you?' Maria asked, caressing his body. 'How can we best make you ready for your task?'

Delaney looked at the Wives, then at Sorcha. His expression hardened and a hungry gleam appeared in his eyes. He clapped his hands and the lamps went out so the only illumination in the chamber came from the candles circling the perimeter and an eerie glow, rising like violet mist from the amethyst symbol on the floor, where the light on the lower level permeated the translucent gemstone. 'Go,' he said. 'I won't need your help.'

Sorcha watched the three women obediently file out, willing them to look at her, willing them to come to their senses and help her. But not one glanced at her as they disappeared down the stairs. Finally, she looked down at her exposed, spreadeagled body and her father silhouetted against the candlelight. In the violet glow his own aura appeared faint and she could barely see his features. When he stepped towards her, she involuntarily recoiled. As she did so, her bound hands pressed hard against the amethyst, summoning an unholy chorus of death echoes. As she watched the Seer walk across the violet gemstone, she could see, hear, feel and smell the imprinted death memories of all those who had died in the tower, swirling in the violet mist around him. It seemed to her then, watching him stride through his sea of damned souls, that he was more than just a demon. He was the devil himself, summoning her to hell.

When he reached the plinth, he stopped and studied her. In the candlelight his face appeared hard and angular and she noticed that his breathing was different, heavier, as if he had been running. She realized that the death echoes were arousing him. He climbed on to the plinth and kneeled between her legs. As he lowered himself, her skin crawled as if a hundred insects were marching over her body. She pulled so hard at the ties that she could feel the silk cut into her skin. Gripping the edge of the plinth to pull away from him, she sensed more death echoes—legions of them. How many people had been strangled in the tower to fill the Seer's gallery of lost souls? As she braced herself for the rape, she wished she was one of them. Death seemed infinitely preferable to this.

Suddenly, she stopped struggling and froze. Among the echoes she noticed one that was more defined—more recent—than the others. She couldn't see him clearly in the violet gloom but she instantly knew it was Fox. He was pulling at a garrotte around his neck in the death throes of strangulation. Immediately she recognized him, she wished again that she might die, so she could join him. As she stared at Fox, she realized that Delaney was studying her face. Slowly he turned and looked over his shoulder in the direction of her gaze.

Then he too saw Fox's death echo and smiled.

*   *   *

Regan Delaney had been worried about tonight, concerned that, like Kaidan, he would be unable to perform the sex act and impregnate Sorcha. But he now realized this wasn't about sex but the ultimate aphrodisiac: power. The Wives had offered to assist him but he didn't need their stimulation: the tower and its death echoes were all he needed to boost his potency. In this chamber, touching the lotus symbol of Sahasrara, the seventh chakra, and sensing the spirits channelled by the amethyst made him feel like a god. Seeing Fox's spirit in its violet glow only added to his arousal.

'We can see you, Dr Fox,' he said. 'In a matter of moments I'll leave my body and join you—if only fleetingly.'

Fox's spirit moved closer to the bed. Then Delaney was sure he heard it speak. 'Please don't do this,' it was saying. The voice stunned Delaney. He glanced at Sorcha and could see from her shocked expression that she too had heard it. The astral bond between Fox and Sorcha must be strong to make him plead for her even after death. A fresh surge of power and rapturous excitement coursed through him. The fact that Fox's astral self had communicated with him not only vindicated everything he was doing but also proved he was getting close. He peered into the violet twilight and gloated, 'I told you you'd be more than just an echo.' He turned back to Sorcha, all fears of not being able to impregnate her gone. 'Now he can watch while I take the next step to immortality.'

As he pushed himself between Sorcha's legs he felt something touch his shoulder. Twisting round, he saw Fox's astral body standing over him and was surprised how close it had come. Then it spoke again.

'You're right,' the spirit said, adopting a strange

388

pose. 'I am more than an echo.' Then a very physical hand shot out and struck Delaney so hard that he instantly lost consciousness.

CHAPTER SIXTY-FIVE

According to Fox's sensei, there were two ways to render someone unconscious with a single blow. The first required strength: if you hit someone's chin hard enough with the heel of your hand, their neck was unable to absorb the impact, their brain shifted in the skull and they dropped like a stone. The second was more reliable but required precision and involved hitting the carotid sinus in the neck, which regulated blood pressure. When pressed hard, the carotid helped reduce blood pressure but excessive pressure, such as a sharp, targeted blow, could cause a blackout. As a doctor, Fox preferred the latter technique—although he hadn't tried either before today.

As he watched Delaney's naked body slide to the floor, and considered Kaidan's crumpled frame on the level below, Fox vowed to buy his sensei a bottle of his favourite imported sake, Tentaka, the next time he saw him. Bending to Sorcha, Fox gently covered her nakedness then cut the silk ties on her wrists and ankles with the dagger-like shard of glass he had gleaned from the broken window in the preparation suite. Then he pulled her to her feet and removed her gag. All the time her eyes watched him, wide and wondering, as if she couldn't believe he was there.

She reached for him and held him tight. 'I hoped

you weren't a death echo when I couldn't sense your suffering. I still can't believe you survived and came back for me.'

'Of course I came back for you,' he whispered. 'Come. Let's get out of here before they come round.' He pulled her to the door and led her down the steps.

'What happened with Kaidan?' she said. 'Where is he?'

As they passed the indigo level he pointed to one of the rooms. 'Out cold, like your father.'

'How?'

As they descended through the blue and green levels, he raised the shard of glass he had taken from the broken window. 'I told you I took out an insurance policy. Luckily the hem in these robes is thick enough to conceal a sliver of glass.'

She smiled, understanding. 'When you fell down the stairs earlier, you did it on purpose. You were cutting the silk tie on your wrists.'

'Just a few threads so I could pull it apart when I needed to. I knew I'd only get one chance so I waited for when Kaidan was alone and had his hands occupied. Then I focused on my target and hit him. Hard.' Fox made it sound easy but it had almost ended in disaster. When Kaidan had spread his arms to tighten the garrotte Fox had tugged his wrist tie but it hadn't broken and for one sickening second he thought he hadn't cut enough threads. It had taken two more tugs to free his hands. When he'd landed his blow, however, Kaidan had collapsed like a rag doll. To extend the blackout, he had tied the garrotte round Kaidan's neck, using the knot to keep pressure on the carotid.

'When we get out of the tower we run for the

forest, right?' he said, panting from the exertion of clattering down the stairs. 'Any more objections to letting Jordache handle it from here?'

'Nope. Not any more.'

When they reached the red level Delaney must have regained consciousness because they could hear him screaming above, demented with rage. 'Stop them. Stop them.'

As they left the stairwell the two Watchers in indigo robes appeared. Both were armed but unprepared: a blow to the throat dropped the first to his knees, a kick to the solar plexus doubled over the second. Fox kept moving forward, dragging Sorcha in his wake. The Wives appeared when they got to the door but Sorcha helped push them out of the way. Then Fox opened the door and they were outside. Never had the fresh night air felt so good. Fox stopped for a second to get his bearings. The crowd of cult members had thinned but many remained, gathered in clusters round the tower. Some were talking, some dancing, others lay on their backs looking up at the moon. No one was paying much attention to them and he could see a path through the groups to the forest. He pulled Sorcha with him. Assuming the horse was where they'd left him, they could make it. They could get away.

'Stop them,' shouted Delaney. His voice sounded incredibly loud. The loose groups of cult members quickly joined together, forming a cordon round the tower and closing the path to the forest. Fox turned and saw Delaney standing in the door of the tower holding a megaphone to his lips. 'Stop them.' More Watchers appeared as the crowd closed in, forcing Fox and Sorcha back.

'Look at me,' Fox shouted. 'I'm an indigo. I'm one of you. We didn't volunteer to be Pathfinders. The Seer forced us. Why do we have to obey him? He's not a god. He has no divine powers or third eye.' He pointed to the tower. 'There's a room in there where he spies on you from cameras he's placed around the settlement. He doesn't care about you. He only wants to control you and use you.'

'I am the Seer,' Delaney boomed through the megaphone. 'Return them to the tower.'

'He is the Seer,' voices echoed from the crowd.

'*Why* is he the Seer?' responded Fox. '*Why* do you obey him?'

'He has the aura,' cried a host of angry voices, as the crowd closed in.

'So have I,' said Sorcha, taking her cue from Fox. Standing in the moonlight in her dazzling white robes, she looked like an angel. 'My aura is purer than his. If my father is the Seer who must be blindly obeyed, then what am I? Why should I not be obeyed? Why should he force me to do *his* bidding? Why does he not obey *me*?'

'He is the Seer,' some shouted again. But as the crowd pressed around them Fox could hear questioning voices. Some began to reach for Sorcha and pull her to them. Others tried to push them back to the tower.

'Bring them to me,' ordered Delaney, as the Watchers and the Wives fought through the jostling chaos and dragged Sorcha back to the tower. Fox reached for her but the increasingly frenzied crowd drove them apart. As Sorcha tried to escape, some in the crowd attempted to help her, while others aided the Wives.

Above the noise of the mêlée, Fox heard another sound. When he looked up into the night sky he saw nothing at first, just heard the rhythmic *whup-whup* of rotors. Then two helicopters appeared above the sequoias, silhouetted against the full moon like giant locusts. Searchlights shone down, picking out the eye on the tower and scanning the crowd. When the lights settled on Fox everyone around him panicked, intensifying the chaos.

'I warned you of this, my people,' Delaney shouted above the noise, as the Wives and Watchers dragged Sorcha back to him and bundled her into the tower. 'The government are coming for us. They're coming for you—the indigos.' Delaney pointed at Fox, dazzled in the spotlight of the helicopter beams. 'He brought them here,' he screamed. '*He* brought them here.' Then Delaney stepped back into the tower and closed the door. Fox tried to follow but the crowd held him back. He heard Jordache's voice, amplified by loudspeakers, rise above the roar of the rotors, appealing for calm and calling his name. But Fox ignored him, totally focused on one aim: rescuing Sorcha. As the helicopters came in to land, forcing the crowd to run for cover, Fox fought his way back into the tower.

CHAPTER SIXTY-SIX

'Come. We must hurry. We haven't much time.' As the Wives dragged Sorcha into the tower, helped by the Watchers, Delaney refused to let his dream slip away. Sorcha belonged to him. As a product of

393

his loins she was born to serve him and realize his destiny. He could still complete the Great Work. He had the Wives with him and three Watchers.

After preparing everything so carefully he couldn't believe it had come to this. Moments ago, he had been on the brink of taking the Great Work to the next stage. And now . . .

Climbing the stairs, he could hear the muffled sound of approaching helicopter rotors. The children of men must have come for Fox but why were they here tonight of all nights, and what right did they have to meddle in his divine business and threaten the Great Work? He couldn't countenance failure. Not after all the time and work. He was the Seer, born of gods. Nothing must stand in the way of his divine birthright.

He was near the top of the tower now. All was not lost. The Watcher above him had only a knife but one of the Watchers following below had a rifle, which should be enough to secure the staircase. When they passed the indigo floor, the heavily pregnant Maria was panting hard but Delaney could hear footsteps on the stairs below. 'Hurry,' he hissed.

'It's over, Regan. Let Sorcha go.' The sound of Fox's voice echoing up the staircase inflamed Delaney's rage. Why was he still interfering? This had nothing to do with him. 'Let her go,' Fox shouted. 'The police will be here in minutes. Sorcha, can you hear me?'

'Nathan, I'm here,' Sorcha shouted, pushing against the exhausted Maria and twisting out of her grip. Immediately her arm was free she turned to Zara, who was gripping her other arm, and lashed out with her free hand. 'Get your goddamn hands

394

off me.' Zara let go to defend herself and Sorcha turned on Deva, kicking and punching in a frenzy, desperate to get away.

'Stop her,' Delaney ordered. As Sorcha ran back down to the indigo level one of the Watchers slammed her against the wall and put his knife to her throat. At that moment, Fox appeared round the curve of the staircase. 'Kill him,' Delaney screamed. 'Kill him.'

The Watcher with the rifle raised it and fired. The shot ricocheted around the enclosed stairwell and Fox jumped back, out of sight. Delaney ran down to Sorcha, filled with a sudden hatred for his daughter. Everyone else on the settlement knew their role in the Great Work and did exactly as they were told. They understood the necessary sacrifices and performed them willingly. But Sorcha had never played her part. She had never done anything for the Great Work. She would learn, though. He would make her understand her place in the world. He took the knife from the Watcher then slapped Sorcha hard across the face with the palm of his hand. As she fell he grabbed her by the throat and pulled her to him. 'You will obey me.'

'Never,' she said, glaring at him. 'Whatever you do to me now, you're finished.'

'You *will* obey me,' he said again. 'You're nothing. You never lost your identity because you never had one. You're nothing more than an extension of me. You belong to me. Your identity is *mine.*'

'No it's not,' she screamed. 'You're history, part of my past. You're *nothing* to do with who I am now.'

'You don't even know who you are now.'

'I'm whoever *I* choose to be,' she roared, drumming her fists against his chest. 'I am what *I* decide.'

'You decide *nothing*,' Delaney said, pushing the knife close to her face until it was inches from her left eye. He wanted to cut her, punish her for defying him. 'You will obey me, Sorcha, or I will blind you.' He began dragging Sorcha back up the stairs, then turned to the Watcher with the rifle. 'If Fox or anyone else tries to come up those stairs, shoot them dead.'

* * *

Pressed against the wall, Fox peered round the central pillar of the spiral staircase and studied where and how the armed man was positioned. He briefly considered waiting for Jordache and his men—who would also be armed—but there wasn't time. He had to get Sorcha away from Delaney now. If the man had had a pistol or a semi-automatic then stepping out would be suicide and Fox would have no option but to stay where he was. But the man had a hunting rifle. Deadly at long range, it was inaccurate and unwieldy at close quarters.

If he rushed the Watcher at the right angle he could reach the rifle before the man could get in an accurate shot. The risk was high but worth it, especially if he could engineer some surprise. He could hear Delaney and his Wives dragging Sorcha up the steps. 'Don't worry, Sorcha, I'll get help,' he called up to her. Then he ran down the steps to the next level, where he stopped, turned and silently crept back up to where he had started. Lying low on the steps, he peered round the column and saw the man had dropped his guard and lowered his rifle. Taking his chance, Fox rose to a crouch then sprinted round the corner and leapt at him.

Or tried to.

Fox was so intent on speed and reaching the man before he raised his rifle that he slipped on the steps, lost his footing and lurched forward on to his knees. Extending his hands to break his fall he looked up and saw the man raise the rifle and take aim at point-blank range. Beyond the rifleman, Fox saw Delaney look over his shoulder and smile, as if Fox had made it too easy. He could hear Sorcha shouting his name, 'Nathan! Nathan!' as she struggled to break free from her father and come to his aid. Then he detected a familiar taint in the air and saw Kaidan step on to the stairwell from the indigo level. In that instant, as Fox looked down the barrel of the gun and the man's finger tightened on the trigger he knew all was lost and he was about to die. This time he had no plan, no insurance. Nothing. It was over.

Suddenly, time seemed to slow and Fox could only look on in helpless amazement as Kaidan threw himself at the gunman, ripped the rifle from his hands and, holding it by the barrel, broke it against the wall. 'It's finished,' Kaidan shouted at his father. 'Let Sorcha go.'

For a second, no one moved. Delaney stood frozen in shock. Only when Kaidan reached for his half-sister did the Seer react. 'How dare *you* tell me it's finished?' he bellowed, face white with rage. 'Just because you couldn't kill Fox it doesn't mean it's over. It's not over till *I* say it is!'

Kaidan stood his ground and prised Delaney's hand off Sorcha's neck. 'Let her go.'

Delaney turned to the remaining Watchers, who stood back, uncertain what to do. 'Stop him, you fools.' The Watcher above Delaney could do little but the other two rushed at Kaidan. Fox didn't hesitate. He swept the first Watcher's feet from under him and pushed him down the stairs. The second was already on Kaidan when Fox punched the Watcher hard in the kidneys and slammed him against the wall. As Delaney released his grip around Sorcha's neck she kicked her father hard in the groin. When Delaney doubled over, Kaidan pulled Sorcha away and pressed her hand into Fox's. 'Take her.' For a second, Kaidan's eyes met his. 'Save the angel.' Then the killer pushed him away. 'Go. Now.'

As Fox pulled Sorcha towards him, Regan let out a howl of pain and rage. 'How could you betray me, Kaidan? You're my son, a part of me. You're *mine*.' Still bent over in pain, Delaney reached up and thrust his knife deep into his son's side, and twisted the blade.

CHAPTER SIXTY-SEVEN

Kaidan fell as Fox pulled Sorcha down the steps, away from danger. When Sorcha saw Delaney bend to stab her half-brother again she stopped running. She refused to be scared any more. She had to end this now.

Breaking free of Fox, she ran at Delaney and pushed him off Kaidan. 'Leave him alone,' she shouted, standing protectively over her brother. 'You've hurt him enough. You've hurt everyone enough. Stop this madness. Don't you understand? Your pathetic Great Work is over.'

Delaney raised his bloody knife and, for a second, Sorcha thought he, along with his Wives and the remaining Watcher, was going to attack her. Then Fox appeared beside her and someone called from below: 'Nathan? Nathan?'

'Up here, Karl,' shouted Fox.

'You OK? You got Sorcha there?' Detective Karl Jordache's voice sounded faint but clear.

'We're fine, but we could do with some back-up.'

Sorcha kept her eyes fixed on her father. 'The police are already in your precious tower and will be up here in a few moments. Like I said, you and your Great Work are finished.'

Delaney glared at her, eyes filled with hatred. Suddenly, Maria collapsed to her knees, supported by the other Wives. The steps beneath her were wet. 'Her waters have broken,' Deva said.

Delaney glanced at Maria and then at the knife in his hand. He seemed to come to a decision. 'Come. There's still time.' He turned to the remaining Watcher. 'We're going to the top of the tower. Let no one pass.'

'Give it up,' Sorcha called after him. 'You can't complete the Great Work now.'

'I can still do it without you,' Delaney spat. 'The Great Work's bigger than you. This isn't over. It hasn't even begun.' Then he hurried up the stairs.

Sorcha let him go and knelt down to Kaidan. He seemed calm, despite the blood pouring from his side and dripping down the steps. As Sorcha touched his wound, he groaned. 'I don't think you'll be able to dress this like you used to,' he said.

Fox crouched down and tried to stem the

bleeding but Sorcha could see that the wound was too deep. Fox shot her a glance and she knew Delaney had struck her half-brother a mortal blow. 'You saved my life, Kaidan,' Fox said. 'Moments ago you tried to strangle me to death and now you do this. Why?'

'I didn't do it for you.' Kaidan smiled at Sorcha. 'I did it for her.'

'Why?' she asked. 'Why did you change your mind?'

*   *   *

As Kaidan looked up at his half-sister he searched his mind for the answer to her question. To his surprise, after he had regained consciousness from Fox's knockout blow, he had felt no anger towards the psychiatrist, only a perverse gratitude. Despite diligently and dutifully trying to do everything his father had demanded of him, Fox had stopped him. And in so doing, Fox had saved him from himself. When Kaidan had heard the faint *whup, whup, whup* of helicopters through the thick tower walls, he had felt no fear, only a surge of relief—almost euphoria. The authorities were coming. He could do no more except surrender. It was out of his hands. It was over.

As he had got to his feet and brushed himself down, he had seen everything clearly for the first time. Fox had been right about the murders in Portland. For the first time in his life he was free to shed the person his father wanted him to be and become himself. When he had heard the commotion on the stairs he had known exactly what he had to do. Even now, after his father had

400

stabbed him and his lifeblood was leaking away, his only regret was that he hadn't acted earlier.

He reached for Sorcha's hand and tried to answer her question. 'When I knew it was over I wanted to break away from my past and be someone different. For once—just once—I wanted to be the angel and not the demon.' He glanced at Fox. 'You were right. We are more than our past. We can become whoever we decide to be—however fleetingly—through the choices we make.' A huge convulsion suddenly seized his body and he coughed up a lungful of blood. Gasping for air, he discovered he could no longer breathe. Then his head fell back, his hand slipped from Sorcha's grasp and he was gone.

*   *   *

Feeling both sadness and anger, Sorcha gently closed Kaidan's eyes. Then she stood and continued climbing the steps. 'Let's finish this.' Fox followed silently behind until they reached the violet door to the seventh level and found their path blocked. The last Watcher stood guard, brandishing a knife. He looked terrified.

Fox groaned. 'You don't need to do this. I don't want to fight you. The police are coming and they're armed. Throw down the knife and step aside.'

Sorcha reached out her hand. 'Give me the knife. My father's no longer in charge. Too many people have died in this tower. You don't need to be another one.'

The man hesitated for a second, then threw down the blade, pushed past them and ran down the stairs. Sorcha reached for the door but it was locked with a conventional lock and key. Through the door she could hear whispering and frantic activity. It sounded like the Wives were trying to placate Delaney as he gave them instructions. With a sickening jolt, Sorcha realized what her father planned to do. She banged frantically on the heavy wood then turned to Fox. 'We've got to stop him.'

'Stop him doing what?' Realization dawned on Fox's face. 'But it won't work. It can't work.'

'I don't care. I don't want him to even *think* he might have succeeded.' Sorcha heard their names being called again. The voices were closer now.

'Nathan? Sorcha? You OK?'

'We're fine,' Fox shouted back. 'There's a guy coming down. He shouldn't be armed.'

'Nathan, there's a body down here. Who is it?'

'That's your killer,' Fox replied. 'I'll explain everything later. Just come up here.' He glanced at Sorcha then examined the lock. 'And bring a gun. We need to get into this room fast.'

CHAPTER SIXTY-EIGHT

'Help me,' said Delaney, frantically. 'There isn't much time.' He turned to Deva and Zara. 'You understand what I need you to do?'

They both nodded silently, too close to tears to speak.

'Which one will do it?'

Zara broke down and started crying.

Deva held out her hand and Delaney passed her the knife. 'Timing is everything, Deva. You know what to look for? You know the signs?' he said.

'Yes,' Deva whispered.

He turned to Maria, who was lying on her back on the amethyst plinth—where Sorcha had lain a short while ago. This wasn't what he had planned or wanted but it was his only remaining hope. It would at least give him the chance to continue the Great Work. He took strength from the death echoes in the amethyst floor and comfort from the devotion and pride he saw in Maria's eyes. Unlike Sorcha, Maria and the Wives appreciated the greatness of his work and *wanted* to help him achieve success. 'Are you ready?' he said.

Maria nodded, eyes bright. 'I'm ready.'

'Then let us begin.'

*   *   *

When Jordache appeared with two police officers, all three were panting from the climb. Immediately the detective saw Fox he gripped his friend's shoulder, relief etched on his face, then patted Sorcha on the arm. 'Thank God you're both OK. Nathan, I'm sorry I didn't believe you when—'

Fox smiled. 'It's OK. You're here now.' He extended his hand. 'I need a gun.'

Jordache nodded to one of his officers, who passed Fox his Glock. 'Why? What's going on?'

'I'll explain later. Now stand back.' Fox removed the safety, fired at the lock then rammed his shoulder against the door. It took two more bullets and all their weight to break the door open. Sorcha had witnessed and experienced many bizarre events over the last few days but what she saw when she climbed the last few stairs and entered the top chamber would stay with her for ever. Even the macabre death echoes that infested the space seemed to recede into the background, as if yielding to the real-time life-and-death drama unfolding before her.

Maria lay supine on the amethyst plinth. Beside her, the Seer lay on top of Zara, gripped in the final throes of passion. Sorcha could see his pupils rolling back in their sockets, leaving only the whites of his eyes visible. Deva stood behind him, pulling his head back with one hand and holding a knife to his throat with the other. The blade was already slicing into his flesh.

Visibly shocked by the tableau before him, Jordache raised his gun. 'Drop the knife and step away.' Ignoring him, Deva continued to pull the blade across Delaney's throat until Jordache fired twice into her chest, throwing her backwards. Her knife, however, had already done its work. Blood jetted from Delaney's severed artery in an orgasm of death. As he fell off Zara and on to the amethyst floor Sorcha saw his lips form a smile of triumph, the curve of his mouth mirroring the curve of the laceration on his throat.

'No!' Sorcha shouted. She threw herself at her father. 'No!'

*   *   *

Still in the throes of sexual ecstasy, Delaney felt no pain, only a euphoric sense of floating free from his physical self. He imagined himself looking down on the carnage within the chamber and merging with the countless death echoes emanating from the violet lotus symbol on the floor. Soon his old body

404

would die and his astral self would transmigrate to its new physical body—that of his own and Maria's newborn child. He was entering the final stage of the Great Work. His journey to immortality had begun.

Suddenly, a searing pain jolted his consciousness and he became acutely aware of his physical self. Was the process meant to be this painful? Perhaps he was experiencing the psychic trauma of transmigration, as his astral self navigated the narrow portal through the crown chakra of his new body? The pain intensified. Perhaps he had already transferred to the infant in the womb and was now being physically born? Was this why we never remembered the moment of our birth, because it was so traumatic? This agony felt more like dying, though. His eyes flickered open and the first thing he saw was his daughter, Sorcha. Her face was pressed close to his and her lips were moving. 'It didn't work. You failed,' she hissed with the whispered urgency of a lover. 'Within seconds you'll be dead. For ever. The Great Work, the murders and all the sick things you did in your life were for nothing.'

At first he couldn't understand what she was saying, then he moved his right hand and felt the amulet. It was still round his neck. Raising it to his face, he stared at his bloodstained fingers clasping the ankh, the symbol of eternal life, and realized he was still trapped in his old body. Panic coursed through him. How could this have happened? How could the Great Work have failed? Deva must have made a mistake. She was supposed to kill him and cut the silver cord while he was still out of his body but she must have mistimed the kill. He looked

405

down and saw he was lying in a pool of blood. His old body was bleeding to death. *He* was bleeding to death. The Great Work was no more. His life and everything he had believed in was over, finished. There would be no immortality. Only extinction. He tried to scream but his strangled cries only quickened the stream of lifeblood pouring from the severed artery in his throat.

*   *   *

When Sorcha had leapt on her father, she had feared he would die during his orgasmic trance, allowing Delaney to convince himself he was transferring to a new host and his Great Work had succeeded. To her relief, his pupils had returned to normal, signalling the end of his out-of-body experience, while he was still alive.

Just.

Now, as she watched the realization of failure dawn on him, she took some satisfaction from seeing his smile fade and the fear flicker in his eyes. Seeing his violet aura dim and watching him die, she felt nothing.

Fox checked Delaney's pulse then Deva's and shook his head. Both were dead. Jordache and the two policemen pulled Zara away from the bodies while Sorcha hurried to help Maria, who lay on the plinth covered in blood, clutching her belly, screaming: 'He's coming. He's coming.'

Zara's eyes widened with wonder and she strained against the policeman's grip. 'It's a miracle. Let me go to her.'

'Keep her back,' Fox said, moving to Maria's side. 'Help me, Sorcha.'

As the policemen constrained Zara, letting Fox and Sorcha tend to Maria, Jordache stared down at Delaney's bloody body. 'What just happened?' he said. 'Why did she kill him?'

'Deva didn't kill him,' Zara said.

'What the hell are you talking about?' Jordache pointed at Delaney's body. 'She cut his goddamned throat. He's dead.'

'The Seer's not dead,' Zara said, pointing defiantly at Maria. 'He's being reborn.'

As Maria pushed her baby out into the world Sorcha couldn't take her eyes off it. In the midst of all the death that surrounded her there was something mesmerizing about watching a new life begin. When it finally emerged, Fox took the baby in his hands and laid it on a pillow on the plinth. Its beauty and innocence made Sorcha smile. Then she looked closer and her smile faded and the room began to spin.

'You OK, Sorcha?' she heard Fox ask, moments before she blacked out.

CHAPTER SIXTY-NINE

As dawn approached, Jordache's men began processing the carnage in the tower while trying to restore order to the rest of the settlement.

After Sorcha had regained consciousness and Fox had settled her in the Great Hall to recover, Jordache took him to one side. 'It's chaos out there, Nathan. Everyone's running around like crazies. The cult's imploding and many of the Indigo Family are looking to Sorcha for guidance. They claim

407

she's the new Seer. I know it's a long shot but once she's recovered perhaps she could talk to them. Just to calm things down.'

Fox shook his head. 'No way. She owes those bastards nothing. They stood by and let her father get away with murder—literally. Delaney would have killed me and raped her and they wouldn't have batted an eyelid. Hell, they would have applauded. After all she's been through she needs to get away from the cult and this toxic settlement as soon as possible.'

'I thought you'd say that, Nathan,' Jordache said. The detective smiled. 'Christ, if this is what you do for an ex-patient then I know where to come when I get a problem. Just fill me in on the weird and wonderful things that happened here, then you can both board one of the choppers and get out of it all.'

'You want the official version or what actually happened?'

'What actually happened, of course.'

'Then we'll only speak to you. Once. And you need to keep an open mind.'

Jordache narrowed his eyes. 'It's that bizarre, huh?'

Over the next two hours, Jordache debriefed Fox and Sorcha on all they knew about Delaney and his cult. When they had finished, the detective, who had seen most things in his line of work, looked shell-shocked. 'I'm trying to be as open-minded as I can, Nathan. I really am. But tell me one thing. Apart from the death echoes, what other weird parts of the Great Work were genuine?'

Fox shook his head. 'None of them. Delaney's cult and the Great Work were based on one flawed core belief: that his unusual synaesthesia meant he was somehow divine and had supernatural powers. Everything flowed from there. He believed in it totally but it was madness.'

'What about the murders in Portland?'

'They weren't part of the Great Work. They were an act of rebellion, an expression of Kaidan's inner conflict between his loyalty to his father—the demon he had to serve—and his love for Sorcha—the angel he wanted to save. Kaidan saw the men he killed as surrogates for his father and their victims as surrogates for Sorcha.'

Jordache studied his notebook then scratched his head. 'You've given me a lot to check out. And think about. I'd better get on with it.'

As Fox watched the detective leave the Great Hall, his thoughts turned to Sorcha. Although her memories were finally returning there was no guarantee she would remember everything from her past, which wasn't necessarily a bad thing. Few of the memories she had from this place were good.

'How are you feeling, Sorcha?'

She walked to the door of the Great Hall and looked out at the settlement. 'I don't know how I feel yet. This place contains all my personal history but there's nothing here I want.' She opened her locket to reveal the photograph inside. 'I came back hoping to rediscover who I was but all I've discovered about my past life is that it's rotten and hollow. I've no foundations here I want to build on: no family or friends. Nothing.'

'Then start again, Sorcha. Let me help you.'

She turned to him. 'You sure?'

'Of course I'm sure. We're in this together now. Come back to Portland. Forget the past, focus on the present and let the future take care of itself.'

She smiled and closed the locket. 'Thank you.'

As they walked outside, Fox saw the police carrying Maria to one of the helicopters. She lay on a stretcher holding her wrapped-up newborn. Sorcha stared at her then marched over.

'What are you doing?' Fox asked Sorcha.

'I want to check the baby.'

'Why?' Fox had initially assumed Sorcha had blacked out because of the intense and bloody nature of her father's death but now he realized she had encountered worse death echoes. Something else had tipped her over the edge. 'What's wrong with the baby?'

'Nothing. I just want to check its colour.'

'I thought all newborns were indigo.'

'They are. Unless . . .'

Fox remembered what Delaney had said. 'Unless they're beyond indigo like you and Kaidan?'

She glanced at him. 'And my father.' Before Maria could protest, Sorcha pulled back the wrap, exposing the baby.

An involuntary shiver ran down Fox's spine. 'What colour is it?'

'It means nothing,' said Sorcha, studying the baby. 'I realize that now.'

'What colour is it?'

'Violet. The baby's violet.'

As a rational man Fox knew the baby's rare aura was an irrelevant coincidence. It was only a question of time before Delaney sired another violet and there was no way the Seer's spirit had transferred to the infant staring back at him. As he looked into the baby's blue eyes, however, and noticed how violet they looked in the fading

410

moonlight, he thought of all the strange experiences he had encountered in the tower and for a moment, just a moment, he wondered.

CHAPTER SEVENTY

Five days later

The movements of the chestnut mare beneath Sorcha felt both natural and familiar as she cantered across the emerald grass. They say you never forget how to ride a bicycle. The same evidently applied to horses. She gave a small tug on the reins and the horse turned obediently in the paddock and headed towards the large clapboard house etched white against the flawless blue sky. Closing her eyes she breathed in the smell of horse, leather and cut grass. It felt a million miles away from her father's cult. If there was a heaven, it might be like this.

'You want to go back to the house?' said the young girl on the pony beside her.

Sorcha turned to her cousin and smiled. 'Race you, Angela.'

The girl squealed with delight, kicked her heels and sped off across the paddock, bouncing in her saddle. Sorcha followed. As they neared the house Sorcha could see Nathan and Samantha talking with her uncle Connor on the veranda. It felt good to know she had other family—good family. When her uncle had showed her around the house she had entered the room in which his father—her grandfather—had died and she had sensed the man's love for Connor as well as his pain. Connor

411

couldn't have been more welcoming to her, insisting she regard his stud farm as her home.

Sorcha's father had hoarded a considerable fortune and once the legalities were finalized she stood to inherit a significant sum. She intended to return part of it to Connor to reinvest in the stud. She regretted not being able to return the family Bible her father had stolen from him. It had disappeared amid the chaos of the collapsing cult, as panicked members of the Indigo Family had scattered. Zara had also disappeared, slipping away from the police and vanishing into the wilderness. Sorcha suspected that Delaney's Wife had taken the Bible and would never be found. Zara and other members of the cult had lived so long off the grid that there was no official record of their existence.

Sorcha, however, was about to enter the grid for the first time.

Samantha waved from the house and she waved back. Sorcha had been staying with Fox's aunt since returning to Portland and was glad Samantha had agreed to come with them when Fox arranged today's visit to Sacramento. Because Samantha and his uncle had saved Fox when he had lost his family, Fox seemed to think her uncle would save her—even though she wasn't a child like Fox had been and no longer needed saving. Evidently worried about her, Fox had been careful—almost too careful—to give Sorcha enough space to decide what she wanted to do next.

Fox didn't seem to appreciate that she was doing fine because of what he had already done for her and taught her. In the same way he had helped her disengage from her death echoes, she had learned

412

to disengage from her painful past. Someone once claimed that 'we are our memories' but Fox had taught her this wasn't true. Memories may inform who we are but they don't define us. Our choices do that. If Kaidan, who had done unspeakable things, could break out of the prison of his past—however briefly and belatedly—then anyone could. Her past, like a foreign country she had once visited and didn't much like, no longer concerned her. Her focus now was on the present and the future.

Another squeal of delight told her that Angela had beaten her back to the house. The excited girl waved at her, jumped off her pony and ran towards the house to tell her father. As Sorcha dismounted and handed the reins to the waiting groom, Fox came down from the veranda. He held a sheaf of papers in his hand. 'You ride a lot better than I do,' he said.

'That's not difficult.'

He laughed. 'You enjoyed it?'

'Loved it.' She pointed to the papers. 'Is that it?'

'Your uncle's signed all the identification forms. You just need to sign the passport application and then soon, for the first time in your life, you'll exist officially.'

She took the papers from him and was surprised how reassuring she found it to see her name written on the official document. Then she realized it would literally confirm who she was. 'Can I sign it now?'

He passed her a pen. 'It might be more comfortable inside.'

'I want to sign it now.' She leaned against a fence post. 'What's my signature?'

'Whatever you decide.'

413

As she signed the form she realized it was the first time she could remember writing her name: Sorcha Delaney. 'Not only does my name taste good when I hear it, I like the colours of the letters when I write it.'

'Good.' Fox showed her the four passport-size photographs she had sat for yesterday. 'We only need two for the application. What do you want to do with the other two?'

She took one, folded it to fit and then opened her locket. She began removing the faded picture of her past self. Then she stopped, replaced it and put the passport photograph over it. She studied her new self for a moment, then closed the locket.

Fox stepped back towards to the main house. 'What do you think of your uncle's place? You like it here?'

'Very much.' She looked at him. 'But you must understand something, Nathan. I like Connor and his family and they have a lovely home. And I love the fact that I have family who are normal but—and it's a big but—I don't belong here. I know you're worried about me, Nathan, but you don't need to be. Not any more. I don't know what my future holds, only that I want it to involve two things. The first is the *mothú*. My death-echo synaesthesia has become such a key part of me that I want to turn it from a curse into a gift. Instead of being scared of it, I want to harness its power and do something useful with it.'

'And what's the second?'

She sighed. God, for a perceptive man he could be incredibly dense. She walked towards him. '*You*, Nathan.' She moved closer, until they were a foot apart. She half expected him to back away but he

414

didn't and she felt bolder. 'Don't you see, Nathan? You've saved me.' She moved closer. 'When I was lost you found me. When I was broken you made me whole again. When I was in danger you came for me.' She moved still closer, until they were touching, his taut body against hers. She looked up and tried to read his blue eyes. 'Now it's my turn.'

For a long moment he didn't react and she realized she was trembling, afraid he was marshalling his defences, deciding how best to reject her without hurting her feelings. Then, as he smiled and leaned his head towards hers, she heard Connor call them in for drinks. 'It's your turn to do what?' Fox teased, lips inches from hers.

At that moment Angela rushed out of the house, grabbed them by the arms and began dragging them inside. Sorcha smiled at Fox and took his hand. 'Save you, Nathan. It's my turn to save you.'

EPILOGUE

The yellow bulldozers and wreckers waiting to begin their work gleam like oversized children's toys in the early light. As a thin blush of pink warms the dawn horizon and the rising sun reveals a cloudless blue sky, it looks as good a day as any to start one's life anew. Fox feels nervous but resolved as he parks by the large sign: *Condemned Buildings. Do Not Enter.*

'You ready?' Sorcha says.

'As I'll ever be.' He opens the car door and gets out.

A man in a construction helmet approaches. 'You Dr Fox?'

'Yes.'

'OK, you've got one hour before we start bulldozing. Like it says in the paperwork, you're doing this at your own risk but don't worry, the building's safe until we send in the 'dozers. We're going in at eight sharp. So be off site by then. OK?'

'OK.'

The man hands each of them a helmet. 'See you in an hour.'

As they pass the first of the disconnected gas pumps Fox casts his mind back twenty years, to the day his life changed for ever. When they get to the kiosk door he braces himself. Then, just as Fox did with Sorcha on the day they met, she takes his hand. 'Come. I'll be right beside you.'

Fox winces as he opens the door, waiting for the sound of the bell he heard all those years ago, but there is nothing, only the squeak of tired hinges as he steps inside. The place has been stripped for demolition and is unrecognizable from that in his memory. It could be anywhere. Suddenly he feels foolish because there is nothing in here to be frightened of. Trying to orient himself, he walks over to where the comic book stand had been. He looks over at where the cash register clerk was shot, and remembers the blood dripping like red treacle off the cartons. Sorcha is already touching the wall, face intense with concentration. Slowly she walks over to the wall against which his family was shot. And he was spared.

Suddenly, the anxiety kicks in. What will she discover? 'Can you sense anything?' She nods but says nothing. For a long while he watches her walk along the wall, shaking her head. He can see her blinking back tears.

'What's wrong?' he says, suddenly wishing he hadn't agreed to do this.

'Nothing,' she says. 'It's OK.'

'Tell me what you see. Tell me what you feel.'

'It's in fragments but when I put them together, it's pretty clear what happened.' Sorcha takes his hand and leads him along the wall: 'After the clerk, the first to be shot was your mother. You saw the bullet hit her and your mirror-touch synaesthesia made you feel the impact and her pain. The shock made you black out. But only momentarily. You regained consciousness in time to see your father shot next—feeling his pain as acutely as if it were your own. The hooded killer laughed as you blacked out again, calling you "a goddamned Jack-in-the-box".

'The next time you came to, you tried to throw yourself in front of your sister. But the killer pushed you away and shot her. Again you watched. It's like you thought sharing their pain might somehow lessen it. When you blacked out again the killer stood over you and waited for you to come to. Then, as soon as you opened your eyes, he pulled the trigger again. But nothing happened. The gun jammed.

'Ignoring him, you clambered over to check on your mother. You were trying to stem the blood flowing from her wound when the killer put the gun inches from your head and pulled the trigger four more times. Each time the pistol jammed. The last words the killer said to you were: "I don't know whether you're a pig like the others or an immortal like us. But whatever you are, boy, you're lucky." Those were the last words each of your family heard before they died. Your mother's last words to you were: "My lucky boy. I love you." After she died you tried to help your father and then, finally, your sister but you couldn't save them.

'The point is, Nathan, I can sense from their death echoes that knowing you survived helped ease their passing. I can feel their love much more strongly than I feel their suffering or pain. You shouldn't feel guilty for surviving. You should feel glad.' Again she blinks back tears. 'You were lucky but you were brave, too. You were only ten but you shared each of their deaths and tried to save them. No one could have done any more than that. No wonder your memory blanked it out.'

Suddenly, she embraces Fox and holds him close. At first he tries to push her away but as the guilt slips from him like loosened chains he feels the tears come in rolling waves. For the first time since they died he surrenders all control, collapses into

419

Sorcha's arms and cries—really cries. Great sobs rack his frame as if purging his body of the years of pent-up sadness.

Finally, the tears stop and he feels a great weight lift from him. He stands and thanks Sorcha, then takes her hand and walks outside. After returning the helmets they stand by the car and watch the bulldozers move in and level the garage. He feels nothing as the building collapses into rubble. Only a sense that a part of his past, which had been mislaid, has been put back where it belongs.

At that moment, a police car drives into the lot and parks beside them. Karl Jordache gets out and hurries over. 'I've been looking everywhere for you.'

'What's wrong, Karl?' says Fox.

'We've got a homicide in the Pearl that's not adding up. I could really do with some help.'

Fox smiles, excited to get back to work. 'Where's the crime scene? Let me take Sorcha home and I'll be right over.'

Jordache shakes his head. 'You don't understand. I was hoping for *both* of you. We've got to do this by the book, though—no spooky archaeosonics or death echo bullshit. No judge or jury's going to buy into that. So whatever weird stuff you guys find we've got to bring it back to the evidence. You understand?'

Fox turns to Sorcha. The gleam in her eye reminds him, momentarily, of her father and the excitement the Seer had shown when talking of the Great Work. 'What do you think, Sorcha? You said you wanted to use your gift to do some good. Are you in?'

She smiles like this is her destiny. 'Oh yes. I'm in.'

420

ACKNOWLEDGEMENTS

My first debt of gratitude is to my wife, Jenny, for her unwavering support and invaluable criticism. Her best work usually ensures that my worst is safely consigned to the bin.

I thank Betty Cordy, Nathan Renard and Valerie Ivens for their time, encouragement and feedback; Heather Bryan for lending me her American ear; my agents, Patrick Walsh and Jake Smith-Bosanquet, for selling the book around the world; and my editor, Bill Scott-Kerr, for improving the story.

Finally, I have to thank my daughter, Phoebe, who invariably chooses the perfect moment to interrupt my writing and make me laugh.

Michael Cordy
London, 2011